HOLD FAST

THE LAIRD'S HOLDINGS

BOOK ONE

ELIZA MACARTHUR

Cover Design by Kelsey Bowman, Let's Get Lit Studio

❀ Created with Vellum

For Julie Garwood, whose Ransom was my introduction to romance.

And for all of us who have found our way back to something we love.

CONTENT WARNINGS

Dear reader,

There are certain elements and events of a sensitive nature that I want you to be aware of before you begin, in case reading them would in any way negatively impact your own healing or mental health.

Within this book, you will find the following:

Before the events of the story:

- Previous sexual assault
- Death in childbirth
- Infant death

Within the events of the story:

- Pregnancy
- Childbirth
- Murder
- Wound stitching
- Graphic sexual content

- Anxiety
- Attempted sexual assault
- Kidnapping

Take care, dear reader. Your heart and brain are worth protecting.

AUTHOR'S NOTE

Hello friends!

Before you begin *Hold Fast* (and after you've read the content warnings), I wanted to take a moment to chat about a few items!

First of all, the kilt as we know it today began as the "belted plaid," and has its origins in the 16th century. I know that the events of this story take place before that date but I took a little liberty with that detail because who doesn't love a kilt? And, as this is a work of fiction (and knees are certainly having a moment), I hope you'll indulge me and enjoy!

Second, our heroine, Una, is a survivor of sexual violence. I am also a survivor of sexual violence and, as such, I tried very hard to take care with Una and her story and I promise you that I did not write anything gratuitously in this book. It was important for me to write a story that demonstrates that healing is not linear, nor does it look the same for everyone. That said, if this story will in any way hinder your own recovery or healing, please, dear reader, take care. Your heart and brain are worthy of protecting.

Finally, I have vivid memories of reading *A Year and a Day* by Virginia Henley, originally published in 1998, which takes place against the backdrop of Scotland's 13th-century wars of independence. It features a handfast which, in Henley's imaginings, was a trial marriage of sorts that lasted for a year and a day. Accurate, historical handfasting did not look like this but I wanted to play with the romance trope of handfasting as a trial marriage as established by those vintage romances but with a feminist twist.

Hold Fast is my love letter to all of the medieval highland romances that served as my introduction to the genre and I am so grateful that you've chosen to pick it up. I hope that you enjoy reading it as much as I enjoyed writing it.

Cheers!

Eliza

PROLOGUE

SCOTTISH HIGHLANDS, 1420

"There's a lass. Dead through the center."

A smile tugged at the corner of Una's mouth. "I'm getting good."

"You've *been* good. What you're getting is deadly."

Blair pulled up from where he'd been leaning against a tree, stalking over to the target and yanking out three arrows, all within the center ring. He brought them to her, his shaggy, dark hair falling around his face, catching in his beard as the breeze blew through the shaking leaves.

She took them, placing two in the quiver at her hip before nocking the third. She drew on the string, feeling the flex of her arms as she did. Her knuckles were cold and chapped, but the wood of the bow was warm in her grip. The fletching tickled her cheek as she took a deep breath and then, on her exhale, let the arrow fly.

There was a satisfying *thunk* as the arrow struck the target, in the center once again. Greer, the white greyhound at her feet, lifted her dainty head at the sound.

"Bloody hell, Una," Blair said, his voice somehow all the

quieter for its depth. "I should put you on the wall. Our enemies wouldnae stand a chance."

She snorted. "Your brother would never allow that."

Blair grunted.

"How could I make myself available for his lairdship's whims if I was murdering intruders on the wall?"

She'd been going for a light tone, but the question had sounded sharp and angry.

Then again, she *was* sharp and angry.

"'Twill nae be long now. You have, what? A week?"

"Ten days."

Ten days. Ten days until she was free and could leave this horrible place. Ten days and her handfast would be over, the contract fulfilled. And, as no heir had been conceived, she would be released from the contract without a fight.

Blair grunted again, sounding like a beast that lived in the dark.

"Ten days," he repeated. "And then what?"

That was the question, wasn't it?

She nocked another arrow, adjusted her stance, and, just before releasing the string, said, "And then I never touch another man as long as I live."

Blair rubbed his mouth with his palm. "Have ye had your courses yet?"

It was an inappropriate question. Or, it *would* have been an inappropriate question for anyone else. But for a healer, the discussion of a monthly flux was as commonplace as the topic of sleep. Besides, her very life relied upon the answer to that question, and Blair knew it.

"Aye. Just this morning."

Una was allowed to leave the walls of the keep once per day, to walk the dog and gather her herbs and roots for medicines. One might think it a position of honor for the laird's brother to be assigned to guard her for those excursions.

One would be wrong.

One day, two months into her handfast, she'd been in especially dark mood after an especially horrible evening and had needled Blair for the entirety of their walk, calling him a guard dog, telling him he must be an utter failure to be tasked with running errands and taking walks with a woman.

He'd surprised her when he muttered, "He knows I willnae touch you."

"And how can he be so certain of that?" she had spat, feeling like a wild animal on a leash. Volatile and unpredictable.

He had shrugged his heavy shoulders and said, with a little flick of his head to the side, "Besides the fact that I dinnae touch unwilling women?"

"Your brother certainly doesnae care whether or nae I am willing," she had countered icily.

He had shrugged again, a casual, careless gesture. "He doesnae care about anyone. Only himself. But even if I loved you with my entire soul—which I verra much dinnae—I wouldnae touch you."

"Oh, really? And why is that?"

He'd looked skyward, his hands clasped behind his back. "Because he swore to me that he would kill any woman I touched."

Her mouth had dropped open. "But... *why?*"

She would remember the haunted look in his eyes for the rest of her days. "Because an heir of mine is yet another threat to him."

"How would he know?"

"He would know. He knows everything. He has rats in every wall and eyes in every corner."

Malcolm Cameron had despised Blair since Blair had drawn his first breath. Blair told her that it was because Blair was their mother's obvious favorite. The second son. Quiet and kind and gentle. He told her that his mother had called him easy to love. Una hadn't known Blair as a child, but she could picture it. Whereas she couldn't imagine Malcolm ever being loveable a day in his life.

But now, the very things that had made Blair so loveable as a child—his kindness, his honor and honesty—made him a threat. It was unfortunate, really, that the entire reason Una had found herself bound in a handfast to Malcolm Cameron was how very much he hated his brother. If Malcolm did not have an heir, Blair would become laird in the event of his death, something Malcolm could not stomach.

"Do ye think he would ever try to have ye killed?

Blair had shrugged but shaken his head. "I havenae done anything wrong. The clan would forgive many of his sins—and they do—but they wouldnae forgive that."

And so Malcolm kept his younger brother under his thumb. The ink hadn't yet dried on the handfasting contract before Una found herself under that very same digit.

But she hadn't been able to recognize that at first and had fought Blair like an angry cat, insulting him, goading him, pouring into him all of her anger and hurt, and he, the noble, gentle man that he was, had taken it.

That was yet another thing they had in common—being on the receiving end of Malcolm's vicious temper, though Blair had insisted she had the worst of it. For the most part, Malcolm left him alone. The same could not be said for Una. Rather, Malcolm came to her every night and exercised his will and wishes no matter how unwilling she was. He was vicious and violent, raging at and mistreating her in every conceivable way short of starving her.

"You belong to me, Una, and I shall do with ye as I see fit," he often sneered in her ear from behind.

And, in the eyes of the law, she *was* his property. For a year and a day. But that time was nearly up.

Ten days.

That day, nearly a year before, when Blair had confided in her, he had asked her if she was angry and, when she'd said yes, asked, "Would you like to do something about it?"

At her puzzled expression, he'd continued. "Some of the young lads get all riled before they are grown. Restless. Angry. Too many feelings they havenae been taught to manage. That's when I start to train them with a dagger."

"Why a dagger?"

"Because after you've stabbed a hay bale a few hundred times, you're too tired to be so fashed."

She had wanted to laugh. It had been *just there*. But laughter was beyond her grasp. "Just a dagger?" she had asked.

"We begin with a dagger. A sgian dubh you can carry in your boot. And when they have a handle on that, we move to the staff or the sword."

"Can you teach me to use a sword?"

"Nay."

Of course he wouldn't teach her to use a sword.

He had sighed then, a gusty, frustrated sound. "I could teach you to *use* a sword. I cannae teach you to *lift* one. But" —a long pause as he rubbed his beard contemplatively—"I can teach you to use a bow."

She'd dropped her digging stick, turning to look at him with wide eyes.

"What?"

"You're all riled. Restless. *Angry*. I can work with that."

She'd narrowed her eyes. "And what will you want in return?"

"Nothing. Nae conditions. You're angry. Sometimes, the best way to move that anger out and on is to strike something. But first, the dagger," he said, pulling a small knife out of his boot and flipping it, deftly catching the blade between his thumb and forefinger, holding the handle out to her.

Now, as she nocked the next arrow, she remembered the first time she'd held a bow in her hands, how hard she'd struggled to pull the string, how Blair had made her draw it back, unloaded, over and over until her fingers bled, to build her strength. She'd had to lie about picking herbs in bramble to explain away the bloody fingertips.

The third arrow slid neatly into the target's center. Blair whistled softly through his teeth.

"You began your courses today? Does that mean you're out of danger?" His voice was low, just in case. It was a traitorous question after all, though not as traitorous as the answer.

"I willnae stop the fennel, just to be certain, but it certainly hints at that."

She went for the last arrow in her quiver.

"Do you have enough? Fennel?"

"Aye," she said. "I do."

A fact that was entirely due to Blair's help. Blair had planted the fennel in a sunny spot away from the keep, and tended it, harvesting it carefully and hiding it here for her to bring back to the keep in her satchel along with her other herbs and medicines.

She owed Blair everything. For the fennel which, when prepared correctly, was a strong contraceptive. For the lessons in archery and blade work. For the friendship.

"I am happy for you, Una. At least one of us will escape this place," he said before he walked the distance to the target to retrieve the arrows.

As she watched his back moving away, a thought formed. Another dangerous, traitorous thought.

What if Blair escaped, too? What if he came with her? What if…

Her mind raced, considering possibilities.

As Blair approached, arrows clenched in his fist, Una whispered, "Blair. You need to come with me."

He snorted. "You're off yer head."

"Nay," she hissed. "You cannae stay here. You deserve better than this. Come with me."

Blair thrust the arrows out and, when she took them, crossed his big arms over his bigger chest and arched an eyebrow. "Och, aye? And precisely how far down the road do ye expect we would get before there is an arrow in my back? Use your head, Una."

She knit her brows together and bit her top lip. If they could find an ally. Or, at least, not an enemy, they could—

"The Stewarts," Una breathed.

"What?"

"I'll go to the Stewarts."

"Why would you go to the Stewarts?"

Her breath was coming faster now, her heart pounding in excitement.

"Because I cannae stay here. I dinnae *want* to stay here. And my da will just marry me off to the first man who offers for the laird's castoffs. I cannae—" She sucked in a deep breath, the plan becoming clear in her mind. "I will go to the Stewarts. I delivered Lady Stewart's babe just before the handfast. She told me if I ever wanted to come work there, she would take me on as her family's personal healer."

It had been more than that. Lady Stewart had begged Una to stay. She was an anxious woman, and the days after birth had not been kind to her. Una had stayed for three weeks, until the worst of the danger was past, but had promised to return if Lady Stewart sent for her.

Blair was rubbing his mouth now, the way he did when he was thinking.

"Aye," he said. "You should go to the Stewarts."

She was breathless now.

"And then, I will convince Lady Stewart to ask her husband to send for you."

"Malcolm would never let me go," he protested. "He likes me where he can see me."

"Then you escape. And Laird Stewart sends him a letter that says you were running away and his men killed you by mistake, believing you to be an enemy."

"Why would Laird Stewart do such a thing? He is my brother's ally."

"He is your brother's ally because it suits him best to have protection against the Campbells. He doesnae have any love for Malcolm. I heard him say so when I was there."

"He told you that?"

"He didnae tell *me*. But people dinnae think much about talking when a healer is present."

He snorted.

"And what would a dead man do at the Stewarts?"

"Whatever you want. Be in the guard. Raise sheep. Find a lass and welp a dozen bairns on her," Una said, so giddy that she was bouncing on her toes.

"You would do that for me?" Blair asked, his hand fumbling.

"After all you have done for me? 'Tis the least I can do. The very least, Blair. You saved my life."

He narrowed his eyes, but she knew him well enough to know that he was caught. Because while she had been bound to Laird Cameron for a year, Blair had been the victim of his caprice and cruelty for his entire life. And the sentence would continue until his death, unless…

"You'll send word when it is time for me to run?"

"I'll find a way. I promise."

He didn't believe it yet. She could tell. But he would. She would show him. She was getting out of here for good and she was taking him with her and they would never, *never* have to think of Malcolm Cameron ever again.

"Ten days, Una," he said quietly.

"Ten days," she repeated, and let the arrow fly.

CHAPTER 1

Ewan MacDonald laid his body nearly flat against his horse's neck. The pair raced through the dense forest, ducking overhanging branches as they followed the wounded stag

"Faster, mo charaid. We cannae lose him," Ewan said into the dappled gray stallion's ear. The horse, understanding the urgency, snorted, lowered his head, and surged forward. Ewan could feel the animal's power beneath him.

It was a perfect day for a hunt, and he and his men had taken advantage. The bulk of the hunting party was tracking a boar at the moment while Ewan cleaned up his youngest brother's mistake. Sometimes as laird, it felt as if all he did was clean up other people's mistakes. Other times, it felt like all he did was make them.

"Keep up, Mathan!" Ewan bellowed over his shoulder, though he did not need to. The massive, shaggy deerhound was just to the right of the horse's flanks.

The low sun glinted sharply through the trees, and the heavy breathing of the two beasts created great clouds of white smoke in the early morning light. The stag ran like the devil before them, leaving a trail of bright blood on the ground.

At last, it stumbled. Ewan squeezed the stallion's flanks with his legs. The horse stopped quickly. The hound stood at attention to his right.

Ewan shaded his eyes and watched as the deer weaved back and forth in the clearing. Its gaze desperate and unfocused as it stumbled again and fell onto the soft leaves beneath its hooves.

Ewan wasted no time. He unsheathed his knife as he jumped down from the horse and strode quietly toward the dying animal. The hound began to follow, but Ewan held up his hand and whispered, "Stay put, Mathan." The dog sat obediently beside the horse.

Moving silently over the fallen leaves, Ewan crouched behind the stag, whose eyes followed him weakly. Taking his knife in hand, Ewan grabbed the stag's antlers with the other and held the head steady as he drew the blade across its throat in one swift motion. He released his hold on the antlers and moved backwards to crouch again at the edge of the clearing.

"Hush. There now. You're nearly home," Ewan murmured softly to the stag as more of its blood rushed forward, seeping into the leaves. He could feel the change in the air. Snow was coming. The stag flinched once, twice, and was still.

Ewan glared at the arrow protruding from the animal's side. It had been a poor shot—a mortal wound, but not one that would deliver a quick death, and certainly not a merciful one. The sight made Ewan's stomach turn. The shot had been one of youthful arrogance as Ewan's youngest brother, Connor, believed himself to be a far better marksman than he was.

Ewan fumed. "I should have made him come finish the

beast himself."

It was one thing to kill from a distance. It was quite another to draw your knife and take a life with your very hands. Ewan knew that all too well.

He waited a few minutes longer, already planning the hours of target practice Connor would be completing as punishment. If Connor wanted to believe himself an ace marksman, he would put in the training until his skills matched his opinion of himself. That's what their father would have done.

In his youthful arrogance, Ewan had believed himself to be a far better swordsman than he was. That had earned him hours in the ring sparring with man after man while his father and the captain of the guard critiqued his form and offered corrections. For years, Ewan had spent his mornings training with the guard and his afternoons and evenings in the laird's solar, learning the "inside work," as his father called it. Every night, he'd collapsed in his bed exhausted and slept like a corpse until dawn.

But he'd learned. The politics. How to manage a large holding. How to wield a sword. He had been well positioned to step into his father's shoes, but that didn't mean he'd been ready. The work of laird was endless, and for all his preparation, he felt woefully unprepared. He missed his father's guidance. He missed his wisdom. He missed *him*.

Ewan whistled sharply and heard the heavy plodding of the gray stallion's hooves moving towards him. The dog stayed where he'd been left. Ewan had just hoisted the stag onto the horse's back when he heard an ear-piercing squeal and the sounds of men yelling. A boar. They would feast tonight.

Ewan turned back to the task of securing the massive stag to his saddle, muttering to himself about the lecture he was going to give Connor when they returned to the keep. He didn't have the heart to thrash the boy, but he'd blister his ears for certain.

He was checking over the fastenings when he heard a human scream of pain.

Ewan flew into the saddle, whistled for the hound, and kicked the horse into a gallop. The forest was quiet now, save for the percussive exhales of the great stallion and the pounding of Ewan's heartbeat in his ears.

Before long, Ewan came upon the clearing where his men gathered in a tight circle. They parted as Ewan ran towards a body, which lay motionless on the forest floor. His worst fears materialized when he saw that it was Connor. Ewan dropped to his knees next to the fifteen-year-old boy and looked across his still form into the eyes of his best friend and right hand, David.

"The lad thought to help us bring down the boar. We had it cornered well enough, but the beast gave us the slip and made right for Connor. We felled it, but nae before it gored him," David murmured.

Ewan ran his hands over Connor's leine shirt. There was so much blood that Ewan couldn't tell the source.

"His leg," David offered quietly.

Lifting up the blue-and-green plaid, Ewan saw a deep gash in his brother's thigh. The boar's tusk had nearly cut down to the bone. Looking up, Ewan saw two of his four brothers standing in the tight circle around Connor, who was pale and unconscious.

"He should never have come with us," Ewan bit out at them, drowning in his own frustration and grief.

Kenneth, two years younger than Ewan, sighed. "You know good and well that if you'd forbidden him to come, he'd have followed anyway."

"We must get him to the keep," Ewan said, his jaw clenched.

"The healer's gone," muttered Angus, born a mere thirteen months after Kenneth.

The MacDonald healer who had served the keep and surrounding crofts for decades had died three weeks before after succumbing to a sudden fever. Cold dread settled in the pit of Ewan's stomach. Of all the rotten, cursed timing.

Ewan pulled his leine shirt out of his plaid and used his knife to cut the bottom several inches away. As he worked, the great, shaggy dog sat next to the boy and whined softly. Kenneth reached out and absently scratched behind Mathan's ears as he watched Ewan.

Wrapping the fabric tightly around Connor's thigh, Ewan wondered what they would do for him once they returned home. How would they stave off fever? How would they treat it if it came? He was a laird, not a healer, and while he had been taught how to cauterize or stitch up smaller wounds after battle, he had nowhere near the skill required to deal with an injury like this. His mind raced as he scooped his brother's body into his arms and stood in one, powerful move.

"Where is Connor's horse?" he asked.

"We moved your stag to it, m'laird," one of his men replied. "We thought you'd prefer your own mount."

Ewan nodded at the man, set his jaw, and walked towards his stallion, Kenneth following close behind. Kenneth took Connor so that Ewan could mount the horse before handing him up to his brother. Connor groaned and protested weakly. Ewan's throat felt full to bursting, and he imagined it was his heart that had lodged there. Heavy snowflakes began to fall as he turned his stallion and made for home.

"Hush now, mo ghaisgeach," Ewan whispered against the boy's blond curls. *My hero*. "You're nearly home now."

CHAPTER 2

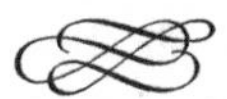

Una banged on the door to her childhood cottage. On the other side, she heard her father grunting and shuffling as he made his way to the door, opening it just far enough that she could see his faded, watery blue eyes. A bushy gray eyebrow rose sharply toward the shiny top of his head, and he flung the door wide open.

He looked unkempt. His trews were dirty, the leine shirt he wore even more so, and the ring of hair that still grew on the bottom half of his head hung long and limp and dirty around his shoulders.

Her father had never been much for tidiness, but it seemed that since her youngest sister Mary had gotten married a few months before and left home, he'd given up on it entirely.

"What are ye doing here, Una?" he asked as she pushed past him into the cottage, which stank of old cooked fat and body odor and musk. Greer followed closely behind her.

"Can I nae visit my father and look after his well-being?"

"You havenae visited this past year. I dinnae ken why you would start now."

Una forced a brittle smile.

"I wasnae allowed such liberties."

He grunted. Una took in the rest of the cottage. Dirty dishes were stacked on the table, and it was clear that Fergus has simply been ladling new food on top of the old without washing. Una's stomach turned to think of it. Clothes lay scattered about the cottage, the rushes were all but gone, and the bed was a tangled mass of dirty linens. Fergus scratched his head, and Una took a careful step back.

"Jesu, Da," she said, noticing the state of the hearth, which had not been cleaned or swept in what looked like months. That the cottage had not burned down around him while he slept was a miracle.

"What?" Fergus said defensively, looking around it. "'Tis fine."

"'Tis filthy," she retorted, tying up the sleeves on her dress.

She only planned to sleep there one night, but if she was to sleep there, she wanted to be sure that she would not be in danger of fleas or worse. The floors needed sweeping and new rushes to be laid, the linens needed washing, the dishes needed scouring, and that hearth needed to be dealt with immediately.

Fergus rested his hands on the table and lowered his body into a chair with a grunt.

"I don't like dogs," he said.

"Greer willnae bother you. We'll be gone by morning."

"Surely you'll be gone before then. I cannae imagine the laird allowing you to sleep away from him."

Una took a deep breath, preparing herself for the row that she knew was coming.

"I am nae going back to the keep."

He blinked at her, confused. "Then the laird is coming to fetch you here?"

She shook her head and began sweeping ashes from the heart into a pile.

"What do ye–"

"My handfast is over today, Da."

He grunted. "Ah. So the laird set ye aside, did he?"

Una's shoulders were so tense that they were making a bid to join her ears at the top of her neck as she worked. Greer whined from the floor at her feet, always so in tune with Una's moods. The white greyhound had been a gift from one of the kitchen boys after Una had cared for his dying mother, and Malcolm had let her keep it in an uncharacteristic act of charity.

"Let's hear it then," Fergus said, scratching at a bit of dried food on the tabletop.

Una continued to sweep the hearth. When he cleared his throat loudly, she rolled her eyes, annoyed but not surprised that he would press for more information.

"Just that, Da. The contract was fulfilled. There was nae heir. I am free."

If she had stopped there, he might have let it go. But instead she added, "And thankful I am for it."

"Thankful? You are *thankful*, Una? You're happy to be cast aside by the laird? Like… like… like a whore he's tired of? I never thought you a fool, Una, but zounds, lass!"

"You signed the contract alongside me. You ken full well that if no heir was conceived within that year, it was finished."

Una kept her face a careful mask as she swept. It had been a long walk from the keep, through the village and past the cottages of people she knew well, people she had known her entire life. Some of the doors had been open, their inhabitants standing in the openings and watching as she passed with expressions that varied from pity to disapproval. She knew what they thought of her. She kept her head high anyway.

"Did you nae do your duty?"

Una whirled around to face him, her black hair like a whip. She was nearly breathless with anger, sharp and glinting like a knife's edge.

"Och, I did my *duty,* Da," she said through clenched teeth. "I tolerated him every night for a year. There was nae bairn, but it was nae because I didnae *do my duty.*"

The last words made her feel sick, the anger and hurt roiling around in her belly along with all of those unpleasant memories of laird Malcolm Cameron.

Fergus narrowed his eyes. "You and that healer you were always hanging about—"

"Agatha—"

"I dinnae give a damn what her name was. Nae doubt she taught ye how to be rid of such things as a bairn."

She felt the tears threatening at the corner of her eyes at the mention of her mentor's name. Agatha had been such a good friend to her. An old woman when Una had met her as a child, Agatha had died in her sleep a few months prior, and Malcolm had refused her request to attend the burial. What would Agatha say to her now?

"You should have begged him for more time."

Collecting the ashes into a pail, she said, "I didnae want more time. A year was more than enough time with such a monster."

Fergus snorted. "He was nae unkind to ye." It wasn't a question.

"That all depends on your definition of kindness, I suppose. But I wouldnae consider it kind to keep one's betrothed as little more than a prisoner, to use and abuse her as he saw fit."

"Ye belonged to him!" Fergus shouted, pounding a fist on the table.

When she first began training with Blair, he taught her how to breathe into her belly. He'd told her to imagine inhaling all of her anger and frustration and worry with it, mashing them all together with that breath, and then, when she exhaled, forcing them all out.

She took a deep breath now, filling her lungs with as much air as they could hold and imagining the white-hot rage that filled her coming together, warming her chest. She would release it slowly. She would be calm. She would not cry in front of her father.

Instead, she felt her face slide into the blank mask that had always so infuriated Malcolm. He hated when she went vacant in the eyes. Often, he had tried to provoke her into reacting by being more vicious than usual. But she had allowed her brain to go somewhere peaceful, somewhere he could not follow, no matter what he did to her body.

She didn't leave the room, not really, but she did let her face go slack as she began collecting dirty dishes from the table and stacking them in a basket.

"Una, did you hear me?"

She hadn't heard the question. She glanced at him out of the corner of her eye.

"You were his intended. You were nae a prisoner. You signed your mark to that paper. He didnae steal you. He didnae abuse you. I willnae have you speaking such falsehoods!" His voice had risen with every word until he was shouting at the end.

Sometimes Una wondered if she had inherited her father's temper because she, too, could rise to anger like a flint strike on kindling. She was dangerously close to such a flint strike now. Had she not been taught to breathe, she would have already erupted. She likely would have shouted that she knew a thousand ways to save a man and at least half that many to take him out of this world.

"Did you hear me, Una?" Fergus said, standing now. "I willnae hear you speak false of the laird in my home!"

She should have known better than to expect any sort of sympathy from her father, a man who had been as hard as stone since her mother died. She stood opposite him at the table, her own hands braced on the top as she leaned forward until they were nearly nose to nose. His breath was foul, but she did not flinch.

In a flinty voice, she said, "You cannae govern me any longer."

"If you mean to remain under my roof, you best believe I can, Una!"

Una straightened and crossed her arms over her chest.

"How fortunate for the both of us then that I willnae be under this roof after tonight. In fact, I doubt you will ever see me again."

Fergus blinked at her like a startled owl. He opened and closed his mouth several times, always stopping just shy of responding.

"I'll be leaving at first light," she said, pulling the wash-basin off the hook on the wall and setting it in front of the fireplace, noting the thick dusk that covered it.

"Where?"

"That is nae business of yours, Da."

Fergus lowered slowly back to his seat, his mulish expression carving deep lines into his face. He suddenly looked so much older than he was. Or maybe he'd always looked older and Una was only just noticing.

Then again, so did she. She hadn't had many opportunities for looking at her reflection before her handfast. Her family didn't own a mirror. But she had been surrounded by mirrors at the keep, had watched her face transform over a year. Her mouth hardening, her brows narrowing until there was a permanent furrow between them. She looked ten years older than she had before, the year feeling like a lifetime.

Then again, it *had* been a lifetime. The life she had lived, the person she had been before, both of them were long gone.

"You've nowhere to go. You have nae prospects. Nae family but me. And after this, I cannae imagine anyone lining up to take you off my hands as a bride. So we're stuck together, you and me," Fergus said, glaring at his hands.

She looked at him. Then she looked beyond him. At the filthy cottage, the dim light. Everything was rough and homespun, nothing like the fine surroundings she'd experienced in the last year. She wore a wool gown today, but Malcolm had insisted she wear silk in the keep. He had given her trinkets and jewels, gifts when he flew off the handle. But she had left them all behind that morning. The gowns. The jewelry. The mirror. The furs.

She didn't want a single thing from him.

She didn't want anything from her father either, she realized. Not his sympathy. Not his care. Certainly not his pity. Such kindness might have made her stay, might have made her worry about him enough that she lingered to help him, to save him.

But this was better. Easier. Because he was wrong about yet another thing. She would never be stuck anywhere ever again.

CHAPTER 3

The MacDonald men, laden with their quarry, returned to the keep at an agonizingly slow pace. Ewan was torn between a desire to return to the keep as quickly as possible and the knowledge that excessive bumping and jostling might cause Connor to bleed more. They continued, Connor in his arms, as the snow fell. He loosened the extra fabric from his belt and wrapped it around Connor to keep him warm.

Connor floated in and out of consciousness. From time to time, he would open his eyes and gaze at the sky, seeming to see and not see at the same time.

"Ewan," he whispered. "Where is Ewan? I must apologize to Ewan."

"Shhh," Ewan said. "Hush now. I am here. I have you. There is nothing to apologize for."

"Can you make it stop hurting, Ewan?" Connor whimpered.

Ewan's jaw was so tense that he wondered how it was that he hadn't broken his teeth. So many failures for one day, all of them laying at his feet and in his lap. He should have forced Connor to practice more. He should have supervised him more closely on the hunt. He should have sent someone else after the stag. He'd just been so angry, *so damned angry*, and he never allowed himself to indulge such a feeling.

It had felt good to ride off after the stag in a fit of temper, to feel his anger punctuated by the pounding of his horse's hooves, to chase and catch.

It had felt good, but for what? What had such temper gotten him? Nothing, other than sending his brother to death's doorstep.

"Ewan," Connor asked weakly, a few moments later. "Am I going to die?"

Ewan choked before answering in a voice that neither sounded nor felt like his own. "Nay, Connor. Why would you say such a thing? That boar merely scratched you. We'll have you patched up in nae time."

Connor nodded and slipped back into unconsciousness. Ewan's heart and hopes sank lower as the gatehouse and curtain walls of the keep came into view. The watchers atop the wall stood silently. There were no whoops or cheers as there normally might have been. Rather, the hunting party rode as silently as a funeral procession into the bailey.

Ewan guided the horse to a stop. Connor was shivering violently in Ewan's arms, both of their clothing completely soaked with blood that had chilled quickly in the cold air. Kenneth pulled his horse up next to Ewan's and dismounted, reaching up for Connor and taking his unconscious body gently into his arms. Ewan dismounted and handed the horse's reins off to a waiting groom before following Kenneth across the bailey.

Just then, the door to the keep burst open and their sister —and Connor's twin—Catriona appeared in the shadowed opening. She hiked her skirts and flew down the steps, racing toward them with tears streaking her face. Ewan had sent men ahead to ready the keep for their arrival.

"He cannae be dead!" Cat screamed. "He cannae be dead, Ewan. Tell me he isnae dead!" She sobbed and hurled herself at Ewan's chest.

He wrapped his arms around her and held her tightly. "He yet lives, Cat. But we must work quickly if we are to save him."

Catriona drew back, her face stained from Connor's blood, which had saturated Ewan's shirt. She looked as if she'd been to war. She walked with them into the keep, up the wheeled staircase, and down the hall to the laird's chamber, where the light was best.

All around them, chaos reigned. Servants bustled back and forth with arms full of linens and boiling water that they carried up the stairs and to the laird's chamber. He heard Fiona, the housekeeper, shouting orders from the Great Hall and hear Fenella's bellow beyond hers in the kitchen. Someone spoke of fetching Father Brian. The cacophony sounded like droning insects in Ewan's ears as he helped Kenneth to arrange Connor's body on the bed.

The room was large, and yet, with so many people, it felt cramped and small as servants hurried to fill the boiling cauldron over the fire and lower strips of linens into it.

"What are we to do, Ewan?" Catriona cried. "The healer's been dead for nearly a month now, and we havenae replaced him!"

"He needs to be stitched," David said from the window, where he was pulling back the fur coverings to let in more light.

"Aye," Ewan said, turning his gaze to his sister. "And by someone with verra fine stitching."

Catriona looked momentarily confused, but she soon caught his meaning and her hand flew to her throat in shock.

"Ewan… nay. Nay! *Nay!* You cannae ask me to do that! I dinnae ken the first thing about stitching a wound like that!"

"There's nae one else," Angus said, meeting Ewan's gaze across the bed.

"Cannae Fiona do it?" Cat protested.

Fiona had been standing by the hearth, supervising two maids in stirring the boiling linens. She crossed to the bed. "Nay, m'lady. My eyesight isnae what it used to be, and I dinnae trust myself with such a task."

"Fenella, then."

Fiona clucked her tongue sadly. "M'lady, Fenella is a butcher with a needle and thread and would tell you as much herself."

"A maid then. Cannae you send for the seamstress? Ewan, please, I cannae–"

"There isnae time, Cat," he said grimly.

She choked on a gasp, her mouth covered by her hands as tears coursed down her cheeks, cutting streaks through the bloody stains. She was panicking. Ewan knew the look well. He'd seen it in enough men before a battle, when they realized that all the training in the world hadn't prepared them to actually run headfirst into a line of enemies with weapons drawn. He'd felt that panic himself. He *felt* it. Every day. Endlessly. Sometimes it felt like panic was his most constant companion.

He realized he was asking her the impossible, tasking her with sewing her twin back together to save him from the brink. But there was no other choice. He trusted no one else.

"Cat, it must be done, and there is nae one better to do it. You are the most skilled with a needle."

"But he is my brother, nae an embroidered cushion! I cannae do it, Ewan! What if I make it worse?" Her voice had risen in pitch with every sentence until she was shrieking by the end.

He held her shoulders in his hands and shook her gently. She sucked in a breath and looked at him, her tears and the ruby red of Connor's blood making her green eyes look otherworldly.

"Cat, you cannae make it any worse." It was the truth. "You can do this. You *must* do this."

During his time as laird, Ewan had found that people responded better to kindness than threats, that if you made a person *believe* they could do something, they were generally more eager to prove you right. But he knew that no amount of encouragement from him would make Cat's task any easier. There was no proving him right.

Cat squeezed her eyes tightly shut and more tears leaked through. But then, as if gathering her mettle, Cat opened her eyes and nodded. "I'll do it."

Ewan squeezed her shoulders. Over her shoulder, he met Fiona's gaze.

"Has anyone told Rabbie?" he asked.

"Aye," Fiona said. "He was fetched from the stables shortly after your arrival."

"We'll need him."

Fiona nodded. "I will go bring him myself," she said before hurrying out of the room.

Cat was fetching her needle, Fiona was fetching Rabbie, Kenneth and Angus were standing at the bedside and staring at Connor with tense expressions. So much stillness and yet so much movement at the same time.

But the wound would need to be thoroughly cleaned before Cat could stitch it. He asked for some of the boiled linens and watched as a maid lifted a steaming strip with a thin metal rod, holding it aloft as the heat rolled off the fabric. When it was cool, Ewan took it and cleaned as much debris as he could from Connor's wound. Connor grimaced as the linen abraded the injury, but did not wake.

Catriona returned to the chamber with her hair pulled back in a tight braid, her sleeves tied up. Rabbie followed close on her heels, his face ashen. He didn't say a word but went to the bed and took Connor's hand in his, rubbing the back of his with gentle strokes.

"Can we give him something for the pain while I stitch him?" Cat asked. "A sleeping draught? Something? *Anything*?"

"I fear it would kill him after losing so much blood," Ewan answered grimly.

"Let us hope I dinnae finish him off, then," Cat whispered and crossed herself quickly.

Ewan climbed onto the bed behind Connor, drawing his brother up so that his back was pressed against Ewan's chest. Ewan wrapped his arms tightly around Connor's thin, still-boyish torso and nodded to his three brothers and David to take position around Connor's legs.

Catriona's hands trembled as she threaded the needle with whisky-soaked catgut. She took a deep breath and began to stitch. Connor bucked, yelling hoarsely as he arched against Ewan's hold.

"Dinnae stop," he commanded as he tightened his hold around Connor.

She ducked her head and continued her grisly work, biting her bottom lip so sharply as she worked that she drew blood. Time crawled as she worked neatly and carefully. Eventually, Connor passed out from the pain. "Thank God," Angus muttered.

Slowly but surely, Cat's even stitches brought the final edges of the wound together. With the last stitch in place and the bandages tied, Catriona stood, walked gracefully as a queen to the corner, and retched into the chamber pot on the floor. Ewan's arms ached, and his leine was soaked through with sweat and blood. His brothers and David stood around the bed, equally gray in the face, equally exhausted.

Wiping her mouth, Catriona turned to them and asked the question that Ewan had been pondering all the while she stitched. "Now what?"

"We wait. And we pray that he doesnae catch fever. Or if he does, that he has strength enough to fight it."

Catriona sniffed and dragged the back of her hand under her nose. Her ladies' maid, Joan, rushed forward with a handkerchief. Ewan hadn't even noticed her come in.

"Beg pardon, m'laird," Joan said quietly as Cat blew her nose into the kerchief. "The Camerons have a healer. A brilliant one, they say. Perhaps they'd be willing to come."

Ewan narrowed his eyes. The Camerons were enemies. They had plagued his father for decades as they tried to encroach on the boundary between their lands.

"Why would I trust a Cameron healer? They're just as likely to finish Connor off and poison the rest of us as they are to help, especially if their laird had anything to say about it."

"But m'laird, they are the best. Lady Stewart said so."

He arched an eyebrow in her direction.

"Laird Stewart's servant told us the story when he paid you that visit two months past. Said that Lady Stewart had called for the Cameron healer to deliver her bairn and would have nae other."

That fact, if true, gave Ewan pause. He didn't trust the Camerons, but he also knew that the Stewart laird would entrust his precious wife—a rare love match—to no one but the very best.

"Ewan! You must beg them to come!" Catriona said.

It wasn't as if he had any other options.

CHAPTER 4

Una woke before the dawn and collected her belongings, meager as they were. Her bow and quiver of arrows, her medicine satchel, a sack of provisions, her wool plaid, a cloak, and the only gown she owned. The laird had sent it down from the keep the night before her handfasting. It was a fine garment, made of soft wool dyed a rich green. And while she hated to keep anything that had come from him, she had no other clothes. Her father had sent hers with her sister when she'd been married. She'd worn this gown into the keep, and she'd worn it out a year later.

She let herself out of the cottage as quietly as possible so as not to wake her father. Greer followed close on her heels as she strode briskly away from her family cottage, making for the burn that ran alongside the forest. The Stewart lands lay to the south. If she walked all day at a strong pace, she should reach the border by nightfall.

After a time, she cut into a wood, grateful for the tall trees that blocked much of the icy wind.

"Go on, Greer," Una said to the dog as she scratched behind her ears. "Have a run. Let's see what you catch."

The lanky greyhound raced joyfully off into the forest beyond. While Una had brought the dog with her on her daily outings with Blair, she seldom was able to let her run as free and fast as she wanted. But things were different now.

Una listened to Greer tear through the brush. Greer was enjoying every single second of her newfound freedom. Yesterday, Una had been practically vibrating with excitement for that same freedom. But now, as she stood beneath the ancient, towering trees, the world suddenly felt very big and she very small.

It was alarming.

For her entire life, her world *had* been small. And for the last year, it had been smaller still. As Laird Cameron's special pet, his handfasted maybe-bride, she had been guarded closely, used with fiendish delight, and then tucked away again until he desired her next.

Until she reached the Stewarts, she was on her own in that great big world she'd barely scratched the surface of seeing. That feeling of smallness, so foreign to her, caused prickle of goosebumps that had nothing to do with the cold. A few months before her handfast, she'd been called to the Stewarts, and gladly gone, but had been accompanied by a full detail of guards. Now, she was utterly alone, which was both a blessing and a concern. A blessing in that she belonged to no one any longer. Her life was her own to live, to save... or to lose. But that last part made her anxious.

Una kept walking, making as little noise as possible as she picked her way through the undergrowth. Greer was far enough away now that Una no longer heard the crackling of sticks and leaves as she ran. She adjusted her heavy medicine satchel higher on her shoulder. Perhaps keeping to the road would have been easier, but her journey needed to be a secret. Her safety—Blair's safety—depended upon it.

She picked her way along a burn, the water ruffling over smooth stones as the wind blew through the tree tops high above. The branches rustled together, and late falling leaves fluttered down to the forest floor. A flock of geese flew overhead, their honks echoing in the cold air. She took a deep breath, appreciating the peace, the *space,* and was comforted by the sounds of the forest around her.

But then, hoofbeats. The nickering of a horse.

Una froze, a desperate sort of panic clawing at her throat. What if Cameron had come for her? What if he meant to bring her back? She'd die before she allowed that to happen.

As quietly as possible, she lowered her satchel and food bundle to the ground. Her quiver was on a belt and at her hip. She reached for an arrow and nocked it in the bowstring before sliding silently behind a tree. With great effort, she slowed her breathing, the way Blair had taught her, making the inhales and exhales silent from her open mouth. Blood was rushing in her ears, but she felt all of her preparations sliding into place, the way Blair said they would.

"Instinct takes over, if you've practiced well enough," he'd said.

It seemed he had been right. Her hands didn't shake and her heartbeat was steady, albeit fast. She felt in control despite her fear. Perhaps *in spite of* her fear. She would never go back to the Cameron keep, would never live under Laird Cameron's cruelty every again. And if she had to kill the laird himself to ensure that, so be it.

The horse was close, and Una could tell from the sounds that its rider had dismounted and was walking beside it. The horse and rider were alone. That fact was almost a relief. Malcolm Cameron never went anywhere without a personal guard of twenty men. Her odds of escape were as good as they could possibly be.

Perhaps it was an outlaw, one of those men who had abandoned his clan or been forced out for sins unforgiveable. A rogue man with no allegiance and a chip on his shoulder was dangerous, to be certain, but she had freedom within her sights for the first time in a year and would not let a lone man stand in her way.

The horse's heavy footfalls closed in, just behind a large bramble and oak. Una drew back on the string, calmed by the muscle memory, just as Blair had taught her. A huge, dappled gray destrier emerged from the thicket. Its shaggy main hung long, but Una could see a bright, white blaze streaking down the length of its nose.

She did not wait for the horse's owner to appear before she said, "Take one step further, and I'll shoot you where you stand."

CHAPTER 5

Ewan passed the bramble and froze, following the line of the arrow shaft with his eyes, up a long arm that belonged to… a woman. She was tall, with glossy black hair plaited and draped over her shoulder. The Cameron plaid had fallen to the leaves at her feet.

With the breeze blowing the loose tendrils around her face and her eyes narrowed, Ewan couldn't help but think of the old goddesses his gran had told him about, relics from a wilder, ancient time in the land, when there was more room for magic. Her chest rose and fell evenly with her breath, and she looked as if she feared nothing. Certainly not him. She looked as if she would have no qualms about murdering him and then stepping over his carcass to carry on her merry way.

"I mean you nae harm," Ewan said, slowly raising his hands to show that they were empty.

She barely blinked. Her lips pressed into an even tighter line.

"I'm going to take off my belt now," he said. *Shite.* She tensed and adjusted her aim. "My sword belt!" he shouted.

He took a fortifying breath, feeling it shake in his chest. "I'm going to take off my sword belt now. To show my good faith. Dinnae shoot. Please."

Saints above, he couldn't imagine this going worse. That is, unless she actually shot him. That would be wildly inconvenient.

Ewan kept his gaze on hers as he unbuckled his sword belt, which held his sheathed claymore and a dirk. After wrapping the leather around the scabbard, he tossed it toward her, the heavy sword landing with a thud in the leaves near her feet. He wondered what she was doing out here alone. It wasn't safe for a woman to go traipsing about the woods alone, especially not on Cameron lands.

"I am looking for the Cameron healer. Do you ken where I might find him?"

She snorted. "You dinnae look in need of healing," she replied acidly.

Ewan's hand shook from holding his arms up. "Aye. I dinnae need a healer for myself. And I'd like to maintain that state of nae needing a healer, if you'd be so kind."

She narrowed her eyes. "Why do you need to find the Cameron healer?"

He swallowed against the lump in his throat. "My brother has been gravely wounded, and our healer is gone," Ewan said as evenly as he could, speaking in the same tone he would use with a spooked colt. "If you cannae help me, then I beg you to let me continue on my way. A boy's life is at stake."

She flinched, and a strange flicker of pain crossed her features.

With his hands still in the air, Ewan dropped carefully to one knee. "I'm going to remove my other dagger and throw it to you."

She lifted her chin once, and he reached down into his

boot and removed his sgian dubh, tossing the small blade next to the sword.

Never breaking eye contact, he rose back to standing. "Now. I am unarmed, as you can see. I mean you nae harm. Will you tell me where I can find the Cameron healer? Or will you at—"

"What's his name?" she interrupted.

"I dinnae ken the healer's name. I've never met the man."

"Your brother," she snapped with a huff. "What is his name?"

The question told Ewan all he needed to know, that the person he sought to save Connor's life was the very same person poised to take his own. The Cameron healer was no man, but this woman, tall and solid, with chapped hands and an enraged look on her face.

"Connor," he said quietly. "His name is Connor. He's fifteen."

There it was again, that slight flinch, the flicker of concern. He decided to try his advantage, to draw her out. With his hands still high overhead, he took a careful step closer.

"He was gored by a boar on a hunt. The tusk cut deeply into his thigh. His twin, my sister Catriona, stitched the wound as best as she could, but, well, I dinnae think you can expect much from a fifteen-year-old lass in the way of healing."

"I was stitching battle wounds and helping with birthings at fifteen. Your sister probably did a fine job," she shot back.

Color rose up the pale column of her neck until it reached her ears, no doubt angry that she had given herself away. Ewan took another careful step forward.

"Aye. Will I have the pleasure of being murdered today by the Cameron healer?"

"That all depends," she replied icily.

Just then, a large, white greyhound burst through the trees, leaping in between Ewan and the healer, standing directly over the pile of weapons he'd tossed her way. The dog snarled viciously, hackles high. How the hell would he be able to protect the healer from a wild beast like this without his sword, he wondered, noting the gleaming, sharp teeth.

But as Ewan hazarded a glance at the woman, he noticed her staring at him, not the hound. For the first time, she looked afraid. But not of him. Good heavens. She was afraid *he* would hurt *the dog.*

What a bloody mess this has turned into, Ewan thought as slowly, inch by inch, he came back onto one knee. He held his arms out, palms up.

"Easy, now," he crooned. "Settle yourself. I mean you nae harm. You have my word."

The dog softened its snarl a bit, though the hackles remained lifted.

"That's a good dog," he continued in a soft, low burr. "I've come to ask your mistress for help. That is all. Will you come to me? You can smell me all you like and see that I am nae anyone to be afraid of."

Out of the corner of his eye, he saw the healer tighten her grip on the bowstring. Sniffing the air as it went, the white hound padded warily towards Ewan.

"Greer, nay!" she cried out, and Ewan heard the bowstring creak.

With great effort, he forced himself to focus on the dog, letting Greer sniff his hands. She circled him as he knelt in the leaves, snorting as she passed, pressing her nose into the side of his plaid, against his hip. No doubt she smelled Mathan on his clothing. Thank heavens he'd left the hound behind to comfort Catriona. Mathan wouldn't hurt Greer, not without being commanded, but he would have added unnecessary complication to what was already an ungodly mess.

Circling back around him, Greer looked at Ewan for a long breath before pushing her delicate head against his chest.

"That's a good girl, Greer, my sweet," Ewan murmured as he scratched behind her ears. "What a beauty you are."

The dog snorted contentedly and pushed harder, nearly taking him off balance.

A laugh burst forth from his mouth. Looking up at the healer, he called out, "As you can plainly see, I mean neither of you harm."

The bow lowered an inch. And then another.

"How far is your brother? What clan?"

"I am Ewan MacDonald. My home lies a full day's ride from here. I've ridden through the night to reach ye." He looked at her pleadingly. "Please," he said, "I need your help. Without you, I fear my brother will die."

Ewan choked on those last words. It was the first time he'd allowed himself to even give them space, let alone voice. The awful truth threatened to crush him.

He was not accustomed to begging. A laird didn't beg. He commanded. He instructed. He directed. He never begged. But he was desperate, more desperate than he'd ever been in his life. And if he must beg her, he would.

He looked into her eyes and let her see every raw, aching bit of his fear. Not of her bow, not of her dog, but of losing yet another person he loved. She *had* to come with him. Without her, Connor would be lost.

She pulled herself up taller, a vengeful goddess in the cold dawn. But then she lowered her bow, and Ewan's sigh of relief was like a thunderclap in the silence.

CHAPTER 6

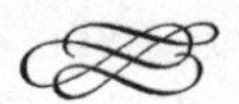

Una replaced her arrow in the quiver at her hip, keeping her eyes on Ewan. Dark blond hair hung in loose, messy waves to his shoulders, the unruly locks shagging over his forehead. The heavy stubble of several days without shaving covered a strong jaw, and his nose appeared to have been broken at least once. His eyes were wreathed by the early wrinkles of a person who spent a great deal of time outside squinting at the sun.

He was filthy, a dirty leine shirt tucked into the MacDonald plaid, which was blue and green with red striping. The plaid was flecked with mud and—Jesu, was that blood?

Ewan sat back on his haunches, petting Greer and crooning soft words to her as she wiggled excitedly. Una could see muscles flexing under his shirt. He was strong, someone who used his body to earn his supper. Perhaps a guard for the MacDonald laird? Why else would he be riding a warhorse?

As she wrapped her fallen plaid tightly around her shoulders, she cursed silently. This was not the plan. She was meant to go to the Stewarts. She was to convince Laird Stewart to send for Blair. She was *not* meant to be side-questing to a neighboring clan.

But she took in the heavy set of Ewan's shoulders, the tense line of his jaw, the way his hands shook slightly as he rubbed Greer's flanks. Connor. That was his brother's name. A boy, he'd said. She couldn't let a child die. Not when there was any possibility of saving him. Agatha would have blistered her ears for even considering it.

She would go to the MacDonalds. She would tend Connor and do what she could for him. And in lieu of payment, she would ask Ewan to escort her to the Stewarts when the job was done.

Resolved to that plan, she gathered up her bundle of provisions, she said, "Come along, Greer, my traitorous sprite."

Greer bounded to her, all long legs and enthusiasm, and shoved her head under Una's hand, nuzzling affectionately. Ewan rose to his feet, and for a moment, he seemed frozen, his eyes unfocused, as if looking *through* her. But then he shook himself.

"Do you ride?"

"What?"

"Horses. Do you ken how to ride a horse?"

"Cannae I just walk?" she asked, sweat prickling instantly.

But Ewan had already turned, whistling loudly. The huge horse lumbered up to him obediently.

"You call your horse like a dog?"

"You say that like it's a bad thing," he said, holding the reins in a loose grip. "Why should a horse nae come when he's called? 'Tis verra useful."

"I suppose," she said, feeling her palms sweating now, her heart pounding.

"So do you ride?"

"I prefer to walk. Shall we?"

She took off, walking in the direction from which he'd come, her pace brisk. She heard the heavy hoofbeats behind her as he followed, catching her easily.

"Are you afraid of the horse?"

"I am fine. 'Tis only that I would rather walk."

"Riding will get us there much faster. You ken better than anyone that time is of the essence with wounds like this."

"I can walk quickly."

"Look," he said, the frustration in his voice evident. "We dinnae have time for this. Is it that you are afraid of the horse?"

She stopped walking, wheeling around to glare at him and coming nose-to-nose with the animal in question, who snorted.

Una shrieked and jumped back, catching her heel on an exposed root and flailing wildly as she fell backwards, anticipating the way the hard ground would send radiating pain up from her tailbone when she landed. But she never did.

Instead, she found herself pulled up against a very hard, very warm chest as Ewan reached and caught her arm, dragging her out of the fall. For the space of a breath, she froze, staring into eyes that she could now see were a mossy green. The wind blew suddenly, and she squinted as a stray lock of hair whipped against her eye. Ewan brushed at the lock with a careful hand, and that touch brought her back to herself.

She flinched and shoved him. He released her, his brow furrowed in obvious concern, and took a step away from her. That step made it possible to breathe again. He was still so close, though. Too close.

"I dinnae ken your name," he said.

"Una," she croaked.

"Una," he repeated, his voice taking on the same timbre he'd used when soothing Greer. He said her name with care, like it was a precious, fragile thing. She shoved that thought away as quickly as it had come. She was not precious, nor was she fragile, and she could not afford to allow him such notions.

She turned and kept walking, not surprised when his long strides brought him easily to her side once more.

"This is ridiculous, Una," he said, obviously losing patience. "We can reach my home twice as fast on the horse as if we walk."

She shook her head. She knew it was ridiculous. Of all things, to be more afraid of a horse than a man—though she had plenty of reasons to be afraid of those, too. She also knew that he was right. The horse *would* be much faster. But she couldn't bring herself to even consider it. The thought of such a big animal. What if... Una quickened her pace.

"Una," he growled. "We dinnae have time! Dinnae be stubborn."

"I am nae being stubborn," she hissed. "I—"

She couldn't answer, because the horse had taken another step closer, his massive head nearly the size of her torso, close enough to touch.

Her breath caught, and she felt the tears flooding quickly to her eyes. *Damn it. Damn it all. Not now.*

He would mock her. He would tease her for such a ridiculous fear. That's what Malcolm would have done. But it wasn't ridiculous. She'd never grown up around horses, but she'd treated many an injury from men being thrown from them. Broken bones, broken necks. And it didn't matter if this one seemed especially tame, that it came like a dog when called.

Her breath was fast and uncontrolled now. The horse took another step, and she squeezed her eyes shut tightly, feeling the tears squeeze through the tight line of her lashes. But then there was a gentle bump at her abdomen. An insistent press that was... much like Greer. She cracked open an eye and saw that the horse had lowered his head and was nudging her, as if he wanted to be pet.

"That's good," Ewan whispered. "You're so brave, Una."

"Dinnae mock me," she said through clenched teeth.

"I speak the truth. 'Tis more than common to be afraid of horses, especially if you havenae been around them. You're brave to face it."

"You havenae exactly given me a choice."

"He wants to be your friend," he said easily, though there was an unaccountable note of surprise there as well.

The horse pushed his nose into her belly again and shook his head.

"What does he want?" she asked, the last word shrill.

"He liked to be stroked down his nose. Gently."

She reached out with a shaking hand, ready to leap away, and pet a hasty line down the nose.

"There. I did it. Is he happy now?"

The horse snorted and nudged her again. Ewan stepped closer and rubbed a long, slow streak down the horse's nose before lifting his hand again to the wide, gray forehead and repeating the motion.

"May I?" he asked, and when she looked bewildered, he took her hand in his. He placed her palm on the horse's forehead, laying his overtop. And together, his hand driving hers, they rubbed down the horse's nose again. The destrier nickered happily, and with Ewan's hand over hers, warm and scratchy with calluses, she felt safe enough to notice how soft the horse felt. Like velvet. And so very warm.

"Good," Ewan crooned and guided her to the side, placing her hand on the horse's neck and showing her how to rub down the long, strong line of muscle beneath her palm. After a few passes, he took his hand away. But Una continued to pet the horse, feeling the muscles twitch and jump under her fingers every so often.

"Ready?" Una heard Ewan say.

"What?" she replied just as she found herself airborne.

She shrieked. His hands were on her waist, and he had hoisted her up onto the saddle. But without being prepared, she found herself clinging to it, the hard leather and wood frame digging into her belly. The horse took a step to balance the new weight, and she screamed again.

"Down! Down! Get me down now!"

"We cannae waste any more time, Una. You can do it. You're halfway there."

The tears were falling in earnest now and her hands shook as she gripped the saddle as if she were clinging to a cliff face over a bottomless crevasse. She felt a heavy hand at her elbow and heard Ewan's low voice through her panic.

"Una, you can do this. Listen to me and do as I say. Swing your leg over his back."

She shook her head.

"Aye, ye can. You were going to shoot me in the throat back there. You can sit on a horse, Una."

Una took a deep breath and lifted her leg that felt as heavy as if it had been filled with rocks. Pulling with her arms, she swung it over the side, finding herself with a face full of the horse's mane, which she gripped in fistfuls.

"Aye, you've done it. Now stay just like that."

It was comical to suggest that she could do anything other than stay frozen where she was. She had no intention of sitting up, of being even more likely to fall. No. She would stay just like this. And as she had no interest in seeing just how far off the ground she was, she kept her eyes tightly shut.

She heard Ewan tying things, buckling something else. And then she felt the warm weight of her plaid tossed over her back, having fallen off. Likely when he tossed her onto the horse's back without warning. She felt him reach a hand under her torso and bristled, but he was only gripping the pommel, his knuckles hard against her belly. And then he was behind her. She tensed again, the feeling of his hips against her backside too reminiscent of...

She vomited into the leaves at the horse's feet so far below.

"God's bones, Una," he said, "Are you ill?"

But she couldn't answer. She was made of terror, with this giant animal beneath her and this powerful man behind her. She shook uncontrollably. Would he shout at her now? Manhandle her upright and take off at a run? What if he—

But then she felt the gentle press of a hand between her shoulder blades, a palm rubbing wide circles across her back.

"I am sorry, Una," he said quietly.

She froze. It was enough to drag her away from her terror. The gentle touch—when had Malcolm ever been gentle with her?—and the apology. An *earnest*-sounding apology.

"Can you take a deep breath for me?"

She tried, her lungs shaking with the effort, but eventually, she felt them expand.

"Good. Verra good. Now another?"

She sniffled, her mouth tasting sour from her vomit, but she did as he asked, the breath coming more easily now.

"That's the way. You are so brave, Una," he said in that careful way. "Do you think you can sit up now?"

She shook her head quickly.

"Shhh," he said. "You can. Take another deep breath, Una, and—"

"I'll fall," she sobbed.

"Nay," he said insistently. "I willnae let ye fall. I willnae let anything happen to you."

He couldn't make such a promise. Not letting *anything* happen to her? When so much had *already* happened to her? But she found that she believed him, believed that this man would, at the very least, try.

And for that reason alone, she found herself pushing her hands against the pommel, allowing him to draw her up with strong hands. She didn't open her eyes, not yet, but she was grateful that he let her sit, let her get used to the way the horse shifted from one side to the other as he stood, patiently waiting.

The horse hadn't flinched when she'd screamed. Hadn't bolted when she'd yanked on his mane. Hadn't done anything more than twitch when she'd vomited at his feet. If anything, he'd stood deliberately still, allowing her to calm down before resuming his side-to-side shifting.

"Good lad," Ewan said to the horse, taking Una's hand in his and placing it against the soft, gray neck, rubbing.

He removed his hand, and she continued to stroke the horse's neck. She did not love the feeling of a man at her back, and she didn't know if she would ever be ready to open her eyes and see how far from her feet the ground was, but she trusted, at the very least, that this horse would not hurt her.

She blinked back her tears, opening her eyes. The ground was indeed *very* far away, but if she looked out, not down, it didn't seem quite as terrifying. Ewan's front was pressed close against her back, but he wasn't grabbing her or manhandling her. In fact, he seemed to be going out of his way to touch her as little as possible.

"Are you ready, Una?"

She knew he was impatient, likely frantic with worry about his brother. And she knew that every minute she spent panicking was one moment more than she'd have to make up for in saving his life. Because Ewan was right, with wounds, every moment counted. Yet she also had the impression that he would give her as long as she needed to be ready, that he could control his temper with the same deftness that he controlled this animal beneath them. She nodded.

"Hand me the reins, would you?" Ewan asked. Una lifted a hand off the pommel to grab the strips of leather draped over the horse's neck and passed them to him. He took them, resting his closed fist against his thigh. His other hand hung at his side. Harmless.

Well, not harm*less*. But not harm*ful* either. At least not now.

This horse and its owner would carry her away from her and then, with any luck, would also deliver her safely to her new life.

"Last chance, Una," he said, and she couldn't tell if she was referring to a last chance for panicking or a last chance for refusing to come with him at all. "Are you ready?"

The sun was in the middle of the sky now. *Jesus, how much of the morning had she already wasted?* She looked to the right and saw Greer standing next to the horse, unbothered and panting happily.

"Nay," she answered. Because she wasn't. "But we must go anyway."

CHAPTER 7

Snow fell, sifting softly through the canopy of trees. They'd ridden through the afternoon, Greer trotting quietly beside them, only stopping once so he could relieve himself. He'd asked Una if she needed to see to similar business, but she had stubbornly clung to the pommel and said, "If I get off this horse, you willnae get me back on it."

He'd hoped to be able to ride straight for home and arrive that evening. But finding Una had been a task, as had convincing her not to kill him. And then she'd been so damned afraid of the horse. But she hadn't vomited until he'd mounted behind her in the saddle, a fact that had rankled him all day.

The day had not gone to plan, although what *had* gone to plan in his life the last few years? His father had died, years before he was meant to, Ewan had been thrust into leadership he didn't feel prepared for, and now Conner might be dying.

They would not reach his home tonight. It would be dark

before long, and while that was dangerous enough, he'd ridden through the night before to find the Cameron healer. The horse was tiring, having gone without meaningful rest. *He* was tiring, having gone without it as well. And the snow made riding at night treacherous. He needed to find a place to stop for the night before the dark swallowed them whole.

Una would not be happy, but she could join him in that sentiment.

Ewan remembered passing a cave on his way early that morning. It wasn't especially deep, but it was wide enough to accommodate a horse, a dog, and two people, and shelter them from the snow. If memory served, they were getting close.

He glanced down at the hooded figure in front of him. Sometime in the afternoon, he'd grown tired of watching her stubbornly shiver and had rummaged in her bag for a heavy cloak, draping it over her shoulders. No doubt she hadn't expected to need it traveling on foot and working up a sweat. But the wind was biting, and she wasn't exerting enough to keep her warm.

He could have kept her warmer, but given how she flinched and tensed every time he shifted in the saddle behind her, he didn't imagine that wrapping his arms around her to share body heat would be welcomed.

There would have been nothing behind it. Ewan didn't have any interest in seducing the woman who would hold his brother's life in her hands. He didn't have any interest in seduction, period, if he was honest. It was a luxury he couldn't afford, even if the price was loneliness.

After his mother died delivering the twins, Ewan had watched his father turn into a hollow shell. In a world where marriage was a tool to establish or solidify alliances, his parents had been truly blessed to find love with one another along the way. The late laird had gone through the motions of life after, but certainly hadn't done anything that remotely resembled living. And then one night, his life had been snuffed out like a candle while he slept, leaving Ewan with yet more howling grief, but also the mantle of responsibility for hundreds.

It was true that, as laird, the burden of expectation surrounding an heir was heavy indeed. But he had four brothers, all of whom he genuinely liked and trusted. Let one of them be laird when he was gone.

He had no desire to feel the sort of shattered heart that had slowly bled his father's spirit dry until there had been nothing left. He could bear no more pain. He could bear no more loss. And so he'd found himself guarding his family like a broody hen, keeping them close where he could protect them. The worry was constant and consuming already, but now, *now*, Connor lay on the brink.

Yet another failure on his part. He should have found a new healer immediately. He should have told Connor to stay home. Or, barring that, he should have kept a closer eye on him during the hunt. Failures were collecting around his feet like kindling.

The sun wrestled with the craggy horizon, just visible through the trees over his left shoulder. He tightened his grip on the reins, feeling the leather flex in his hands. The muscles of his torso were sore from holding himself upright and away from Una. Well, as away as one could be with their hips crushed together into a saddle. Through the gloaming, he glimpsed the cave in the distance.

Ewan leaned as forward as he could without pressing his chest against her. "Do you see that cave ahead? We must stop there for the night."

She sat as straight as a caber. "You told me we would make for your home with all haste. That we wouldnae be stopping."

He sighed, his breath sending forth a cloud of white that wreathed her hood. "Aye. We've made good time. But we were... delayed." Before she could protest, he continued. "I cannae risk the horse on this path in a snowstorm with nae moon. He's tired and willnae be as surefooted as he would be rested. It would be dangerous for us all."

He heard the shuddering sound of her breath. "I understand."

There was still enough light that he could see her hands trembling as she took down the hood of her cloak. Then there was the set of her body, even more rigid than before. Next to them, Greer whined, looking up at her mistress with obvious concern.

Understanding dawned, and with it, horror. The vomiting, the way she'd held herself as straight as the sword at his side. Una was afraid of *him.* Not the horse any longer. *Him.*

"I meant what I said, Una. I willnae allow any harm to come to you."

Her silence was an answer.

"I swear it, Una. And *I* willnae harm you."

"I've heard that before."

They rode in silence until they reached the cave. Ewan swung down from the horse and reached up to help her dismount, but she did not relinquish her tight grip on the pommel. Her breaths were coming faster again, the panic rising.

"Una," he said softly. "Let me help you off the horse, and then I willnae touch you again. I'll give you my weapons. All of them."

That seemed to settle her slightly. She turned and looked down at him.

"I know all the best places to stick a dirk, Ewan," she said.

"I dinnae doubt that, Una," he said with an unbidden smile. "I dinnae doubt that at all."

He held his arms up for her, and she turned, bracing her hands on his shoulders as he lifted her off the horse. But the light was dim, and he misjudged his distance from the animal. In the confined space between man and beast, Una slid against his body as he lowered her to the ground. Her body went rigid again, and he practically leaped backwards. She stumbled, wheeling to grip the saddle for balance.

"My legs are stiff from riding so long," she said. The horse swung his head around to look at her, and she reached out hesitantly to stroke his nose.

With the snow falling softly on her windswept black hair, wisps framing her face, Una looked like a faerie queen in the coming night, taming a wild creature of the forest. He had the strangest urge to rub one of those loose tendrils between his thumb and forefinger, to feel the satiny lock slip through his open fist. And wasn't that odd?

Ewan coughed. "I'll go gather wood for a fire," he said, thrusting the reins into her hands.

"Wait!" Una called. "What am I to do with him?"

Ewan took back the reins and led the horse into the cave's opening.

"Will he nae run? Should you nae tie him to something?"

"He will nae run. Just… I will return soon. Stay put."

She made a sound of protest, but Ewan had already turned and stalked away from the cave. He went farther than he needed to, farther than perhaps was wise. But he found himself filled with a twitchy sort of energy that was hard to shake, no matter how briskly he walked. His mind kept wandering the way Una's backside had felt pressed between his thighs.

Oh no. That would not do.

"Goddamnit," he muttered.

The light was almost completely gone, the forest a tangle of dark shadows and deeper hollows. He hastily gathered enough wood that he fervently hoped would be dry enough to light. The snow was falling in earnest now, melting against his face and eyelashes. Through the curtain of fat, heavy flakes, he spotted the silvery gray horse against the darkness of the cave.

But where was Una?

The horse nickered a greeting as Ewan entered the cave, but Una was nowhere to be found.

"Una?"

No answer.

"Una?" he said, louder now.

There was no response. Only the sounds of horse and night forest.

"Una?" he called out, fighting against a rising panic. How could he have lost the damn healer already? "Una?"

From behind a boulder outside the cave, he heard a disgruntled huff.

"Dinnae fash yourself," she grumbled. "I'm right here."

"What in hell were you doing back there? And why didnae you answer when I called?"

She was a shadow, the night too dark to make out her face. But he could see her hands move to her hips.

"I had to see to some business, and I felt it best to do while you were away," she said peevishly. "I didnae think I required an audience."

There was a long span of silence as they stood, not looking at one another.

"Ah," Ewan said, clearing his throat. "My apologies."

She sighed. "'Tis fine. I am sorry I worried you. I ken ye have enough to panic about without thinking that I tumbled down a hill in the dark."

He grunted.

"Did you find good wood?"

"Nothing dry. But we'll do our best, aye?"

Ewan knelt at the mouth of the cave, fumbling at the bottom of his bag until his fingers closed around his flint. He hadn't planned well or packed—there hadn't been time. It wouldn't have been a problem for him alone, but he had Una to take care of. She'd need a fire. She'd need food.

He heard her shiver behind him.

"Go and stand by the horse, Una. He's plenty warm."

As she hesitantly picked her way past him, approaching the horse, he attempted the impossible task of lighting a fire with damp wood in a snowstorm.

Ewan was in the middle of a long, elegant stream of curses under his breath when Una said, "What's his name?"

"Who?"

She huffed. "The horse, of course. What is his name?"

"He doesnae have one."

"What? How do ye refer to him? You cannae just call him horse."

"I dinnae call him anything," Ewan said with a shrug, striking the flint, the sparks dying as soon as they touched the damp kindling. "I just say, 'Ready my horse.' The stable master calls him Lucifer, though, on account that he's such a devil."

Ewan wished he had thought, even just a moment, before saying that. She was afraid of the horse. He didn't need to add more fuel to the fear. But it was too late now.

He sighed. "This horse is... high-spirited. He willnae let anyone but me ride him. Doesnae take orders from anyone else without some cheek."

"He let me ride him," Una said quietly.

"Aye," Ewan said, rolling a shoulder to ease the tension. "He likes you, it seems."

From the soft sounds, he could tell she was petting him. And from the answering sounds of the horse's snorts, he wagered she was stroking his nose again, the way he'd shown her.

"He also likes to be scratched beneath his chin," Ewan said, striking the flint again.

"Everyone needs a name," Una said. "And that includes you, horse."

The horse snorted.

"You are a verra good boy. Mo sneachda, mo luchag."

"Well, which is he? A snowflake? Or a mouse?" Ewan asked, sounding surly. He *felt* surly, his temper rising hotter with every failed flint strike.

He *needed* a fire. With a fire, Una would stay reasonably warm. Without one, well… the night would be long. Huddling would be required, which he imagined was the last thing Una would want. She'd probably rather freeze.

"Such a big, strong boy," she said softly. "Perhaps you should be called Larann. What say you, Larann? Is that your name?"

The horse whinnied and shorted.

"Nay to that, then," she said with a chuckle. "It is such a hard name. And you are such a sweet boy. Aye. You are. So verra sweet."

Ewan stopped his flint strikes, transfixed by the conversation between Una and his horse. She had been terrified of the animal just a few hours before. But she had faced her fear and ridden him all afternoon anyway, and now she was petting him and speaking to him like a bairn. She had threatened to murder Ewan—and he had no doubt she would have followed through on that threat if provoked.

She was a collection of sharp edges. But between the jagged, armored plates, there was a softness. Agreeing to help a boy she'd never met. Speaking gently to a horse that terrified her in a busy, melodic voice, calling him one ridiculous pet name after another.

And the horse, a renowned grump at best, a menace at worst, was putty in her hands.

As he listened to her talk to the horse, Ewan couldn't help but wonder if Una used that voice when she was healing, or sitting with the dying. Did she speak sweet words to a person to ease their leaving, soothing them the way she gentled the horse? Ewan felt a sudden tightness in his chest and a lump in his throat as he remembered whispering into Connor's sandy curls. *"Hush now, mo ghaisgeach. You're nearly home now."*

The horse snorted happily, and Una chuckled.

"I have it. What say you to Calman?"

"You're naming my warhorse after a dove?" Ewan spat in disbelief.

But the destrier pranced happily in place and snorted his approval.

"He chose it for himself, Ewan. You heard him."

Ewan cast his gaze to the heavens before stuffing the flint back into his bag and rising to his feet.

"Too wet for a fire?" Una stated more than she asked.

He approached Calman—for it seemed that the horse had indeed chosen—and rubbed his neck.

"Aye," he said. "We'll have to rely on our gentle dove for warmth. I'll just rub him down first so he's dry."

Ewan took a cloth from his saddlebag and carefully rubbed the sweat from the horse's body, going by feel since he could not go by sight, taking his time. Once the task was done, Ewan felt his way to Calman's head, taking the reins and gently pulling, encouraging the horse to lie down.

"Down you go, laddie," he said. "If we lean our backs against him, we willnae freeze to death. Are you hungry?"

"Aye," came the quiet response. "Starving."

They sat, backs against the horse's warm side. From his bag, he pulled out two apples, some oatcakes, and two leather flasks.

"Hold out your hands, Una."

Ewan reached to place the oatcake in what he thought was her hand, but instead brushed against what could only be her breast. She tensed and hastily reached for his hands, fumbling for the oatcake and snatching it from his grip.

"Shite," Ewan cursed. "I didnae mean to— I couldnae—"

But there was no reply. Only the sounds of chewing and the faint smacking of her lips as she ate with the hurried gusto of a child.

"More?" he asked, holding out another oat cake.

"Aye," Una replied hastily, her mouth half full, before adding, "Please."

With groping hands, she found his arm and felt her way to her his hand, taking the cake. The feel of her strong fingers against his body made him feel flushed.

Ewan ate his oatcake, listening to the sounds around him: Calman's breathing, the quiet wheeze of the falling snow, Greer's scratching as she turned in circles, and Una's chewing. She hadn't been kidding. She *was* starving.

"Apple?"

Her mouth was full when she answered with a muffled "Mmphmm."

Ewan couldn't help but smile. The smile turned quickly to a grimace, however, as her nimble fingers grazed down his arm again before closing around the apple.

"When was the last time ye ate, Una?" he asked as he heard the snap of her teeth breaking the apple's skin. She chewed and swallowed before answering.

"Yesterday noon."

"Why nothing today?" he asked, shocked.

"I was in a hurry."

He didn't press further. It wasn't his business anyway.

He swallowed another bite of his oat cake. "As long as you

are with me, you willnae go hungry. You have my word on that."

The responding silence was thick. No chewing. None of the endearing lip smacks. Just the sounds of a horse and snow and his own breath.

Finally, blessedly, he heard a deep inhale. "Thank you, Ewan. I hope your laird is as generous with you as you have been with me."

Ewan was confused for a moment until he remembered that he hadn't actually gotten around to telling her that *he* was the laird. He'd meant to open with that information, to use it as leverage to convince her to come with him. But then he'd nearly walked into an arrow shaft and it had been all he could do to give her his name.

Ewan cleared his throat. "I… I am the laird."

"Verra funny, Ewan."

After a few long moments of his silence, she scrambled away from him. Calman snorted.

"You didnae tell me you were the laird," she hissed.

"There was nae time, what with you trying to shoot me and all."

"And this entire afternoon? You've sat behind me for half a day, and you could nae have found a single moment to tell me that I was sitting in a *laird's* lap?"

"What difference does it make?" Ewan asked, exasperated.

"It makes every difference!"

"Why? I didnae come to you as a laird. I came to you as an older brother. I came to you frantic about my kin. What does that have to do with being a laird?"

"You could have forced me to come. Ordered me about all high and mighty, your *lairdship*." He could hear the sneer in her voice, the anger. And maybe… the fear.

"I wouldnae have commanded you."

She snorted. "Right."

"I wouldnae have!"

"Bah."

Ewan clenched his jaw, feeling angry and defensive.

"Have I threatened you? Have I nae fed you and kept you safe thus far, helped you, respected your boundaries? Have I nae shown myself to be a good laird? A good man? You have no reason to accuse me of being such a horse's ass."

A long, heavy moment passed before she answered him.

"I have been treated thus before. And then, when I ceased to be useful or meet expectations, I have seen how all that care can turn to cruelty."

"Cameron?" Ewan asked, because what other laird would she have met? She was common-born, a crofter's daughter perhaps, but not a lady. A lady would never have been allowed to assume a trade like healing. As such, her world would have been very small. She wouldn't have traveled to the king's court. She wouldn't have traveled anywhere.

"Aye," she whispered.

"What business did you have with Cameron?" He felt her shiver next to him. "Are you cold?"

"I am fine," she said in a muffled voice, obviously talking into her cloak.

He huffed. Whatever else she might be—and he was still trying to figure that out—she was stubborn as a mule.

He scooted closer to her and spread the spare plaid overtop of them. "We'll have to share. You are nae good to anyone frozen solid."

She was rigid as the stone around them. With his free hand, he reached for the smaller of the two flasks, pulling the stopper out with his teeth.

"Here," he said, holding the letter flask out for her to take.

"What is it?"

"Whisky. It'll warm your blood. Soothe your nerves."

"Nay, thank you," she said. "I want my wits about me. Especially if you plan to partake."

He took a long drink from the flask, his eyes closed in frustration, and leaned his head back against Calman's warm side. The whisky was spicy on the back of his tongue and burned a delightfully warm trail down his throat. He corked the flask and sighed.

"I willnae touch you," he said.

Another disbelieving snort.

He choked on the insult. Because he knew he didn't have any right to feel insulted. It wasn't *him* she was talking about, after all, but a specter of Cameron. The bastard.

"I am nae Cameron," he said through his teeth. "I cannae imagine a worse insult than to be lumped into the same batch as him."

When she didn't answer, he said, "Try to get some sleep. We'll leave at first light."

Ewan pulled his side of the plaid up to his chin, scooting down and leaning fully back against Calman, feeling the comforting tattoo of the horse's steady heartbeat behind his back.

She took in a shaky breath. "I was handfast to Laird Cameron."

His eyes flew open, but he didn't move a muscle otherwise.

"You were?" he asked, forcing his voice to remain low and calm.

"Aye," she whispered. "For a year. I was freed from my indenture to him yesterday."

He heard her swallow.

His hands were balled into fists in his lap. "And I take it… it didnae go well?"

In a thick voice, she answered, "Nay."

Ewan stared into the darkness for a long time. Eventually,

he felt Una's body relax against his, her breathing becoming deep and steady. At some point, she listed to the side and her head landed on his shoulder with a soft thud.

Sleep eluded him for a long time, even though he couldn't remember ever being so tired. But he couldn't seem to settle his mind long enough to drift off, replaying the day in his mind. Una's anger. Her fear. Her sickness. The distance.

But it wasn't his business. None of it.

CHAPTER 8

Una drifted into consciousness with the slow, ruffling manner of a leaf tumbling to the ground from a high branch. The air was cold against her face, but beneath the plaid, she felt as warm as a kitten. Warmer, in fact, with a solid wall of heat at her back. *The horse,* she drowsily thought, remembering how warm his side had been to lean against the night before.

In front of her, Greer's body twitched in sleep, her legs kicking as she chased something in her dreams. Una reached out to stroke the dog's velvet ears.

Still half asleep, she shifted her body and burrowed her nose deeper into the warm wool. It smelled like horse and soap and heather, almost as if its owner had spread it on the ground and let it soak up the smell of flowers and sunshine before the weather had turned cold. The plaid had a comforting weight to it, pressing down on her torso.

She could easily go back to sleep. It was so nice to be warm, to rest. Una wiggled again, trying to make herself more comfortable on the hard stone of the cave floor. She felt a warm gust of air against her neck.

"Have mercy on me, Una," a strained voice groaned in her ear. "You cannae wriggle about like that."

Una's eyes flew open wide and she froze, her body breaking into a cold sweat as she realized that the solid heat behind her was not the horse but *Ewan,* and that the weight slung carelessly over her waist was not a heavy plaid, or not entirely that, but his *arm.* Una hurled herself clumsily away, elbowing Ewan in the face and nearly kicking him in the groin.

"Bloody hell, Una," Ewan groaned, holding his nose and curling in on himself.

She saw drops of blood seeping through his closed fingers before dripping onto the ground.

"What *the hell* do you think you were doing?" she seethed.

"Nae freezing to death," he grumbled, sitting up and leaning against Calman's side with his head tilted back, pinching it with bloody fingers.

Greer licked her hand, scooting closer to rest her head on Una's leg.

"Was there nae other way to prevent freezing to death?"

"Believe me, Una, I didnae do it on purpose. We must have moved that way in our sleep."

She snorted. "Pfft. A likely story."

With another groan, he stood and folded the plaid, tucking it into the saddle bag. Calman rose as well, with as much grace available to such a large animal. Una felt herself losing control of her breathing. He'd been so close. He was so much bigger. He could have—

"Una," he said and snapped his fingers. She shook her head, her eyes refocusing on him. "I promised I wouldnae hurt you, and I *meant it*. God's bones, Una. What kind of monster do you take me for?"

She wrapped her arms around her bent knees and glared at him. But he was right. Nothing had happened. Nothing at all except sleep. Sharing warmth. She watched Ewan press his forehead to Calman's nose, speaking to the horse in a voice so soft she couldn't make out his words. He scratched under Calman's chin, the way he'd shown her yesterday.

"Catch."

Una barely had time to register the command before an apple nearly hit her on the chin. But she did catch it, which made Ewan smile. She'd never seen him smile before. The fine lines around his eyes crinkled deeper, and though the reddish-brown stubble on his jaw had grown even more, it was not yet long enough to block a glimpse of his teeth. It was a warm expression. Her mother would have said he had a kind face.

He scratched his head and drew his hand away with a twig pinched between two fingers.

"We should go," he said, tossing the twig aside.

"Aye," she said, her voice shaky. "We must."

"I'll take the horse and dog to the burn for some water so that you can tend to your business."

She recognized it for the kindness it was. He whistled as he left the cave, and Una watched Calman and Greer follow without being commanded, the dog bounding happily after him into the woods, darting between the sharp sunbeams piercing through the woods from the horizon.

Greer trusted him. Perhaps she could try too.

Una ducked behind the large boulder to relieve herself. As she walked back to the mouth of the cave, she combed her fingers through the tangled mess of her own hair, removing three twigs of her own. A comb would have been better, but her satchel was tied to the horse, and so she did the best she could with her hands before plaiting it into a long braid.

The trees were nearly bare, save for a few clinging, brown leaves. The ground outside the cave was blanketed with a brilliant snow that sparkled in the rising light. The sun, still climbing over the mountains, offered no actual warmth, but the sight of it brightened her spirits nonetheless. It was the first day of her new life, she thought, as she tied her braid with the same old strip of Cameron plaid.

She heard Calman snort in the near distance and turned to see Ewan climbing the hill, dog and horse close on his heels. His leine shirt was filthy, his knees scraped and scabbed, and from this angle, the bump where his nose had been broken before was more pronounced. Una couldn't figure him out. What sort of laird ran his own errands? What sort of laird went out in public looking like he lived in the mountains and hadn't seen soap in months?

He looked up and locked eyes with her.

For a moment in that quiet, early morning brilliance, they stared. Una sucked in a breath, feeling tingles rush down to her toes, making her shiver. She told herself it was the frosty morning. Nothing more. Certainly not the way his eyes seemed to be looking *through* her.

Greer ran to her side, rubbing her sleek flanks against Una's skirts. She bent down to pet the dog.

"Did you eat?" Ewan asked.

Una remembered the apple, which she had put in her pocket.

"Nay. Not as of yet. I can eat as we ride."

He nodded and held out his hands, reached for her to lift her onto Calman's back. But he didn't touch her.

"May I, Una?" he asked.

She nodded and, with a squeak, found herself airborne. Though she was far more prepared for that sudden rise that she had been the day before and swung her leg over Calman's back as Ewan hoisted her up.

"Verra good, Una," he praised. "You're a natural."

Ewan grunted as he climbed up behind her, settling against her backside as he'd done yesterday, his thighs snug around hers. But she found that she didn't feel the violent nausea this morning that such proximity had caused yesterday. Still, she tried to sit as straight as possible in the saddle to avoid leaning against him. She shivered again.

With one deft motion, Ewan reached into the saddle bag, extracted his spare plaid, and whirled it to wrap around them both. He tucked the ends around her, making an obvious effort to touch her as little as possible as he cocooned them both in the horse-warmed wool.

It was so tempting to remember how warm he'd felt at her back. That memory was almost enough to make her relax, ever so slightly, into that solid chest behind her.

Almost. But not quite.

CHAPTER 9

If Una sat any straighter, Ewan was certain her spine would snap in two. It made riding immensely uncomfortable as it required him to sit equally stiff in the saddle in an attempt to give her space. As they rode in silence, Ewan pushing the horse as fast as was safe, he was flooded by endless thoughts of Connor lying in his bed, feverish and dying. It made his stomach roll. Needing to distract himself, he decided to talk to Una.

"How came ye to be a healer? Is yer father in the trade?"

He almost didn't expect her answer, but then she turned to look over her shoulder enough that he caught a glimpse of a blue eye.

"Nay," she said. "He couldnae find good bedside manner if his life depended on it. I learned from a woman named Agatha. She was our healer. I was always lurking around her cottage as a child, peeking through the window as she worked. One day, she flung the door open and grabbed me by the arm before I could run. She looked down at me and said, 'Either you help me, lassie, or you stop skulking about like Lucifer himself.'" She shrugged. "So I helped."

He grunted. "How old were ye?"

"Och, I dinnae ken. Eight or nine? She said she'd take me in on a trial basis. But on my first day, one of the blacksmith's sons came to her with a nasty burn. When she saw I didnae grow faint at the sight of blood—or even a bad burn—she decided to keep me on."

Calman's breath sent fog rushing into the cold air.

"Where is Agatha now?"

"Dead," Una said flatly, seeming to grow smaller in the saddle. "She was old when I met her, and I suppose the years finally caught up to her. She died in the summer while I was... away. I was nae allowed to attend the burial."

"Bastard," Ewan cursed through his teeth.

"Aye," she said. "At first when she died, I planned to take up residence at her cottage and continue her work there."

"And now?"

"Now I am here, with you, headed to the MacDonalds."

It was an evasive answer.

"But that wasnae your plan. You were nae headed for the MacDonalds when I found you."

"Nay," she said with a sigh. "I meant to go to the Stewarts. Lady Stewart said I would always be welcome."

"Alone?" Ewan asked, unable to hide his shock. "Ye meant to go to the Stewarts. On foot. *Alone*?"

"Aye," she said, stiffening and pulling even farther away from him. "'Tis but a day's walk."

"Aye," he answered sarcastically. "'Tis but a long day's walk over rough terrain where anything could happen to you with nary a soul to help."

He heard her slow, controlled inhale.

"Christ, Una. You cannae be so foolish as that. Whatever would possess you to undertake such a journey alone?"

She sniffed, as if she was fighting back tears and all the fight left him. He felt like a bastard. A whole herd of donkeys.

"Una, I—"

"I didnae have a choice," she said, her teeth clenched tightly around the words.

God's bones, he thought to himself. Could he do nothing right? *Say* nothing right?

"I am sorry, Una. I meant nae offense. I—"

"'Tis nothing, Laird MacDonald," she said softly. "Best to forget it and move forward."

Through the cage of his own teeth, he muttered, "Verra well."

They rode through the morning, and Ewan's spirits sank lower with every step Calman took. A cold dread snaked through his belly as he wondered just how badly Connor fared. He tried to squash the rising panic. Una would save Connor. She *would.* All would be well. But no matter how many times he repeated the litany, he couldn't make himself believe it.

When the sun was high above, Ewan reached forward and directed Una's gaze. "There is the MacDonald keep," he said, pointing at the stone keep in the distance, surrounded by a large curtain wall. The stones looked colder and more foreboding than usual, as gray and hard as the bedrock of the mountains themselves.

Una was silent, her eyes fixed ahead. She leaned forward in the saddle, over Calman's neck, as the horse climbed a rocky hill.

He cleared his throat. "You will be meeting a great many of my family in short order."

"Aye?" Una said, a bit breathlessly, as she clung to the pommel.

"There are six of us in all. I am the oldest, of course. Then there's Kenneth, Angus, and Rabbie. And then, seven years behind him, Connor and Catriona. And then there are the servants and staff of the keep and stronghold."

They reached the top of the rise, and Calman picked up his pace, eager to be back in his stall. They rode briskly through the cottages that clustered more and more tightly together the closer they were to the wall. Una's head swiveled from side to side, taking it all in.

Her back was straight as a poker as they rode into the bailey, and from over her shoulder, Ewan could see that her knuckles were white from gripping the pommel.

"Laird MacDonald! Ye are returned!" someone shouted from across the bailey.

Upon hearing Ewan's name, Mathan bounded out from the stables, stopping short in front of Greer and cocking his head to the side. Calman tossed his head, happy to be home. Ewan dismounted and handed the reins to a waiting groom, who would take the horse off to be groomed and, no doubt, pampered with oats and apples. Ewan reached for Una as he'd done before, holding his arms up and waiting.

She gripped his biceps like a vise as his hands closed around her waist, and he brought her down from the horse's tall back without delay. As he set her down, his eyes snagged on the tiny triangle of flesh visible above the bodice of her dress and below the clasp of her cloak. Her skin was pale, contrasted all the more by the green of the heavy wool.

The groom led Calman away, and Mathan trotted off after them, stopping to look back at Greer, who remained at Una's side. He issued a short bark, and Greer bounded over to him, the pair following Calman neck to neck. For the briefest moment, Ewan was amused by the pair. But then he heard Una's hissing breath.

"What is amiss, Una?" he asked, instinctively cupping her elbow in his palm and squeezing gently.

She closed her eyes tightly. "Nothing. Nothing at all."

He didn't believe her.

"Una—"

"What if he dies?" she blurted out. "The MacDonalds are nae friends of the Camerons. What if you decide he died because of me? What if you seek revenge upon me? What if—"

He bent his knees so that he could look into her eyes.

"You willnae kill him, Una."

"Of course I willnae kill him," she snapped. "But what if I cannae *save* him? Will that nae be the same to you?"

The members of his clan, occupied within the walls, had all slowed their business or stopped it entirely, curious about the scene unfolding.

"I promised you safety," he said in a whisper. "I promised you nae harm would come to you, Una. I gave you my word. You—"

"I have three conditions for doing this," Una choked out.

Conditions? She had *conditions*? No doubt she wanted coin. But what else could she want?"

"First, I come and go as I please. You dinnae lock me in the keep. You dinnae lock me in a chamber. You dinnae restrict my comings and goings in any way."

For a moment, the briefest of moments, Ewan wondered if he was dreaming or at the very least, delirious. Restrict her comings and goings? Lock her in a chamber? What sort of monster did she think he was? But then he remembered to whom she'd been yoked for the past year, and that confusion turned to a flash of rage.

"Una, you are nae a prisoner. Of course you'll have your freedom."

There was a flash in her eyes. One he would have missed it if he hadn't been paying attention. She was surprised by his easy answer.

"Alright then," she said, pulling herself up taller, emboldened by the victory. "The second condition is that I willnae stay in the keep."

"You will need to be close to Connor to do your job, Una. I cannae have you running back and forth between the keep and somewhere else. 'Tis a waste of energy. I will find you a place to sleep close to him."

"With a bar on the door," she said, her voice as hard as the stones surrounding them.

A sudden horrified sympathy washed over him. *God's bones.*

"All the doors have bars," he said quietly. "I assume the third condition is coin? You will want to be paid for your labors?"

"Nay," she said. "That is, I *will* want to be paid, but that isnae the condition."

He would more than pay her. If she saved his brother's life, he'd have to fight the instinct to empty the clan coffers and drape Una with every jewel to be found therein. And it still wouldn't be enough.

Una shifted uncomfortably on her feet. Whatever she was about to ask was more than simple coin.

"Come now, Una. It cannae be as terrible as all that. Out with it. There isnae time."

"I am well aware of the time, *m'laird*," she snapped, the title sounding distasteful, as if she couldn't wait to spit it out. "My third condition is that ye must take me to the Stewarts when the business is… finished. Either way."

"But—"

"I must go to the Stewarts, m'laird. I am expected there. You will see me safely escorted."

In the grand scheme of requests, it was not so very large. The Stewarts were friendly, often called upon to mediate between the Camerons and the MacDonalds, and Laird Stewart had been a good friend of his father's.

"Verra well," he said and did not miss the way her body

seemed to sag with relief, as if there was far more at stake than she'd let on.

But it wasn't his business. *She* wasn't his business. And he would do well to remember that. Just then, Fiona appeared at his side.

"Welcome home, m'laird," Fiona panted, clearly having run to him from wherever she'd been. "Have you brought us a healer?"

"Aye," Ewan said with a pointed look. "I have brought a verra skilled healer to care for Connor. Una, this is Fiona. She is the housekeeper and in charge of everything, including myself."

Fiona's cheeks grew pink with a pleased blush before she curtsied low, and Una made a strangled sound of protest.

"You've come nae a moment too soon, m'laird," Fiona said gravely, rising again.

Ewan felt as if his innards had been hurled off a cliff. He cleared his throat. "Then we best go to him. At once."

CHAPTER 10

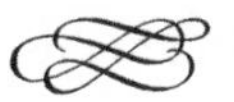

"Come, milady," Fiona said, reaching for Una's satchel. "I shall take ye to him."

"Please call me Una."

"Verra well, Lady Una. If ye'll follow me."

Una took a deep breath, willing herself to speak gently. "Nae Lady Una," she said with forced calm. "Just... Una."

When she'd been handfasted to Laird Cameron, the staff had been instructed to call her Lady Una. Not because she was a highborn lady, but because for all purposes, for the duration of the handfast, she was Laird Cameron's lady. The honorific made her skin crawl with memory.

Fiona stopped at the door, turning to look at her. The older woman narrowed her eyes and knit her brows together, pondering. "Alright then, *just Una*. Connor is in the laird's chamber. This way."

Una followed her into the keep's entrance hall and to the right, ascending a wheeled staircase. They climbed to the top floor, stepping into a hallway with seven doors, three on each side and one at the end. Fiona's shoes scraped quietly on the stone floor, the sound echoing throughout the hallway, which was wide enough for two men to stand shoulder to shoulder with room to spare.

Torches hung in intervals on the wall, and in the flickering orange light, Una saw a man sitting on the floor outside the door at the end of the hall, his forehead resting on crossed arms overtop his bent knees. Fiona hurried to his side and rested a gentle hand on his shoulder. She murmured something, her voice so quiet that Una couldn't make it out, but the man's head shot up, bleary eyes fixing upon her.

Dark shadows clung beneath his eyes, mirroring Ewan's. The resemblance was strong. He staggered to his feet and shuffled toward her.

"Una, this is my brother, Rabbie."

Una nearly jumped out of her skin as Ewan's sudden voice filled the hallway. How long had he been there? He brushed past her and wrapped the younger man in his arms, clutching him tightly and rubbing his back. Rabbie pressed his face into Ewan's shoulder and let go of a low sob.

"Th-th-th-thank God y-y-y'ouve brought her, Ewan. Th-th-thank God."

Una's heart broke with that plaintive cry and braced herself for Ewan to scold his brother. It would break her heart to hear. Instead, Una heard him murmur comforting words in a low burr, his soft, deep voice sounding like far distant thunder, muffled by a forest between.

Una remembered Blair telling her the story of his mother dying. Of how his brother had come upon him weeping in the buttery and boxed his ears for being weak. This man, this laird MacDonald, whatever he might be, was not Malcolm Cameron.

Ewan squeezed his brother tightly before releasing him, gripping Rabbie's shoulders and looking into his eyes. "Get to bed, Rabbie. You're exhausted. I'll wake you if anything changes."

After an affectionate clap on the shoulder, Ewan gently pushed him down the hall towards Una. Rabbie bowed his head and said, "M-m-m'lady," before shuffling into the room nearest the stairs on the right.

Una turned and found herself snared in Ewan's intense gaze. His eyes glittered in the torch light, his jaw was tight, and the dancing shadows made the deep purple beneath his eyes all the more visible.

"Are you ready, Una?" he asked, lifting the latch on the door and beckoning her through.

Una registered the stench of Connor's wound before she even crossed the threshold. She rushed to the bedside. The bedclothes were tangled around one of his legs, and he moaned fitfully, his leine drenched in sweat.

There was always a moment, a scant collection of seconds, before the healing began where she felt a bit unmoored. Either by the age of the patient, or the severity of the malady or injury, or, in this case, both. But in every case, she knew to take a deep breath and to remember that she had been taught by the very best, to remember that in this room, in this moment, she was the one most likely to be able to help. That knowledge was enough to help her shake off the nerves and settle into the familiar rhythm of her work.

Clasping his limp hand in both of hers, Una chafed it gently. "Connor, my name is Una. I am a healer, and I must have a look at your leg."

His sandy blond hair was soaked and clung to his forehead and cheeks, which still held a remnant of youthful roundness. He mumbled incoherently, semi-conscious. Regardless, Agatha had taught her to talk to the patient whether they could hear or not, and describe what was happening to them.

"We cannae ken for certain what a person may hear between the veils, Una," she had preached.

Una drew back the sheet and choked on her gasp as she beheld a tusk goring that stretched from the top of the boy's knee nearly to his groin. Tidy, even stitches held the wound closed, and Una recalled Ewan telling her that his sister, Catriona, had put them in.

Unfortunately, for all that the stitches were neatly placed, the wound needed to be reopened and cleaned. Una set her satchel down on a small table near the bed and began pulling out bottles, vials, and pots, arranging them hastily on the polished wood surface.

"Give me something to do," Ewan said in a hoarse voice behind her. "I beg of you."

She understood the request. Being busy helped to keep the mind from entertaining the worst possible thoughts. Thoughts which, it occurred to her, had likely been rattling around in Ewan's brain ever since he had left his brother to find her.

She turned. Ewan looked haggard standing before her, his eyes glassy with tears, fists clenched tightly at his sides.

"Please," he said, his voice breaking.

Una sighed. "I must reopen the wound, but I cannae give him anything to sedate him for fear he willnae wake from it. He's lost a great deal of blood and has been weakened by the fever."

"Aye," Ewan replied, scrubbing a hand roughly over his face. "I didnae drug him during the first stitching for the same reason. I will… hold him."

She nodded, pleased that he had shown such good instincts. "You did right," she said grimly.

He closed his eyes, pained, and without thinking, she reached out and took his hand in hers, squeezing it with all her might. His eyes opened and he stared at their joined hands, looking as surprised as she felt.

Una cleared her throat. "Fetch your men, m'laird. We shall do our verra best."

"Aye," he said quietly, squeezing her hand, before stalking from the room.

And if Una had felt a shock of heat from that press of fingers against palm, she ignored it entirely. It meant nothing anyway.

"Una, what may I do?" Fiona asked, standing by the fire and wringing her apron with shaking hands. She appeared to be holding onto her composure by mere threads, but she was holding onto it nonetheless. Another worried heart. Another person in need of a job. But another set of hands to help.

"The laird has gone to fetch the muscle, so you may help me with the medicine. We'll need more cool water to bathe him to bring down the fever."

"I've had a maid replacing the cool cloths day and night."

"Good," Una said, pleased. "I will need water boiling at all times and clean linen as well."

Fiona marched swiftly toward the door, turning just before leaving through it.

"I shall return shortly with cool water and something for you to eat. You'll need your strength. I'll set Fenella to work on the rest. The keep is at your service."

The door closed behind her with a dull thud, leaving Una alone with Connor. She returned to the bedside, smoothing her hand over his forehead and pressing his hair back and away from his eyes. He was a strong, resilient age. Young, but not too young. If anyone had good odds to come out of this alive, it was a hearty, hale lad like him.

Una crossed to the window and lifted the fur covering, tying it up and away. She would need all the light that could be had. A gust of icy wind blew through the open window, whipping Una's hair, and she couldn't help but remember how windy it had been as she'd walked away from the

Cameron keep. Had it really only been two days ago? It felt like a lifetime.

And yet she had commitments to keep. She needed to reach the Stewarts. Blair was counting on her. And while she wanted to believe in Ewan's integrity, that he meant it when he promised to take her there regardless of whether Connor lived or died, she couldn't trust it. She couldn't trust *him*. Not completely. Not yet. Probably not ever.

Failure was not an option. She could not afford for the boy to die. She wanted him to live because he had a lot of life ahead of him to experience, but she *needed* him to live to protect her future. It felt selfish and perhaps it was, but she could live with that.

Selfish, perhaps, but not unreasonable, she reminded herself.

Una forced a cheery expression onto her face as she turned back to the bedside.

"Well, Connor, we're in this together now. Let us both do our verra best, aye?"

Connor was delirious with fever, but he nodded his head slightly, fingers fluttering restlessly over the sheets.

"Glad I am to hear it, Connor. You'll be good as new in nae time," she said, forcing even more cheer into her voice as she went back to her medicines and began placing them in the order they would be needed.

Deep in the bottom of the bag was a very special jar filled with a salve made from wine, garlic, onion, and oxgall. One of Agatha's creations. The preparation was left to cure in a bronze vessel for exactly nine days. Una had made a large batch the week before the end of her handfast after using the last of it on a particularly nasty knife wound on one of the kitchen maid's hands.

The door creaked open behind her, and Ewan stepped into the room, followed by three men and Fiona. Two of the men were clearly Ewan's brothers, the resemblance uncanny with sun-bleached, oat-colored hair and heavy eyebrows. The third man had short, dark hair and dark eyes. Not family, but close, given the ease with which he held himself around them.

Fiona scurried over, setting a basin of water on the side table before thrusting a piece of bread into Una's hands.

"Eat," she commanded.

When Una opened her mouth to protest, Ewan repeated the command. "Eat, Una. That's an order."

Her eyebrows flew toward her hairline, but he crossed his arms over his chest and stared her down. She bristled at this man thinking he could *order* her about. But there wasn't time, and so Una tore a bite of the fresh bread with her teeth. After eating she dusted the crumbs from her clothing and washed her hands in the basin in the corner.

As she dried them on a new cloth, she turned to Ewan. "Are you ready to hold him?"

He nodded and came to the bed, gently lifting Connor's torso and sliding behind him on the bed so that he could hold him against his chest. The other three men arranged themselves around the bed, holding him but leaving her access to the wound. She took the sgian dubh from her boot and carried it to the hearth, crouching low and thrusting the blade into the flames, praying for steady hands.

By the time she finished the grisly task of removing the stitches, cleaning the wound thoroughly, applying a thick portion of salve, and restitching, her back and shoulders cried out for relief. Blood and sweat drenched her gown, and loose hairs were plastered to her face. Her hands shook as she applied more salve to the closed wound before bandaging it in clean cloth.

She staggered away from the bedside, and Fiona dove to take her place, cool cloth in hand, crooning softly to Connor as she bathed his face. The men filed stiffly from the room without a word. Except for Ewan, who stepped closer. So close that his broad chest filled her vision. His leine shirt was like a second skin, soaked with sweat and clinging to his chest.

"And now we wait?" he murmured,

She cleared her throat and shook herself, bringing her attention back to his face. "Aye. I can give him tinctures for the fever, and we will keep bathing him in cold water to bring it down. But beyond that, all we can do is wait."

Una raised a hand to brush the sticky hairs off of her forehead when, in a flash, she found herself pressed against Ewan's wet chest. His arms wrapped tightly around her back and squeezed her against him. She flinched, her whole body going rigid in his arms. She was frozen, her breath trapped in her chest as the panic began to rise. What was he doing? What in God's name was he *doing*? She had to get away. She had to fight.

She wiggled in his hold to push herself back when he dropped his forehead to her shoulder and she felt his body shake around hers, his breath shuddering. And then she felt the hot, silent tears drip down her neck, between her breasts, soaking into the blood and sweat already drenching her gown.

He was weeping.

Like water leaking through the weave of a basket, her panic drifted away, leaving her exhausted and shaking. Una took a fortifying breath and carefully brought her arms around him, patting him on the shoulder with one hand and rubbing between the blades with the other. His heat enveloped her, making her feel feverish in the already warm room.

This close, she could smell him. Sweat, mostly, but also blood, leather, and the scant trace of horse. It was an over-powering combination and not a terribly pleasant one either, but she allowed him to hold her because she had the suspicion that Ewan didn't have anyone else to hold him while he fell apart. She knew that feeling. She knew it well.

And so she held him until his shaking body solidified again, and as she did, she let go of the tension that she'd been holding since first taking her knife to Connor's wound. Ewan released her, stepping away quickly, as if he'd forgotten himself. His gaze was intense, entirely focused on her, and she struggled to look away.

"I shall find you a chamber nearby," he said gruffly. "You must rest."

"Nay, m'laird. I must stay close to Connor. Perhaps someone can bring up a pallet."

He scowled but didn't argue.

"Verra well," he said. "But I have three conditions of my own as long as you stay here."

Una tensed, fear tingling once again at the base of her skull. Of course there was a catch. Wasn't there always?

"Let's hear them," she said, mustering her courage to hear it.

He coughed into his hand. "First, you are to eat and rest when you can. You strike me as the type to forget herself when caring for others, and I willnae have you falling ill because of your devotion to your work."

She wanted to protest on principle alone, but she couldn't. Because he wasn't wrong.

"I agree to that," she said easily. But surely the rest of his conditions could not be so straightforward as the first.

"Second, as we have ruined your frock, you will allow my sister to find you a new one."

There was nothing wrong with her dress. It was perfectly serviceable, albeit stained. But it would be stained again and again in her line of work. She could wash it, and it would be as good as new. Or as good as it had been anyway.

"I dinnae want—"

"Una," he interrupted, his voice low. "It is a gown, not a fortune. Please."

It was the *please* that did it, gentle and sincere, and she found herself nodding.

"Fine," she spat. "But it must be a sturdy gown. Nothing that can be ruined easily. And something dark that willnae stain. Wool. Nothing fine. I'll work in my shift before I ruin a fine gown," she said, clutching for the upper hand.

There was a spark in his eye, the briefest flash and that little tic in his jaw. Did he like the challenge? Or was it the suggestion of working in her shift? Either way, the look was gone as quickly as it had come.

"We cannae have that now, can we?" he muttered.

She felt goosebumps prickle across her skin. What was this feeling? Not desire. It couldn't be that. Not with this man. Not with *any* man, for that matter. Not after she'd just freed herself from one. Not when she was standing eight feet away from a boy fighting for his life. Not when she was so close to her new start.

And yet, her body felt almost liquid as he reached up with a hesitant hand and swept a wet lock of hair away from her forehead, brushing it behind her ear, as if the soft animal of her body *wanted* him to touch her. Which was impossible.

He looked as confused as she did, the two of them staring at each other, like creatures across a clearing, sizing up the relative danger.

"And the third condition, m'laird?"

He shook himself and took a half step back. "You must make me a promise."

He spoke barely above a whisper, and Una felt her blood go cold again. This was where he would make demands. Of her body. Of her time. Any number of promises he could exact from her, things she did not want to offer, in exchange for her safety.

The bread roiled in her stomach as she lifted her chin. "And what promise might that be?" she asked through her teeth.

He cocked his head to the side, a confused look on his face. "'Tis an easy promise, Una."

"Then spit it out, m'laird," she said, the word *laird* sounding like a knife in her mouth.

He sighed, his shoulders rising with the air, his huge hands hanging by his sides. "You must promise to never call me that again."

CHAPTER 11

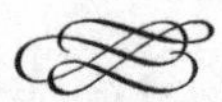

Ewan didn't know what had possessed him to make such a request. It was his title. It was his due. And yet the word always sounded like a sneer when she said it, as if she could barely stand the taste of it in her mouth. For some reason that he had not yet had time to dissect, he didn't like that. He didn't like it at all.

Una was clearly as confused as he was. "But you *are* the laird."

"Aye, but I am nae *your* laird," he said, cursing the flimsy logic.

What could he say? *I dinnae want you to call me laird because I want us to be friends? I want you to* like *me?* What the hell was that? And yet it was true. He found that he *did* want her to like him. Almost as much as he wanted to brush another errant lock of hair away from her cheek. Perhaps his knuckles would graze against her soft skin.

It was all a lie. Or, if not a lie, an *untruth.* He wasn't her laird, that much was true, but he would be. Hang the Stewarts. He needed a gifted healer who could care for his clan and his family, and she was already here. Why couldn't she just... stay?

That was the reason he wanted her to like him, to trust him. It certainly had nothing to do with wanting to hear his given name slide off her tongue. *Laird* did not do the same things to a mouth that *Ewan* did. But that was ridiculous.

"That is," he began, trying to salvage the situation, "I *would* be your laird, if you agreed to stay."

"I am bound for the Stewarts."

"Are they expecting you? Is there an emergency?"

Her hesitation was answer enough. He forged ahead. "What can the Stewarts offer you that I cannae provide? Safety? Meaningful work? You are needed here, Una. I can provide it all. And keep you safe."

"Other people are counting on me. People who would join me at the Stewarts."

"Your family?"

"Nay," she said, looking at her feet. "A... friend. In need of a new situation."

"She would be welcome here as well, Una."

Una looked at him. "What would *he* do here?"

The word *he* was a much-needed dousing of cold water on his racing brain. Perhaps she had a sweetheart, some poor bastard who had pined away for her throughout her handfast to another man. Ewan hated the idea, though he recognized that that wasn't remotely fair.

"That depends. Has he an occupation?"

Her eyes darted to the left before she answered. A flick. Perhaps nothing more than a trick of light.

"He's a soldier. He trains the new guards."

"There is always room for good men in the guard. Would he be staying in the barracks? Or... would you and this *friend* require a cottage and a priest?"

He regretted the question before it had even left his mouth. *What does it bloody matter, ye riddy bastard?*

She narrowed her eyes. "He sleeps in the barracks now, so I doubt he will expect anything different."

Ewan's heart was pounding, and he couldn't account for it. It didn't matter who this man was. It didn't matter what he meant to Una. What mattered—the only thing that mattered—was taking care of his clan. That required a healer. *He* required a healer.

"I want you to stay," he blurted out, coughing into his fist after. "That is, *we* want you to stay."

She arched an elegant eyebrow, seeing too much. He remembered the last healer, a crotchety old man named Mason who, for all that he had the people skills of a distempered goat, could read people like scripture. He never missed a thing. And neither, it seemed, did Una. *Healers*.

"Stay," she repeated flatly. "For good."

"For as long as you like."

He was nervous. More nervous than usual, which was saying something. Since his father died, Ewan felt as if he was built brick by brick from nerves.

"You will be safe here. There will be plenty of work for you, especially the way my family seems to be in scrapes more often than nae. And for the rest of the clan as well. And your"—he coughed—"friend will have work, too. We can always use a hand training the young ones."

She sucked on the inside of her right cheek, pondering, staring *through* him and taking his measure.

"Verra well, m'laird. I will stay for a trial period. So long as you promise to deliver me to the Stewarts should I choose to leave."

"Fair enough," he answered easily.

"And you will send for my friend when I ask you to?"

"I can write whatever missive you require."

"Nay!" she blurted. "Nay. It cannae be written. It must be done… another way."

He didn't like that. He didn't like any part of that. But what choice did he have? Better to agree to the demand and sort out the details later.

"I agree."

"Then we have a deal, m'laird," she said with a nod.

He still didn't like the sound of his title in her mouth, the way she seemed to spit it out like a rancid morsel.

"My third condition stands, Una. I dinnae want you calling me 'm'laird.'"

"But—"

"Call me by my title when others are around, but when we are alone, I would prefer that you use my name."

"When we are alone?" she repeated, eyes wide in horror.

"As friends," he hastily added, raking his hands through his hair and pulling at the roots. What a day it had been and it was not nearly over yet. "I wish you to call me by my name as friends."

She took a step back, eyes narrowed in suspicion, but eventually, after an eternity, she nodded.

"I have duties to attend to. But I will instruct my sister to attend to you, and one of my men will be outside the door. If you need anything at all, ask him, and it shall be delivered."

A small nod. He stepped around her, moving toward the door.

"I will return later to check on Connor. But if anything changes before then, I want you to send for me."

"Aye, m'lai—" she stopped short and her gaze flicked to his. "Ewan."

A smile teased at the corner of his mouth, but it twisted to a grimace as Connor groaned on the bed.

"Hold fast, Ewan," Una said, his name coming more easily

off her tongue than the last time, and he allowed himself to smile weakly. "I have faith in him."

As he closed the door gently behind him, he heard Una humming a soft, lilting tune. He nodded to the guard in the hall before knocking on his sister's door.

Catriona wrenched it open, her eyes red and puffy, tear tracks staining her cheeks.

"I heard him screaming, Ewan," she cried, launching herself against his chest. He caught her and held her, his own heart feeling as if it would eat him alive from the inside.

What a messy, bloody day.

"Aye. He did. Una had to remove all of your fine stitching to drain the wound," he said, resting his chin on the top of his sister's head and wishing, for the second time in only a few minutes, that he had changed shirts.

"I told you I was nae fit to stitch him! I've killed him for certain!" Cat wailed, bursting into fresh tears.

"Cat," Ewan said, cradling her cheeks gently in his palms and looking into her moss-green eyes. "Our new healer bid me to tell you what a fine job you did. She said it was a pity that she had to remove your stitches."

Catriona gasped. "*Our new healer*? But I thought you fetched the Cameron healer!"

"I did. But I convinced her to stay."

For a trial period, he thought to himself. But he did not say that out loud. Let him worry about how to convince the new healer to stay. That was a future Ewan problem.

"Thanks be to God!" Cat said, hastily wiping at her tears with her sleeves.

Ewan nodded. "I want her to feel welcome here. At home. That's why I came to find you. Her gown was in sorry shape to begin with, but 'tis ruined now. I want her to have something… nice. She deserves something nice."

"We can find her something nice," Cat said, sniffling. "Right, Joan?"

Joan sat sewing next to the hearth. "Of course, milady," she answered brightly.

"I am afraid she is a fair bit taller than you are, Cat," Ewan said. "I thought perhaps we could—"

He stopped. It didn't seem fair to ask his sister to part with one of their mother's gowns, the only things she had left. Cat had never worn them as she would have had to alter the length significantly, something she insisted she could not stomach doing. They remained neatly packed in a trunk beneath the window, safe and stowed.

But perhaps Cat could *find* her a gown. Perhaps there was an extra lying around the keep somewhere.

"Mother was tall," Cat ventured. "I have all of her gowns in the trunk."

"I cannae ask you to give up such a precious item. Surely there is another gown to be had."

But Cat made that *pfft* sound that she often made when she thought one of her brothers was being especially ridiculous. A hard, suffocating lump rose in his throat. He had not looked at his mother's gowns since they'd been packed away after her death.

He looked down at his own clothes, at the white lawn of his shirt and the blue and green of his plaid, both drenched in Connor's blood, and his stomach turned as he remembered entering the laird's chamber after the twins had been born. He'd found his beautiful, gentle mother's sheets and shift soaked red with blood, the bright stains contrasting with the blue-and-green plaid wrapped around his tiny new siblings. She had not survived the night.

"Ewan? Ewan, where have you gone?" Cat asked with a loud clap of her hands.

He startled and shook himself, returning to the present.

Cat was rummaging through the chest under the window, handing parcels to Joan, who arranged them neatly on the bed.

"Ewan, I have been asking you questions this whole time. What color is her hair? Her eyes? And what did you say her name is?"

"Una," he said, feeling how his tongue cupped to cradle the first syllable.

"Una. A beautiful name. And her hair color? Och, pfft. You likely didnae even notice."

Today had been impossible. Yesterday even more so. Overwhelming. Devastating. Exhausting. Seeing Connor so very ill, so very bloody, in the same bed in the same chamber where their mother had died bringing him into the world had been too much. He hadn't made the connection until just now, until seeing his mother's gowns removed from the trunk. His throat felt tight, as if it might close, and he sucked in a raspy breath.

It was all too much. And yet, through the haze of panic, Ewan could still picture in vivid detail what Una looked like.

"Her hair is dark," he said hoarsely. "Black, like a raven. Her eyes are a verra light blue. Like—"

He'd been about to say *like a clear winter sky*.

His sister grinned.

"What?"

"Oh, nothing at all, brother," Cat said with a smirk. "I believe I've found just the thing."

She pulled a bundle from the trunk, letting the gown unfurl as she pinched the shoulders between her fingers. The dress was made of a fine wool, dyed the color of bluebells. He remembered his mother wearing it often, one of her favorites, and his mouth went dry as he imagined Una's glossy black hair cascading down in sharp contrast to the soft color.

"Well?" Cat asked, interrupting the daydream. "Will it serve?"

Una had insisted the gown be a dark color. Something that wouldn't stain or be easily ruined. *"I'll work in my shift before I ruin a fine gown with my work,"* she had declared. This gown would show every speck, every drop, every smudge.

But he wanted to see her in it anyway, wanted to see if it made her eyes look even more blue like he suspected it would. He wanted to give her something fine, something that she could wear to feel pretty, not just serviceable.

"Aye," he said, swallowing thickly against the tightness in his throat. "'Twill more than serve. Will you take it to her?"

Cat draped the gown over her arm, placing her other hand on her hip. "Leave Una to me. I'll make sure she feels welcome. You have more important things to attend to."

He did. Hundreds of them. And yet none of them seemed *more* important than making Una feel safe and welcome. There was much to do. Eventually, once Connor recovered, as he could not bring himself to imagine any other outcome, Una would need a home. She could not stay in the keep indefinitely or she would become the subject of gossip. He could find her a cottage, something close to the wall and the keep. He pictured her cooking her supper alone, sitting alone by her hearth at night, climbing into her bed alone. The thought rankled him.

But that would not be the case. Una was young and beautiful. No doubt someone would ask for his permission to seek her hand before the end of the week. And he would have to grant them permission to court her because denying that permission would indicate that he'd set his own cap at her. And he hadn't. He wouldn't. He *couldn't.*

And yet that rankled him, too. He did not want a wife. He did not want to love yet another person who could be taken from him. But the thought of another man building a home with her made him want to put his fist through the wall.

He tried to regulate his breathing as he ran down the wheeled staircase. He tried to calm his mind as he stomped out of the keep into the blinding, frigid air.

But he could not stop thinking about Una wrapping her long arms willingly around the neck of a faceless man. Of that man stroking her hair, rubbing the slick strands between his fingers.

"Enough," he growled, the word leaving on a puff of steam in the cold.

But it wasn't, and suddenly, Ewan didn't know how anything that had once been would ever be *enough* again.

CHAPTER 12

Una sat in a chair next to the hearth, trying in vain to warm her chilled body. Her dress and shift were soaked through to the skin, smelling sharply of sweat and blood. She needed new clothes or she would never get warm, but she didn't have another gown. She shivered and wrapped her arms more tightly around herself.

Someone knocked on the door, a gentle tap before the heavy door creaked open.

Una shot to her feet.

"Knock knock," Fiona said as she entered the room.

She was followed by a young woman with wild, golden curls. Her eyes were swollen and red-rimmed. She could only be Ewan's sister. Fiona stoked the fire, sending sparks shimmering high in the hearth. The young lady stood frozen in the doorway, her eyes locked on Connor's sleeping form in the bed.

"He lives, m'lady," Una said softly. "He is feverish, but he is resting well."

Sharp green eyes flashed in Una's direction.

"Thanks to you alone, Una," she said. Una wondered how

she had learned her name. "I dinnae ken how we will ever repay you."

"I cannae be certain that he—"

But she fell silent as the young lady waved her hand.

"You are a blessing to us, Una," she insisted. "And thanks to you, Connor will live. I feel it in my bones."

Una was humbled by Catriona's confidence, even if she didn't share it. Connor was much weakened by fever and blood loss, and she had put his body through yet another ordeal to tend to his wound. The next few days would be critical. She clasped her hands and chewed on her bottom lip anxiously, wincing as her teeth bit into the chapped skin.

"I have forgotten my manners. I am Catriona, the laird's sister, though you doubtless put that together already."

Una curtsied, her knees aching. "Lady Catriona."

"Oh, none of that, please. Everyone calls me Cat."

"I couldnae do that, m'lady," Una protested.

Fiona cleared her throat and arched an eyebrow at Una, no doubt reminding her of a similar exchange between the two of them mere hours before. But this was different.

"Pfft. Please call me Cat. I want you to. I want us to be friends."

Friends. There was that word again. She could count her friends on one hand with fingers to spare. Blair. Maddie, the Cameron housekeeper who had taken such good care of her. Once, she would have counted her childhood best friend, Joan, among the list, but Joan had disappeared in the middle of their sixteenth summer, and she'd never learned where she'd gone.

But Una nodded. She was not in a position to refuse either friendship or kindness.

The door opened once more, and another woman entered. She was short and plump, with curly chestnut brown hair wrestled into a knot at the nape of her neck. A halo of unruly curls wreathed her face, and as she turned to look at the assembled group, Una could not believe her eyes.

"Joan?" she shrieked, clapping her hand over her mouth, her eyes wide.

Joan's face split with a wide smile. "Una!" she answered happily, rushing forward and wrapping her arms around Una's waist in a tight hug. Una held her just as close, her chin resting on top of Joan's head, fighting back tears and eventually surrendering to them.

Joan held her close and let her cry, rubbing her back with gentle soothing passes of her hand. Eventually, Una's sudden tears gave way to embarrassment and she released Joan, stepping back quickly and wiping her eyes with the backs of her hands. She saw that some of the blood from her dress had stained Joan's beautiful gown, and she winced.

"I have stained your gown with my mess, Joan," she said. "I am so sorry. I should have thought before I—"

"Before you hugged your lost friend? Think nothing of it. I certainly dinnae mind."

"What are you doing here, Joan? Of all places. You disappeared and I didnae ken where you went and—" She couldn't continue.

"You know each other?" Cat asked, and Una nodded.

"My mother was a MacDonald, m'lady," Joan explained. "But my father was a Cameron. Una and I grew up together. She was my very best friend."

"How did you end up here, though, Joan?" Una felt as if her head was spinning.

Joan reached for Una's hand. "When my ma left, Da sent me here to live with her people. Did he nae tell you?"

"Nay," Una said, feeling the tears collecting again at the corners of her eyes. "I had nae idea where you'd gone. And he wouldnae tell me anything. He only said you were dead to him the way your mother was. We all assumed you went with her."

Joan's mother had famously run away with a traveling musician, and for years, Una had sought Joan among every caravan that passed by her cottage. It wasn't as if Joan could have written a letter. And even if she had, Una couldn't have read it. The lack of closure had been a wound that had never quite healed.

Joan looked sad. "He couldnae stand the sight of me after she left. Said I was the spitting image of her and that he wouldnae sit by and watch me grow up to be just like her. He brought me to the MacDonald keep, and somehow I became Lady Catriona's maid."

"How I have missed you," Una said, and Joan stepped closer, as if to hug her again.

Una stepped back. "I am soaked to the skin with blood, Joan. I already stained your gown. It wouldnae do to ruin it entirely."

Cat clapped her hands. "That, Una, is precisely why we've come. We have prepared you a bath in my chamber and have a new, dry gown waiting."

Una's aching body felt weak at the thought of a proper bath. Not washing her face in the icy burn or hastily bathing from a basin, but soaking in water as hot as she could stand it. How long had it been?

But Connor groaned and tossed on the bed, and Una shook her head. A bath was a luxury she couldn't afford, not while her charge lay so ill.

Fiona clucked her tongue and rested a hand on Una's arm. "I am nae stranger to sitting beside a MacDonald man recovering from injury. You willnae be gone long and will be just down the hall. I promise to shout if the slightest thing changes."

Una hesitated.

"Go," Fiona insisted with a wave of her hand. "We cannae have you taking ill from catching a cold."

As if dreaming, Una followed Joan and Catriona down the hall to Cat's chamber, a cheery room with bright tapestries and weavings and a crackling fire in the hearth. A tub of steaming water sat in front of the fire. Joan's nimble fingers unlaced Una's dress while Cat pulled the hem of both gown and shift upwards until Una was forced to lift her arms overhead and duck. The dress flew off, and Una winced as it landed on the stone floor with a wet slap.

Una felt as if she was covered in six layers of dirt and grime and blood. Her cheeks colored with shame. But when she looked at Joan, she saw her friend smiling.

"Come, Una," Joan said softly, offering her hand and helping Una to step over the rim of the tub.

She sank down, moaning as the hot water covered her aching shoulders.

"May I wash your hair, Una?" Cat asked. "'Tis the least I can do."

Una nodded. Cat tied up her sleeves and unbraided Una's hair, combing through the tangles with her fingers before working through them with a wooden comb.

"Duck your head, Una," she commanded, and Una obeyed, relishing the feel of the hot water closing over her head.

She stayed underwater for a few moments, feeling warm for the first time since she'd woken in the cave next to— Una burst to the surface and shook her head. She wiped the water away from her eyes and leaned back so that Cat could reach her more easily. Cat passed a ball of soap between her hands until she had a lather and scrubbed at Una's scalp.

The smell of the soap took her back in time, to her childhood, to nesting against her mother's neck.

"Lavender?" Una whispered.

"Aye," Cat replied. "'Twas my mother's favorite, and so I use it as well. Makes me feel close to her."

They were quiet for a time, as Cat washed her hair and Una scrubbed her body until she was clean.

"I am sorry," Una said. She meant it. She had lost her mother too, but she had at least known her. She couldn't imagine never having known her, only having soap and scent to meet her.

Cat sighed. "I never knew her. I miss the idea of her, but I miss my father so much more. All I have of my mother are stories and her keepsakes that she kept in her trunk. But my father was flesh and blood. He died when I was thirteen," Cat said in a distant voice, her hands pausing from their gentle scrubbing. "'Twas a difficult time. Father's death took all of us by surprise. Though, I suppose it was hardest on Ewan."

"What do you mean?" Una asked.

Another sigh, longer this time.

"He'd been raised for it, trained since birth to become laird. But I dinnae think he wanted it. At least nae so soon. And I ken that it weighs heavily upon him. Duck your head again, Una. We must get you out before the water grows cold," Cat commanded, and again Una obeyed.

When Una surfaced, Joan stood next to the tub with a large drying cloth warm from the fire. She wrapped it around Una, helped her out of the tub, and pushed her gently towards a chair by the hearth. Una sat, and Joan squeezed the water out of her hair with another cloth before running a wooden comb through the ebony locks. Soon, Una was warm and practically pink from the fire, her long hair gleaming behind her.

"I thought it was you," Joan said as she ran the comb through her hair.

"Who?"

"Laird Stewart's servant spoke of the Cameron healer and

how skilled they had been, how much Lady Stewart trusted her. I thought it must have been you. I told the laird to fetch you."

Una's throat tightened with emotion.

"I am glad you did," she whispered.

She was. Sitting before a fire, having been tended with careful hands and treated with kindness from the moment she had arrived, Una realized that she *was* glad. She had found her lost friend. She had been assured safety. Perhaps she didn't have to go to the Stewarts.

Joan guided Una to stand and removed the drying cloth from around her torso.

"Arms up," Joan said brightly.

Una raised her arms and bent her knees so that Joan could slip a fine linen shift over her raised hands. Joan guided the fabric as it cascaded down Una's body, over her breasts and the softness of her belly. She shivered.

"Here we are," Cat said, approaching with a pale blue gown. Una could tell without touching it how soft the wool would feel.

"This color will make her eyes look even more stunning, aye, Joan?"

"Aye," Joan agreed readily.

They worked together to tug the gown into place, lacing it up the back.

"It fits you perfectly!" Cat exclaimed.

Una smoothed her hands down the exquisite fabric, feeling her callouses catching on the fine weave.

"'Tis beautiful," she said softly. "But I shouldnae wear something so fine. I *cannae* wear something so fine. I will ruin it within a day. Within the hour!"

"Pfft," Cat said. "'Twas my mother's gown, and it has sat in this trunk all these years. A gown like this should be worn to turn heads, nae sit in a chest tempting moths."

"We can find you another dress for your bloodiest work, and you can keep this one for the rest of the time. I'll loan you an apron in the meantime," Joan said, tugging on Una's hand. "Now come and sit and I'll braid your hair."

Una allowed herself to be led back to the chair in front of the fire and sat. Joan made quick work of plaiting Una's hair.

Squeezing Una's shoulder's tightly, Joan said, "There. You always were such a beauty, Una."

Una lurched to her feet at the memory of Malcolm Cameron muttering those same words to her as he kissed her hand before their handfasting ceremony. He had leered up at her, hovering over her knuckles, a cold glint in his eyes. *"You always were such a beauty, lass."*

Una felt the blood drain from her face. Suddenly the room felt too small. She backed toward the door. "I thank you for the bath, but I must see to Connor," she stammered before wrenching open the door.

She ran out the door and straight into a wall. A warm, solid wall that wrapped itself around her. She gasped and flinched away.

"Easy, Una," Ewan said. "What is amiss?"

His hair was damp and he smelled clean, wearing a fresh leine and plaid.

"Nothing," she snapped.

"Then why did you race out of Cat's room like hell is on your heels?"

The door behind Una flew open, and Cat exclaimed, "Ewan! Isnae she beautiful? The gown may as well have been made for her."

Una noticed a slight flush around the collar of Ewan's shirt. He lifted a big, tanned hand to the sleeve of her gown, rubbing the soft material between his thumb and forefinger.

Una opened her mouth to protest, but Ewan coughed and said, "It suits you. Do you like it?"

Una was dimly aware of Cat and Joan in the doorway behind her, but it felt as if they were leagues away at the same time. She had worn fur-trimmed silks as Malcolm Cameron's handfasted betrothed. She had worn the finest of gowns at his command. She had liked them well enough. But she didn't just like this gown. Soft and warm and so special for having belonged to such a beloved woman, it was the finest, loveliest thing she'd ever worn.

What was more, she didn't deserve it. She didn't deserve to wear the gown of a laird's wife, a beloved mother, dearly missed. She was a healer. A common-born woman with a job to do. She deserved homespun in a sturdy, practical color that would show neither dirt nor blood.

But she didn't know how to say that. Not with Cameron's voice so fresh in her mind. *"Ye always were such a beauty, Una."*

And so she didn't answer. She didn't say a word as she ducked around him and raced into the laird's chamber, slamming the door behind her.

CHAPTER 13

Later that night, Ewan came to sit watch by Connor's bed. When he entered the chamber, he found a sleepy Fiona bathing his face with cool cloths. She held a finger to her lips and canted her head toward the fireplace where a pallet lay. Sleeping atop it, huddled under a blanket pulled up to her nose, was Una.

"I had to threaten her to rest," Fiona whispered. "I told her that if she refused to sleep, then so would I."

Ewan nodded. "She needed the sleep."

"Aye. She has been through a great deal, I fear."

"What has she told you?" Ewan asked, wanting to follow the breadcrumbs wherever they might lead.

"Nothing with words," Fiona said carefully. "But she ran in here after her bath as if escaping a bear and begged me to find one of the servants to lend her a work dress. She couldnae get yer mother's blue gown off fast enough. Nearly ripped a seam. When I asked her what was amiss, she got very quiet and said that she didnae feel comfortable attracting as much attention as such a fine gown would earn.

She wore naught but her shift until Mary could bring a work dress for her."

Ewan felt sick.

"I dinnae ken what happened to her before ye found her, but she's as skittish as a colt and as prickly as a hedgehog. She didnae want to speak any more of it, so I left it alone."

"She was handfasted to Cameron," Ewan said through clenched teeth, his jaw so tight that he could hear his molars squeak together. He looked over at Una, half expecting her to fly off the pallet in a rage, but she only snored softly.

"God's bones," Fiona breathed.

"Aye."

"He is a verra cruel man, is he nae?"

"He's a tyrant," Ewan agreed.

"What did he do to her?" Fiona asked, the mending clenched tightly between worried fingers.

"I dinnae ken. But I doubt verra much he was kind to her."

Fiona nodded, her lips pressed into a tight line.

Ewan relieved Fiona of her post so that she could eat a meal in the kitchen and rest for a few hours herself. He bathed Connor's face with cool water and stared broodily at the way the firelight made Una's hair look like gleaming obsidian, thinking about the gown and wondering if he and Cat had overstepped horribly. It bothered him.

When she'd woken an hour or so later, she'd taken over the cool cloths with quiet thanks before turning her back on him and setting to work redressing Connor's wound. He, the laird of this keep and clan, had been dismissed.

That had bothered him, too. So much so that he'd sparred with David late into the night in the torchlit bailey until he was bloodied and could barely lift a sword. It had been beyond stupid, but he'd been so full of restless, thrumming energy, the panic sitting on his chest like a bull, and he knew that the only way he would sleep was if he gave his body no other choice.

The next morning, he awoke aching from head to toe. Groaning, he rolled out of Connor's bed, his for the time being, and dressed in the near darkness, with only embers to light the room. He strapped on his weapons and crept down the hall, easing open the door to the laird's solar. Fiona sat in the chair beside the bed, but the pallet by the fire was empty.

"She went to the chapel, m'laird," Fiona whispered, not missing the flare of panic he'd felt seeing her missing.

"Oh," he said. "I didnae come to… that is, I came to see Connor."

"He is asleep," Fiona said, resting a gentle hand on the boy's forehead. "His fever is still high, though Una believes he is fighting it with strength. He took a bit of broth in the night, and she was pleased by that."

"Aye," Ewan said, forcing the word over the hurdle of the lump in his throat. "That is verra good."

"Perhaps you should check on Una now?" Fiona said, her eyes squarely on the mending in her lap.

He rubbed the back of his neck, noting that even that ached. "Aye, I will. You will alert me if anything changes with Connor?"

"Of course, m'laird," Fiona said.

The sky was turning pink and the mountains looked as if blanketed with a dusty velvet in the early morning light as Ewan walked briskly through the empty courtyard. The chapel was a small, stone addition to the keep. Inside, there was enough seating for a laird's large family with a few extra pews for guests. It was primarily used for individual prayer as the MacDonalds shared a priest with a few neighboring clans and did not have one in residence.

As he closed the door behind him without a sound, he saw the lone figure sitting in the second pew in the dim chapel. She had lit two of the candles and one of the wall torches, which made the sharp, flickering stabs of brightness tremble and dance across the stone walls.

He approached her with quiet care, clearing his throat when he was a pew behind her.

"You're up early, Ewan," she said in a soft voice.

For a moment, he was struck by the fact that she had known it was him without turning around, as if she could sense him. He thought he might be able to sense her too, that he could find her even blindfolded if only he let the animal of his body find the animal of hers.

"As are you, Una," he replied, taking a seat next to her. Close, but not touching.

"I didnae ken what else to do."

"For Connor?"

"Aye. I am doing everything I ken to do. Everything that has ever worked."

"And so now you come to pray?"

"Something like that," she said with a sigh. "And you? Do you come to pray as well?"

"Something like that," he said.

But he had hesitated too long, and she noticed.

"Something like that, but not exactly like that. Why are you really here?"

He pinched his bottom lip between his thumb and forefinger, something he did when he was thinking, a habit his father had tried in vain to break, telling him it revealed too much.

Ewan looked up at the stone ceiling as he said, "I see you changed your frock."

She whipped her head away so that she was staring at the crucifix hanging behind the altar.

"Why, Una?"

It wasn't his business, and yet he found that he wanted to know. He *needed* to know.

"'Twas too fine a gown," she answered stiffly. "I told you I wanted something in a dark color that wouldnae stain. Something fit for work. I am nae a lady of leisure. You—"

Her voice shook at the end with barely controlled anger, and Ewan held up a hand.

"Una. Please. I didnae come to fight you. I came to apologize. Because you're right. You did ask for a dark gown. You asked for a work gown. But I saw that one and… I wanted you to have it."

She angled her face toward him. "But why? It was your mother's gown, Cat told me. Why would you give me such a precious gift? 'Twas far too much."

Ewan ran his hand over his mouth before rubbing his chin.

"I dinnae ken how to explain it," he said, which was true. "I just did. But it made you uncomfortable, and for that I am sorry. Can you forgive me?"

She looked at her hands in her lap. "There is nothing to forgive. I… appreciate the kindness for what it was."

They sat in silence for several minutes. In his periphery, Ewan saw her chest rise and fall with her quiet breathing. Her hands were folded in her lap as she glided the pad of one thumb up and down the length of the other. He had a sudden urge to rub his own thumb down that track of skin. He wondered if it was as soft as it looked.

After a time, Una asked, "Do you come here often? To the chapel?"

A threat of a smile tickled the corner of his mouth. "I cannae say I do."

"You are nae a devout man then?"

Ewan snorted. "Nay. Does that offend you?"

She took her time answering, and though the light was dim, he saw her eyes flick toward the cross over the altar.

"It doesnae offend me at all. My own notions of religion are admittedly... unorthodox."

"Unorthodox?" Ewan repeated, loving the experience of saying that word.

"Aye. Likely heretical, if I were to be technical."

"A healer and a heretic," he mused, giving in to that threatening smile for a moment. "You have captured my curiosity."

He didn't look at her, and she didn't look at him. They were simply two people sitting on a hard pew in a cold chapel in the early morning hours staring at a bare altar.

She sighed. "I struggle to reconcile what I am *told* is true with what I *believe* is true."

"And what do you believe to be true, Una?"

"I believe it's far simpler than we try to make it. I believe that we are here to ease one another's suffering, to prevent it where we can. I believe in focusing my sights on this life, not what lies after it."

"You dinnae believe in heaven then?"

She shrugged. "Who can say? I dinnae ken for certain if heaven exists, but I dislike it when we are told to live our lives as if heaven is all that we should care for, as if what we do every day doesnae matter more than as a means to an end."

He made a noise of agreement in his throat.

"I suppose I do believe in heaven. I've seen enough of it, after all," she continued. "When a lovestruck groom first sees his bride. When a mother first holds her bairn in her arms after the laboring is done. When the heather blooms on the hills and the wind blows it in waves. I dinnae ken what lies beyond this, but this life is filled with heavenly things aplenty."

Ewan was struck. Heretical indeed, but he couldn't disagree with her either. He'd seen it too. Sunrises over the snowy peaks, waves crashing against rocky shores, the look on Rabbie's face when he held the new lambs. They had reminded him of precisely how small he was, how insignificant in the grand scheme of things, no matter how strong and important he might have once felt.

"And hell?" Ewan asked, his voice catching.

"I certainly believe in hell," she whispered fervently, her voice nearly a hiss in the silence.

He reached out to lay his hand over her clasped ones but stopped, his palm hovering over hers. She held her breath.

"Una," he said, feeling strangled by his own words, wanting to say something but having no idea where to begin.

"Please, Ewan," she said her voice breaking. "Please dinnae ask me."

For a heartbeat, it seemed like she might say more, like she would unburden herself. But then she fairly jumped to her feet.

"I must see to Connor. I bid you good day, Ewan," she said with a hasty curtsy before side-stepping down the pew and sweeping out of the chapel. A cold gust of wind blew down the aisle as the door closed behind her. Ewan remained in his seat, his fists clenched so tightly that his knuckles cracked.

As the sunrise cast its brilliance through the chapel windows, illuminating floating, shimmering dust, Ewan dropped to his knees on the chapel's cold stone floor. Bowing his head, he prayed. For Connor. For Una. For himself.

CHAPTER 14

As Una made her way across the courtyard, shrugging against the icy wind, she couldn't help but think of Ewan's hand, hovering over hers. He'd meant to offer her comfort. It was a gesture that she practiced at nearly every healing, squeezing her patient's hand to reassure them that all would be well.

But he'd stopped. Close enough that she could feel the warmth radiating from his palm but far enough away that she could have moved her hands away. A very small part of her wished that he *had* touched her. She knew that his hands were calloused from the way they had scraped against the fabric of her gown as he lifted her up and down from Calman's back. She knew they would be warm because all of him was warm.

It had been five days since that morning in the chapel with Ewan. Five days of Connor battling through a raging fever. Five days of little sleep and sharing the watch with Fiona and Ewan's siblings. Five days of morning prayers in the chapel. Alone, after that first day.

Last night, she'd dreamt that he was behind her, holding

her close from head to toe, as he'd done in the cave. He had whispered beautiful, soft things in her ear and rubbed his large hands gently up and down her arm. The dream had been so real that when she'd woken, she'd reached behind her, expecting to feel his large body nestled there. But her hand had brushed nothing but air.

It wasn't the dream itself that had unnerved her, but rather her disappointment that it had only been a dream. That same small part of her that wished he had taken her hands had also wished to find herself held against his warm chest. Surrounded by his strength. Safe.

The past days had been a blur of activity. In addition to tending Connor, she had been called upon to tend to other minor injuries and maladies as word spread of the new healer at the keep. None as severe as Connor, but she was kept so busy that she collapsed into immediate sleep the moment her head hit the pillow. She knew Ewan came to visit Connor, but he did so when she was sleeping or down in the kitchens, eating or preparing medicines. She hadn't seen him since their conversation in the chapel, and she was surprised to find that she wished he *would* come when she was there.

The keep was warm, and she untied the strings of her cloak as she climbed the wheeled staircase. When she entered the laird's solar, she hung the cloak on a peg driven into the wall. The sun was up and shining through the window. Fiona sat stitching in the chair by Connor's bed.

"Any changes while I was gone?"

"Nay," Fiona said with a sigh. "He is as he has been. How was the chapel?"

"Bleak," Una said, and Fiona snorted. "I must go see Fenella about the makings of more salve. It must cure for nine days, and I dinnae want to run out. You will send for me if anything changes?"

Fiona nodded and returned to her knitting.

Una made her way down to the kitchen, where she'd prepared medicines many times before during the week, but never with these particular ingredients.

"I'll be happy to help you get your ingredients, dearie," Fenella said as she drove a sharp knife into a particularly stubborn turnip. The head cook was a stout, red-faced woman. "But I willnae get you a single thing until you've had breakfast."

Moment later, Una sat at the worn, wooden worktable, eating a bowl of steaming porridge with dried berries, and watching the kitchen women bustle about, stoking fires, peeking under cloths to peer at rising loaves, and scouring pots.

The table's surface was scarred by the slices and gouges of knives and worn smooth in others, the wood eroded into a concave from years and years of kneading dough in the same, favored spot. She smiled at the thought of decades' worth of bread being shaped and kneaded there, the hands changing over the years but the work, the bread, remaining exactly the same. In some ways, healing was like that\ too. Certainly, discoveries were made all the time, and yet she relied heavily on the medicines that Agatha had taught her, remedies that Agatha had learned from her grandmother.

Time didn't move in the same way down in the kitchens as it did above them, and Una quickly lost track of it. She was separating wedges of onion, peeling the petals away from the bulb before dropping them into a bronze vessel when she heard heavy footfalls moving quickly down the stone stairs descending into the kitchen.

Every head in the room turned as a guard burst through the door, skidding to a halt and nearly toppling over.

"Milady!" he shouted, and all the eyes turned to Una. "You must come at once!"

"Holy God," Fenella whispered under her breath.

Una shot to her feet and raced past him, taking the stairs two at a time as she ran around and around the wheeled staircase. She stopped briefly at the top to regain her equilibrium before tearing down the hall and throwing open the door to the laird's solar.

Fiona stood weeping next to the bedside, her face buried in her hands, and Una felt as if she would lose her breakfast.

"Is he dead?" Una asked in a choked voice.

Fiona turned to her, tears streaking down her cheeks. A wide smile stretched across her face.

"Nay, Una! His fever has broken!"

Fiona burst into a fresh round of sobs. Una rushed to the bed, pressing her hand against Connor's face. His skin was warm, but not the boiling misery it had been the past five days. More importantly, it was dry. He wasn't sweating or thrashing with delirium. Una turned to Fiona as Connor groaned loudly, mumbling about something to eat.

"Nothing but barley water and broth!" Una commanded Fiona, breathlessly tripping backwards toward the door. "And only small sips at a time!"

"Where are you going?" Fiona shouted after her, but she was already gone, racing down the hall, down the stairs, and out into the frigid morning.

She had forgotten her cloak but wasn't about to turn back now. Connor was not totally free of danger, but if his fever had broken, the worst of the dangers were past. Hope bloomed in her chest as she ran through the bailey and to the gate. Greer, who had been nosing around the courtyard, bounded after her, barking happily. Una felt a momentary pang of guilt. She had hardly seen the dog since their arrival.

"Come, Greer. We must make haste!" she panted, and the dog barked again.

She stopped at the gate where a guard told her that the

laird was training with his men in the fallow field past the cottages. She ran as fast as her legs would carry her down the road, clutching fistfuls of her skirts to keep from tripping over the hem. When she reached the hill overlooking the training fields, Una shielded her eyes with her hand and tried to spot Ewan among the men. Greer panted next to her.

A man on a black horse cantered close, stopping a few feet away. Una recognized him at once as the man who had helped Ewan and his brothers to hold Connor while she tended to his wound. David, she thought his name was.

"Are you well, Lady Una?" the man asked, his dark eyes narrow with concern.

"I need to speak to Laird MacDonald," she said around her gasps. "'Tis urgent."

"Is aught amiss?"

"Nay. Nothing is amiss. Only I must find him. Do you ken where he would have gone?"

David pointed behind her. "He went to the loch. Just beyond that hill."

Una grabbed her skirts and took off again, Greer close on her heels. Behind her, she heard David shout, "Let me send a man for him!" but she did not stop. She could not stop.

The cold air seared her lungs and stung her nostrils as she sprinted, grateful that she had forgotten her cloak after all, but she kept moving, feeling the hard ground underneath her feet as she tore across the field. As Una ran, she realized that she was bursting with eagerness to tell Ewan the news herself. That kept her feet moving, one in front of the other, long after her legs began to ache and her lungs felt as if they would burst into flames.

The loch grew closer, the water shimmering in the morning light. Calman stood nearby, lazily grazing on what was left of the grass. His mane fluttered in the breeze, and he lifted his head as she drew closer, nickering happily. Ewan was nowhere to be seen. Greer raced to the water and drank.

"Where is your master, Calman?" Una asked, trying to calm her breath as she stroked the horse's long nose. He bobbed his head up and down eagerly before pressing against her torso, looking for a treat.

"You're a greedy one, my darling," she said, her eyes scanning the loch for any sign of him.

A sudden splash had her whipping her head toward the loch, where a figure burst from under the water with a sputtering roar. Greer yelped and scrambled away, hiding behind Calman. There, in the frigid morning light, was Ewan. Standing waist deep in the loch, water streaming down his torso in rivulets around the hard contours and soft spaces of his body. He shook his head like a dog, cursing. When he saw her, his eyes went wide, and he charged out of the water.

"Una! What is the matter? You look as if you've seen a ghost."

"I… You…. I … You're naked," she stammered as she spun quickly around.

"Goddamnit," Ewan cursed loudly. "A moment, Una."

She felt her cheeks turn pink and grow hot with her blush, which was ridiculous. She was a healer, for God's sake. She had seen a hundred naked men. *At least.* Calman whinnied as if he found the entire scene hilarious before returning to his grazing.

Behind her, she heard mumbled curses and the rustling of fabric. Satisfied that it was only Ewan, Greer lay down and began rolling, rubbing her back against the scratchy, dead grass.

"There. Now, what has happened?" he asked. Una turned, startled to see that he stood less than a foot away. Ewan had put on his leine shirt but not his plaid. The bottom hem barely reached the middle of his thighs. It covered the bits that most needed shielding, but only just.

Una felt the blush rising from her chest to the tops of her ears. As a child, she had been teased about them turning as red as a fire poker.

Ewan placed his hands on her shoulders, shaking her gently and bringing her back. "Una! What has happened?" he shouted, sounding wild and desperate. She did not flinch away.

She forced herself to keep her eyes on his face. Not on his broad shoulders. Not on the way the fabric clung to the strong lines of his torso. Definitely not on his bare thighs.

"Una," he repeated. "Talk to me."

Tears sprang to her eyes, and she shook herself. "Oh, Ewan," she said thickly. "'Tis Connor—"

He was silent, standing still as stone for two or three breaths. "Och, Una. May I… may I hug you?" he whispered.

It was easy, far easier than she thought it would be, to step closer, to let his arms slide around her and hold her close. He smelled like water. Una's arms moved hesitantly around his torso, and she allowed herself to relax against the soft dampness of his shirt.

He felt so good. So strong. So *safe*. How long had it been since she'd felt truly safe? How long since someone had held her like this and she'd been unafraid? At least a year, but it felt like a lifetime. Una took a deep, shuddering breath.

"There now, Una," Ewan said, his voice thick as he rubbed a hand up and down the length of her spine. "You did your verra best."

Una shook herself, hearing the mournful tone. "What?"

"I will be forever grateful that you came and tried to save him."

She pushed against his chest and stepped back so that she

could look him in the eye. Her heart splintered when she saw the tears coursing down his cheeks.

"Nay! Ewan! I didnae— Saints, what a damned mess I made of this," she said. "Connor isnae dead! His fever is broken!"

A strange look crossed Ewan's face, and his eyes went wide, brows arching high. He opened his mouth to speak, squinting at her, before closing it again.

She took his hand in hers, shaking it. "Ewan?"

He stared at her, dazed. She had seen this many times before as a healer. Sometimes when a person received unexpected good news, they were shocked speechless. Others fainted dead away. Some dropped to their knees, clutching at her skirts and offering thanks to both her and God in the same breath. One man had danced such an aggressive jig that he broke a chair and a broom.

She chafed Ewan's hand, feeling the callouses against the pads of her fingers. "Did you hear me, Ewan? The fever has broken. Connor is awake and speaking."

"Aye," he rasped, his shocked eyes never leaving hers. As if he didn't trust his ears to have heard correctly, he asked, "You are certain?"

"He will live, Ewan," she said, a rare smile spreading across her face. "I willnae have it any other way now."

Before she could exhale, Ewan had snatched her around the waist, lifted her, and began spinning her wildly around, wheeling fast over and over again, whooping loudly. Her feet flew out behind her and the wind blew her hair loose from her braid, but she couldn't seem to care. She felt weightless—she was *flying*—and she laughed for the first time in a very, very long time.

With every shout and spin, her heart felt lighter and lighter. She imagined that if Ewan were to let go now, she would sail away over the clouds. He slowed his spinning, and

Una came back to the ground, her feet catching on the uneven earth. He held her against him by her waist, steadying her. The muscles of his arms bunched against the protesting fabric of his shirt. Una became painfully aware of the sensations of her body as she felt his hands clasping her just above her hips, their chests barely parted.

Una took a step backwards and Ewan followed, closing the gap and taking her face in his hands, his thumbs pressing gently into her cheeks. She realized distantly that she wasn't afraid of him and blinked, eyes wide, lips parted, gazing at his face, noting the muscle that ticked just below his ear.

"Ewan—"

The rest of the thought died when Ewan pressed his mouth hard against hers, and she went rigid in his arms.

CHAPTER 15

Ewan sprang away from Una as if she'd bitten him. He dragged the back of his fist against his mouth. *Shite.*

"What the hell was that, Ewan?" Una's arms gestured wide.

He didn't have an answer. He hadn't spoken to her in five days, hadn't seen her awake in as long. It had been a week filled with various anxieties causing varying degrees of panic. The endless worry had accumulated until he felt as if he carried a millstone on his back.

He'd come to the loch to cool down after a frustrating morning. The icy water had shocked his system, so cold that it stole his breath when he first dove in. He had stayed beneath the surface until his lungs burned and his head tingled before he'd burst through the surface with a shout.

Only to see Una, standing next to Calman in a brown work dress, her hem and hair flapping wildly in the breeze. Her cheeks were red and she gasped for breath, and he had been able to think of nothing but going to her.

She'd told him that his brother would live, and for a

moment, for the scantest of time, all of his other worries slid away like water off a duck's back. There had been no clan to manage, no winter to plan for, no enemies to consider, no brother to grieve. There had been only joy. And her.

"Una, I—" His face scrunched in frustration. "I beg of you, please forgive me. I shouldnae have done that."

She glared at the middle of his chest, where his damp leine gaped open. It offered no warmth, and he felt the goosebumps spread across his skin like a wildfire as the excitement of the moment wore off and the cold dread from what he'd done settled.

"Una, please. I dinnae ken what came over me."

"That makes two of us," she spat.

He should back away further, keep stepping backwards until his feet reached the loch and then continue in until the water swallowed him whole. He certainly shouldn't have looked at her, especially in the wake of this, his most recent failure, more monumental than most.

But he couldn't help himself. She was so beautiful, even angry, with her cheeks flushed and her lips berry-red, as if they'd been bitten, her chest rising and falling with hasty, uncontrolled breaths. Her wide blue eyes nearly brought him to his knees begging her forgiveness.

What the hell had he been thinking? He hadn't. That was the bald truth. He had been so consumed by joy and relief, and she had been *there,* so close. So warm, so lovely, so *Una.* But that didn't excuse it. Nothing did.

"Una, I beg yer forgiveness."

"'Tis fine," she said tightly.

"It isnae fine, Una. It isnae fine at all. I took something that you didnae offer. I am ashamed of myself."

He looked at the ground between his bare toes and the dark brown of her dress. He rolled his right shoulder toward his ear and back, wincing as the joint crackled like a branch snapping.

"You are sorry, Ewan?"

"Aye. I am mortified."

"You regret kissing me," she said matter-of-factly, as if she were telling him that she liked pigeon pie.

He looked her in the eyes, the blue looking otherworldly as it reflected the glass surface of the loch and turbulent sky behind. But for all that she looked ready to shout at him, she didn't look afraid.

"Aye," he said and he meant it.

"Because you didnae want to kiss me."

Ewan willed his eyebrows to stay in their given places. Had he wanted to kiss her? He'd thought of it many times since meeting her. She wouldn't want to know that. Her eyes were wide as a doe's before flight.

He pinched his bottom lip between his thumb and forefinger and stared at the skirt of her dress, rough and patched, and wished that she would allow him to provide her with better. He had a sparking desire to provide her with far more than a better gown. She would never allow it. And besides, he didn't *really* want that. Did he?

No. Of course not.

But he could give her this at least.

He cleared his throat. "You should take Calman back to the keep. You dinnae have a cloak, and I cannae have you catching a chill."

"You could ride with me," she said, rubbing Calman's neck.

"I need to walk and clear my head."

He went to Calman's side and waited. Una placed her hands on the saddle, and he hoisted her by her waist. She swung her leg over Calman's back, and as his hands slid away, he unintentionally grazed the line of her long leg through her skirts.

"You could catch chill yourself, Ewan. I..." Her sentence faded on the breeze.

Ewan shook his head. "Go on, Una. We can speak more later."

He gave Calman a slap on the rump and watched as the horse and dog trotted across the field toward the keep. His own walk back was long and cold, and he spent every single moment of it wishing he had better controlled himself. She had endured the attentions of Malcolm Cameron for a year. He *knew* this. And yet he'd forced a kiss upon her without even thinking.

Halfway home, a terrible thought wiggled into his consciousness. She had a horse. What if she'd left? What if he'd hurt her so badly or frightened her so much that she took Calman and went to the Stewarts?

He ran then, racing back to the keep, the cold air burning his lungs and chapping his lips. If she had run away, it was because he had driven her to it, frightened her to it. She could be out in the world alone, unarmed and unprepared. If anything happened to her, it would be on his head.

By the time he reached the courtyard, his jaw was clenched so tightly that he felt a muscle cramp in his cheek. Everyone in his path leapt to clear the way. He raced to the stables, frantically throwing the door open wide. Calman poked his huge head out of the last stall, and Ewan's knees went weak with relief.

"Oh, thank God," he said around his heaving breath.

He went to the horse, stroking his neck. Calman nickered happily, and Ewan rested his forehead against the horse's. He was feeling too many things at once, and they were making him dizzy. Relief that Una had come back, that his brother would live, that he had another chance to make things right with her. But along with that relief was panic, because he *did* need to make things right with Una. He needed to see Connor with his own eyes.

He gave Calman one last pat and made his way out of the stable, planning what he would say when he begged Una again for her forgiveness. Ewan was almost out the door when he heard heavy panting. He took a step back and looked into the empty stall to his right. Mathan was draped heavily over Greer's slender form. She did not seem to mind Mathan's attentions.

Ewan rolled his eyes and saluted Mathan. "I'm glad one of us managed to be charming, ye bastard," he said before striding out of the stable and into the cold.

CHAPTER 16

Fiona had been more than happy to surrender her post to Una. The evening meal was being served in the Great Hall, and the housekeeper was eager to check in on the household. She had been especially eager to look in on Fenella who, she insisted, was lost without her. While Una had been at the loch, Connor had taken some more broth and managed to keep it down. If he continued to do that, Una would allow him some porridge in the morning.

They had played a guessing game for a while before he had fallen asleep in the middle of his turn. Una sat in the chair by the hearth, watching his chest rise and fall rhythmically. Her stomach growled, and she wondered if she could ask the guard in the hall to fetch her some supper. As soon as her backside left the chair, the chamber door opened. Ewan slipped through and closed it softly behind him. She sat back down.

Ewan crossed the room on silent feet and approached the far side of the bed. Una watched as he carefully lowered his weight to sit on the mattress. He looked older than he had an hour before and certainly more haggard, as if he'd been given an extra weight to carry upon his already burdened shoulders. After a few moments of sitting and watching, he eased his body down to lay next to Connor, pressing his forehead into the side of the boy's shoulder, his hand resting on his brother's chest.

Una sat frozen to her chair, stunned by the tenderness of the moment and gaping outright.

She had known he was a big man, but he looked even more solid and broad next to Connor's lankiness, made even thinner by days of raging fever. She remembered how solid Ewan's thighs had felt bracketing hers, and her stomach dropped. But not from fear. It was something else. Something beyond her memory.

In the firelight, tears glittered in Ewan's eyes. Connor lifted his hand, reached across his own body, and rested it on Ewan's head. Ewan squeezed his eyes shut, and Una heard a choked sob. Connor tilted his head so that it rested against the top of Ewan's, and Una shot to her feet, suddenly feeling very much an intruder on such a tender, vulnerable moment. She crept to the door.

"Una, wait," Ewan said, his voice thick from his tears.

She stopped and turned. He climbed off the bed, gently ruffled Connor's hair, and came to her.

"Thank you, Una," he whispered. "I am forever in your debt."

She felt the blush heating her cheeks. She cleared her throat. "Of course."

Just then, her stomach growled, the gurgle sounding dreadfully loud in the quiet room.

"Have you eaten?" Ewan asked.

"I will eat later in the kitchen."

His heavy brows pinched together and his mouth tightened, displeased.

"Wait here," he commanded before striding quickly out of the room.

Barely a few minutes later, he returned with a plate of bread and cheese, fruit, and roasted venison. He thrust it into her hands and nodded toward the chair and table next to the hearth. Una was prepared to snap that she was perfectly capable of feeding herself and that she had no need of being ordered to meals like a child, but just as she opened her mouth, her stomach growled again, even louder than before.

"Una, please dinnae be stubborn. You are the most important person here, and you need your strength."

The most important person here. It was nonsense, of course, but even more ridiculous coming from the *laird*. And yet she couldn't help the butterflies that swarmed in her belly as she held his gaze.

Ewan arched an eyebrow and cocked his head. With a sigh, she sat and ate while Ewan returned to sit on the edge of the bed.

She had just finished her meal when someone knocked on the door. It creaked open and Angus, one of Ewan's brothers, poked his head in.

"Fiona tells me it is my turn to sit by him."

"You dinnae have to," Una said. "I am here. Go about your business."

"This is my business," Angus said, coming into the room. "She also bid me to tell you that you will be sleeping with Joan and in the bed, nae on a pallet on the floor."

"Certainly Joan doesnae want an intruder."

"I am told it was Joan's idea to begin with."

Angus seemed to wear a permanent scowl. Always serious, always reserved. Grumpy, Cat once called him in passing. But he looked downright cheerful as he took the chair next to the bed.

"Evening, Connie," he said brightly. "How do you fare? Do

you care for a nap, or would you like to hear about how Kenneth got tossed into a pig sty this afternoon?"

Connor's smile was weak but bright. "Tell me the story, brother."

Ewan stood and stretched, groaning as he reached his arms high in the air, an action that made his chest look impossibly even more broad.

"May I walk you to Joan's room, Una?" he asked, standing a respectful distance away.

After receiving assurances from Angus and giving him more detailed instructions than were necessary, she followed Ewan into the hall. The guard that had been stationed outside the door for the entire week was nowhere to be seen and the hallway was empty. He led her to a door that Una remembered leading to Cat's chamber and knocked. When there was no answer, he opened a door and ushered her in, opening another door in the interior wall and revealing a quaint little chamber with a wood posted bed, a cheerful fire in the hearth, and dozens of skeins of yarn looped around hooks on the walls.

"This is Joan's room?" Una asked, knowing the answer. The riot of color had Joan written all over it.

"Aye," Ewan answered. "This was my mother's dressing room, but Catriona decided she couldnae bear for Joan to sleep below with the servants, and so she insisted Joan make it her own."

"How thoughtful," Una said, and she meant it.

The room was silent except for the crackling fire, and Una became very aware of how small the chamber was because of how large Ewan loomed within it. He took a step closer, looking into her eyes.

"I am so sorry, Una. Again. I was an ass. Can you forgive me?"

Though he had apologized already, Una was not yet

accustomed to men apologizing at all. For anything. She blinked.

"Forgiven, m'laird," she whispered.

He reached out and took her hand in his, chafing her knuckles with his thumbs.

"Ewan," he replied, his voice soft but firm. "Or have you already forgotten your promise to me?"

"Ewan," she breathed.

"Can we be friends again?"

She smiled and nodded. "Friends."

He had not let go of her hand, and she did not pull it away. He was so close, close enough that she could see the fine weave of his shirt, the stubble on his jaw. She could feel the warmth of his breath and body.

The animal part of her, the voice in her brain that ran on instinctive fear alone, screamed at her to run, to get away before he could hurt her. But she found that there was another voice, a softer voice, one she had not heard in a very long time, that whispered, *"He is nae Malcolm Cameron."*

He wasn't. He was Ewan MacDonald, a gentle man who didn't behave as if he was owed anything or entitled to anyone, who treated his people with kindness, who wept.

She remembered the way it had felt when he kissed her, the heat from his mouth, for that split second before he leapt away from her as if she'd been on fire. And she thought... maybe... perhaps, it wouldn't be so bad to be kissed by him again.

He lifted her hand, his lips skating across her work-roughened knuckles and her breath caught in her chest. They stood like that for several long breaths. But then he pulled and she allowed herself to be towed closer. She rested her other hand gingerly on his chest, feeling the strong staccato of his heart beating beneath her palm. Una felt his ribs expand under her hand and inhaled deeply herself, the breath feeling like a wheeze.

"You asked if I regretted kissing you because I didnae want to."

She swallowed against a thick lump and nodded.

"Una," he whispered. "I shouldnae have handled you the way I did. I shouldnae have taken what you didnae offer."

Oh. That was an answer. She was surprised by her disappointment.

But then he shifted impossibly closer. "But you make me want things I shouldnae have. I shouldnae want to kiss you, but I *do*. I want it so badly I can feel it in my bones."

Una allowed herself to soften, to feel the strength of his body surrounding her. She found that she *wanted* him to hold her, to wrap her in a tight clasp and clutch her against him so that nothing could harm her ever again. He inclined his head, his lips close to hers, and closed his eyes before groaning softly, like a contented beast.

But then he released her hand and stepped away, and all the warmth left with him. She opened her mouth to protest, but before she could find the words, Ewan had spun on his heel and stalked out the door. Una sat heavily on the side of the bed, her heart pounding, her armpits sweating and her hands shaking.

I want it so badly I can feel it in my bones.

She brought her trembling fingertips to her lips and contemplated everything that she might want but was too afraid to reach out and take.

CHAPTER 17

The following day, Una was in the kitchen crushing coriander seeds to give to a guard whose daughter was running a fever. There was something deeply comforting in the familiarity of the work. Grinding herbs and seeds had been one of the first tasks Agatha had assigned to her in her apprenticeship. Even as a child, she'd found something highly satisfying about watching the whole materials slowly break down into a fine, uniform powder. It hadn't required her full attention, and so she'd been free to daydream while she worked.

As soon as she'd taken the pestle in hand that afternoon, her mind had wandered back to the day before. To the abrupt, stolen kiss, the way he had held her hand in his, the feeling of his lips brushing against her knuckles. She'd been startled by how much she liked the feeling of his fingers wrapping around hers, the way his heart pounded beneath her hand.

But more than the kiss or the gentle touches, Una kept replaying the apology in her mind. Both of them. No man had *ever* apologized to her for anything, and yet Ewan had managed it twice. *I shouldnae have handled you the way I did. I shouldnae have taken what you didnae offer.*

He'd whispered it like a prayer. Like a confession.

She glanced down at the mortar, examining the nearly ground coriander. She breathed in the clean, strong fragrance and sighed.

"What has you smilin' like that, Una?" Fenella's gravelly voice asked, breaking through the haze of Una's daydream.

She shook her head and looked across the work table at Fenella, who wore a smile of her own as she stared back at Una with a raised eyebrow. She was mixing pastry crust, her meaty hands pinching and working fat into the flour.

Una liked Fenella. She had a booming laugh, a bawdy sense of humor, and a temper that flashed hot like grease in a fire but burned off just as quickly. Una could relate. Fenella ran the kitchen with the precision and skill of a seasoned battle commander. The room was always clean and warm, and her charges worked efficiently but with excellent support and care. Fenella made sure everyone was fed, everyone sat and rested at regular intervals, and never turned away the children who seemed to always find their way into the warm sphere of her domain. Whenever Una came to the kitchen, there was always at least one child sitting on a stool at the long work table with a bowl of food and a large hunk of bread.

Una felt the hot blush creeping up her neck.

"What's their name?" Fenella asked.

"Whose name?" Una said, pounding the coriander with more force than necessary, her ears hot and throbbing now.

"Dinnae lie to me, lass. I ken that look on your face."

"Perhaps I am just happy," Una replied saucily. "Is that nae allowed in the MacDonald clan?"

"Och, you verra well may be happy. But you had a secret

smile just now. Like you were thinking about a tumble you took."

"I havenae taken any tumbles, Fenella," Una said, her eyes wide with protest. "With what time?"

Fenella laughed, her bosom quaking, and shook her head. "Fine. Keep your secrets then. The keep is full of them. But you might be interested to know that a little birdie told me some verra interesting news this morning." She winked.

Una narrowed her eyes. "What?"

Fenella shrugged, her eyes on the lard and flour before her when she casually said, "Something about a certain bonny healer being lodged with Lady Catriona's maid just down the hall from the laird himself?"

Una felt her mouth go dry.

"Is everyone talking?"

"Nay. Only one little bird," Fenella said with a warm smile. "But it willnae be long."

Una's face felt unbearably hot. She stopped her grinding. Fenella's smile was easy and genuine, but a year in the Cameron keep had made Una suspicious in a way she'd never been before.

"What else did this little bird tell you?"

Fenella shrugged her broad shoulders again and pursed her lips. "I have heard tell that our laird is often verra interested in the whereabouts and well-being of the bonny healer."

"Fenella—" Una began, but the words died on her tongue.

She could imagine what the gossip would become, what people would say about her. How very unfair for her to have been here less than a fortnight and there already be rumors swirling about her relationship to yet another laird. A relationship that, unlike the last one, did not actually exist. Una swallowed against the lump in her throat.

Fenella smiled at her across the table, her eyes bright and

kind and full of mirth, without a hint of malice, and continued to rub the globs of fat into the flour. "I remember the laird as a lad. Always with a smile on his face. He had a new joke for me every day. And hungry. Och, he was always so hungry. I teased his mother that her boy had a bigger appetite than my husband, Big Hew. God rest him."

Una relaxed in spite of herself, resuming her grinding. "What was his mother like?"

Fenella's smile softened, a wistful expression crossing her face. "My lady was the kindest. She didnae set herself apart. She was the laird's wife, but she often made her way down here to have a cup of ale with me and the maids. She would ask after us, our bairns, our troubles. And it was a common thing for a maid who had complained of a sick child or a pished husband to find a basket on her doorstep the next morning."

Una smiled.

"She loved children. All of them. Of an evening, she sat in a chair by the hearth in the Great Hall and told faerie stories to the wee 'uns. She—" Fenella cleared her throat, her eyes shining.

"She sounds wonderful," Una said.

"Aye," Fenella said with a cough. "She was. She was the beating heart of this keep. When she died, the keep died a bit as well, I think. The laird—Laird Ewan's father, that is—was never the same. And our Laird Ewan wasnae ready for the title when it fell to him. Though he is the best man for it. He has all of his mother's kindness. All of her heart. All of her worry too."

Una looked back at the coriander grounds.

Fenella sighed and added water to her pastry. "If only he had someone to ease his heartache. To make him smile. I havenae seen that smile in a verra, verra long time."

Una's stomach tightened.

"Imagine my surprise when that little bird told me that he smiled when asking after the bonny new healer."

Una's heart was pounding now. She was saved from having to reply by Fiona appearing in the doorway.

"Well!" Fenella exclaimed happily, "if it isnae my little bird! Hello, Fifi! We were just speaking of you."

Fiona approached the table and stood next to Fenella. Very close to Fenella, in fact, who smiled warmly up at her.

"That cannae be good," Fiona grumbled with a smile and roll of her eyes.

"Psh," Fenella said. "As if we could say a bad thing about you. You're an angel. Nay, I was just telling Una a wee story to pass the time."

"I've heard yer stories," Fiona said. "All of them. And if you have been telling her a story, I'm surprised she hasnae turned inside out from embarrassment."

Fenella barked a laugh, her eyes crinkling with mirth.

"I was about to ask her a question, actually. Perhaps you'd be interested in her answer as well? I was about to ask how a certain bonny healer might react if the laird set his cap at her."

Una's eyes went wide and she looked around the kitchen. It was remarkably empty for the afternoon, with only a cluster of maids scouring pots in the corner. *Thank God,* Una thought.

Fiona nudged Fenella hard with her shoulder. "Fen," she said, her voice full of warning.

"You ken you want the answer as much as I do, mo cridhe."

Una's heart was pounding now. "I— I— I—"

She felt sick. She felt nervous. She felt… something that almost resembled excitement?

Fiona and Fenella looked at her expectantly, and she opened and closed her mouth over and over, feeling like a fish on the shore. She was saved from having to answer as a voice echoed from the hall and a gangly, red-headed boy flew into the kitchen, red-faced and out of breath.

"Fenella!" he shouted. "Have you seen the healer?"

Fenella stood and wiped her hands on a cloth. "What is the matter, Rory?"

"The laird is injured!"

"Saints' bones, cannae these MacDonald men give us a day of peace?" Fenella muttered at the exact moment Fiona screeched, "What's happened to him?"

Rory gasped for air, clutching his side against a stitch. Una's blood ran icy cold. Through his heaving breaths, the boy said, "He was helping with the roof thatching on the widow Bertie's house. The roof gave way and he fell."

"Jesu," Fenella said. "Surely he cannae be badly injured from a fall. He's a big, braw man, our laird."

"Aye," Rory said, "But he landed on a sickle! Bleedin' like a stuck pig, Fenella! There was blood everywhere! I havenae ever seen so much blood! Da told me to run for the healer. Said she lived up at the keep."

Worry clawed higher, every one of Rory's sentences acting like a new ladder rung for the tightness in her chest to climb, until she could hardly swallow. Where had he been stabbed? How much blood had he really lost? She shook herself out of her daze.

"I am the healer," she said, dropping the pestle and rushing around the table.

Rory's eyes went wide as platters. "You're even prettier than Douglas said," he whispered in a reverent voice.

"Where is the laird?" Una asked impatiently.

"They've put him on a cart and are a'comin' this way now. He wanted to ride that big gray beast of his. You ken the one who willnae let anyone else touch him but the laird? But David wouldnae let him. Told him he was aff his heid, and the laird didnae cuff him or anything. Can you imagine? He's cussin' like the devil, though. I learned a new word, Fenella," he said, his excitement temporarily overriding his concern. "Do you ken what a swi—"

"That's more than enough of that," Fiona interrupted, glaring at Fenella who was suddenly very interested in something on the ceiling. "Rory, I want you to meet them in the bailey and tell them to bring the laird to Connor's chamber. That's where he's staying."

"I will!" Rory said importantly, dashing quickly away.

"Aye, and when ye're done, come back here and I'll have a pie for you," Fenella shouted after him.

Fiona sighed heavily, and Fenella draped a strong arm around her shoulders, squeezing her tightly to her side.

"Dinnae fash yerself, mo cridhe," she said affectionately as Fiona rested her head on Fenella's shoulder. "Have we ever gone a week in this keep without one of them getting stitched? Besides, if he can curse creatively enough to teach *Rory* a new word, he cannae be so beyond repair."

Then Fenella clapped her hands together loudly. "Well, I believe you birdies have an enraged laird to tend, and I have to make this pie so that I can have a long chat with young Rory about the new word he learned and when nae to say it."

"That's a wee bit hypocritical, dinnae you think?" Fiona asked with an arched brow as Fenella returned to the table with a booming laugh. "*You* teachin' him nae to swear?"

"I didnae say I would tell him *never* to say it. Just nae to say it around *you*."

Fiona huffed a long-suffering sigh, and Una thought that it was no wonder Ewan had spent so much time in the kitchen as a boy. She could picture him, blond shaggy hair and lanky body, sneaking into the kitchen to sneak scraps from the table behind Fenella's back.

"Come, Una. Gather what you require," Fiona said, and Una obeyed.

When they reached Connor's room, Una and Fiona made preparations for Ewan's arrival. Fiona spread clean linens on the bed, and Una sent a maid down for the boiling water Fenella had promised before they'd left, then arranged her medicines on a table near the bed.

A commotion in the bailey sent Fiona flying to the window, pulling aside the heavy coverings and peering down. "He's here. It looks as if David and Rabbie are helping him. Saints, but that is a lot of blood, Una."

Una joined her at the window and watched Ewan hobble toward the keep, an arm slung over both men. While she was gratified that he was both conscious and strong enough to walk, she hissed between her teeth at the sight of his bloody clothes and body.

"Foolish man," she said "Struggling up all those stairs willnae make him bleed less. Cannae they carry him?"

"Aye, they could. Especially if Angus or Kenneth or one of the others helped. But do you think the laird would let them?" Fiona asked with a maternal look, both fond and frustrated.

Una blew her breath through pursed lips, her cheeks puffing. "Perhaps David should have knocked him out. That would solve both problems, the carrying and the shouting."

Fiona snorted a laugh.

Moments later, curses echoed from the stairs and then the hallway just before the chamber door burst open and the men entered the room, seeming to take up every inch of space. All three were panting, and Ewan's head hung low as he grunted, pained.

"Where is the wound?" Una asked.

Rabbie bit his lips. David said, "Right at his hip, m'lady. He fell off the roof and landed on a sickle. Thank God his belt caught it so the blade sliced his side rather than piercing him through."

"That was fortunate," Una said. "Can you remove his plaid and leine so that I can see the wound?"

"M'lady," David asked, shocked. "Strip him to his skin?"

"How else am I to examine and stitch a wound at his hip?"

"Aye, but—"

"And that leine is *filthy*. Cover him as you see fit, but I must have unfettered access to the wound."

David nodded, and Ewan cursed loudly as they maneuvered him toward the bed. With more shouted curses, they got him onto the bed and reclined, but nobody moved further. Una rolled her eyes and turned her back on them.

"I'll give you some privacy then, m'laird," she said, and Ewan growled. That was gratifying enough to send a small smile tugging at her lips.

Una heard the rustle of clothing being removed, the scraping of a belt through a buckle, more shuffling. And then David said, "He is ready, m'lady."

Rabbie stood next to the bed, pale as a ghost and clearly shaking. Fiona looped an arm around Rabbie's waist, guiding him away from the bed. "Send for me if you have need, Una. Rabbie and I will go to the kitchens to see if Fenella has an extra pie and then check on Connor."

Una was prepared to tell David to sit when Ewan grabbed his wrist with a shaky hand. "David, go be sure it's finished. I dinnae want Bertie and her wee 'uns without a roof tonight."

David nodded and squeezed Ewan's hand. A maid entered with an ewer of boiled water, and David held the door open for her to leave after placing the ewer on the table. The door closed with a dull thud, and she was alone with Ewan, naked except for the sheet tucked around him.

CHAPTER 18

Ewan lay in the bed, panting and in pain. The sickle had sliced him across his side, a cut that was several inches long and a good half-inch deep at least. David had covered his left leg and groin with a sheet that was pulled up to his armpits and tucked there, leaving his right hip, side, and leg exposed for Una's examination.

His hair was dirty, drenched with sweat and bits of thatch stuck in the waves. Hell, all of him was dirty, and he wished he'd instructed them to visit the well before coming upstairs and poured a bucket of water over him. He was sure he smelled like a sty in August.

Una approached the bed slowly. "How is your pain?" she asked.

He grit his teeth. "I have certainly been in *less* pain."

"Fenella tells me she cannae remember a week when one of you didnae require stitches."

Ewan chuckled, but the laugh turned into a groan as a bolt of pain lanced through him. He shifted on the bed. "Aye. Why do you think I sought to steal a healer?"

Una leaned over the wound to examine it more closely.

"You didnae steal me. You asked me quite politely, in fact. Though you did use a heavy hand with the guilt."

"I didnae steal you," he agreed, his teeth clenched against the pain. "But I would have, if I'd had to."

She looked at his face, her mouth a hard, concerned line, and even through the pain-fueled waves of nausea, there were butterflies in his stomach. She placed a clean piece of linen against the wound, applying pressure, and just like that, the butterflies were gone.

"Fuck!" he cursed

"I am sorry," she said, "but I must slow the bleeding enough that I can check for any debris in the wound."

She pushed the cloth into a different spot, and he groaned between his teeth, the sound rising to a near squeak.

"Are you wounded anywhere else?"

"Besides my pride?"

She smiled. "I believe your confidence is strong enough to survive such a paltry thing as wounded pride, m'laird."

Damn her. She was baiting him. Here he was, writhing in agony, and she was *teasing* him. There was a ghost of a smirk at the corner of her mouth, and she seemed softer than usual, more at ease. He was unaccustomed to seeing her without a frown at best, a scowl at worst. But now, her mouth was relaxed, her eyes focused on the task before her. He couldn't help but stare.

"You're beautiful, Una," he said.

She ducked her head, but he reached out with a hand that was shaky from blood loss and exhaustion and placed his fingers under her chin, coaxing her to look at him.

"You are."

She looked away again, back to his wound.

"And *you* are lucky it was a sharp sickle and nae a pitchfork," she said, using a damp piece of cloth to clean around the edges of the wound.

It hurt, and he shifted uncomfortably.

"You're right about that. Better a gash than to be skewered."

"It makes my job much easier."

She leaned to the side and reached for a dark bottle on the side table. When she pulled the stopper, he smelled vinegar. She poured it into the wound, and he nearly flew off the bed from the way it burned.

"God's bones, Una! Do you really hate me so much?"

"Shhh. This part will be done soon," she said, pouring another splash of vinegar and wiping it away, her brows knit tightly together in concentration. After a while, she said, "And I dinnae hate you."

"You fooled me," he groaned.

She placed her free hand in the center of his chest and applied gentle pressure. His heart beat fast beneath her palm. She pressed another linen square hard against his wound. She was bent over him now, one hand on his chest, the other wedged between her body and his as she leaned firmly into his side.

He felt a stirring beneath the sheet. *Dear God, not now. Not now, I beg of you.*

But it was too late. The sheet rose away from his body. He'd hoped she wouldn't notice, but he should have known better. Una noticed *everything*. She kept her eyes locked on his wound but he saw her cheeks turn red as roses.

"Christ," he said through clenched teeth. "Strike me dead now."

"And ruin all my hard work?" she said in a tone that was impossible to decipher as jab or jest.

He covered himself with his hand. Or tried. Una closed her eyes, and Ewan could not remember ever being so mortified.

"It seems that 'tis true what they say about there being a

first time for everything," she said, pulling the linen away from his wound and stepping away from the bed. He saw her measuring out a long length of cat gut. Her needle glinted in the light.

"What do you mean?"

She bit her lip and turned toward him, her eyes very carefully fixed on his. "In all my years of healing, I have nae ever witnessed a man become… like that… from having a wound cleaned."

Ewan kept his eyes focused on the ceiling, one fist clenched at his side, the other still cupping his… *Goddamnit.* He tried to think of something to kill it—*anything*—to no avail.

"I dinnae think you could do anything to me without my body responding to you," he confessed quietly.

She froze, and he growled, frustrated that he'd said such an inappropriate, honest thing.

"Ignore it," he growled. "It will go away on its own."

"I'll make it go away," she replied.

Ewan's eyes flew wide, and he croaked, "What?"

Her cheeks became even more red and she tripped over her words as she said, "I mean, that is, what I meant was, I will make it go away with what I'm about to do to you, which you willnae find arousing in the least."

"Stitches are nae so bad," he said, his voice strained.

She seemed to deliberately keep her eyes trained on his face, ignoring the tented sheet.

"I suppose we will get to test your theory."

She arched an eyebrow, and it struck him that while she was obviously embarrassed, her posture was relaxed, her eyes focused on him, not darting about looking for an escape the way she usually did.

"I'm sorry, Una. I— you deserve double your usual fee for having to put up with me."

"Ten times over," she said and he rolled his eyes.

"Between all you've done for Connor and now this, you'll impoverish me within a month."

She was quiet for a moment as she prepared the catgut and her needle.

"You dinnae have to pay me in coin."

"Oh? And how else am I meant to pay you?"

"A cottage. I want a cottage."

"A cottage?" he boomed, struggling to sit up but groaning and falling back.

"Dinnae do that!" she scolded, pushing hard on his chest. "And aye, I want a cottage of my own."

His head was spinning, from pain, from exhaustion, from blood loss, yes, but also from the thought of her leaving the keep, of her being… away.

"Why? Why cannae you stay here?"

"I cannae live in the keep any longer," Una protested. "There will be talk. I'm surprised there hasnae been any already."

"Hang the talk. It doesnae matter."

"It matters verra much to me," she said, her mouth returning to that hard, angry line.

She was silent then. Truly silent, and he had the sense that she would not speak again for the rest of this encounter if he did not fix things. *God's bones.* Could he do nothing right?

A cottage. She wanted a cottage. She didn't want to be the source of gossip. He wanted to tell her that she shouldn't concern herself with talk, but that didn't seem fair. It certainly didn't seem considerate. And he wanted to be considerate with her. He wanted to take care of her.

"Ye can have the cottage," he said with a sigh.

"Thank you," she said, and he was miserable.

"But nae too far away," he insisted because the truth was

that it would drive him mad to not be able to check on her, to see how she fared.

"It *cannae* be too far," Una agreed. "If Fenella is telling the truth and I am to stitch a MacDonald at least once a week, 'twould be terribly inconvenient to have to travel verra far so often."

He snorted a laugh and then groaned.

"It will be a few days before I can have something ready for ye."

She nodded. "I understand. But perhaps before Connor is fully out and about?"

Ewan clenched his jaw again. "As you wish."

Una stitched him quickly. He watched her face as she worked, noting the way she stuck the tip of her tongue out of the corner of her mouth when she concentrated, the way her blue eyes darted quickly. From time to time, she would check in on him, and his answer was always the same. *"I am fine. Carry on."*

But he wasn't fine. He couldn't remember the last time that he had been *less* fine. Her hands were all over him, holding the wound closed and stitching with the other. The room felt as hot as the fires of hell itself, and he wondered if it was his body's response to the injury or to her. And though it felt unspeakably good when she smoothed the salve over the stitches, the pain of being sewn whole again outweighed any pleasure he might have derived from looking at her, from her other touches.

He felt feverish by the time she had finished dressing the wound. She pulled the sheet up to the middle of his chest, straightening and smoothing the material and resting her palm over his heart. He couldn't look away. She leaned down and pressed a long kiss to the center of his forehead. He sucked in a surprised breath, and Una pulled back far enough to look him in the eye.

"Una," he rasped.

She shook her head. Leaning closer again, she kissed his cheek. Then the other cheek. She pulled back, the tips of their noses touching, and he could feel her mint-scented breath on his lips. He tipped his chin up, and his lips met hers. He half expected her to bolt, but she didn't. Instead, with a sigh, she kissed him back.

It was a tender kiss, a lover's kiss, and he felt as if his heart would pound its way out of his chest to rest in peace and pieces in her hand. He lifted a shaky hand and cupped the back of her head.

She tensed and pulled away.

He wanted to shout, *"I'm sorry! Come back! I beg of you!"*

But she surprised him again by kissing his forehead once more.

"Rest," she said, smoothing her other hand over his wild hair. "You must rest."

She took a step back. She would leave. She would gather her medicines and walk out that door and leave him alone with the knowledge of how her lips felt, how they *really* felt. And she would go about her magical day, healing and tending and he would be stuck in this bed, caged and *aching*

"Dinnae leave," he said, his voice a hoarse whisper.

"I must finish making a remedy for one of the kitchen maid's daughters."

He nodded. She was important. People depended on her. People depended on him too, but she moved through that need with a grace and confidence that he envied. He'd never felt so at ease in all his life as she looked while she worked.

"But," she said, and he froze. "If you rest, if you *promise* me that you willnae get up and rip all my fine stitches out like I ken you're itching to do, I will come back and sit with you when I have finished."

"Whatever you ask. Whatever you want," he blurted, not

caring in the least how very much like a lovesick youth he sounded.

She squeezed his hand before taking her leave, and Ewan allowed himself to slide into a shallow, dreamless sleep. When he blinked his eyes open, it was dark outside the window and the fire blazed high in the hearth. He was still exhausted and in pain, aching with disappointment that she had not come. Or, if she had, she was gone.

But then, from the shadow beside the bed, he heard a hum. Not a tune as much as the impression of one. He looked out the corner of his eyes and saw her there, sitting next to the bed and darning a sock.

"You came back," he said, his throat dry.

"I promised I would," she replied, lifting a cup of water to his lips and tipping it gently in. He swallowed the cool water. "Now, back to sleep. We heal when we sleep, and you must rest so that I have a chance at any peace at all."

He smiled before closing his eyes and diving back into oblivion, her soft humming showing him the way.

CHAPTER 19

In the hours just before dawn, Ewan sprawled naked on top of his bed. His skin was hot, and he was certain he was still feverish from his wound, but he'd been feverish like this before and was not afraid. He felt the cool air of the chamber against his overheated, overstimulated skin. He had slept like the dead, lulled deep by Una's humming before she had left him sometime around midnight. He wondered if she was sleeping. He hoped she was. He pictured her on her side, the blanket pulled up past her nose, her black hair fanned out behind her on the pillow.

How many times had he imagined combing his fingers through those long, silken strands? How many times had he imagined holding her while she slept, her hair pressed between their bodies, as sleek and slick as a crow's wing?

Wispy tendrils of hair had escaped her braid and framed her face yesterday as she'd worked to stitch him back together. One of them had tickled his chin when she'd kissed him. *God's bones, that kiss.* It had been so tender, so tentative, and yet so pure. So earnestly and freely given.

He'd been desperate for another, but she'd left him to go about her work. Just like she would leave the keep soon to live in the cottage he'd promised her. He would have no excuse to see her every day, no chance meetings in the Hall or stairs. Once he released her from his sight, that would be it.

No more moments alone, certainly no more kisses. He scrubbed his hand over his beard and closed his eyes against that thought. He didn't regularly keep a beard. He found them itchy, and until a year or so ago, his whiskers had grown in patches. Kenneth had teased him that he looked like a mangy dog.

This beard was entirely accidental, a result of not taking the time to shave during Connor's illness and the days following. He pulled at the ends and imagined Una tugging on it, using it to tow him close for a kiss. A beard like his would make her lips pink, would rub at the delicate skin around her mouth and turn that pink too. What would it feel like against her delicate skin, he wondered. Against her throat, her breasts. He pictured Una on her back, his head between her thighs, the beard chafing at her delicate, private skin as he tasted her. He was hard in an instant.

"Fuck," he groaned, taking his cock in hand.

He stroked his fist up and down his length once, twice, three times, imagining Una's breathy cries as he worshipped her with his mouth, her petal pink center blooming brighter, abraded from his beard. He gripped his cock roughly, gritting his teeth as he increased his tempo. His wound pulled and ached, but his bollocks ached worse.

Would she cry out? Or would she bite her lip and fall apart in silence? Would she grip the sheets in tight fists or yank his hair at the roots, pulling him closer and closer until he could hardly breathe before pushing him away when it all became too much? He was painfully hard now, consumed by the need for release. How long had it been? Days, at the very least. Perhaps weeks?

He panted, grunting softly and blind to everything but the sensations in his body. At some point, he stopped thinking of Una, his focus narrowing on the way his bollocks tightened up against his body. He increased the pace of his hand and ground his teeth, ignoring the lancing pain in his side as his abdomen clenched. He felt his seed rising until it boiled out, splattering hot on his belly as he gasped for breath, squeezing his cock to ground himself.

"Goddamnit," he muttered as he used a spare rag to wipe the sticky spend from his body and hands, glad that he had missed the wound dressing.

What a wretched conversation that would have been. *"Aye, Una, I ken you just dressed the wound last evening, but I need you to change it again as I went and drained the moat all over myself."*

Ewan stood from the bed, wincing as his stitches pulled tightly, and crossed to the window. He saw the torches glowing brightly atop the wall, the men keeping guard. He bit back a smile as an idea came to him. He'd promised her a cottage outside of the keep. He'd never promised that it wouldn't be in the shadow of the walls, where she could be guarded. Where she could be safe. Where he could visit to check on her and make sure she didn't have needs that weren't being met. Where she could still take her meals in the Great Hall and worry for nothing.

At least, those were the noble reasons, he told himself as he dressed quickly in a clean leine and plaid. Ewan left the chamber, closing the door silently behind him. The keep was quiet, save for the murmurings of servants as they shuffled in and out of the kitchens. He hurried along the corridor, eager to find the perfect spot for this cottage.

David lived in a cottage just next to the curtain wall of the keep. He'd built it there so that he could be close in case he was needed but also have the benefit of being in the village. There was a space behind his cottage, tucked close to the wall. If Una could not be under his protection day and night, David would look out for her.

David agreed readily, and they began planning. The morning passed quickly. Due to his wound, Ewan could not lift any timber, but he helped direct a small group of men in beginning to frame the cottage.

He came back to the keep at noontime to grab a bite to eat and check on Connor. On his way to the Great Hall, he bumped into Joan, who was carrying a basket of mending. Upon colliding, the basket flew out of her hands, thread and scraps of fabric scattering across the floor.

"Oh!" she squeaked. "Good afternoon, m'laird. Beg pardon!"

Joan was short and plump, with wild chestnut curls that never wanted to stay in their bun or braid and surrounded her head like a bramble. But what she lacked in height, she more than made up for in presence.

"'Twas my fault, Joan," Ewan said as he knelt to help her collect the scattered sewing. "I was lost in my thoughts."

She smiled, as she often did, revealing the small gap between her front teeth.

"How do you fare this day?" he asked.

"Och, it has been quite a busy morning!"

"What is happening?" Ewan asked, curious. They were expecting no guests, there was no feast, and the harvest was done.

"Well, one of the maids, Sarah, was asking Fenella for a few days' leave so that she could clean out her late father's cottage. Do you remember old Gavin down in the village? Anyway, Fenella said that she could do better than that and offered her two kitchen boys and a whole score of maids to help so that Una can take it."

Ewan froze, his eyes widening. Words escaped him, which was just as well since Joan didn't seem to require his response.

"We've been there all the morning. The old man was just like a squirrel, he was, hoarding everything. But between us all, we got it emptied and scoured and open to air out. Fiona and Cat are collecting linens for her, and Fenella sent a few of the lads around the village to ask if anyone has any goods to spare to make a home. Una is delighted." Joan stopped to sigh wistfully. "I always wanted a home of my own, and now she has one! Can you imagine how—"

"Joan," Ewan croaked, feeling as if he were coming back to the surface after hearing the conversation from deep underwater. Old Gavin's cottage was at the far end of the village, farthest away from the keep within that immediate cluster of homes. Unprotected, the first to be reached from the road. His stomach turned.

"Aye, m'laird?" Joan asked, cocking her head to the side like an inquisitive dog.

"Where is Una now?"

If Joan thought anything of the question, she didn't show it, her face as serene and happy as it always was. "She is in with your brother, m'laird. I believe she meant to get him to stand today. 'Tis—"

But he was off, lunch forgotten, the cottage forgotten, as he raced up the wheeled staircase to the top and into the hallway. He stalked to the end of the hall and threw open the door. Una stood close to Connor, one arm around his waist and the other holding his hand, which was slung over her shoulder. Connor stood next to the bed on thin, shaky legs. His face brightened when he saw Ewan.

"Brother! Look!"

Ewan made a sound that was not a laugh, not a sob, not a groan, but something very much birthed of all three. "You are up, Connor," he said, forcing himself to speak actual words. "Praise be to God."

"Praise be to Una!" Connor said, and Ewan saw her cheeks flush red.

She shook her head. "Dinnae speak blasphemy in the face of such a miracle, Connor. I willnae have you tempting that on my head."

Connor snorted a laugh. Ewan watched his brother stand until Connor's knees began to shake.

"Verra good!" Una praised, her voice light and cheerful in a way he hadn't heard before. "You did so well! You should be verra proud of yourself. And now you can rest."

She coached Connor to slowly lower his backside to the mattress and then helped him to lift his legs onto the bed, arranging pillows and bedclothes around him.

"Una, may I… may I speak with you?" Ewan asked, his mind whirling.

She looked puzzled, but nodded. "Of course, m'laird." She rested a hand on Connor's forearm and said, "I willnae be long. Shout if ye have need of me."

When Una came to Ewan's side, he grabbed her hand and tugged her out of the room.

"Ewan? What is the matter?"

He pulled her to Connor's door and opened it, pulling her inside after him.

"M'laird, you had best have a good reason for dragging me away from my work and bringing me to your bedchamber."

He couldn't tell if she was angry or teasing. Perhaps it was both. Ewan fought for calm. He felt like shouting, but it wouldn't do any good to shout at her. She hadn't done anything wrong.

"Joan tells me that you mean to take Old Gavin's cottage."

She blushed. "I wondered how long it would take for you to hear about that."

"Until noon," he said mulishly.

"Gavin's cottage is lovely, with plenty of room for an herb garden out back. I shall be quite happy there."

"You didnae want to tell me yourself?"

"I would have. I planned to. But you were gone this morning, and there was much to be done."

"I told you I would find ye a cottage. I began building it just this morning!"

"And now you dinnae need to go to the trouble."

He paced away from her, dragging his hands through his hair. He could feel it sticking up at odd angles.

"'Tis nae good enough."

Una laughed, a bright, sharp sound. "And why is it nae good enough? I am a crofter's daughter, Ewan, and I assure ye that Gavin's cottage is far nicer than my childhood home."

"I was building you something new," he muttered.

"And how long would that take? A week? Two? I told you I wanted to be out of the keep by the time Connor was up and about, or else there would be gossip."

"Hang the gossip!" he said, his voice a near shout. He took a steadying breath and fought to regain his composure. "Why do you care about the gossip? Why does it matter what anyone would say?"

"Because I have nae interest in being the source of gossip again," she snapped.

"Again? Have ye been accused of seducing a laird before?"

He regretted it the moment it was out of his mouth. But it *was* out of his mouth, and he couldn't take it back. Una's eyebrows slammed together and her eyes narrowed. Her mouth was pinched in a tight line and fury radiated off of her like the crackling after a lightning strike.

"That is nae any of your business, *m'laird*," she hissed.

"Goddamnit, Una. You promised me you wouldnae call me that," he said through his teeth, scrubbing his hands over his face and pacing like a caged beast, the stitches in his hip tugging painfully with every agitated step.

She turned to leave, and he darted around her, blocking the door with his body.

"Let me go," she said.

"We need to talk."

"I think you've said quite enough, *Ewan*."

He didn't like that either. He didn't like the way her tongue sliced his name to ribbons. He didn't like having made her angry. He didn't like having hurt her. He didn't like being so out of control that he spoke without thinking. He didn't like the thought of her being far away and unprotected. He didn't like any of it.

And nobody could fix a mess of his own making but him.

"Please, Una," he said. "I didnae mean that."

"Aye, you did. And aye, *they* did. They *did* accuse me of seducing the laird. And worse. But I didnae seduce him. I didnae want anything to do with him. My father offered me up when the laird asked, without a single care for what I wanted."

His stomach roiled.

Una drew herself tall, looking into his eyes. "It was hell. He was cruel and violent. He treated his dog better than he treated me, which is nae saying much. But the gossip was insult to injury." She contorted her face into a sneer. "'Poor Una. This is what happens when you aim above your station.' 'Poor Una. He wouldnae beat her so if she only did her duty.'"

His blood ran cold.

"*I did my duty*," she said, her voice as hard as a blade. "Every night, even in my courses. I did my duty. But I didnae seduce him. I didnae ask for it. I didnae *want* it. And yet they talked anyway."

Her chest heaved, and he felt her breath on his face. His own breathing was just as labored. The enormity of the moment was too great for calm.

"I want to ride there right now and kill him with my bare hands," he said in a tight voice. "I want to wrap my hand around his throat while you watch and make him beg you for forgiveness while I watch the life drain out of his eyes. And then I want him thrown to the crows."

Una gasped.

"I hate him, Una," he whispered. "I have hated him since I was a lad, since I learned what hate was. Or so I thought. But it seems that I have only harbored mild dislike for him all my life because it pales in comparison to what I feel now, how I *hate* him now."

Una took a step back, and he resisted the urge to grab her and pull her close. Her eyes welled with tears, and she clutched her apron in her hands. But she shook herself, swiping at the eyes and clenching her jaw.

"I willnae be the source of such gossip again, m'laird."

"Ewan," he said gently.

"Ewan, I willnae do it. I cannae bear it. I need people to trust me. They willnae bring me their sick if they dinnae trust me."

"It doesnae matter what they think of you," he said stubbornly, knowing it was the wrong thing to say but believing it nonetheless.

"It matters to me! Are you nae listening to me? It matters to *me* what they think of me!"

"What about what *I* think of you?"

She squeezed her eyes shut and shook her head.

"I'm going to tell you whether you want to hear it or nae."

He saw the moment she armed herself, the moment she

donned her shield. She stood taller and her eyes went cold as she glared.

"Say it, m'laird," she said through clenched teeth.

He stepped closer and lifted his hand to cradle her cheek, swiping a thumb over her tears. She didn't flinch.

"I think," he said, pausing for breath, "I think that you are the bravest person I have ever met. I dinnae ken how you survived a monster like him. I dinnae ken how it is that you're here with me—"

Una sucked in a breath.

"But I dinnae care. Because you *are* here with me. And I am sorry. I shouldnae have spoken to you as I did. I have been… worried of late. I cannae have eyes on everyone and everything at once. I wanted to keep you close, to keep you safe. When I heard that you meant to take Gavin's cottage, I —" He swallowed thickly. "I lost my senses. His cottage is on the outskirts of the village, farthest away. I cannae—" He heaved in a breath. "I cannae promise you safety there. The thought made me half mad."

"I can take care of myself," she said quietly, and he remembered first meeting her, her arrow trained on his heart.

"Aye," he agreed. "You can. You are more than capable of taking care of yourself. You are more than capable of anything you set your mind to."

Her blue eyes went wide. That lump rose higher in Ewan's throat, making it difficult to speak at all, and his voice caught. "You're so brave, Una, and I—"

The thought died when Una launched herself at him, cutting off his words with her mouth pressed against his.

CHAPTER 20

Una gripped Ewan's cheeks between her palms and kissed him. She could taste the saltiness of her own tears, of his sweat. But Ewan's mouth did not soften, did not kiss her back. She squeezed her eyes shut, filled with the most sudden, horrifying sense of embarrassment.

She dropped her hands and moved to push away when Ewan groaned and banded his arms tightly around her, crushing her to his chest. His hand tangled in the braid at the back of her head, gripping her tightly.

Nobody had grabbed her like that since Cameron—and certainly no one before. Her skin prickled and she felt the panic rise, but then Ewan's tongue swept at her lips and she tasted him. Laird Cameron had always tasted of whiskey or wine. Ewan tasted like mint, as if he'd chewed it before coming to find her. That taste, that scent alone was enough to remind her, yet again, that Ewan was not Malcolm Cameron. She was *safe*.

Una let out a small sob, almost collapsing into the kiss.

Ewan kissed her like a man leaving for war. He kissed her without restraint, without guile or finesse, as if he were trying to join the very fibers of their bodies. He was a man possessed, bent on erasing every kiss that had come before and ruining every kiss yet to come with anyone that wasn't him.

Una wrapped her arms around his neck and grabbed at the sun-bleached waves that hung past his collar. Ewan's hand slid from her low back down to cup her arse, pulling her roughly against him. She felt the hard planes of his body, the soft places, too, against her own. The muscles of his shoulders bunched and flexed under her wrists, and she became more aware than ever of the raw power of his body.

It made her feel wild. His body was a weapon, and she suspected that all she would need to do is ask and he would wield it for her however she commanded.

He brought his other hand from her hair to the other cheek of her backside, squeezing it roughly as he ground his hips against her. Una felt the hard line of his cock against her belly and moaned as he bit her lower lip.

He held her jaw in his hands, angling her head back to give him greater access to her mouth. Ewan began to walk, pressing her with his body under she felt the cold stones of the wall at her back.

"Is this good? Are you well?" Ewan panted against her mouth, and she nodded rapidly.

It was true. Wedged between Ewan's body and the stone wall, she wondered why she didn't feel frightened. After all, Cameron had pushed her up against a wall many times and it had always made her feel like being buried alive.

But this felt nothing like that. If anything, she wished Ewan would press in closer. The yielding hardness of his body at her front and the unyielding solidity of the stone at her back made her body feel positively alive with sensation, as if lightning crackled under her skin.

"Una," he whispered huskily, his lips against her throat. "I didnae plan to fall on you like a beast. God's bones, Una, I—"

"Aye," she said and kissed him again.

Una slid her hands away from his hair, down his chest, around his waist, and then back up to grip his shoulders. As he sucked gently on her tongue, she lifted her right leg, wrapping it around Ewan's calf. That small gesture seemed to bring out even more of the beast in him as he began quickly rucking the skirts of her gown and chemise up in greedy handfuls, like a parched man hauling a bucket up from the well.

The fire was low in the hearth, and the room was cold. Una's skin erupted in goosebumps as the fabric lifted higher and higher. When her skirts were around her waist, Ewan gripped her bare backside, pulling her hips roughly against his.

"Christ, Una," he moaned, caressing her arse. "You are so soft."

She lifted her leg higher, hooking her calf around the back of his thigh. A low growl sounded in Ewan's throat, and he lifted her from the floor. He grunted, sounding pained, and her eyes flew open as she remembered his stitches.

"Your wound! Ewan, put me down!"

"Not if God himself told me to," Ewan said against her lips as he pinned her to the wall with his hips, grinding roughly against her.

"But—"

He looked at her with narrowed eyes. "I said, if God himself told me to put you down, I wouldnae do it."

"And *I* willnae let you do something so stupid as to rip out all of those stitches," she said as he buried his face in her neck. "Put me down this instant."

He complied, but he grabbed her thigh and wrapped it

around his waist on the side where he was not injured and continued to grind against her. The rough stones dug into her back and scalp, but she didn't care. With her leg wrapped around his waist and nothing on under her gown and shift, the feeling of the rough wool of his plaid, the only thing that separated her center from his cock, made her desperate with need.

As Ewan broke away from her mouth to kiss across her jaw to her ear and then down her neck, the scratch of his beard followed immediately by soothing sweeps of his tongue, Una gasped for breath. She'd never felt this way before. Gone for the moment were the memories of Cameron and his clumsy roughness, which had made her skin crawl. Ewan made her feel as if she glowed white-hot everywhere his mouth and hands touched.

Una gasped as Ewan's length, still concealed behind his plaid, pressed hard against her pearl. And then when he thrust against her again, she stifled her cry against his shoulder, biting down, feeling his muscle between her teeth, tasting the fabric of his leine. He groaned and dragged her face back to his, kissing her with abandon.

He was so close. So very close to her. If the fabric of his plaid parted, he could fill her in an instant. That thought sent frissons down to her toes, and she realized that, yes, she wanted that. She wanted that more than she'd wanted anything in a very long time.

As if he read her thoughts, Ewan broke the kiss, pressing his forehead to hers and breathing as hard as if he'd run around the curtain wall ten times.

"Una," he gasped, sweat beading on his forehead, making her own skin slick.

"Ewan, please," she breathed. "Please."

"Una, are you—"

A sharp knock sounded on the door, echoing in the chamber. Ewan's fingers dug sharply into her backside as he whipped his head to look at the door.

Una became suddenly very aware of her body in space—her leg wrapped around his waist, her gown bunched around her hips leaving her completely exposed below her middle, Ewan's hips pressed into her core, anchoring her to the wall, the way their chests rose and fell heavily in unison.

She thought that maybe she should be ashamed of the position in which she found herself, but she couldn't bring herself to feel that way. She wasn't ashamed. She was on fire, and this interruption made her want to scream in frustration.

"What is it?" Ewan barked.

Through the door, a voice said, "There is a Cameron man downstairs demanding to see you. He says he willnae leave until you speak to him."

Una felt all the blood drain from her face as Ewan turned back to look at her. The voice belonged to Kenneth. For Ewan's own brother to deliver the message instead of David or a guard was troubling.

"You dinnae think…" Ewan whispered, his brows knit together.

A strangled sound escaped her lip and her leg dropped like lead in a pool. He held her close when her knees nearly gave out.

Ewan clutched her to his chest and said, "Show him to the Hall and give him a meal. Clear everyone else when they're through eating. I'll speak with him there."

"Verra well," Kenneth replied and then Una could hear his steps retreating down the hall.

When Ewan turned back to her, his face had a feral look about it. Una noticed that muscle twitching in his jaw beneath his ear, his brows still close as he stared down at her.

"I willnae let him hurt you," he said through his teeth, gripping her upper arms in his hands. "I willnae let you go back."

And then, with a crack in his voice, "I willnae let him take you away."

CHAPTER 21

Ewan delivered Una to Joan's small chamber. He wondered if she still planned to move to the cottage in the morning. He would give her anything she asked for, even if the only place that felt remotely right in his mind was in the keep. But he couldn't worry about that right now. That particular worry had been shuffled to the bottom of the ever-growing pile. At the moment, the only thing he *could* worry about was which Cameron man waited downstairs and what to do with him.

After Una had closed the door, Ewan practically raced down the stairs, his heartbeat thundering in his ears. *"He willnae take her,"* he thought. *"I'll kill him first."*

When he reached the bottom of the stairs, he saw Kenneth and David standing near the door to the Great Hall.

"Well?" Ewan said. "Who is the man?"

"He's a crabbit auld git to be sure," David said with a snort.

"Och, aye," Kenneth said, his eyebrows going high on his forehead. "Making demands like the king and criticizing the ale, accusing the serving women of giving him the worst stock."

Ewan clenched his fists tightly, the knuckles cracking. Only a laird would come with such a presence. Only a laird would dare. But had Malcolm Cameron changed so much that Kenneth and David did not recognize him? Was he disguised?

"How many men accompanied him?"

"None," David replied.

"None?" Ewan said in disbelief.

"Nary a one."

"And you—"

"Aye. I ordered patrols to search the woods around the keep. He came alone."

That made no sense at all. Even disguised, Laird Cameron would not travel alone. But he wouldn't get any answers standing out here. He gripped the hilt of his sword with one hand and took a deep, fortifying breath.

"Verra well. Let us nae keep the man waiting," he said as he pushed open the doors to the Great Hall and scanned the room for the visitor, who was sitting at a trestle table just next to the dais.

It was an old man, with a leathery, tanned face and a halo of long, lank gray hair around his head below the tops of his ears. The man looked as indolent as he did inconvenienced.

"Who are you and what are you doing here?" Ewan asked, his voice sharp like a whip strike.

"My name is Fergus," the man said with a broad smile, revealing several missing teeth. "I am Una's father."

Ewan blinked at the man. *Una's father?*

"You were expecting someone else?" Fergus said with a smirk.

His own father would have dressed the man down for talking to him as though they were equals, but Ewan didn't know how to deal with this sudden, unwelcome stranger. Especially not so close to hearing Una confess to him that her father had all but sold her to Malcolm Cameron.

"What do you want?" Ewan said, his teeth clenched. He'd done so much of that the past few weeks, both waking and sleeping, that his jaw hurt.

"What do I want?" he asked, leaning forward on his elbows over the table. "I came for my daughter, of course."

"She isnae here," Ewan lied.

"Och, m'laird, dinnae take me for a fool. Word has travelled far and wide about Laird MacDonald's new healer, a bonny young lass with black hair and a temper like Cain. How many of those do you think there are in the Highlands?"

"I wouldnae ken," Ewan said, keeping his face placid.

"Because there's only one," Fergus said, leaning in. "And she is my daughter. I'll be takin' her home with me."

"You cannae take her," Ewan said flatly, glaring at Fergus and crossing his arms over his broad chest.

"You mean to keep her here then? 'Tis improper. She belongs with her clan," Fergus scoffed.

"She is with her clan."

"She's a Cameron!" Fergus snarled.

"Nae anymore."

"You think that just because a lass runs away from her clan that she cannae still be claimed by the people who raised her?"

"Nay, I think she shouldnae be claimed by the people who raised her because they threw her to the wolves," Ewan said, his voice a sharp bark.

Fergus assessed him with water, bloodshot eyes before leaning back in his chair. "Ah, I see what is going on here. You want her for yourself."

"You're aff your heid," Ewan spat.

"You willnae make my daughter a whore," Fergus sneered. "So if you think I'll be leaving my unwed daughter here to live among enemies, you're daft. 'Tis unseemly. Laird or nae." Fergus took a deep drink from his flagon of ale. "Unless, of course..."

Fergus trailed off, tenting his fingers in front of his mouth. Ewan felt the muscles of his arms, still crossed, tense underneath his own hands.

"Speak," Ewan said.

Fergus broke his hands apart and stroked down the length of his bard. Taking another sup of ale, he looked into Ewan's eyes. "I suppose I could be persuaded to sign for another handfasting."

Shock and outrage boiled through Ewan's body. Had this man no conscience? Ewan dropped his arms to his sides, squinting his eyes and furrowing his brow as he searched for words.

"You would handfast Una to *yet another* man?"

Fergus sat preening, looking utterly satisfied with himself. "Nay. But I would handfast Una to yet another *laird*."

Ewan wanted to tackle him. He could throw Fergus out into the night, tell his men never to let him near the keep again. Hell, he could throw him in the dungeons and let him rot. But he wouldn't do that, not the dungeons at least. He didn't know if Una harbored any love for her father, and he would do whatever was in his power to spare her pain.

But if he let him go, Fergus could just as easily go to Cameron and tell the bastard that Ewan had kidnapped Una. Cameron could declare war. Blood would be shed. Una would once again be a pawn that could fall into Laird Cameron's clutches. He couldn't risk it.

He could send Una to the Stewarts. It was where she'd been headed in the first place, before this all began. She would be safe there. Yet the thought of her leaving made his chest ache.

But Una deserved more than a handfast. She deserved more than to be traded about like a herd of goats or a chicken. She deserved everything. But chief among the things she deserved was safety. And for that, he was responsible. He had made her a promise. Several of them, in fact.

Slowly, all of the sediment that normally roiled around in the waters of his brain settled to the bottom so he could see clearly. He had to protect Una, and he knew just how to do it. Yes, that was the best course of action.

"I willnae handfast Una."

Fergus pushed on his thighs to stand. "Well, then, I'll be taking her with me. Tonight."

"You will do nae such thing."

"M'laird, I've been clear. If you dinnae mean to handfast her—"

"I mean to marry her." That feeling of rightness grew stronger.

Fergus squinted at him, as if questioning his sincerity. After a moment, his face lit up and he rubbed his pals together greedily.

"This is a happy turn of events indeed, m'laird," he crowed. "Have you a priest? You could say vows tonight, and I'll be gone with the bride price by morning."

"Una deserves more than hasty views in an empty hall after dark."

Fergus rolled his eyes so hard it was a wonder he didn't topple over. Ewan couldn't remember ever wanting to hit someone so badly.

"She deserves flowers and a feast and a gown and anything else her heart desires," he said, his heart pounding in his chest, the excitement rising. It was the perfect solution. She would stay. She would be *safe.*

"If you say so, m'laird. I've never been one for sentiment. But you can afford it, ken. When will you wed?"

"I'll send for Father Brian in the morning."

Fergus smiled his rotten, gapped smile, and Ewan nearly joined him when the doors to the Great Hall were thrown open behind him. He wheeled around and saw Una striding toward him, looking more furious than he'd ever seen her.

CHAPTER 22

Una gave Ewan the benefit of a five-minute head start before creeping down the stairs and walking straight past Kenneth and David to press her ear to the door.

"M'lady," David gently said, "I dinnae think that you —"

"David, if you try to stop me from hearing what's going on in there, I'll scream so loudly that the laird will come running. And what do you think he'll do?"

David crossed his arms over his chest and glared down at her.

"Please," she begged, looking back and forth between the two men. "This concerns me. I cannae stay upstairs and wait."

David and Kenneth exchanged a long-suffering look before David lifted his hands in surrender.

"Verra well, m'lady. But if the laird discovers you, I willnae take a crumb of the blame."

Una nodded, pressing her ear to the door, fully expecting to hear Malcolm Cameron's sneer on the other side.

When she heard her father's gravelly voice instead, she gasped.

"That isnae Laird Cameron," she whispered, eyes wide.

"Of course it isnae Laird Cameron," Kenneth scoffed, looking at her as if she'd suddenly grown a second head.

"But you said—"

Ewan's bellowed from the other side of the door.

The worn wood was cold against her cheek, but she didn't care. Her father? Why on earth had her father come? And alone? It made no sense. Either way, from the sound of it, Fergus had not come as an emissary of peace.

Una imagined Ewan and her father facing off like bulls. She smiled as she heard Ewan tell her father that he deserved her far more than the clan of her birth. She bit her bottom lip to contain her wide grin and pressed closer against the door. But the rest was unintelligible when Kenneth began scuffing his feet back and forth across the floor.

"Shhht. I cannae hear what they're saying with you shifting about!" she hissed at him. Kenneth made a mocking face and took an even more mocking bow, rolling his eyes as he returned upright. Una stuck her tongue out at him before crouching lower. There was a small notch in the door and, if she knelt, she could press her ear to it and perhaps hear better.

"Unless you handfast her."

Una's stomach plummeted, and her eyes went wide with horror.

"He cannae handfast me!" she whispered, to no one in particular.

Kenneth suddenly took great interest in the cleanliness of his nails, and David wiped his dirk with the hem of his plaid, the two of them looking anywhere but at her.

"Nay, nay, nay, nay. He cannae. He cannae do this to me again."

Una pressed her ear so hard into the notch in the wood

that she could nearly feel the grain of the ancient door imprinting in the softness of her cheek.

"M'laird, if you dinnae mean to handfast her—"

"I mean to marry her."

Her fingers slapped over her mouth as she gasped. She felt her breath coming in sharp bursts, the air not moving into her lungs the way it ought. No matter how hard she tried, Una couldn't drag in enough. She pulled herself to stand on shaky legs just in time to hear Ewan declare that he would send for the priest come morning.

Ignoring the protests of Kenneth and David, Una flung wide the door to the Great Hall and stormed through it.

"You will do nae such thing, Ewan MacDonald!"

Una felt her limbs shaking from her fury as she strode quickly across the rushes to where her father and Ewan stood.

"You didnae think I would like a say in whether or not I'll be marrying you? Which I willnae do!"

Ewan's shocked expression hardened as he crossed his arms. She stood as tall as she could and crossed her own, glaring back at him.

"You willnae marry me?"

"Nay!" she spat at him. "And shame on you, Ewan MacDonald, for letting that old goat trade me about like chattel. *Again.*"

"Och, chattel, are you? You think that I dinnae care more for you than I do my sheep?" her father asked smugly.

"You dinnae ask your sheep if they want to be supper," she said before wheeling on Ewan, "And you didnae ask me if I want to marry you!"

Through gritted teeth, Ewan said, "Una, a word."

Una opened her mouth to tell him exactly which part of her anatomy he could converse with when he jerked his hand toward the far side of the hall. He stalked into the buttery, leaving behind a satisfied-looking Fergus, who sat down at the table and poured himself more ale from a pitcher. Una rolled her eyes and followed after Ewan. When she entered the buttery, she found him pacing like a wild animal, anger and frustration radiating off of him like steam from a boil. But she did not cower. She was not afraid of him.

How very refreshing.

"Well, *m'laird*?"

He wheeled on her, his hurt feelings only barely concealed by his anger. "I willnae remind you of your promise. Which you *insist* on breaking to bait me."

She crossed her arms over her chest.

"What is it, Ewan?"

Abruptly, he stopped pacing and turned to her. "What is so damned offensive about marrying me?"

"Nothing!" she snapped.

"Then why do you refuse?"

"Because I willnae be traded about like livestock *yet again*, Ewan!"

"You would be safe as my wife!"

"Aye. And under your thumb!"

He reared back. "That isnae fair, Una. I havenae once tried to control you, and I wouldnae start now."

"Perhaps you havenae tried to control *me*, but you tried to fix it so that if I wouldnae stay in the keep, that I would be close enough to the walls that your guards can spit in my garden to water it. You made arrangements for a cottage without talking to me. You made arrangements with my father without even *thinking* to talk to me. He doesnae care one bit about what I want, and neither, it seems, do you!"

"I thought you made it pretty clear what you wanted upstairs when you climbed me like a tree," he said in a low voice.

"You swiving bastard!" Una shrieked, turning to leave, but

he grabbed her hand and pulled her back. She spun around and landed against his chest.

"You did, Una," he barked before lowering his voice to barely above a whisper. "And I have never experienced anything like it."

She snorted in disbelief and pushed him away.

"Believe it or nae, Una, I am nae in the habit of rutting against lasses like a beast in heat." His voice was soft now, smooth. Coaxing. The same tone he'd used to earn Greer's trust. "You make me burn."

She looked up into his eyes, a shifting, subtle green, like the moss-covered rocks at the bottom of a burn. His heavy eyebrows were drawn close together, and she could almost see him trying to work it out in his mind.

"Una," he said in that same gently voice. "I am *asking* you now. Will you marry me?"

"Nay," she bit out, sounding more petulant than she intended.

He dropped her wrist and took a step back. "God save me from stubborn, impossible women!"

"And by that you mean a woman who willnae be ground under a lairdly boot again!"

Ewan's brow furrowed and mouth hung open as he dragged heavy breaths into his body.

"Is that what this is about? Why you refuse me? You think I would treat you like he did?" he asked in an agonized whisper. "You think I'd abuse you? Lock you away? Try to break your spirit? Is your opinion of me truly so low, Una?"

It had been a lethal blow. Because, as she had acknowledged to herself so many times, he was not Malcolm Cameron. He was not a threat or a boor or a monster. He was a man. Flawed, up to high doh with worry, to his detriment. But safe. Good. *Kind.*

Part of her wanted to touch him, to reach out and bring

him close again. But she couldn't. She couldn't afford to lose focus.

"Nay," she murmured. "You are nae a monster. I know that."

Ewan ran his hands through his hair, clasping them behind his neck as he so often did when he was frustrated, his forearms pressing into his temples.

"Then I'll ask you again, Una. Why will you nae have me?" His voice was quiet, his restraint returned. "I've asked you. I'm damn near begging you. At least tell me why? What more must I do? Carve open my chest and serve you my own heart? Here," he said, taking his dirk from the sheath at his hip and holding it out to her, the point of the gleaming blade pinched between his fingers.

"Goddamnit, Ewan," she said, closing her eyes in frustration. "Put the dirk away."

The knife clattered to the floor, and then there he was, filling her vision, her nostrils, all of her senses with his presence. He cupped her jaw in his hands, lifting her face to look at his.

"Dinnae you want me, Una?"

"It isnae that simple."

"Do you want me?"

The lump in her throat threatened to choke her as tears sprang to her eyes. She didn't want to look at his anguished face, but she also couldn't turn away. She squeezed her eyes shut as her bottom lip quivered.

"I only wanted to keep you near so I could keep you safe. Anything to keep you safe, to keep you away from *him*," Ewan said in a strangled voice.

Una reared back, confused. "Why would you worry about that?"

"Your father found out where you were because of talk traveling. If someone misrepresented the facts and Cameron believed I had kidnapped you, he might retaliate. He might try to steal you back."

She was going to be sick.

"I willnae let it happen," he said insistently, ducking down to look in her eyes. "If you married me, he couldnae take you. You would be mine, under my protection, safe in the keep."

He heaved in a deep breath that Una felt as much as she heard. He brought her closer, so close that her chest was pressed against his, their noses touching.

"Ewan," she breathed, his name a breath, a prayer. His thumbs pressed into her cheekbones as he held his mouth just a breath away, waiting for her to go the rest of the way to meet him.

"Una, mo cridhe," he murmured into that space, making her feel the gentle percussion of every breath against her lips.

But the endearment wrenched her back. It might be true that Ewan MacDonald would never physically hurt her, she believed that with her whole heart. But that didn't mean she should marry him. Nor did it mean that she *could*.

"Or you could take me to the Stewarts," she said, the words nearly choking her.

He dropped his hands and stepped back, looking as if he wanted to speak. In fact, he opened his mouth as if he would, but he clamped it shut before striding out of the buttery. Una heard his footsteps in the rushes, the creaking of the door on its hinges, and the bang as it slammed behind him.

An hour later, Una sat next to the hearth in Joan's small room, braiding her hair and watching the sparks pop. Joan was asleep in the bed, snoring softly. When she had returned to the room, red-faced from weeping, Joan and Cat had fussed over her like she was a child. After a while, she had waved them off and begged them to sleep.

"All will be better in the light of a new day," she had insisted.

Now, hours later, Una still could not sleep. The keep was quiet, the silence only broken by the occasional man's voice, drifting up from the bailey. She wondered where Ewan had gone but scolded herself for the thought. She didn't have any right to wonder where he was. She had refused him.

She felt the sting of fresh tears gathering in her eyes and fought against them, losing far too soon. He was a good man. He was a *great* man, perhaps. Hot, heavy tears fell from her eyes and down her temples. She had to talk to him. Perhaps his temper would have cooled enough that they could hear one another. Perhaps they might even come to an understanding.

Una rose silently from the chair, wrapped a MacDonald plaid around her shoulders, and slipped from the small chamber and into the hallway. The torches in the wall sconces burned brightly, casting long shadows on the stone floor, as she crept down the hall and knocked on Connor's door, Ewan's door for the time being. Her quiet taps were met with silence.

She waited as long as she dared and had just turned away from the door when it creaked open a few inches, revealing Ewan. He was fully dressed except for his bare feet, his hair wild and tousled, as if he'd done nothing but rake his hands through it.

"You'll snatch your head bald if you keep up like that," she said, going for a teasing tone but failing.

"What are you doing here, Una?"

She hesitated. What had she been thinking? Coming to the laird's bedchamber in the middle of the night in nothing but her shift? *To talk*? As if it couldn't wait until morning. If she'd been worried about baseless gossip, she'd give them something to talk about in truth if she wasn't careful.

And yet she could not make herself leave.

"Una?" Ewan asked, peering around the doorframe and into the corridor. "Is aught amiss?"

"I— I wanted to speak with you."

Ewan looked at her, an unreadable expression on his face. But eventually, he opened the door wider and stepped aside. Wordlessly, she slipped past him and into the dark chamber.

CHAPTER 23

Ewan had neglected to feed his fire, and as a result, the chamber was cold and dark, his figure barely visible. She shivered, grateful for the wool plaid wrapped around her shoulders. In a sliver of moonlight that came through the window, she saw him move toward the hearth.

"I'll stoke the fire," he said.

"Nay," she blurted in response. "That is, I dinnae want to inconvenience you."

She heard the mattress creak as he sat on the edge of the bed. "Will you sit?"

Una debated. She could sit. But she didn't want to sit next to him. Especially not on a bed. He was too warm, too wonderful. Too tempting.

"I willnae touch you," Ewan said softly. "You have my word."

Una sighed and used that small moonbeam to creep to the bed, sitting on the mattress near him. She pulled her legs up and sat with them crossed and tucked under her nightgown, the plaid pulled tightly around her.

"Are you cold, Una?"

She didn't have a chance to answer. The dark shadow of him loomed closer, followed by the heavy weight of a blanket dropped around her shoulders. She gripped the edges in her chilled fingers and pulled it close.

Neither of them spoke, the silence almost its own entity in the darkness. But it wasn't a companionable silence, not like when they'd been silent together before. This silence was thick with words unspoken.

"I am sorry, Una," Ewan said, his voice hoarse.

Una wished she had let him build that fire, if only so that she could see his face.

"I am sorry too."

In the scant moonlight, she could see him leaning forward, his elbows resting on his knees, head in his hands.

"I want to understand, Una. But perhaps you need to understand me as well."

He took a deep breath.

"My mother died when I was fifteen. She had such a hard time with Rabbie that the midwives told her that if she had another babe, it would kill her."

"The twins," Una whispered, her hands clutching the covers.

"Aye. Six years later, she found herself with child again. No matter how many times my father begged her to purge her womb, she refused. She told him that all would be well, that she held fast to her faith so he should hold fast to her."

She heard Ewan swallow heavily before taking a long breath in. She wondered if Ewan's mother had had a good midwife, if someone had taught her about fennel. She imagined not.

"My father grew more and more despondent by the day, terrified of losing her. And then her time came. He sent for the best midwives, the best healers from every ally. Connor was born without issue, but Cat...."

Una reached out and rested a hand on his shoulder.

"The midwives were able to deliver Cat, but the birth injured her shoulder permanently. And my mother…" he trailed off.

"She lost too much blood."

"Aye," he said bitterly. "She died shortly after naming them and took my father's will to live with her. He poured his love into Catriona and Connor, and I'm grateful to him for that, but he was a shell of the man he had been. He became a ghost."

Ewan shifted on the bed and turned to face her. His knee pressed into the juncture where her shins crossed.

"I have lost much, Una. I lost my mother. I lost my father the day she died, and then I lost him again years later after watching him slip away. Here and gone at the same time. I couldnae bear the thought of loving someone the way my father loved my mother and losing her the same way. That's why I havenae married yet. And, to be truthful, it was nae such a sacrifice. Until recently."

"Until recently?" Una felt her heart hammering behind her ribs.

"I never even considered it until I met ye. I dinnae ken why. You've wiggled your way beneath the armor. I cannae sleep for worrying about you. I cannae focus for thinking about you. You've consumed my waking thoughts and my sleeping dreams. I find myself wanting to seek you out, to hear about your day, to help you where I can."

Tears welled in Una's eyes, and she choked on a sob.

"Una," he said quietly, reaching out and resting a large, heavy hand on her knee. "Please dinnae cry, Una. I willnae ask you to marry me again. You said nay, and I respect your decision. I ken I worry too much. I cannae seem to stop. But when I close my eyes, I see everyone dead and myself powerless to have stopped it. Sometimes I feel like I'm going mad."

He took a deep breath, his hand falling away from her knee. "When you refused me, after I finally decided to cast my worries to the wind, I didnae handle myself well. I'm sorry."

She wept in earnest now, tears sliding between her fingers.

"Please dinnae cry, Una. Please. I beg of you. I'll take you to the Stewarts. I'll send you to court if you'd rather." The words sounded stuck in his throat.

"That isnae what I want," she replied, shaking.

"Then tell me what you do want," he said gently.

"I dinnae ken!" Una cried. "I dinnae ken what I want besides the fact that I dinnae want to be traded back and forth like my wishes dinnae matter! I ken you are nae like him. You are a good man. But I survived a year with him, and I am nae well, Ewan. I have nightmares. I'm afraid of everything. Sometimes I am so angry I want to stab something. And you. I make you feel crazed. You said it yourself. You would be better marrying a woman who didnae inspire such intensity. And I—" She didn't know what she was about to say.

Una suddenly felt as if she hadn't slept for days, as if she'd raced to the loch and back. Her body trembled with exhaustion and nerves and something else. Ewan rose from the bed and crossed the chamber. She waited for him to open the door and tell her to leave. It would break her.

But he didn't. Instead, he put two logs on the fire, crouching to stoke the embers and blowing gently, encouraging the small flames until they lapped greedily at the wood. When the fire burned brightly once more, bathing the room in soft light, Ewan returned to sit on the bed. He rested his hands on either side of his body, governed by the tension and restraint that Una recognized so well.

"Was there a babe? With Cameron? Or did you…"

Una blinked at him, the question feeling sudden and abrupt, but perhaps it wasn't so abrupt after all. Perhaps he'd wondered this whole time. She swallowed heavily. "Nay."

"I wouldnae judge you if you had."

"One cannae get rid of a bairn they deliberately didnae conceive," she replied. "But I left the Cameron keep in disgrace. The common wench who seduced a laird and failed to bring him an heir. People talk. They will continue to talk. And before long, that talk will reach a MacDonald's ears, and yer clan will find out that their laird married his enemy's previous handfast."

He made a noise of protest, but she pressed on. "Ewan, ye need a better wife than me. Someone people will respect."

"People respect you—"

"Someone that will strengthen an alliance or help your clan—"

"You will help my clan. You—"

"Someone who isnae a castoff from an enemy clan's laird."

With the speed and grace of a cat, he was close, cupping her cheeks in his hands and lifting her face so that her eyes met his. Una squeezed her eyes shut and bit her lips between her teeth.

"Castoff?" he asked, so gentle with his words and his touch as he brushed the tears off her cheeks with his thumbs. "Castoff? How can you say such a thing about yourself?"

Una shrugged, her tears gathering again. "I dinnae see myself that way. But others will." And when he began to argue, she pressed, "They *will,* Ewan."

"Una," he said, his voice a hoarse rasp. "Why does it matter what people think? What good is being laird if I cannae marry whoever the hell I choose? Because I think you're the most remarkable person I've ever met."

She blinked her eyes open, shifting her gaze to his. He was so close.

"Una, mo cridhe, cannae you see what a gift you are?" he whispered, pressing his lips to the knot between her eyebrows.

Mo cridhe. His love. Her heart threaded to burst forth from her chest. He didn't mean it. He couldn't. But she relished the feel of his kiss on her forehead anyway.

"Can I ask you another question?" he whispered, the words formed against her skin.

She nodded.

"Do you feel safe with me?"

She nodded again, reaching up with a shaky hand and caressing his cheek. She touched his lips with her fingertips, smiling when he sucked in a breath.

"So stay. Stay in the keep. Stay with me. Let me keep you safe."

CHAPTER 24

Let me keep you safe.

Una tipped her chin up, their lips so close that she could feel Ewan's breath fanning against her face. She brushed a stray lock of hair off his forehead, trailing her fingertips down his cheek.

The calluses of his thumbs scraped at her temples, catching the fine hairs there as his strong fingertips pressed into the back of her neck, but he didn't come closer. Through the tumult of her thoughts and feelings, she realized that he was waiting for her to choose.

Una closed the distance and kissed him, her tongue licking hesitantly at the seam of his lips. A shudder wracked his body, and a low sound reverberated in his chest. She felt the echo of that sound in her own chest as his tongue rushed to meet hers.

She pressed her palms against the hard plane of his chest before gripping his shirt in her fists. His mouth broke from hers, and he kissed along her jaw to the sensitive place just below her ear. He nipped her earlobe before kissing down the column of her neck to the hollow at the base of her throat.

His unruly hair brushed against her chin, and Una sucked in a breath, inhaling the smell of him that she'd come to know so well. He kissed up the other side of her neck, pressing his lips to the corner of her jaw. Una sifted through his hair, and he moaned softly. With a strength that never failed to surprise her, he pulled her into his arms so that her knees straddled his broad thighs. She felt his erection beneath his plaid pressing hard against her center.

He kissed her languidly, a tangle of lips and teeth and tongues, as if he had all the time in the world. Perhaps they did. Or, perhaps, he simply kissed her as if it was the last thing he would do on this earth and, therefore, the only thing that truly mattered. Una felt like she was flying.

Ewan's hands glided up and down her back beneath the plaid wrapped around her shoulders. One hand traveled lower and gripped her bottom, waiting. She shifted closer, grinding her center against his groin in a rhythm. His other hand roamed up from her hip to cup her breast. He rubbed her nipple with his callused thumb, and it tightened to an almost painful peak. He pinched it, and she groaned loudly into his mouth.

He kissed down her neck, his mouth leaving a scorching trail to the exposed expanse of her chest, stopping at the edge of her shift, which rested just barely above her nipples. Ewan pressed a hand against the middle of her back and drew her up and close, taking one of the straining buds into his mouth, sucking hard. The fabric of her shift between his mouth and her nipple increased the sensation tenfold as he flicked his tongue back and forth across the stiffened peak.

When Ewan drew back, the cool air of the chamber met the wet circle of her shift. She shivered and gasped. But then he closed his mouth over her other nipple, sucking even harder before taking the stiff point between gentle teeth. She found herself pulling on his hair, anchoring him to her. She rocked her hips, rubbing her core against his length, her body desperate for more.

"We can stop, Una," he said, bringing his mouth back to hers and speaking the words against her lips. "I can take you back to your room."

"Now?" she whined. "You want to stop now?"

"I *never* want to stop, Una," he said and kissed her hard. "*Never*. But I dinnae want to overwhelm you. I want you to want this. For yourself. Nae for me."

He was rubbing his hands up and down her arms. His body was like a furnace beneath her. Like the bedrock of the keep. Hard and strong and *safe*.

Una gripped fistfuls of his shirt in her hands, yanking on it until it came free from his belt. He grabbed the shirt behind his neck and, in one baffling movement, swept it over his head before stopping it on the floor.

She had undressed men before. Laird Cameron had enjoyed the subservience of her undressing him before he had his way with her. Just another means of showing her her place. Before that, in her work, she'd undressed dozens of men before treating wounds or assessing conditions. There had been a similar clinical capacity to both. When undressing Cameron, she had tried to touch his body as little as possible. She'd tried not to look. She'd tried to be quick and perfunctory because the sooner he was disrobed, the sooner he would be done and she could be away from him.

But there was nothing familiar about undressing Ewan. She wanted to touch him. She wanted to look her fill, to watch the firelight dance across his skin, the hair on his chest that tapered and blazed a trail that disappeared in the fabric of his plaid, still belted around his hips. She traced the hard muscles of his chest and stomach, smiling as they tensed under her touch.

"I willnae push you, Una," he whispered, kissing her forehead.

She believed him, which made her feel wild. She knew that she could take this as far as she wanted and that, no matter what, if she told him to stop, he would stop. What would it be like? To be cared for like that? To be given pleasure instead of having it stolen from her? She couldn't fathom, but if being with Ewan felt even half as good as being kissed by Ewan, she wanted to try.

With sure fingers, she fed the leather of his belt through the buckle until the belt fell away. She tossed it behind her, smiling at the satisfying thud it made as it hit the floor.

"Ewan?" she said, kissing the corner of his mouth and circling her hips slowly.

"Aye?" he croaked.

"I trust you."

Ewan was panting now, his chest rising and falling rapidly against hers. She untied the bow that held her shift, the fabric still clinging to her shoulders.

In a hoarse whisper, he asked, "May I?"

She nodded.

Ewan slid his fingertips up her thighs, hooking them under the hem of her shift and drawing it slowly up her body, his fingers dragging gently over her hips, up her sides, even across the ticklish plane of her armpits, driving the shift up her body. She lifted her arms, and he drew it up the long lengths of her arms as carefully as if handling a holy relic. He groaned at the sight of her naked body and squeezed his eyes tightly shut.

She paused, worried suddenly. But then his eyes flew open and he shot to his feet, taking her with him. His hands gripped her arse, and he held her close against him. Her legs wrapped instinctively around his waist. He turned, depositing her in the middle of the bed. The plaid, unbelted, had fallen to the floor around his feet when he'd stood, and Una couldn't help but stare as he crawled toward her.

Una parted her thighs, leaving room for Ewan to settle between them. He kissed her deeply, and she melted into that kiss. The textures of his body felt so different against hers, hard where she was soft, callused where she was not, hair in different places, heat in different places too. She knew the body well. It was her trade. But she'd never known the body like this. She'd never known what it was to have every single part of her body alight with sensation as his tongue delved into her mouth and his hands roamed.

Ewan shifted his weight to the side so that he could slip his hand over her hip, stopping just above her mound.

"Una," he panted, looking into her eyes. "Are you well?"

She nodded, feeling itchy and hot, needing something. Knowing that he could give it to her. "Touch me. Touch me, Ewan. *Please.*"

He slid a finger against her slick seam.

"God's bones, Una. You're soaking," he groaned against her ear. "Can I—"

"Please!" she cried out, cutting him off.

She was tired of talking. She was tired of thinking. She wanted to feel good, for her *body* to feel good. He slipped a thick finger into her sheath and she gasped. He added a second, his thumb grazing just above the hood of her pearl. Una's back bowed off the bed with a moan.

"Shhh, mo cridhe," he whispered into her mouth. "You must be quiet. You are nae supposed to be here. I may be compromising your virtue, but I ken you dinnae want the whole keep hearing it."

"What virtue?" Una protested, her breath coming in short, insufficient bursts.

How was she supposed to stay quiet with his fingers moving in and out like that, gentle but insistent? He pressed them even deeper, curling them toward a place within her that made her toes curl so tightly that her feet cramped. He beckoned and swallowed her groan with another kiss.

"You dinnae want there to be talk. I respect that. So we must be verra, *verra* quiet, Una."

Pleasure shot through her limbs and her legs quivered around his forearm from where she'd clamped them shut against the rising tide.

"Can you be quiet, mo cridhe?"

Breathless, she clutched at him and nodded, hissing through clenched teeth as he thrust his fingers deeper and beckoned with them again, alternating that pattern until she was shaking. *Thrust. Beckon. Thrust. Beckon. Thrust. Beckon.* All the while, he traced featherlight circles around her pearl with his thumb.

Una had touched herself before. She had brought herself to silent climaxes in the dark emptiness of her bed. But those climaxes had always been short, white-hot bursts of feeling rocketing from her head to her toes, there and gone in an instant, satisfying, but not sating.

As good as her fingers had felt, it had done nothing to prepare her for the lightning that Ewan was creating in her body. Her muscles were tight, every one of them, and she fought against the pleasure—too sharp, too consuming, too *much*. But he was there, his lips against her ear as he circled his thumb, never changing the speed or pressure, a constant that she could cling to as her body fell apart.

"Let me take care of you, mo cridhe," he whispered in her ear.

With those words, what had begun as a writhing, almost torturous heat liquified and spread, a sizzling wave that traveled down her body, making her feel almost suspended in space, hovering above the bed, above the world. She bucked her hips against his hand and gasped, arching her neck and driving her head back into the mattress. She bit her bottom lip to contain her cry with such force that she tasted blood. All the while, Ewan kissed her throat and crooned in her ear as she rode his hand until the tremors subsided and she drifted back to earth.

Una felt a drunk, hazy euphoria settle over her. Ewan withdrew his fingers from her channel with great care. In the firelight, she saw her arousal glistening and her mouth fell open as he sucked on his fingers, closing his eyes as he groaned.

"You taste so good, Una," he growled before bending his head to kiss her, letting her taste her own sharpness from his tongue.

Una reached down and wrapped her fingers around his cock, sliding them from base to crown, catching a bead of his own arousal on the pad of her thumb. He gripped her wrist.

"Nay," he groaned, pressing his forehead against her shoulder.

"You dinnae want me to touch you?" she asked, surprised, momentarily hurt.

He huffed out a breath, sounding very much like Calman. "Una, I want you to touch me more than I want to take my next breath. But I dinnae want you to pleasure me like that. Nae this time. I want you to come with me."

"So I'll come with you," she said, kissing his cheek.

He dragged his mouth to hers, his lips never leaving hers as he rolled onto his back, taking her with him so that she sprawled over top of him. She pushed against his chest and rose upright, sitting tall, his cock nestled against her folds, her knees squeezing his ribs.

She'd never been on top of a man like this. Malcolm Cameron had certainly never given her the position of dominance. She looked down at Ewan, at his rumpled hair in the tangled bedding, his mouth slack and his eyes intense as he met her gaze.

"I want ye to feel so good that ye forget about ever feeling anything else, Una."

Experimentally, Una rocked her hips, and the head of his cock rubbed against her over-sensitive pearl. She gasped.

"Aye," he said, nodding, before threading a hand into her hair and pulling her down to his chest. She went willingly, loving the way his other arm banded around her back and held her close. She kissed him until she was breathless and writhing, her hips circling hungrily. She pushed up tall again, her palms on his chest as she ground against his length. They both stifled groans.

She rocked back and forth, over and over, the friction of his length sliding against her pearl was almost more than she could bear but, at the same time, felt so good, so decadent, that she didn't ever want to stop.

He offered his hands and she placed hers atop them, palm to palm, their fingers locking together. She used them for leverage and rocked against him harder. This time, her climax took her by surprise, rushing through her body with the suddenness of a burst dam. She clapped a hand over her mouth to cover the sound of her shriek as her body shook and her toes curled.

In an instant, Ewan lifted her by her hips, setting her back on his thighs far enough that he could wrap his hand around his cock, working it in frenzied strokes. He locked eyes with her, and he groaned low in his throat as the hot splatter of his seed burst forth and painted her belly.

Una panted, eyes wide, unable to look away from the sight of his cock emptying in ropes against her. He collapsed back, his chest heaving, his cock slapping against his own stomach as he flung his hand away.

Spent. That was what they called it. She understood why now.

Ewan drew her gently down, rolling them to their sides, face to face, and pulled her close against him. They stayed like that for a long time, until their breathing slowed and Ewan's cock softened against her hip.

It might have been minutes, it might have been an hour later when Ewan rose and went to the washbasin, wetting a cloth and returning to the bed. He cleaned his seed from her belly with gentle, thorough strokes, before using the cloth on himself. He tossed the rag into the corner and climbed back into bed, pulling her against him, her body half covering his with her head on his chest.

Una felt his body cool down against hers, tracing his lines and contours with a single finger. His solid chest. The hard yet undefined belly. The sharp line above his hips. She sifted her fingers through the damp waves tangling around his head. He kissed her softly.

He drew in a breath so large that her head rose with his ribs. "Are you well, Una? Truly? You…" He paused. Swallowed. Shook his head. "You didnae think of him?"

From someone else, in another context, the question might have reeked of jealousy. But Una recognized it for what it was. Deep, consuming worry. Ewan was back to himself, the distraction of his own need dissipated enough that his worry, his anxiety, could rise to the top of his brain once more.

She rested her hand over his heart, feeling the steady tattoo beneath her palm.

"'Tis strange," she said, her voice barely above a whisper. "I thought for certain that I wouldnae like… to be touched. That I wouldnae ever *want* to be touched again."

Ewan didn't say anything. He let the silence breathe.

"But there was nae a single moment tonight when I

didnae want you to touch me, when I forgot that it was you, when I didnae think you would take care of me."

He kissed the top of her head, holding his lips there for another deep breath.

"You honor me, Una. With your trust. With your body. I dinnae take either for granted."

The fire crackled, and though the room was chilly, she was warm in Ewan's arms. He yawned and her own mouth stretched wide in response, the yawn overtaking her before she could stop it. With one hand, Ewan drew the covers over top of them, tucking them carefully around her.

"Sleep, Una. I'll see you back to your chamber before the keep wakes."

She allowed the smile this time, her grin spreading into another yawn. She sighed and relaxed against him again, letting sleep take her.

As she hovered in the misty space between sleep and waking, just before drifting into dreaming, she heard him whisper, "Hold fast, mo cridhe. You're stuck with me now."

CHAPTER 25

Through the crack in the window coverings, Ewan watched as the sky lightened, the deep, inky black of night fading to the dusty pink of dawn. Una's head rested heavily on his chest, her body curled into his. He tucked her closer against his side and traced lazy swirls up and down her naked back under the covers.

"Una," he said quietly, lifting his head to kiss her hair.

"Go back to sleep," she said grumpily, burrowing closer against him.

"The keep will soon be waking, and we must talk before I return you to Joan's room."

She groaned and rolled off of him, flopping onto her back and flinging her arm over her eyes. "'Tis too early to talk, Ewan."

He couldn't help but smile. But she was wrong. They needed to talk *now*. He needed things settled between them.

"Una, I need to know if your answer is the same as it was before."

Her arm fell away from her face. "I havenae the slightest

idea what you're talking about," she said, rolling over and showing him her back.

He vaulted over her and out of bed. She squeaked in surprise. Ewan knelt beside the bed, his face inches from hers. He covered one of her hands with his.

"Una, on my knees, I'm asking you again if you will marry me."

Her face fell, and Ewan forced himself to remain calm, to not let the threatening panic rise and run away with him. Again.

"I cannae marry you, Ewan," she said. "I told you that."

He stood, suddenly aware of his nakedness in the cold room. Una held onto his hand, though, and tugged on it.

"At least nae yet."

"What the hell does that mean?" he asked, pulling his hand away and raking it through his hair.

Una sat up, clutching the blanket to her chest.

"Handfast me."

"Christ, Una," he gritted out, throwing his hands up in frustration. "A handfast? Why in God's name would you want a handfast when I'm asking to *marry you*?"

Una sighed and picked at a loose thread of the blanket with long fingers. "I want you to be certain," she replied, staring hard at the wool beneath her hands. "*I* want to be certain."

Marshaling every bit of control he had learned in his life, he kept his voice low. "You think me the sort of man to propose marriage without being certain?"

"Of course you are nae that sort of man," she said. "But you've gone from never wanting to marry at all to insisting that I marry you in a verra short amount of time. And I have gone from swearing off men entirely to spending the night in your bed in naught but my skin. Let us take the year and a day. *Be with me* like that for a year and a day. And at the end of it, if you still want a wife and I still want you like this, I'll marry you that verra day."

"Una," he said, a near growl.

"Please, Ewan," she begged, coming to her knees, the blanket falling to the bed. He was momentarily distracted by her lush, naked body. But she pulled his attention back to her face with a snap of her fingers. "I need this. Then I will be certain. About me. About you. About *this.* I'll willnae doubt it ever again."

"And if there's a babe? What if there is a bairn and you still decide you dinnae want this?"

It was a fair question. She looked down. He wouldn't like her answer. "Then you'll take me to the Stewarts, and it will be as if we never met."

He crossed back to the bed and took her face in his hands.

"You expect me to take you and my child to the Stewarts and leave you there? Abandon my child and their mother with another clan? To care for? God's bones, Una."

"You wouldnae be abandoning us. You would be holding us safely there. I ken that many lairds send their heirs to grow up with other clans, and they return when they are old enough to learn with their fathers. We could come back after a time. You could raise your son to be the next laird and I could do my work, and enough time would have passed that people would have something else to talk about."

He didn't have time to discuss all the holes in this plan, all the ways it would fall apart, the ways *he* would fall apart. Then again, it didn't matter. There was no way that he wouldn't want to marry her at the end of the year. He just had to make sure that *she* wanted to marry him.

God help him.

"Fine. I'll agree to your handfast. But I want you to understand that I dinnae do it for my certainty, but for *yours*. Mark my words, I will still want to marry you in a year and a day."

He kissed her, and she wrapped her arms around his waist, holding her body against his. He wanted to push her back onto the bed and cover her with his body. He wanted to spend the entire day beneath the blankets learning every single freckle, every dip, every curve. But he wanted to do this properly, too. Or as properly as she would allow.

"Today, Una," he said huskily against her mouth. "I willnae sleep another night without you in this bed."

"Today, Ewan," she whispered, kissing him again.

CHAPTER 26

The handfasting was over in a matter of minutes, though she was bewildered to find that Ewan had indeed fetched a priest as witness, making it feel far more like a wedding. She wore the pale blue gown, which Ewan had returned to Cat for just such an occasion. Her father had served as a witness and, though the mechanics were so similar to the last time, the tone could not have been more different.

Ewan was not happy about it. He wanted a wedding. He wanted a *marriage*. But there was something that felt safer about this. Her last handfasting had been a nightmare from beginning to end, but there had been a safety in the knowledge that it would eventually end. And while she knew that Ewan would never mistreat her, there was a certain peace in knowing that she *could* leave if she wanted to.

After she and Ewan had made their marks, he with a flourishing signature and she with an X, the priest signed as witness. Ewan broke with formality and sealed the arrangement with a kiss that had him bending her over backward and blushing so furiously she didn't know if she'd ever be right again.

No sooner had the ink dried but the doors to the Great Hall had been thrown open and scores of people rushed inside. The MacDonalds, come to wish their laird well. Out of the crowd came a low bellow followed by the reedy, high pitch of the pipes. A drum joined the lively tune.

Kenneth clapped his hands on Ewan's shoulders and said with a wink, "I arranged for the music, big brother. We'll be dancing till morning."

Ewan looked down at Una, who still clung to his hand. "Shall we?"

She bit her lip and grimaced. "If we must."

"Nae much of a dancer, Una?"

"Nay."

"Well then," Ewan said with a smirk before sweeping her into his arms and whisking her into the space that had been cleared in the center of the hall while his clansmen cheered loudly. "'Tis a good thing indeed that ye are a healer and can mend my broken toes tomorrow."

They danced, together and with members of the clan. Even Fergus asked Una for the courtesy of a dance and she found herself laughing at how clumsy he was as he spun her chaotically around the space. They feasted. They received the many wishes for health and wealth and a gaggle of sons. The hour grew late, the celebration as strong as ever. A cask of ale had just been tapped and the music was loud and joyous.

Ewan bent his head to hear ear.

"'Tis time to go, mo cridhe."

She felt her cheeks turn cherry red as he led her out of the hall. The crowd erupted into hoots and cheers as they passed. When they stepped off the top step and into the hallway, Ewan pressed her against the wall, his mouth crashing down over hers at the exact moment she wrapped her arms around his neck and pulled him close. She was too warm and too full and too *empty* all at once.

He followed her down the hallway to the Laird's chamber, which Connor had vacated that morning to continue his recovery in his own room. As she pushed open the door, she looked over her shoulder.

"Are you coming?"

"I certainly hope so, Una," he growled, stalking after her.

She laughed as he picked her up and tossed her over his shoulder, giving her a hard swat on the backside and kicking the door shut behind him. He set her down and backed her into the door. She felt the hard wood behind her and Ewan's scorching heat at her front. The way he kissed her felt almost desperate, his rough hands holding her face as though she would slip through his fingers if he wasn't careful. Una certainly felt as if she might, as if her body might just dissolve into a flash of fire and blow away on the breeze of his breath.

She clutched at his shirt, and he gripped the skirt of her gown in one hand, using it to anchor her tightly against him. He had been so gentle last night. She didn't know what she had expected this evening. Not carrying her across the threshold like a bridegroom, perhaps, but she had not predicted the clumsy tripping up the stairs, being slung over his shoulder like a sack of grain. And being devoured against the door? She had never imagined such a thing.

But his desire didn't frighten her the way she had once worried it would. There was that pervasive feeling of safety that surrounded her when he was near. And in the midst of his passion, he still took care with her. The way he gently set her down and rested his hand behind her head before he had pushed her against the door so she would not bang it on the hard wood. The way he clutched her dress in one strong hand while tracing the lines of her face as gently as if she was a newborn with the other.

She wrapped her arms around his neck. He groaned into her mouth as he thrust his hips against hers, too many layers of wool between them.

"Una," he said, his voice hoarse.

An impish idea took hold, and she reached around and smacked Ewan's arse the way he'd done to her moments before.

A wicked smile crossed his face. "Now you've done it, Una," he said before he bent and picked her up, tossing her over his shoulder again and swatting her even harder. She shrieked with laughter. He tossed her onto the bed and practically leapt to cover her, and she squealed. But that sound turned into something else entirely when Ewan slid down her body, causing the fabric of her gown and shift to drag against her breasts.

He sat back on his heels and gathered handfuls of her skirts.

"I want this off. Can I take this off of you?" Ewan asked, eyes bright and hair wild from her hands.

Una nodded. She took the hand he offered and let him pull her up to sit. With reverent care, he undid the laces on her gown before lifting it over her head. He untied the knot on her shift, his eyes flashing as he watched the fabric drop, revealing her breasts. Ewan traced a tight, aching nipple with a gentle finger. She gasped at the sensation of his rough fingertip against her delicate skin.

He leaned closer, taking the taut peak into his mouth and sucking harder than he had before. Her head fell back, and she gripped Ewan's strong arm as her breath sawed in and out. Ewan nipped her with his teeth and she whispered his name, begging. He sat back with a devilish smile on his face.

Una pulled at his leine shirt, needing to feel his skin, and he obliged her by removing it. He pressed a hot palm into the middle of her chest, coaxing her down onto her back. He shifted his big body, kissing around her breasts again before dragging his lips down her belly, toward her intimate center.

"Ewan?" she asked breathily, pushing up onto her elbows.

"Aye?"

"I... I have nae experience with that," she said, blushing feverishly.

He smiled. "But are you opposed? Is it a nay?"

She shook her head slowly. "You dinnae have to though, Ewan. I ken—"

"Shhh. I want to make you ready, mo cridhe," he whispered against her hip bone.

"But I am ready now," she protested, trying in vain to pull him up, to bring his face back to hers. She wanted to kiss him. She wanted to hear him say her name against her lips. She wanted to *feel* him say it.

He smiled, looking up the length of her torso, and said, "Then you'll be doubly so when I'm through with you," before lowering his mouth, his tongue licking a hot stripe against her seam. "Besides, I didnae have any dessert downstairs. Surely you wouldnae deprive me of it now."

CHAPTER 27

If Una had thought it felt good to hear him speak her name against her mouth, she was made nearly delirious by the feeling of him speaking against her slick, aching core. She fell back against the mattress with a squeak. He gently parted her folds with his thumbs and licked from her opening to her pearl, flicking gently over the aching bundle of nerves. Una moaned, squeezing her eyes shut. He moved away from that most sensitive spot, thrusting his tongue inside of her before coming back to lick at the apex of her sex. He took his time with his explorations until Una was writhing, arching off the bed.

When she was gasping and unable to lie still, he focused his tongue on her pearl, gently circling and flicking. She gripped his hair in her fingers to keep him from moving away again. He chuckled, and she felt the vibrations of that laugh against her sex. The climax rose steadily within her, so close and yet just out of reach at the same time.

Ewan reached up with one hand to lazily play with her breast as his tongue flickered deliberately where she needed it most. With his other hand, he inserted two fingers in slow shallow glides, crooking them towards his mouth and beckoning from deep within. Una shattered like glass, her release sharp and shocking. Her mouth opened wide on a soundless scream as the orgasm rocked her body. Her toes curled and her thighs clamped tight around his ears. He wrapped an arm around her thighs and followed her as she bucked her way through it.

She was left panting and feeling as if she was floating, as if her body hovered above the sheets instead of resting tangled among them. Ewan crawled up the bed and lay beside her, his head resting on his hand as he watched her collect herself. Una turned her head to look at him.

"See?" he said, an eyebrow quirked high with a smug look on his face. "Doubly ready. Aye?"

She was boneless, brainless, and in that moment, it was all she could do to close the distance between them and press her mouth to his, tasting herself on his tongue. He rolled onto his back, taking her with him so that she straddled his hips.

"What are you doing?" she asked, her lips moving over his face.

"I want you to take me, Una," he said between kisses.

"Isnae that your job, m'laird?" she teased, nipping at his plush bottom lip.

"Next time. But I want you to do the taking."

She pulled back to study him. He ran a big hand through her hair, the beautiful braids Joan had plaited for her no doubt destroyed by now. He had such a soft, earnest look on his face. He wanted her to be in control. Of her body. Of this first time. Of every time if she wished it, she had no doubt.

He cupped her cheek. "And if you dinnae want this tonight, I will wait until you are ready. I willnae make demands of your body, Una. It isnae mine to command."

Una blinked back tears. His belly was hot beneath her,

and she felt the gentle swell of his abdomen against her slick center with every deep breath he took.

"If you want to stop, we'll stop. Now or at any point. I swear it. I willnae lose myself. I willnae make you—"

"Shhh," she said, pressing a finger against his lips. He kissed the pad of her fingertip. "I want you, Ewan."

With a nod, Ewan reached between them. She rose up higher, watching as he lined up the blunt tip of his cock with her opening. But he went no further, holding her gaze and waiting. She slid down a small measure, and her body encompassed the broad head. Ewan groaned low in his chest. He moved his hands to her hips as she sank lower, inch by inch, not daring to breathe until he was fully sheathed within her.

Una felt incomparably full. It took her breath away. Ewan seemed similarly at a loss, panting, his eyes squeezed shut.

"God's bones, Una. You nearly undid me with one stroke," he said through gritted teeth.

She bent to kiss him, and he met her mouth eagerly. His strong shoulders flexed under her hands.

"Are you well?"

She nodded and began to ride him, lifting and lowering her body over the anchor of his cock. It felt good. So very, very good. Ewan rubbed his calloused palms up her thighs. She wiggled, desperate for… *something.*

She rode him harder, until her thighs trembled and her body was covered in a sheen of sweat, chasing after that elusive peak but never quite finding the right rhythm to reach it.

"Ewan," she whined. "I need more."

"Tell me what you need."

"I dinnae ken!"

He brought his thumb to her pearl and began to circle. She felt her body fluttering around his, the sensations almost too much. And yet it still wasn't enough. It wasn't what she needed.

"I want you to do it," she begged. "Please, Ewan. Please. I cannae... I cannae..." she couldn't draw in enough breath to speak. Or perhaps it was that her brain was so alive with *feeling* that words were fully beyond her grasp.

"You are certain, Una?"

"Please!"

Ewan pulled her off of him quickly and flipped them, entering her again in one long, smooth stroke. Her legs wrapped around his waist, her heels dug into his muscular backside, and she moaned at that full feeling, so similar and yet so different like this.

"Are you well, Una?"

"Aye," she breathed, clinging to him as if he was the only thing keeping her from being swept away.

He ducked his head, burying his face in the crook of her neck and dragging his nose up her throat. Ewan began to thrust, his mouth fused to hers in a searing kiss. He moved slowly, but he wasn't gentle, bottoming out every time with a powerful, forward lunge of his hips that made her gasp as he pressed deep. She felt her body tighten around him.

"Christ, Una, just like that. You're perfect," he said into her ear as she dug her short nails into his back.

He picked up his pace, thrusting faster, in and out of her body. She felt feverish. She felt overwhelmed. And yet she never wanted to stop.

"Ewan," she mewled, her hands scrabbling across his shoulders.

"Aye?"

"I need—I need—I still need—" She couldn't speak. It was as if she'd forgotten every word she'd ever none, or at the very least, the ability to express them.

But Ewan must have known because, in an instant, she

found herself moving again. He had brought his hands under her back and pulled her upright. He knelt, sitting back on his heels so that she sat on his thighs, still firmly anchored on his cock. He shifted his pelvis back and forth, thrusting with small movements as he pressed one hand to the middle of her back.

With his other hand, he grabbed one breast tightly and lowered his mouth to the other. Una gasped as his mouth closed around her nipple and sucked hard. She found herself meeting his thrusts, lifting her hips and driving them down hard against him. His answering groans around her nipple spurred her on. She had never felt anything so good in all her life.

Or so she'd thought until he released her breast and trailed his hand lower, his thumb tracing lazy circles once again against her pearl. She cried out, but he tore his mouth away from her breast and kissed her roughly, his tongue thrusting into her mouth. She thought she would die from pleasure.

"I am yours, Una," he said, his lips against hers. "Tell me I am yours."

She couldn't answer, clinging to him like a piece of driftwood in a stormy sea, her head barely above the waters of pleasure. He pressed harder, thrust deeper, as he nipped at the skin of her neck, soothing the bites with his tongue.

"Say it, Una. I need to hear you say it. I'm *begging* you to say it," he said roughly, pressing his face into the crook of her neck.

At that moment, the dam burst and her release rushed over her with twice as much force as the first had. She dropped her head back, her hair cascading behind her.

"*Mine mine mine mine mine mine mine,*" she sobbed over and over as the tremors rocked her body. The word seemed to light a fire in Ewan who shifted forward, dropping Una onto her back again as he braced himself on his forearms on either side of her head and thrust hard and fast.

Una wrapped her legs around him and gripped his back tightly with her arms, clinging to him as he bucked and panted. His face was still buried in the space where her neck and shoulder met, and she felt his sweat dripping onto her skin, his breath coming in hot rushes.

"Please, Ewan, please," she said, clutching him tightly to her.

He groaned and shuddered, thrusting once, twice, three times before burying himself deep within her. Una felt the hot rush of his seed filling her, the warmth seeping into her as she dug her fingers into the contours of his muscled back. The room was quiet except for their panting, both of them gasping as if they'd just run to the loch and back.

Una still felt dazed when Ewan gently slid out and away from her body. He gathered her close, his arms wrapped around her, and placed a long, tender kiss against her hair, squeezing her tightly in his arms.

"Well, m'laird," she said, making circles in his chest hair and biting back a smile, "I suppose we ought to sleep."

"Will you never keep your promise, Una?" he said drowsily. He covered them with the blankets, tucking her into his side.

"Goodnight, Ewan," she said.

He kissed her forehead and lingered there. "Goodnight, Una," he whispered.

She smiled, tipping her head up to kiss his jaw before snuggling closer with her head under his chin. Just before she drifted off to sleep, she thought of the does in the thickets in the woods, safe and hidden, quiet. And then all was still.

CHAPTER 28

On a Tuesday, four months after the handfasting, Una woke to a frigid morning and an empty bed. Ewan had stoked and built the fire before he left, but she still shivered as she dressed quickly, her limbs feeling sluggish in the chill.

Upon entering the Great Hall, she saw that Ewan and his brothers had already gone, but Catriona sat at the laird's table atop the dais. She waved to Una. The hall was mostly empty save for a few serving women and old men. Their chatter was a quiet drone in the background. Cat dished steaming oats into a bowl as Una took a seat. Una's mouth watered as she smelled them. She'd missed supper the night before, having gone straight to bed after a long day of stitching and bandaging a group of young boys who claimed to have fallen out of the same tree, though no one had believed the story.

Una had just raised the spoon to her lips when she heard the door to the hall thrown open. A frantic, booming voice pierced the quiet.

"I need the healer!"

Una dropped her spoon and stood quickly, too quickly, and braced her hands on the table to steady herself as little black flecks filled her vision. A young man threaded his way through the tables, his plaid soaked with rain, his leine plastered to his body. He was big, broad in the shoulders and very, very tall. Long, straight blond hair hung limp around his face.

Her vision swam as the young man finally reached the dais and dropped to his knees before Una. She watched the water drip off his body and into the rushes.

"M'lady," he panted. "You must come at once."

"What has happened?"

"'Tis my brother's wife, m'lady. Her first babe is coming, and she has been in labor for too long. Her mother and sister sent me to fetch you. Please," he said, his voice breaking on that last, plaintive syllable.

Una wrapped her plaid more tightly around her shoulders and stepped down from the dais, steadied by a sudden rush of purpose.

"Up, Duncan," she said, pulling firmly on his arm. She could just as easily have moved a boulder. "Let us go see to—what is her name?"

"Mary, m'lady," he choked.

"We must see what must be done for Mary. I'll just fetch my cloak and medicines."

A few minutes later, Una walked next to Duncan out into the frigid, rainy morning, her satchel over her arm. The air was not quite cold enough for snow, but more than cold enough to make the rain feel like a weapon.

"How far?" she asked as they crossed the courtyard.

"Three miles, m'lady," he answered forlornly. No wonder he was so out of breath. Going by foot was not an option.

"Come with me," she said, entering the stable.

As soon as she stepped into the dry warmth, Mathan and

Greer trotted up to her. Both dogs pressed their heads against her thighs, and Una scratched behind their ears as she walked to the large stall in the back corner, praying that Calman was not out with his master. She sighed with relief when the giant's gray head poked out over the rail as she approached. She was still uneasy around the horses, but she trusted Calman. She had no other choice.

"I am sorry to take you from your warm bed, but I need your help, sweet boy," she crooned as one of the grooms saddled him. "You may be saving two lives."

Calman stamped his feet importantly but settled when the groom came to saddle him. Una felt a moment of panic. She had never mounted Calman before and had only ridden him alone that once. How was she to climb on without someone to lift her? Her question was answered when the groom brought a wooden box and held the stirrup out for her foot.

"Hurry," she said to Duncan, gesturing behind her. He hesitated.

"But that is the laird's horse, m'lady. I couldnae take such a liberty."

"He's the only horse I trust, Duncan, and time is of the essence. We must go to Mary, and I dinnae ken the way."

Duncan hesitated only a moment longer before hoisting himself up behind her.

They galloped through the gates and down the road that wound through the village, riding as quickly as they could through the driving rain, the dogs close on their heels. Una leaned over Calman's neck, his mane and the reins clutched in her fists, urging him faster. Duncan shouted directions behind her but was otherwise silent, gripping the saddle behind him.

"It is just there, m'lady," Duncan yelled gesturing at a croft with barn in the near distance. Una pulled on the reins, and

Calman stopped in front of the house. Outside, a man who looked like an older version of Duncan paced frantically, soaked by the rain and starved of the good sense to seek cover. This could only be Mary's husband, a man without a country, banished from the birthing room but unable to leave her completely.

Duncan threw himself off of Calman's back and Una followed, forgetting for a moment how far away the ground was. She stumbled but caught herself on the saddle.

"Take him and the dogs to the barn, please," she said, handing the reins to Duncan before running into the cottage.

A blast of heat shocked her. The room was stifling, the fire burning as high as was possible for the hearth. A brown-haired young woman lay in the bed weeping loudly, her shift soaked with sweat so that it clung to her shape. An older woman, likely her mother, bathed her face and crooned to her while another, barely grown, stood in the corner, her face ashen, her lips moving in a litany. Una rushed in and immediately uncovered the far window.

The older woman shrieked, "Dinnae open that window! A faerie will come and take the child, or she'll die of the vapors!"

Una ignored her. She was well accustomed with superstition. She worked amidst it every day.

"How long?"

The older woman blinked at her.

Una washed her hands in a basin of clean water. "How long has she labored?"

"Since yesterday morning," the older woman replied hoarsely.

At that moment, Mary moaned loudly. Una rushed to the bedside, gently touching Mary's bent knee.

"Mary," she said, "Mary, my brave darling. My name is

Una. I'm the healer, and I'm going to have a look at you. Can I do that?"

Mary nodded, and Una placed her hands on Mary's swollen belly, pressing gently. The problem was readily apparent. The babe was not completely turned, which explained Mary's stalled progress. Una needed to turn the baby, or it would never be born.

"Mary, darlin,' I need you to get up."

"She is meant to labor in bed! 'Tis improper to do otherwise!"

Una turned to the older woman. "What is your name?"

"Margaret."

"And hers?" Una asked, gesturing to the panicked young woman in the corner.

"My youngest daughter is called Elsbeth."

"Margaret, I ken you may never have seen a woman labor out of bed, but I promise you that it is the only way to get things moving along. We must encourage the babe to turn. Will you help me?"

Una was no stranger to women like this. Well-meaning women who wanted the best for their daughters but had been raised a certain way and were afraid of deviating. Una was never cruel to them, but she did not pander to their stubbornness or fear either. She was direct and firm, and she found usually the woman in question was grateful to not be in charge any longer.

If Margaret had any such qualms about relinquishing control of the room, she certainly did not let on and scuttled over to help Una coax a resistant Mary from the bed. Una led Mary to the eating table in the center of the room and told Elsbeth that her responsibility was making sure that there was water boiling at all times. Elsbeth jerked to attention and rushed outside with a bucket, obviously glad for a job to do.

Some said that idle hands were the devil's tools, but Una

knew better. Idle hands were the fastest way to a total collapse in one's ability to function. Better to give a person a job lest they focus too long on worst-case scenarios. This, of course, including laboring women.

"Now, Mary, I want you to hold onto this table. Aye, just like that. That's good. Now, I want you to make circles with your hips. Big, smooth circles. Dinnae stop. Aye. Aye. Just like that. Verra good."

"I'm going to die," Mary wailed. "I know it. Just leave me to die!"

Una had never once attended a first birth where the mother did not scream that she would not survive it. Agatha never even dignified the claims with a response, but Una was not Agatha. Like it or not, and though she would never admit it, she was made of softer stuff. Una rounded the table to stand across from Mary. She took Mary's cheeks in her hands, drawing the young woman's gaze up.

In a quiet, firm voice, she said, "Mary, mo cridhe, I know you are exhausted. You have been working so hard for so verra long. But you cannae give up on me now."

Mary's lip quivered, and fresh tears welled in her eyes.

"Are you with me, Mary? You can do this. You can and you will," Una said, gently pressing her thumbs into Mary's cheeks. "We will do it together."

Mary took a deep, shuddering breath. "Aye," she said, new determination in her eyes.

The moments crawled, but the hours flew by as Mary stood, circling her hips, pressing her weight into the solid table while her mother and sister bathed her face with wet cloths and Una pressed her knuckles into Mary's lower back. She had manually turned the baby, which had not been enjoyable for any parties involved, and Mary's labor was progressing again. Una's gown was soaked, though it was impossible to tell anymore whether from rain or sweat. In the end, it didn't matter.

All of a sudden, Mary began to keen loudly.

"Una! I think he's coming!"

Una undid the knot tying the girl's shift and let it fall to the floor. Firelight flickered across her pale, naked form, the skin stretched taut over her rounded belly. Sweat rolled down her body as she gripped the table and panted.

"Do you feel like you must push, Mary? Like you cannae bear not to?"

"I must! I cannae not," she sobbed at the same moment she dropped to her hands and knees in the rushes on the floor.

Una crouched behind her. "Verra well. We will do it here."

Mary pushed with all her might.

"It hurts!" she screamed.

"It will hurt until 'tis done, Mary," Una barked back, "and then you will think of it nae more!"

"I cannae do it. I cannae do it any longer," Mary said, her voice thick with tears.

Between Mary's legs, Una could see a shock of blond hair covering the baby's head.

"Mary, my beauty, I see the head. He has hair as fair as your husband's, Mary! Dinnae give up now!"

Mary panted heavily for a few moments before pushing again, yelling loudly as she strained.

"Good girl, Mary! His head is out! Give me one more push, one more and we'll have him!"

Seeing her grandchild's head must have spurred something in Margaret because she took her daughter's face in her hands, chanting encouragements in her ear and stroking her hair. Mary screamed and, with one more push, delivered a robust, squirming baby boy into Una's arms. After an eternal moment, a piercing cry rent the sudden silence.

Mary wept, loud sobs wracking her body. All Una could do was laugh as tears streamed down her own face.

"Stay where you are, Mary, just a moment longer," Una said before asking Elsbeth to place fresh linens on the bed. Margaret bathed Mary's face with a dry cloth, a proud look in her eye. Una wrapped the babe in a clean cloth and handed him to his grandmother so that she could tend to the afterbirth.

When Una was done with the necessary ministrations, she and Elsbeth helped Mary into a clean shift and then into the bed. Margaret placed the babe in his mother's arms.

Mary looked at him as if he had fallen from the sky without warning, her eyes wide with shock and amazement. Una's heart seized, as it always did in this exact moment. Every time. That first look. The first time the babe curled a tiny fist around his mother's finger. The look of complete bewilderment and utter peace all at once.

Smiling through her tears, Una went to the basin and rinsed the blood and fluids off of her hands and arms. Now that the birthing was done, she felt her exhaustion keenly. She whispered a few instructions to Margaret, who wrapped Una in a tight hug, and made her way to exit, promising she would return in the morning to check in on the pair.

Una opened the door, and Mary's husband nearly fell in. His face was gray and haggard. She smiled at him.

"Go. Meet your son," Una said, placing a hand on his shoulder.

The big man stumbled into his cottage and fell to his knees beside the bed, clasping Mary's hand in one of his and stroking his son's downy soft head with the other. Margaret and Elsbeth were busy setting the cottage to rights when Una slipped out the door, closing it silently behind her. She shook her head, her vision suddenly going dark around the edges again as she remembered that she'd left without breakfast that morning and it was now nearly dark.

As she turned away from the cottage, she ran into a wall. Strong hands gripped her arms to keep her from stumbling back as arms she knew so well banded around her.

"Una," Ewan groaned against the top of her head. "I've been worried sick."

"Worried?" she gaped, still trying to steady her vision as the world spun around her.

"You took my horse, and I heard from the watch that you rode off at breakneck speed with Duncan behind you. I—" His voice cracked.

"His sister-in-law was in labor," Una murmured, her words feeling thick in her mouth. "I dinnae ken her husband's name."

"Lodan."

"Mary was in labor," Una repeated, the ground feeling unsteady beneath her feet.

"I ken that now, lass. Cat tried to find me to tell me, but we kept missing one another."

"I took Calman because he's the only one I trust."

"Did everything go... well?" His voice was husky as he spoke against her temple.

Una pressed her forehead against his chest, soaked from the rain and yet, impossibly, warm. Her head was swimming.

"Aye," she said, her voice feeling miles away. And then she was weightless, falling, falling, spinning downward before the world went dark.

CHAPTER 29

A week had passed since the birth of Lodan and Mary's son, which also meant that a week had passed since Una had fainted dead away in his arms. It had planted a new seed of worry deep in his guts that was watered daily by the constant shower of his own panic. Una had insisted that she never got sick, and yet she had lost consciousness and collapsed like a boulder off a cliff. Had he not been there to catch her, she could have hit her head on a stone. She could have died. She— he couldn't bear to finish the thought.

But Una had no sympathy for his nerves. She insisted upon checking in on Mary every day that week, which meant that Ewan had, in turn, insisted upon being the one to bring her. It didn't matter that she had been right as rain after some bread and broth and tea. It did not matter that she had not fainted since. It didn't matter that she insisted that she was fine. He could not convince himself to believe her.

He was distracted, delegating more and more of his tasks and losing focus because he couldn't bear to go more than an hour without checking in on her. He wanted to believe her. He wanted to believe that she was hale and healthy and that all was well. Yet the worry nagged at him, ever present and growing ever louder.

Since their handfast, Una had practiced her archery nearly every day. He remembered being delighted when she told him she wanted a place to practice. He had set up a permanent target for her in the open green space outside the curtain wall. It was far enough away that there was no danger of an unsuspecting person walking in front of her but close enough that the guards atop the wall could keep watch over her.

Since she had fainted, however, Ewan wanted her nowhere near a bow and arrow. Or any sharp objects for that matter. It had been easy enough with the weather being as poor as it had been. The driving rain from the day of Mary's labor had carried on for a week, drenching everything and turning the courtyard and roads into muck. But yesterday had been dry, and when Ewan woke that morning to see the sun striking out from behind the mountains into a cloudless sky, he cursed to himself because there would be no stopping Una today.

He wondered if he could keep her in bed all day, but then he remembered the mountain of correspondence that had piled high on his desk that week and the fact that he had promised to speak with a group of farmers about a new plan for better drainage in the fields.

It was not uncommon for him to rise and break his fast before she did. Una did not sleep late as a general rule, but nor did she wake before dawn as he did, restless and unable to go back to sleep. In fact, once Una fell asleep, an avalanche could bury the keep and she would not wake up. He rose and broke his fast in the Great Hall before going to meet with the farmers. The meeting took far longer than he anticipated and then there had been more things requiring his immediate attention.

It was late afternoon by the time he rode around the wall to where his instincts told him Una would be practicing. As he rode Calman around the corner, he saw her. A light breeze blew the loose tendrils of hair that had escaped her braid. She stood tall and strong, shoulders pulled back with the bowstring, which she released, sending an arrow flying into the dead center of the target where it joined a cluster already there.

She strode to the target and yanked them free, spotting him as she turned. Even from a distance, he saw the smile that spread wide across her face. Those smiles came more easily to her with every passing day since they'd been handfasted.

He dismounted and walked Calman the rest of the way, not stopping until his chest nearly touched hers. She walked into him, having stowed the arrows in her belt quiver, and rested her head on his chest.

"How are you, Ewan?"

How was he? He was tired, hungry, and feeling as if a prize bull was sitting in the middle of his chest.

"I am well, mo cridhe. And you? How do you fare this day?"

Ewan couldn't decide if her complexion was paler than usual. He did note the tiny pinpricks of sweat around her brow and across her nose. But perhaps she had been practicing for a while. Perhaps she had exerted herself.

She didn't answer him right away, which did nothing for his worry. She began swallowing, and Ewan could see that, yes, in spite of the flush from the cold, she did look paler. Ewan took her face in his hands and lifted it to look closer.

"Are you well, Una?"

"Ewan, I… I…" she began, but wrenched her body to the side before vomiting violently onto the ground beside their feet.

"God's bones, Una!" he exclaimed, jumping behind her, supporting her with one arm and grabbing her hair with the other as she heaved.

Standing shakily, Una dragged the back of her hand across her mouth, closing her eyes tightly as she gasped for air. Ewan whistled, and Calman hurried to his side.

"Hang on, Una. Christ," he hissed under his breath. "Can you hold onto him until I can climb behind you?"

She nodded.

"Good lass."

Ewan lifted her onto Calman's back and scrambled up behind her, drawing her into his lap and shifting her legs so that he cradled her in his arms.

"Home, Calman," he said, and the horse began a steady walk back to the keep.

Ewan held her close, trying his best to shield her from the damp chill. Perhaps she had eaten something disagreeable. Or perhaps she had gotten overheated. Sometimes people simply cast up their accounts, he reminded himself, forcing himself to breathe normally. One bout of sickness was not enough to cause alarm.

Una groaned, and Ewan tensed as she buried her face in his chest.

"We're almost home, mo cridhe. Stay with me."

His voice sounded as taut and strained as a bowstring, but he tried his best to keep the terror at bay. Una stirred in his arms.

"I am fine, Ewan," she protested weakly, not opening her eyes. "I missed breakfast again this morning. I was too excited to be in the sunshine. That is all."

He scowled down at her. "All the same, you'll be in bed the rest of the night and all day tomorrow, Una."

"Ewan, dinnae be ridiculous," she protested, but without strength. "A piece of bread will set me to rights."

"Bed, Una. And you'll stay there if I have to tie you to it," he growled.

She opened her mouth to protest again but snapped it closed just as suddenly, clapping a hand over her lips.

"Stop!" she cried through her fingers, and Calman skidded to a halt before Ewan could even pull on the reins and command him. And not a moment too soon, either. Una twisted away from Ewan and retched.

The fear that he had kept reined in broke free from its bonds and ran amuck in his heart.

"You are ill."

"I'll be fine, Ewan," she said, patting his chest, but her eyes were closed and her skin had a gray pallor.

He wanted to believe her. He wanted to laugh at how grumpy she sounded but his mind whirred. As they rode through the gates and into the courtyard, the dogs ran out to meet them. Ewan hadn't paid much attention lately, but as the dogs approached, he noticed that Greer's belly appeared somewhat distended.

A nagging thought came. *It cannae be that. She cannae.... Could she?*

Fiona's shout pierced through the other sounds of the courtyard. David approached with a groom, who took Calman's reins as David reached his arms out to receive Una while Ewan dismounted. He took her immediately back. Fiona fussed and followed as he strode into the keep, not stopping until they were in their chamber where he began to, without ceremony, strip off her wet clothing. Una swatted his hands away ineffectively, but he had her bared to her skin before she could stop him. Fiona dragged a dry shift down over her head.

Ewan immediately picked her up despite her protests and carried her to the bed, placing her gently in the center. Fiona tucked the blankets around Una's legs.

"What happened, m'laird?" Fiona asked as she pressed her hand to Una's forehead and looked in her eyes.

"She hasnae eaten since yesterday. She's cast up her accounts twice in the past few minutes. This after she fainted a week ago. 'Tis obvious she's taking fever."

"Give me some bread, and I shall be as I ever was," Una snapped.

"Well, now, I dinnae think that's quite true, Una—"

"Of course it's true, Fiona. If you dinnae believe me, give me a crust and I shall show you."

"Verra well." Fiona sighed as she went to the side table to retrieve a piece of bread.

Una took a bite and then another, chewing with a smug, triumphant look on her face as she stared at Ewan. His pounding heart slowed a bit as she swallowed and took a third bite. But then her eyes flew open wide and she pointed frantically towards the wash basin. Fiona thrust it into her hands just in time for the bread to come back the way it had gone.

Ewan roared, dragging his hands through his soaked hair and pulled hard on the ends.

"What were you thinking, Una? You ken better than to tromp about when you havenae been well."

"I didnae tromp!" she spat. "And besides, I *am* well!"

"You've taken ill."

"Perhaps we should leave it to the *healer* to determine that? I wonder who that could be. Och, aye, *'tis me*!"

"You are nae well!" he shouted, each word a staccato.

"I am fine!" she returned with just as much emphasis.

"Och, aye. As ever you were," Fiona said lightly, her eyebrows high. "Would either of you stubborn mules care to hear what *I* think is the matter?"

Ewan shot Fiona a glare, and Una smirked. He crossed his arms over his chest and leveled a look at the housekeeper.

"'Tisnae obvious? The lass is with child. When I had my bairns, I was the same way at first. Tired, crabbit, couldnae keep a bite down for weeks. You've been dragging yourself around the keep lately, Una. Going to bed early, rising late. Aye, I'd say there will be a little lairdling come autumn."

Fiona kept chattering happily as she moved about the room, but Ewan locked eyes with Una and felt the world around them go completely still. As if time stopped marching, he heard everything in minute detail—the tiny pops and crackles of the log in the hearth, the wind against the walls of the keep, his own ragged breath, the relentless pounding of his heart in his ears.

"Nay," he whispered, barely, but from her gasp, he knew Una heard him. "You cannae be..."

"I could," she said, taking a deep breath, her eyes going wide with wonder and surprise. "I am."

"But you... you prevented it with... you havenae?"

What was he saying? Had he truly thought she was? Whatever he had thought, whatever had had tried to say, it was the wrong thing. Her eyes narrowed in anger and her mouth dropped open.

"Nay," she said. "I didnae ken you wanted me to."

He backed slowly towards the door, never blinking as he stared at Una. Because he hadn't wanted her to. Had he? Or had he simply assumed she would do it on her own, that she would want to wait until the year was up before any lasting decisions were made? The floor began to go out from under him; he felt as if he were falling feet first into a chasm. His ears rang; his breath came in short, insufficient bursts.

"Ewan," Una said, reaching for him.

Ewan's hand shook as he reached behind him for the latch, fumbling to open the door, and then fled into the hall.

"Ewan!" he heard her shout just as the door shut behind him.

Suddenly, time snapped back in place, the words, *I could. I am,* echoing in his brain as he ran.

CHAPTER 30

Ewan descended the stairs in a daze, feeling his pulse in his ears, barely breathing, eyes wide. Sounds from the evening meal in the hall drifted into the stairwell. His stomach turned from the smells of roasted game and fresh bread, but he found himself opening the doors to the Great Hall and striding toward the dais. His siblings were all seated and enjoying their suppers.

"Ewan! You look as if you've seen a ghost," Angus said, standing and placing a hand on Ewan's shoulder.

For the first time in his twenty-five years, Kenneth had the good sense not to crack a joke. He stood and tried to push Ewan into a chair, but Ewan shook his brother off.

"Have you seen David?" he asked. "I must speak with him."

"He's at home," Angus replied, peering around Kenneth. "Said he wouldnae be in the hall tonight."

Ewan nodded to Angus, grateful that his brother paid such close attention to those around him, and stepped off the dais.

"Ewan—" Kenneth called after him, but Ewan shook his

head and kept walking. He needed to talk to David. He needed his best friend.

David's cottage was near the curtain wall, and as he approached it, Ewan couldn't help but remember the day he'd spent planning Una's own cottage behind it. David's home was neat and spartan, with no hint that a woman had ever lived there. Though one had.

Five years before, David's wife delivered a babe sleeping and lost her life in the process. David and Ewan never discussed it. The reason was as obvious as it was shameful to Ewan. David never brought Isbel up in conversation because he did not want to add to Ewan's grief. But Ewan had also not created space for David *to* speak of her.

What a piss-poor friend I am, Ewan chided himself.

And yet here he was, knocking on David's door, seeking out friendship that he had not offered the way he should have. David answered, clearly surprised to see him, and invited him in without word.

They didn't speak. Ewan had always appreciated that about David. He was a man who could talk for hours but who never felt the need to fill silence just for the sake of speaking. David turned to the hearth and stirred something in a pot, crouching low before the fire.

"Una's with child," Ewan said, breaking the expectant silence.

"Oh?" David said, looking over his shoulder.

"Aye."

David rose and clapped him on the shoulder with a bright smile. "Congratulations, Ewan! What happy tidings!"

Ewan raked his fingers through his hair. David returned to the fire. Sitting on his haunches, David grabbed two bowls, ladled stew into them, and stood. He placed them at the table and sat, gesturing to the chair across from him. The chair that always sat empty.

Ewan had never eaten a meal at this table. David took most of his meals in the hall. And yet here they were. Ewan sitting in Isbel's chair, eating from Isbel's bowl, sharing the space with his best friend that should have been occupied by his best friend's wife. Fear rolled deep in Ewan's belly.

It suddenly occurred to Ewan that perhaps David went out of his way to do so much for the clan so that he didn't have to spend much time alone in his cottage, surrounded by nothing but the empty space where such possibility once lived, sitting across from the empty chair where Ewan now sat. Ewan understood this. It was the very reason he had filled his days from beginning to end for so many years.

"How is Una?" David asked around a mouthful.

Ewan dropped his spoon into the bowl and pressed his face into his hands. "I dinnae ken."

David put his spoon down, but gently. "What do you mean, you dinnae ken?"

"I dinnae ken how she is because I turned tail and fled as soon as I heard the news."

David surged to his feet, slamming his hands on the table. The movement seemed so much larger, so much louder in that quiet, small space. "You did what?"

"I panicked!"

"You panicked? *You panicked?*" David roared, disgust written plainly all over his face. "What did you expect to happen when you go at each other like rabbits in spring at every opportunity? Have either of you done aught to prevent it?"

"Nay," Ewan mumbled.

"Louder."

"Nay! There have been nae precautions," Ewan said. "I didnae ask. I assumed she—"

"You're a godsdamned fool, Ewan MacDonald," David snarled.

Ewan groaned into his hands, pounding the heel of his right hand against his forehead. David raked his hands over his close-shorn hair, clearly trying to pull at it.

"My God, Ewan. Where is your head? The moment you learn you've fathered a bairn upon her, you run off and leave her alone?"

Ewan couldn't remember his friend ever being this angry with him. He groaned. "What am I to do, David? What if she..." His voice cracked, and he sucked in a breath. "I—I—I cannae lose her."

David sighed a gusty exhale, the angry wind gone from his sails in an instant. He dropped back into his seat. "You can. You can lose her, and you *may* lose her. And if nae now, then someday for certain. Someday, one of you will have to say goodbye first." He paused, and Ewan choked on a sob. "But nae today, Ewan."

Ewan folded his arms on the table, dropped his forehead to them, and let the tears fall. He heard the scraping of David's chair as he dragged it close and felt the heat of his friend's body as he leaned in, wrapping an arm around Ewan's back.

"Now you listen to me," David said quietly. "Una is probably terrified. Not only of the idea of becoming a mother, but also because the bairn's father ran away from her like she was cursed."

Ewan felt his cheeks grow even hotter with shame.

"She is about to lay her life on the line to give you a gift. Maybe you willnae get to keep it. Maybe you willnae get to keep *her*."

Ewan took a deep, shuddering breath and looked up at David. Tears glittered in his friend's eyes in the firelight and his bottom lip trembled as he went on, "None of it is fair. But she's a gift nonetheless. As is every single day you get with her."

David squeezed Ewan's shoulder so tightly it hurt.

"You've wasted too much of your life worried about who else you might lose. Cling too tightly, and it'll all slip through your fingers. Just love people while you have them, and all will be well in the end."

Ewan sniffled loudly, his thoughts returning to Isbel's chair, the wood beneath him almost possessing a life of its own.

"And for you? Is all well for you?" Ewan murmured.

David swallowed hard, and Ewan could feel the weight of David's arm on his back grow heavier. "It isnae how I pictured my life. Living by myself in an empty cottage with nothing but my memories. But I am still here. I survived it. I survived losing them. And that cannae have been for naught."

The quiet settled between them again. Ewan sat up and pressed the heels of his hands to his eyes, wiping the tears.

"I dinnae deserve your friendship, David."

"None of us deserve any of the good things we have."

Ewan nodded. "Still. You are the verra best man I know."

David's smile was watery. He pulled Ewan against his chest and hugged him tightly. They stood like that for a long time, their chests pressing together as they breathed, their tears falling silently in unison.

Before he pulled away, Ewan squeezed David closer and said, "David, you are nae alone. And you can always talk to me about… about any of it. Anything."

Ewan felt David nod. "You are nae alone either, Ewan. I will stand beside you come what may."

CHAPTER 31

"What do you mean he left?" Joan asked, seething.

"Just what I said. He stared at me as if I were a ghost and then ran from the room."

Joan cursed as she stomped around the chamber. Una sat on the bed she shared with Ewan, her knees drawn up to her chest, her plaid wrapped tightly around her shoulders and clutched in a fist at her breast.

"Joan," she cried, overwhelmed by the sheer number of emotions crowding into the exact same space in her heart. Fury, fear, elation, all pressing in close upon her. Joan hurried to the bed and tucked Una against her chest, rubbing large, gentle circles on her back as she crooned.

"Are you happy about it, Una?" Joan asked, gently tipping her chin up.

"I dinnae ken how to feel," Una said through tears. "For the longest time, I worked and prayed to ensure it didnae happen. But now... It isnae that I am nae happy. 'Tis only that I am afraid to do it alone."

Una buried her face in her hands and sobbed.

"He is a good man, Una. A coward, apparently, but a good man. He will come around," Joan said as she gently pulled Una's hands away from her face and wiped her cheeks with the corner of the plaid. "And if he doesnae, you've got me. And I am nae afraid of anything."

Una laughed. "Aye," she said, wiping her nose with the sleeve of her shift. "But God save us if 'tis a boy and it comes to that."

"You dinnae think we can raise a proper man, Una? I have been less than impressed with the men I've met who were raised by other men. Between the two of us, I'd say we could do the job credibly," Joan said with a wink. Una smiled.

Someone knocked on the door, and Catriona peeked timidly into the room.

"May I come in?" she asked.

"Of course," Una said, patting the bed beside her.

Cat climbed in and sat cross-legged across from Una.

"He still isnae back then?"

"Nay," Una replied.

"What happened, if you dinnae mind my asking?"

Una traded a look with Joan and then sighed.

"There's going to be a babe come autumn."

Cat hopped to her knees and bounced on the bed in excitement. "Una!" she squealed.

Una laughed ruefully. "Your brother didnae take the news so well."

"How did he take it?"

When Una didn't answer, Joan said, "He ran out of the room as if she'd lit his arse on fire."

Cat rolled her eyes and blew a gusty breath out of pursed lips. "Surely it isnae because of our mother."

"Perhaps," Una said. "I ken he is afraid."

Cat didn't say another word. All three of them been orphaned by their mothers in one way or another. One at birth and the others as children, one to death and one to abandonment. Una *was* afraid of birth. She'd seen firsthand how quickly it could go terribly wrong. She would be off her head *not* to fear it. But it was the sort of fear that made a person more aware, a fear that had somewhat soft edges and often looked like something else entirely.

True, a birth could go badly. But so, too, could riding a horse or shearing a sheep or even walking in the wrong place at the wrong time. Childbirth was a hazard, but life itself was a hazard. Una's fear felt so companionable because it was bound to something far more buoyant.

Hope.

Hope had been the unflappable bird that had beat its wings inside Una's chest every day since leaving Malcolm Cameron's clutches. She would not let go of it now.

Una squeezed Cat's hand. "All will be well."

Cat nodded. "I am sorry that Ewan didnae take it well, though, Una. It is such happy news."

"You understand men like your brother, m'lady," Joan said, wrapping an arm around Una and hugging her into her side. "They're the first in line when something needs to be stabbed, but the last in the room to sort out how they feel about anything."

Cat laughed. "Unfortunately, Una, you've yoked yourself to a long line of stubborn men. They'll never forsake you, but they'll drive you mad."

"Perhaps I'll be lucky and have a daughter."

With that, Cat came to her knees dramatically, her hands pressed together and her head bent in prayer. "Holy Mother, watch over us in our hour of need. Keep us ever in your sight. Give us the strength to live among the MacDonald men and the patience to keep from smacking them daily. Pray for our souls, Mother of God, that we may one day walk beside you having already atoned for our sinful ways by living among these goats. And let Una's child be a daughter so that we may begin to even out the numbers around here. Amen."

Cat endeavored to keep a straight face as she prayed but collapsed back onto the bed in a fit of giggles immediately after. Una also laughed until her sides hurt, tears streaming down her cheeks as she gasped for breath. Then Joan snorted, which only made them all laugh harder.

Slowly, the chamber door opened again, and Ewan's head poked around it. He peered toward the bed, his eyes landing on Una. The room fell silent.

He cleared his throat. "Beg pardon, ladies. But I wonder if I might have a moment alone with my"—he cleared his throat again—"with Una."

Joan looked at Una, her eyebrows lifted. Cat sat up abruptly, her hair a tangled halo around her shoulders. Una nodded to them both, and Joan hopped off the bed and sauntered over to the doorway.

She dropped a curtsy and breezed past him, saying, "Beg pardon, m'laird," as she knocked into him with her shoulder.

Cat climbed off the bed with far less grace and stomped over to her brother. She reached for him as if to embrace him and, when he bent his tall form down towards her, smacked him hard against the back of the head.

"Damnit, Cat! That hurt!" he said, rubbing his skull.

"Good," she said tartly before turning to look over her shoulder at Una. "I believe I get that one for free. No penance, aye?"

"I'd say our Lady will give you that one, Cat," Una said seriously, suppressing a smile.

With that, Cat breezed past Ewan, also knocking him with her good shoulder as Joan had done. Una had to double her efforts to stifle her smile when she saw the look on Ewan's face.

"I have lost all respect from the women in my house, it seems, if Joan and Catriona are any indication. Best nae go find Fenella and Fiona, or they might gut me on the spot."

"Cat had a special, holy dispensation. And Joan was prepared to be a father to this babe in your absence so I dinnae think ye can press her either. But you're right about Fenella. Best stay away from her for a while. She doesnae care much for cowards."

His face fell. "I deserve that."

"I was comforted to know that Joan would stand by me, though."

He moved toward her and, in the light from the hearth, she could see his face. It looked drawn, his eyes rimmed in red. He'd been crying, and the knowledge of that softened her. Part of her was still furious for his earlier escape, but a larger part of her knew that he had punished himself that last hour more than anyone else ever could. But she wasn't quite ready to forgive him yet.

"Aye. We had it all worked out. If it is a boy, Joan thought we should name him after my father. And if it's a girl... we thought we'd name her after my father as well. Fergus is such a fine name, even for a lass."

He gaped at her for a moment.

"Dinnae you agree, Ewan?"

"Aye," he said, wiping tears from his eyes, "Fergus is the finest name for a lass."

He hesitantly came to her, going to his knees beside the bed.

"I'm so sorry, Una. I shouldnae have left."

She nodded, running her fingers through this thick, wavy hair. He bent his head and his shoulders relaxed as she gently dragged her fingernails across his scalp and back again.

"Where did ye go?"

"I went to see David." He sighed. "He's a widower. Did you ken?"

"Nay," Una said quietly.

"She died in the birthing," Ewan said, hanging his head.

Una nodded slowly, understanding taking shape. "I take it the bairn didnae survive either?"

Ewan shook his head and then grabbed her hand with his, pressing his cheek to her palm.

"And?"

"And he told me what a horse's ass I was."

"I like David."

"Aye," Ewan snorted. "He's quite fond of you, himself."

He took her hand in both of his, turning it over so her palm faced up. Una felt more tears welling in her eyes. She nodded, ducking her gaze low. He reached a big, calloused finger under her chin and tipped it up.

"I'm sorry if this isnae what you wanted," she replied, her lip quivering.

Ewan climbed onto the bed and gathered her into his arms. He tucked her head under his chin.

"Och, Una. It isnae that I dinnae want this. 'Tis only that it scares the piss out of me. But you are such a gift to me, Una, and I ken this bairn will be as well."

"Do you mean that?"

"Aye," he said, kissing the top of her head. "You'll never be rid of me now."

They were quiet for a while, Una appreciating his solid warmth and the steady beating of his head beneath her cheek.

"Do you remember when you told me that you were far too stubborn to let Connor die?"

"Aye," she said, snuggling closer.

"See that that same stubbornness applies to yourself. Alright?"

"Of course," she whispered, turning her face up to him.

He kissed her gently, threading his fingers through the long strands of her hair. She gripped his shoulders and tried to deepen the kiss, but he pulled back and murmured against her lips, "Shhh. Just let me love you, Una."

He kissed her lips twice and then kissed the tip of her nose and her forehead before wrapping his arms around her and tucking her into his side. As Una heard his breaths deepen and felt his body relax, she felt his hand shift on its own to cover her belly. She smiled and surrendered herself to sleep.

CHAPTER 32

As a general rule, Fenella had a "nae dogs in the kitchens" policy. It made sense to Una, especially when the dogs in question were as big as Mathan and his familiars—deerhounds so tall that their heads could easily rest atop the table and steal food from it. But from the moment Una had encountered Greer in the bailey earlier that day, the dog would not be parted from her. Fenella had begrudgingly allowed Greer entrance into the kitchen but had chased Mathan away when he tried to follow.

"The expectant ladies may stay in the kitchen, but you have nae business here, you hairy brute," she had scolded good-naturedly, herding him away. "Go and fetch your master!"

Mathan hung his head and trotted off to do just that.

Now, Una sat at the large worktable with a cup of tea, helping Fenella to peel apples for the apple muse Catriona had requested. Greer was turning in restless circles, pacing around the table but never letting Una out of her sight.

"She's right fashed, aye?" Fenella asked as a long peel of apple dropped from her knife onto the wooden table.

"Aye," Una answered, chewing on a bit of peel. "A lady gets restless before she drops pups, I suppose."

"Today?"

"I believe so," Una replied with a small smile.

It had been a few weeks since learning about her own pregnancy, but, to be truthful, she hadn't had much time to consider it. The MacDonalds had outdone themselves with their need for a healer, and the past three weeks had been filled with setting more broken bones, stitching more wounds, and assisting in more births than had ever clustered together before, if Fenella was to be believed.

Una liked to be busy. She liked to feel useful. What was more, she liked feeling like she belonged among the MacDonalds. She was making friends and building a life for herself. She could hardly believe how happy she had been.

"I should take Greer out to the barn, I suppose. To get ready."

"You mean for her to whelp those pups in a stall? With *horses?*"

Una laughed at Fenella's horror. "Aye, in the usual way. Where else does a dog drop pups?"

"Our beauty isnae going to have those wee pups in a filthy stall. She'll have them right here in the kitchen where it's warm and we can keep an eye on them."

"Fenella, that isnae—"

But Fenella was already hastening to the doorway, where she called out for help. A half breath later, a young man was in the doorway.

"Aye, Fenella?" he asked.

"We'll be needing a box," Fenella commanded. "A big one."

He blinked at her.

"A box. A big box," Fenella repeated.

"Like a chest?"

"Nay. I dinnae want a chest. I want a box. A birthing box."

"You mean for someone to give birth in a box?" he asked, horrified.

"Aye," Fenella said matter-of-factly.

"But...how will they breathe? How will the bairn get out?"

Una swallowed her laugh as Fenella looked skyward.

"It isnae for a bairn," she said, with exaggerated patience and gritted teeth. "'Tis for a dog."

The lad looked doubly confused now. "So you want to put the dog in the box while someone gives birth? Cannae you just send it outside?"

"God's bones, lad! Get David for me," Fenella shouted, moving to stir something in a pot. When she looked over her shoulder and saw the young man still standing in the doorway, looking at Una for clarification, she barked, "Get you gone! Go fetch David!"

Una smiled as she watched the lads flee up the stairs and away. A short time later, David strolled into the kitchen, bringing the smell of woodsmoke and the outdoors with him.

"Good day, Fenella, Una." David dipped his head at each of them in turn. "What's this I hear about you giving birth to a dog in a box?" he said, winking at Una.

At that, Una could contain her laughter no longer. Fenella threw up her hands.

Una said, "David, we need a pen. A large box will do if we can build it, but Fenella has decided that Greer shall have her pups in the kitchen, and we need to contain them."

"Aye," Fenella said with a fierce nod just as Fiona rushed into the kitchen.

"What's this I'm hearing about you locking a dog in a chest until she gives birth?" Fiona panted.

Fenella whirled around, brandishing a large, wooden

spoon, which she waved around as she spoke. "You," she said, pointing at David, "Build us a pen over there. It only needs two sides since it is in the corner. Is that simple enough now?"

He nodded and strode with purpose from the kitchen. Fenella then pointed the spoon at Una, "And you will eat something, Una, because I willnae have you keeling over whelping a litter of pups and have our laird all over me for allowing you to come to harm. As for you," she said, looking at Fiona, her face softening, "if you'll be a dear and gather up rags and old linens for our darling Greer, I would be much obliged."

Fiona smiled and nodded before following after David. Fenella thunked a bowl of stew down in front of Una with a large piece of bread slathered with fresh butter. "Eat," she commanded before returning to the hearth. Una did as she was commanded, keeping an eye on Greer, who continued to pant and pace in the kitchen.

After a time, David returned with several boards under his arm and Rabbie on his heels. Rabbie waved shyly at Una before dropping to his knees next to David and helping to fit together the cut slabs.

"It isnae much," David said, "and you'll be needing a more permanent solution before long, but it will do for today."

"I thank you, David," Una replied. "'Tis perfect."

And it was. Large enough for Greer to spin and lay fully on her side with Una in the box next to her, but not so large that she would feel separated from her pups or lose track of them. It was close enough to the hearth to be warm, but not so close that anyone would be overheated. David brushed off his hands and stood, bidding them all farewell before striding off to manage the next crisis that demanded his attention.

Una smiled. She imagined that David spent his days in

much the same way she did, only instead of setting bones and stitching wounds, he solved problems great and small. Una expected Rabbie to follow after David, but when she looked up, she found him sitting on the floor, gently stroking Greer's ears and whispering to her.

"She likes you," Una said.

Rabbie looked up, a shocked look on his face, as if he'd forgotten she was there.

"Do ye like animals, Rabbie?"

He nodded. She knew he didn't like to speak except around close family, that he was sensitive about his stammer.

"Would you like to help me? I'll be in the box with Greer, and Fenella will be busy feeding everyone. If you would help me, I'd be in your debt."

Robbie smiled shyly, nodding. "I w-w-would l-like that," he said quietly. "Verra m-much."

Fiona bustled into the kitchen with an armful of cloths. Una spread a layer of soft fabric in the bottom of their pen and gestured to Rabbie, who gently led Greer to the box. She followed, licking his hand affectionately.

It wasn't long before Greer lay down on her side. Una watched her belly tighten with contractions.

"Have you attended a birth before, Rabbie?" Una asked as she stroked Greer's side.

Rabbie nodded. "I spend a l-l-lot of time with the horses. I've helped with the f-f-foaling the past th-three years."

Una smiled. She could picture Rabbie with the horses, stroking their long, velvet noses and playing with the long-legged colts while their mothers grazed.

"Then none of this will surprise you in the least," she said. "This is the first dog birth I'll be attending, but I cannae imagine the main principles are any different from sheep or people."

At that moment, Greer began licking at her back end.

Una noticed a small puppy head, still encased in the sac. A few breaths later, the puppy slid out and into Una's waiting hands. Greer immediately began licking the puppy, and Una helped to clear the puppy from the membrane. Una held the umbilical cord tightly between her fingers while Greer chewed it away from the placenta so that her teeth didn't accidentally hurt the puppy. Once the puppy was clean, Una helped it to find its way to one of Greer's teats to nurse.

The puppy, a male, was round and soft, his eyes tightly closed. He was light gray, though that wasn't an indicator of what he would look like when it was older. Una smiled, imagining a litter of puppies with Greer's grace and Mathan's shaggy coat running roughshod around the keep.

Rabbie handed her a clean bit of toweling, and Una traded him for the dirty one. A small while later, the process began anew, this time with a female pup that was white with gray patches. She was even bigger than her brother and yipped angrily until she was settled in and nursing.

And so the afternoon passed, with Una helping to rub the puppies clean and make sure their airways were clear before Rabbie helped to settle them against Greer's teats. It was evening when Greer delivered her eighth puppy. The litter of tiny, round puppies were nursing happily, squeaking and making the most adorable racket.

Word had spread about the kitchen puppies, and Fenella shooed everyone away with her spoon, saying that there would be no visitors or gawkers until Una said they were allowed. Una was grateful to have such a fierce ally in Fenella. The only other two people she allowed into the kitchens besides the kitchen maids were Fiona and Ewan, who came by just after supper had been served in the hall.

"When did you last eat, Una?" Ewan asked, looming over the pen.

"Midday," she answered distractedly, working with Rabbie to rearrange the puppies to give Greer more room.

"Come, lass," Fenella commanded, setting two plates on the work table. "Eat."

Greer's contractions had eased, and while she couldn't be completely certain, Una thought she might be done. It was as good a time as any to take a break and Rabbie seemed more than happy to climb into the box while Una ate. She was filthy, covered in blood and birthing fluid and the Lord only knew what else. She went to a basin to wash her hands well before returning to the table.

"How many?" Ewan said around a mouthful of bread.

"Eight."

Ewan nodded. "And they are all well?"

"Aye," Una replied. "All fat and lively, knocking and pushing to get to their mother."

They ate in silence for a moment. Ewan looked troubled.

"Are you well, Ewan?"

"Aye. Do you think… och, never mind."

"Out with it, Ewan."

"Do you think that Mathan could see her? He's been a mess all day. If he hasnae been tripping me from following so close, he's been sitting at the keep's door howling. I feel bad for the poor bastard. He hasnae seen Greer all day, and I am certain he believes aught is amiss."

Ewan hadn't looked at her when he'd asked, staring down at his plate instead, but Una's heart went out to him. Mathan was such a good dog and very attached to Greer. Of course he'd been concerned. No doubt he could smell the birthing. But it was more than that, wasn't it? Whelping puppies was not nearly the danger that birthing a human baby was, but Ewan likely couldn't help to connect the two in his brain.

Perhaps Mathan *was* anxious, but Ewan was a nervous wreck.

Una reached out and grabbed for his hand, squeezing it gently. "Go and fetch him," she said.

"Aye?" Ewan asked, looking up and meeting her gaze.

"Aye. Let him see with his own eyes that all is well."

CHAPTER 33

It took Ewan no time at all to find Mathan. His trusty companion was at the bottom of the steps that led into the keep, howling mournfully.

"Do you want to see your lady, Mathan?" Ewan asked, crouching down to look in the dog's eyes as he scratched behind his ears. "And your pups as well?"

Mathan barked loudly once.

"Alright, laddie," Ewan said with a laugh, standing. "Let us go."

Mathan stuck to his heels as they climbed the stairs into the keep, crossed the Great Hall, and descended into the kitchens. As he walked, he thought about his younger brother. It was strange seeing Rabbie there, in a whelping pen, cradling a squirming pup in his overlarge hands.

Rabbie had always been quiet, but his stammer hadn't developed until their mother had died. And now, outside of his family and a few select others, Rabbie didn't speak to anyone. Many in the clan believed that he couldn't.

Being a laird's son was an interesting business. The heir was raised to lead. The second son might join the church, if he felt so inclined, or marry into a neighboring clan to solidify alliances. Ewan had always been the heir. Kenneth loved to joke he was the spare. And then there was Angus, third in line. All three of them had followed after their father like, well, puppies. Learning how to wield a sword, how to fight, how to lead, each with their own strengths.

But Rabbie had always been different. He'd worshipped their late father, but he hadn't been a part of the business of learning to lead. Instead, Rabbie had always preferred the company of animals. And here he had been, sitting on the kitchen floor with a healer, a dog, and a litter of puppies.

Ewan had felt a burning in the corners of his eyes, wishing that his mother could see it. When the older boys would tease Rabbie for always having a kitten in his pocket or not wanting to wrestle, his mother had always defended him. She'd always shown a keen interest in that kitten or listened to him talk about the twin lambs he'd helped feed or the foal that had been born.

When she'd died, Rabbie had scarcely left the stables unless forced, except for meals and any mandatory assembly the laird had commanded.

Whelping a litter of puppies was a usual sort of thing. Nothing extraordinary about it, truly. And yet, to watch his brother deftly arranging the pups, looking after Greer, consulting with Una, and tidying up the pen, you would have thought it the most holy of occupations for the amount of care Rabbie gave to every minute gesture and activity.

Ewan was bursting with pride for his brother, and for Una too, and meant to tell them so as he reentered the kitchen on Mathan's heels. But the sudden silence upon reentering the kitchen stopped him. Ewan had been gone no more than a handful of minutes, and yet the cheerful atmosphere he'd left in the kitchen was gone.

Rabbie was crouched next to the pen, his head bent close

to Una's over a small, gray pup. Unlike their siblings, this pup was not squirming or squeaking. It was quiet and still. Mathan rushed to the pen, nosing at Greer's face and neck. Ewan stood frozen in the doorway, watching Una gently but steadily rub the puppy with a soft cloth.

"What has happened?" he asked, feeling the rasp in his voice.

Una looked at him with sad eyes. "She had another. The ninth. She's smaller. Too small, perhaps. And nae verra strong, it seems."

Una's tone was sad yet matter of fact. It *was* a matter of fact. Sometimes foals and pups and lambs and kits didn't survive long in this world. Didn't Ewan know that better than anyone? Hell, sometimes *people* didn't survive long in this world either. Ewan felt his blood go cold as he watched Una stroke the little, gray head, crooning softly to the pup. Greer was hale and healthy, fussing over her other pups and letting Mathan fuss over her with a beatific look on her face. But the pup. What if the pup didn't make it?

Six months prior, if someone had told him that a dog would lose the smallest of nine pups in a litter, he would have shrugged a shoulder and said something like, "Och. 'Tis the way of it." Because it was the way of it, for some pups to be born sleeping or die shortly after.

But the horror washed over him as his brain slid from dogs to people. Because it was *also* the way of it for bairns to be born sleeping. Or to catch fevers or sickness, to fall from great heights, or to meet other grave misfortune. Or for fully grown, fully capable people to drop dead. God's bones, he'd been so worried about Una surviving her delivery that he'd forgotten about all the dangers that could happen before or after the event.

Jesu, Una was sitting on a drafty stone floor. What if she caught a cold *now*? What if she took a fever? Or fell down the stairs when she was rushing about to see to the wounded and broke her own neck? He brought a shaky hand to his mouth, covering his lips with his fingertips.

"Mathan," Rabbie called, breaking the quiet.

The great, shaggy dog hopped over to Rabbie. Una showed him the pup, and Mathan began to lick it. He licked the puppy's ears and nose, its chin and back. Una flipped the pup over, and Mathan licked the underside and feet before coming back to the nose and mouth.

The kitchen was quiet except for the sounds of puppies nursing and Mathan's licking. Fenella stood by the hearth, chewing on a thumbnail with Fiona by her side, leaning her head on Fenella's shoulder. Una and Rabbie were bent close over the puppy and Mathan's head.

As the minutes passed, the pup appeared to be breathing better and making more noise.

"Good boy, Mathan," Rabbie murmured, pressing his forehead against the dog's.

"Does it live?" Ewan croaked from his place by the door, his feet still frozen on the spot.

"Aye," Una replied, sounding tired. "But someone will need to monitor her to make sure she gets to eat. Keep the others from bullying her away."

"Maybe s-some g-goat's milk as well," Rabbie offered, and Una nodded.

"Aye," she said. "This wee 'un will need our help, won't you, my darling?"

The pup squeaked, and Rabbie reached over Una to shuffle the oldest puppy away from Greer, picking it up and cradling it in his hands so that Una could press the runt to the now-available teat.

"Una, you are tired," Rabbie said quietly, and Ewan shook himself back to the present. "I'll s-stay tonight."

"I can stay with you," she protested. Ewan had taken the

step forward to drag her away from the pen if he needed to, but Rabbie spoke before he could.

"I c-can do it. I w-want to do it."

"Are you certain?" Una asked, but the last word was broken by a jaw-cracking yawn.

"Aye. Go to bed."

Una nodded and rose to her feet, and Ewan wanted to know what magic Rabbie possessed to make his stubborn, defiant Una so readily compliant. Ewan crossed the room in two strides and took her hand to help her out of the birthing pen. Rabbie took her place on the floor, leaning against the wall with his long legs outstretched. Mathan lay down in the pen with his head on Rabbie's thigh.

"Send for me if you need anything," Una said.

"Aye," Rabbie said with a smile. "I'll t-take good care of them. Go and sleep."

It wasn't lost on Ewan that Rabbie had already developed a particular fondness for the smallest pup. It also wasn't lost on Ewan that Rabbie's stutter was slighter than he'd heard it in a very long time.

"Verra well," Una said, leaning into Ewan's side. "Take me to bed, m'laird."

She continued to lean heavily against him as they climbed the steps out of the kitchen, as they crossed the Hall, as they climbed the wheeled staircase to the bedchamber. She sat on the side of the bed and allowed Ewan to remove her shoes, her stockings. She held her arms up while he guided her dress over her head. Ewan took the comb from the bedside table and climbed onto the bed, kneeling behind her as he combed her hair and then rebraided it, tying it off with a scrap of ribbon.

Una crawled beneath the thick covers, pulling them up to her nose. Ewan undressed and climbed in behind her, gathering her solid warmth against his chest. In her sleep, she grabbed his arm and wrapped it around her, bringing his hand to her abdomen. Her belly was normally soft, but beneath his hand, beneath the usual softness, it felt hard.

He'd never noticed before. Her belly had looked much the way one's would after a large meal. But it wasn't that, was it? It was the baby. *His* baby, making her body change and exhausting her completely. He marveled at it, allowing himself, for the very first time, to imagine what it might be like to have bairns running around the keep, shrieking, chasing their uncles and harassing Fenella and Fiona into spoiling them rotten.

The crushing panic from earlier loomed close over his shoulder, like another person in the room. But he forced it back. He simply wouldn't let anything happen to them. He'd kept his siblings safe all these years. He would keep Una safe. He would keep their bairns safe. No matter what it took. No matter the cost.

That settled in his mind, he held Una closer and could almost forget the panic of earlier. Almost.

CHAPTER 34

A week later, Ewan was in the bailey, watching Angus spar with Rabbie. As Angus circled Rabbie, lunging toward and away, he softly called out instructions and corrections. Angus was a patient teacher. He never belittled a person for their mistakes but encouraged them to try again and again until they got it right. He'd been working with Rabbie for a few years now. For all that Rabbie absolutely detested violence, he showed great promise with a sword.

"He looks good," David said, coming to stand next to Ewan, the pair of them leaning against the wall of one of the outbuildings.

"Aye," Ewan replied.

"He doesnae enjoy it, though," David said. It wasn't a question.

"I believe," Ewan said after a long pause, "I believe he enjoys spending time with his brother. He enjoys the exertion. He enjoys learning and being good at something."

"But..."

Ewan sighed. "But he cannae stomach the thought of another man on the other end of his sword."

They were quiet. Ewan didn't relish either the thought or the reality of a man at the other end of his own sword, but there had been many times when it had been necessary. A laird had to defend his clan, which could not always rely upon diplomacy. Ewan didn't have much of a stomach for those bits of his job either.

"God willing, he'll never have to experience that," Ewan murmured. David nodded.

Just then, Rabbie maneuvered quickly, and the sword flew from Angus's hand. Angus cursed.

"Aye, Rabbie! There you go!" David crowed.

Rabbie looked over his shoulder at David and smiled, his cheeks a splotchy red from exertion.

"I'd say that's as good a place as any to stop for a rest," Angus said, stooping to pick up his blunted sword and clapping Rabbie on the shoulder as they walked toward the water barrel next to Ewan.

"You're getting good, my friend," David said, ruffling Rabbie's hair affectionately.

"He's better than any of us were at his age. Including you," Angus said, pointing the dripping wooden dipper at Ewan.

Rabbie blushed and looked at the ground, digging the toe of his boot into the hard dirt.

"You are right about that, Angus," David agreed with a laugh.

"Nae offense, Ewan," Angus said, his mouth against the dipper to drink.

"Why would I be offended? My pride isnae so fragile as that. Besides, I am proud to have such an excellent swordsman at my side, aye?" Ewan slapped Rabbie on the back, and Rabbie blushed an even deeper shade of red.

"I d-d-d-dinnae w-want to be g-g-good at it," he said.

Ewan's heart clenched sympathetically. "I ken you dinnae want to be good at it," he said. "I ken you dinnae like the thought of ever needing to use it. But someday, you might be called upon to protect something or someone you hold dear."

Rabbie looked miserable.

"Rabbie," Ewan said, resting his hands on his younger brother's shoulders, "should the time come, who better to protect Una? Or Cat? Or Fenella and Fiona and the others in the keep? Or my—" He broke off suddenly, swelling the thickness in his throat. "My children," he finished quietly.

Rabbie lifted his head and looked at Ewan, their green eyes so similar.

"Would you protect them?"

"Aye," Rabbie said without hesitation.

"Then you will keep practicing, aye?" Ewan said. "Nae because I plan to put you in harm's way, but should the need arise, I need you ready to protect all that we hold dear."

Rabbie nodded, wiping his mouth with the grimy back of his hand. He took the dipper from Angus and drank, his throat bobbing, before he picked up his sword and walked back to the training circle. Ewan watched as Rabbie flung himself at Angus with more strength and ferocity than before. Angus grunted as Rabbie's blunted sword came down hard at the juncture of his shoulder and neck.

"Goddamnit, Rabbie," he shouted, but Rabbie backed away from him, his sword gripped tightly in his hands, his eyes bright with determination. David looked at the scene pensively as Angus advanced on Rabbie, forcing him to move swiftly out of the way.

"Perhaps he never had stakes to imagine," David said quietly.

Ewan clenched his jaw tightly. Rabbie's eyes were wild, his hair sticking out at odd ends around his head. He looked possessed as he circled, waiting for Angus's attack, and Ewan knew he was picturing Una with a baby in arms, Fenella and Fiona in danger, Catriona, the other servants, the pups and horses and sheep. He was imagining himself as the last defense between them and doom.

There was commotion at the gate, and Ewan saw one of his men rushing through the portcullis, making his way into the bailey with great speed. He spotted Ewan and David against the building and hurried toward them.

"M'laird," the man panted.

"What news?" Ewan asked quietly, beckoning the man close.

"Cameron scouts in the woods," he said, breathless but quiet. "We saw two of them, but they slipped us."

"You are certain it was Cameron men?"

"Aye, m'laird," he replied. "One of them tore their plaid getting away." He handed a scrap of wool to Ewan, the Cameron tartan clearly visible.

"You dinnae think—" David said, breaking off abruptly.

"I dinnae ken," Ewan answered. "A few scouts at the border isnae so unusual."

"But they were nae at the border, m'laird," the man said, his breath returning to him. "They were within sight of the keep."

Ewan's blood ran icy cold. It was unspeakably bold to send men that far into an enemy's territory. A laird wouldn't dare try it unless he wanted to send a message.

"Tell the men on the wall to look sharp," he said and the man nodded, rushing away to see it done.

"Cameron's up to something," David said, and Ewan nodded, watching as Rabbie advanced on Angus, his innocence being shaved away with every slash of his sword. It made Ewan want to weep. Nothing was safe from a man like Cameron. Not Una. Not his clan. Not even his brother's gentle heart.

CHAPTER 35

The sun was bright and a light breeze blew down from the mountains as Una lay on her back in the grass beside the loch. The clouds in the sky cast fast-moving shadows on the grass around her, dappling the land in various shades of light and dark green, and she closed her eyes, watching the play of light and shadow against her lids.

She stretched like a cat, reaching her arms as far above her head as she could, relishing the pull in her shoulders and ribs as she did. She'd been busy. The sickness that had come upon her so suddenly at the beginning of her pregnancy had finally abated.

Greer lazed beside her in the grass, her month-old puppies flopped around her. Una lifted one hand to the rounding of her belly and the other to scratch behind Greer's silky ear. She heard a horse approach and cracked an eye open enough to see that it was Calman. She sighed. So much for peace. Ewan would be furious. She'd slipped her guard and gone to the loch alone, which was strictly against his orders.

For the past month, she had been forbidden to leave the

walls of the keep without a guard. That rule had extended to Catriona as well, but Una knew that was only to prevent a mutiny on her part. But no matter how many times she asked him to explain why, he always dodged the question.

Ewan brought Calman to a stop and dismounted. The horse ducked his huge head and nudged at Una's face, nibbling at her hair. She laughed, taking his velvet nose between her hands and stroking it.

"Dinnae eat my hair, precious boy," she said. "There is plenty of grass for you."

Calman snorted happily and then began munching at the grass a few feet away from her, his large body blocking the sun. Ewan crouched down next to her.

"Una," he said, his voice tight. "You promised you wouldnae leave the keep alone."

"I am nae alone," she replied, her eyes closed again. She didn't want to see his disapproval. "Greer is with me and nine other dogs. And now you're here. And Calman."

Hearing his name, the horse nickered happily.

"Una," Ewan said with an exasperated sigh. "You ken good and well what I mean."

"Tell me why," she said, her eyes open now and gazing into his.

"'Tisnae safe," he replied.

"Aye, but *why* isnae it safe?" Una insisted. "All of a sudden? It has never been unsafe before."

Ewan sighed again and rubbed his palm down his face.

"I need you to trust me, Una. Please? I cannae manage everything else if I'm sick with worry over your safety all the time. Have mercy, lass. I hardly sleep as it is."

He wasn't exaggerating. He hadn't been sleeping much at all. He came to bed far later than she and was always out of bed before her, as well. Always busy. Always taking care of something or conferring with David. He was wound too tightly, the cordage of his body near to snapping from the stress. She knew there was something going on that he wasn't telling her, some unnamed danger that kept him up at night. That annoyed her. But she worried for him, too.

Una couldn't make him talk and she couldn't take away his burdens, but she thought she might be able to ease him, if only for a short while, and Lord knew he needed it. She yanked on his collar, pulling him off balance and sending him toppling to the ground. He gathered her to his chest and rolled so that he didn't land on top of her. Her laugh was bright and loud, so loud that Greer rolled to her other side with an annoyed groan.

Ewan tried to rise, but she held fast to his shirt. "You will break if you get any more tense. We need to relax you, m'laird," she said, her voice husky and soft.

"Una," he groaned and tried to rise again.

"Dinnae go," she said, and she could see him at war with himself, between going and staying. She rubbed her calf against his and stroked a palm down his chest. She kissed his neck, licking the salt that clung to his skin. He grew hard against her hip.

"Una," he rasped against her ear as she glided her hands from his collar up his neck and into his hair, pulling his face toward hers.

He kissed her then, his lips warm and soft against hers. She savored the taste of him as her tongue met his. She nipped at his lower lip with her teeth, and he broke away to trail soft, slow kisses across her cheek and down her neck as his hand reached under the hem of her gown and travelled up her leg, bringing the heavy fabric with it as it went.

Una sighed happily as his fingers reached the apex of her legs and delved into the softness between. She mewled as he gently pressed a finger into her sheath, worrying her pearl in slow circles with his thumb. She arched her back when he added a second finger, relishing the stretch.

She was so much more sensitive lately. Or perhaps Ewan had just become a master proficient at playing her body like a well-loved instrument, one that was almost an extension of his own body. He kissed down her chest, crawling down, down, down her body until his tongue slid along her slick seam. She gasped, threading her hands tightly into his hair.

With his fingers in her sheath, gently stroking, he ran the tip of his tongue over her pearl, making quick, soft flicks against it. Una's mewling grew more pitched, mingling with her heavy panting as she writhed beneath him. She wanted to touch him, but she couldn't reach more than his head. She felt herself climbing the peak, growing desperate for relief as he continued to play her body. She felt herself squeezing tightly around his fingers. She knew he knew what she needed, but he was refusing her, refusing to let her have it. At least not yet.

Just as she felt herself nearing the precipice, Ewan ran the flat of his tongue down her slit to where his hand rested, fingers buried deep. She moaned in frustration, and he chuckled in response, the vibrations against her sex driving her wild.

"Ewan," she panted. "Dinnae make me beg."

He was teasing her, tightening the strings of her arousal until they threatened to snap. And then they did. She cried out with a sudden wail as he sucked her pearl into his mouth and she came undone, her legs shaking as she sobbed his name into her fist. He wiped his mouth against her inner thigh and smiled, crawling up the length of her body. Ewan captured her mouth with a deep kiss and Una tumbled headlong into it, relishing the feel of his weight above her, around her, the way she tasted on his mouth.

"Well, I feel better, but what about you?" Una asked with a

smile as she levered herself up, pressing him into the grass and climbing on top of him. She gathered her skirts out of the way as she straddled his body, until nothing remained between them but the rough weave of his plaid. As she adjusted her body to move the fabric, she felt a sharp punch from within. She gasped, her hands flying to her belly. Ewan sat up with a start, looking quickly around her before his hands ran down her sides, assessing.

"Una," he barked at her, concern heavy on his face, clearly believing her to have been harmed. "Are you hurt?"

"She kicked me!" Una exclaimed with a laugh.

Ewan stared at her with that same, intense frown he'd been wearing when he arrived. She smoothed her hand over his brow and down his cheek, trying to soothe him. She'd known it was coming. She knew that she'd feel the baby in earnest any day, not just the butterfly fluttering she'd felt for weeks prior. But it had still taken her utterly by surprise. She was delighted. Ewan clenched his teeth.

"Ewan," she said, turning his face towards hers, "Did you nae hear me? She's moving! That's the first time I've felt her do that."

"Aye," he choked, looking miserable.

"'Tis a good thing, Ewan," Una said quietly, feeling a threatening rush of tears gathering behind her eyes.

He must had heard the tremble in her voice because his gaze softened and he kissed her, trailing his lips over her cheeks, her forehead, her chin, before settling again on her own lips.

"I am happy, Una," he whispered. "It only took me by surprise. You promise you are well?"

"I am well. I dinnae ken that I have ever been so well in all my life. But there is something that could make me even better..." she said, arching an eyebrow as she circled her hips against his groin.

He groaned. "Are you certain it is well? You are certain it is safe?"

She nodded and he kissed her again, his mouth hungry against hers as she pressed herself tightly against his chest, feeling the hard ridge of his cock beneath the plaid again, rubbing herself against it. He gasped into her mouth. She shifted away to move the plaid and had nearly succeeded when a voice shouted from across the grassy space.

"M'laird! The scouts have a report!"

He stiffened in her arms, all of his ease and good humor gone like the flame of snuffed candle. He shifted her off of his lap and stood, bending down to pull her to her feet.

"Come," he said. "We must return. It isnae safe out here like this."

"I dinnae want to go back just yet," she protested.

"It wasnae a request, Una. Come. We're going home."

He was ordering her. Commanding her. She didn't like it.

"Nae until you tell me what's happening"

Ewan clenched his jaw and squeezed his eyes shut as he took a deep breath. "What is happening is that I told you it isnae safe out here. That is all you need to know. I can protect you, but only if you listen. Come, we can ride back to the keep together."

He wasn't going to give her a real answer. She could see that. And there was no use arguing with him because he'd only hoist her into his arms and carry her back if she protested too much.

She lifted her shin and strode past him. "I'll walk."

Greer followed close at her heels, the puppies gamboling behind her. She heard Calman and Ewan following after her, walking briskly until they had caught up. He took her hand in his. She was angry, and a very large part of her wanted to yank her hand away and storm off ahead, to stew in her anger and make him feel it. She didn't like being kept in the dark, and he *knew* that. Surely he had to know it. But the way he gripped her hand gave her pause. He held her hand as if he was clinging to the side of a boat in an angry sea, as if she was the only thing keeping him afloat. And so she wrapped her fingers around his and allowed it.

When they reached the courtyard, he drew her close, wrapping his arms around her and kissing her forehead gently before letting his hand drop to the swell of her belly.

"Una, I am asking you to trust me," he said, his forehead resting against hers. "Please. There is naught that you need worry about. I will keep you safe. I swear it."

She didn't believe him. His eyes were too strained, his jaw too tight, his pulse too fast in his throat. But she nodded, knowing that he wouldn't tell her then, no matter how much she protested. She climbed the steps to the keep, but before she disappeared inside, she looked into the bailey, where Ewan was listening to a report from a cluster of his men. Judging by the way his eyebrows had slammed together and his fists clenched at his side, there was much for her to worry about.

CHAPTER 36

Months passed. More Cameron scouts had been seen too close for comfort and each time, Ewan's men had not engaged. Not because they weren't capable, but because Ewan believed that making Malcolm Cameron believe that he was complacent and unworried, open to attack, would encourage Cameron to take bolder action. The MacDonalds would be ready.

There were many preparations being quietly made, weapons and armor forged, increased training that took place now in the bailey instead of the grassy spread outside the wall, away from spying eyes. The men faced the looming threat with a grim determination that made Ewan proud at the same time it made panic a permanent fixture in his chest.

He was hardly sleeping now, not catching more than a few hours a night, though he had begun going to bed at more regular hours to appease Una. She did not believe him when he told her nothing was wrong. Why would she? If nothing was truly wrong, he wouldn't have placed so many restrictions on the keep and its occupants, but especially Una.

He had mandated that she bring Joan or Cat with her

wherever she went, and now they were to be accompanied at all times by at least three guards. No matter what. If she went to take a nap, the three guards waited outside. If she was tending a wounded MacDonald, the three guards would stand close at hand. If she attended a birth outside the keep, he sent ten men to surround the cottage.

His men followed her everywhere, not only for protection from Cameron, but also because his anxiety plagued him. All night, as he lay next to her sleeping body, he battled visions of her falling down the stairs or meeting some other dreadful harm. Earlier that day, he'd forbidden her from going to the stables. She hadn't ridden in months, but she liked to visit Calman and the other horses and bring them apples and carrots. But he'd had a dream of her being kicked by a horse and had been nearly sick in the bed upon waking. Enough danger lurked outside his control; he would mitigate whatever threats he could within his sphere.

He knew that he should tell her about Cameron's scouts. But the last thing he wanted to do was frighten her. Because she didn't have to worry. He would protect her. With his dying breath, he would protect her. And so long as she continued to follow his rules, she would be safe.

But it had been months of balancing Una's growing frustration with Cameron's continued threat. Ewan felt the tension rising around him, like the sparking heaviness in the air just before a summer storm. Something would happen soon.

As autumn began, he began to feel as if he would snap. Every groan, every sharp intake of breath, every contortion of Una's face as she learned to navigate her new body made him jump to attention. She was more ungainly than she'd been, which made sense, as her belly was big enough to make Fiona speculate that she was carrying twins.

"All women carrying at this stage are clumsy," Fiona had

reassured him. "I couldnae keep hold of anything without dropping it when I neared birthing my bairns."

She'd said it cheerfully, as if it were a simple fact, easily shrugged off. As if the thought of Una tripping or losing her balance and falling down the stairs wasn't enough to send him spiraling. And so he also ordered two servants to follow her in addition to the guards and Joan, to ensure that she did not fall.

He knew she resented it, but he couldn't seem to stop himself. They had fought daily. Una was as mad as a cat in a sack, and he couldn't blame her.

It was a blustery day, and Ewan had missed supper in the Great Hall because he'd been called to settle a dispute between two neighbors in the village over who had rights to the litter of piglets that had been born late, as one owned the sow and one owned the sire. He was bone-weary and irritable as he entered the keep. A guard named John met him at the door and took his cloak.

"Tell Fiona I'll be taking supper in my chamber," he said, his tone far sharper than he intended.

"M'laird," the man said, "I am to tell you that my lady has already ordered you a supper and that it is waiting upstairs."

Ewan nodded his head. "You have my thanks, John."

He dragged his weary body up the stairs and down the hall. When he opened the chamber door, he saw Una arranging food on a small table by his chair near the hearth. She looked up when he entered and smiled. How long had it been since he had seen her smile?

She gestured to the chair before the hearth, and he went to it. He dropped into the seat and bent down to unlace his boots.

"You look tired, Ewan," she said, her voice honeyed.

She stood behind him, her hands on his shoulders. He grunted as she began to work the knots with her fingers, pressing against his resistant muscles, digging into the burls of tension with her thumbs.

"Eat, Ewan. You need your strength," Una murmured, a hint of a suggestion in her voice. Ewan felt his blood heat in response.

There was a platter of cold meats and cheese, sliced apples, fresh bread with thickly slathered butter, a mug of ale. He ate it quickly, famished, as Una's hands worked their way from his shoulders and to his neck. She massaged his neck, raking her knuckles down the tight cords of muscle and then shifted her hands to his scalp, her fingers raking through his hair and pressing gently at his temples, making slow circles.

If he'd been a cat, he'd have been purring loudly by the time he finished his simple supper and she shifted her hands down to his chest, slipping beneath the dirty fabric of his leine shirt.

He closed his eyes, his head listing to one side. She pulled at his leine until the hem came free from his plaid and lifted it until Ewan was forced to raise his arms so she could sweep it over his head. She dropped it to the ground and circled him, coming to stand between his spread knees.

Una bent and pressed her lips to his, bracing her hands on the arms of the chair. He leaned forward, meeting her kiss with enthusiasm. Between the advanced stage of her pregnancy and how furious he had made her of late, she had not come to him like this in a long time. He groaned and thrust his tongue into her mouth, drawing her closer. She straightened and he pressed his forehead, his lips, against the large swell of her belly as she sifted her fingers through his hair.

"I've missed you, Una," he whispered, burning for her.

"Aye," she answered. "I've missed you as well."

Una lowered herself to her knees, rubbing her palms up and down his thighs beneath his plaid. He held his breath as she reached beneath it and took his cock in her hands. After a few strokes, she released him, unbuckling his belt with quick, impatient hands. She yanked the fabric of the plaid apart, revealing his naked body, his stiff arousal. Before he could say a word, she had the swollen head in her mouth. Una lifted her lashes, meeting his eye, and he groaned. She sucked, her tongue rubbing along the slit at the tip.

"Una," he breathed, "Are you certain?"

This was the first time she had ever taken him into her mouth. Once, she had confided in him that Malcolm Cameron had demanded such attentions whenever she was in her courses and that, out of necessity, she had learned how to finish the deed quickly. She had never offered to pleasure Ewan this way, and he, always wanting to be sensitive of her past, had never asked.

She nodded and slid her mouth down his length. When the tip of his erection came to the back of her throat, he heard her gag. She froze, and his gut clenched. He placed his hands on her shoulders and drew her gently off. "Una, you dinnae have to—"

"Nay," she said vehemently. "I want to."

"But you—"

"You are nae him," she said, her eyes focused on his face.

"I am nae him," Ewan repeated carefully, cursing the fact that he couldn't seem to escape Cameron. The threat of him loomed outside the walls, the ghost of his cruelty haunting within.

"But could you… speak to me?" Una whispered. "To remind me?"

As if he could refuse her anything she asked. As she took him into her mouth again, he told her how good she was, how beautiful, how brave, how strong. His voice was a rasp. She moaned loudly around him, and it was the vibration of that sound, coupled with the image of her bright eyes gazing up at him, her mouth stretched around him, that made him buck his hips and groan like an animal.

"Sorry," he hissed. "Sorry. I promise nae to use your mouth like that."

But she lunged deeper against him, and Ewan gripped the arms of the chair.

"Una," he growled low in his throat.

She slid her mouth up and down his length, one hand squeezing the base of his cock while the other gently fondled his bollocks. He felt his breathing grow ragged, his body tight as a bowstring from head to toe.

"Una, I dinnae want to spend like this," he said through gritted teeth. "I want to come with you."

But she ignored him, bringing the head of his cock into her throat and swallowing. He shouted. The pain of holding back his seed was all-consuming, but he forced it back, gently pressing her back far enough for his arousal to leave her mouth with a pop. She whined, but before she could come back to him, he'd bent and scooped her into his arms, standing quickly and striding to the bed.

He placed her on the mattress and helped her to remove her shift before he gruffly said, "Turn over."

With a gasp, she did, shifting onto her hands and knees. The urge to thrust into her was intense as he climbed into the bed behind her, but he would never do such a thing without her leave, not without discussing it beforehand.

He ran a trembling hand up the long length of her spine, gathering her shift and guiding it over her hips as he asked, "Are you ready?"

She nodded and he entered her with shallow thrusts of his hips. Una dropped her face to the mattress, her weight on her forearms, and moaned. He fucked her slowly, reaching around and wedging his hand between her thigh and the swell of her belly to fondle the bundle of nerves at the crest of her sex, which had her keening and clenching around him in a matter of moments.

It didn't take long. The effort to resist spending in her mouth had drained him, and so, as soon as he felt the flutter and squeeze of her sex around him, signaling her release, he bucked and let go, his own release pulsing so violently that he collapsed to the bed beside her when it was done, utterly spent.

He did force himself to rouse after a few moments, cleaning them both with a wet cloth, before he returned to the bed and tucked her against him, her belly round and big propped against him and her head on his shoulder. She fell asleep almost instantly, and for the first time in as long as he could remember, Ewan felt as if he might sleep as well. She was safe in his arms, he'd received no report of any looming threat that day, and he was just so relaxed, his body so heavy and sated. She was safe, and he would continue to keep her safe.

CHAPTER 37

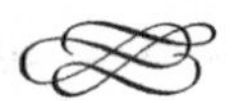

For the past few months, Una had awoken in an empty bed with a fire blazing in the hearth. Ewan stoked and built it up before he left so that she would be warm in his absence. But the next morning, Una woke with Ewan wrapped around her like a vine. The fire in the hearth had all but died. The faint light through the window coverings told that it was nearly dawn. She smiled as she realized that he had gone to sleep with her and had not woken up at some ungodly hour to see to whatever business had made him look ten years older than he actually was. He had stayed with her.

She had also slept better than she had in quite some time. Ordinarily, she woke several times a night to use the privy or to cushion her belly differently as the baby kicked and rolled. But propped against his side, she'd slept deeply until morning. She wanted nothing more than to huddle down deeper in the blankets and closer to his body, but she desperately needed to use the privy.

Una crept out from beneath the covers, crossing her arms

tightly over her chest, her skin erupting with goosebumps from the cold and she shivered. She had her shift on the floor, but Ewan's plaid, discarded on the chair, with its yards and yards of fabric would be so much warmer wrapped around her and it would cover enough to keep her decent as she went to the privy down the hall.

The room was dark and Una couldn't see where she was stepping as she hurried across the room to the chair, her bladder full and aching. Her discarded shift had tangled around her ankles and she was halfway to the ground before she registered that she was falling. Time slowed down as she careened toward the floor. A soft cry flew from her mouth as she landed in a heap on her side, the fabric still wrapped around her legs, the stone floor icy cold against her bare skin. With a shout of alarm, Ewan flew from the bed and landed naked in a half crouch behind her, no doubt woken from a dead sleep expecting an attack.

"Ewan," she whined pitifully from the floor, not because she was in pain, but because her bladder was near to bursting now and she had no idea how she would be able to stand on her own without it releasing. "Privy," she said, panting.

"Una, are you hurt?" Ewan shouted, dropping to his knees beside her and running his hands all over her to assess what it was too dark for his eyes to see.

"Privy!" Una wailed.

Ewan scooped her into his arms and strode quickly down the hall, the two of them naked as the day they were born. He sat her gently on the stone privy seat and, at her urging, left. He returned a few moments later with his plaid bunched in his arms, still without a stitch of clothing on himself.

"You're naked."

Ewan looked down, as if this was the first he'd noticed it. His gaze was intense, all of the relaxed peace from the night before gone. After completing her business, Una stood slowly, wincing when her hip pinched, as it sometimes did when she stood up. Ewan wrapped the plaid around her and, before she could protest, swept her up into his arms again and stalked back down the hall to their chamber.

He deposited her on the chair and rebuilt the fire, the muscles of his back bunched with tension. Una sighed, seeing all of her hard work from the night before destroyed. Fighting him hadn't worked, and so she'd meant to try diplomacy instead. She'd meant to ease and relax him enough that he might confide in her and help her understand what had made him so fearful and preoccupied.

When the fire burned brightly in the hearth, Ewan stood and turned to face her.

"What happened, Una?"

"It was dark. I had desperate need of the privy and I was hurrying to reach it. I tripped over my shift on the floor and fell."

"You're injured."

"I am fine, Ewan. I'll have a bruise or two, but I'm fine."

"But you could have been injured. Or the bairn—"

"Is fine," she cut him off. "We're both fine."

He began to pace, stalking back and forth across the room, dragging his hands through his hair and muttering to himself. Una started to stand.

"Nay," he bit out with a sharp gesture. "Stay."

"I'm thirsty," she said, pointing to the pitcher and cup on the bedside table.

"I'll get it," he growled and pointed his finger. "You stay put."

Una settled back into the chair, watching as he poured water, half worried he'd break the cup in his hands if he gripped it any harder. He stomped back to her, handing her the water with care before he resumed his pacing. She drank, stretching her toes out toward the fire and relishing the warm tingles that crept beneath the plaid as the chill slowly left the room.

After a while, Ewan stopped pacing. "I've decided something," he said, grabbing his discarded leine from the pile on the floor and dragging it over his head.

"Why do I have a feeling that I willnae like whatever you've decided?"

"You willnae leave this room until after the babe is born."

She laughed.

"What is so funny?"

"You cannae be serious. You want to confine me to this room for another few weeks? Ewan, dinnae be ridiculous."

"I am nae being ridiculous," he said through his teeth. "I am trying to keep you safe. You could have been seriously injured."

"I fell *in this room*."

"Aye! And imagine if you'd fallen outside of it! You could have fallen down the stairs and broken your neck. 'Tis settled. You will stay here where I can be assured you are safe."

White hot fury coursed through Una's body with a suddenness that left her breathless.

"Nay," she said, her voice low and steady amidst the torrent of her feelings.

"Nay?"

"I willnae stay in this room until I deliver. And you cannae make me."

"I can lock you in. I can instruct the guards to prevent you from leaving."

"Lock me in? Like a prisoner?" The effort to keep her voice under control was exhausting. The last word was shrill as it left her mouth.

He scrubbed a hand over his face. "Nay," he barked. "You are nae a prisoner. But by the saints, lass, have mercy on me. I cannae let anything happen to you!"

"By locking me in a room?" Una spat. "Just like Malcolm Cameron did?"

He glared at her. "You compare me to that man?" His tone was so quiet she had to strain to hear. Then he shouted, "I am nothing like him!"

She struggled to her feet, standing belly to belly with him. "He made me a prisoner, and that's exactly what you aim to do. I've tolerated your daft restrictions and your men and brothers following me around like baby ducks because I ken that you're terrified and you're trying to control everything you can. But I willnae stand for this, Ewan MacDonald. I willnae stand for it!"

As they glared at each other, Una remembered the date. Their handfast would end tomorrow. And then what? He would want to marry her. He asked her early every day. And she knew that, if she said yes, he would cart her off to the nearest priest without a moment's delay.

But did *she* want to marry *him*? Was it to be like this for the rest of their lives? Him keeping secrets, boiling in his own anxiety without sharing it with her? Restricting the lives and freedom of her and their children because the only way he could sleep at night was to carefully control their every move?

She couldn't live like that. She *wouldn't.*

"Ewan," she said, placing a palm against his heaving chest, trying to reason with him. "You must listen to me. I am fine. I am careful. And, except for this morning, I've never given you a single cause for worry. You can keep the baby ducks following me and I willnae say a word, but I'll go mad if you keep me in here. 'Tis bad for both me and the babe to put me in that situation."

"'Tis bad for both of you if you leave and fall," he said mulishly.

"I am fine! We are fine! I can climb stairs and stitch wounds and walk the bailey and, heaven forbid, pet a horse just fine, Ewan! Nothing is going to happen to me! I am as healthy as ever!"

"Then why do you wince and groan and act so verra much in pain? Dinnae think I havenae noticed, Una!"

"Because I am in the final weeks of carrying a babe, you foolish man! It is hard on the body to carry one this large! But that doesnae mean there is something wrong with me! Certainly nothing that setting every man in the clan to guard me would solve."

"You dinnae ken that," he growled.

"Why willnae you listen to me?" Una's patience, as thin as it had been, was gone, leaving her with only that molten anger. "I dinnae tell you how to make war or use a sword or govern a clan. And yet you seem hell-bent on telling me what I can and cannae do as an expecting woman."

He opened his mouth to respond but she charged ahead. "I want nae part of this version of you, Ewan. You may want different things than Cameron did—he kept me trapped because he was jealous, and you would do it because you're afraid—but I willnae stay here for you to make me a prisoner, no matter how much you believe it is for my own good. You ken nothing about my own good, and you dinnae trust me to know either. You may be doing the wrong thing for the right reason, but it is still wrong!"

She stepped away from him, and he followed, trying to close the distance, but she flung out her arm, stopping him in his tracks. "Nay," she spat, tears falling from her eyes. "Dinnae follow me until you're ready to pull your head out of your arse and *listen* to me. *Talk* to me. Nae order me about. I willnae hear that."

As Una walked quickly down the hallway, she heard a frustrated roar. She knocked on Joan's chamber. Her friend opened the door to her and ushered her inside. There, wrapped in Joan's embrace, she wept in earnest.

CHAPTER 38

The next morning, Una woke long before the sun. She had come to bed late and found the chamber empty. At some point, Ewan had returned. She had a hazy half-memory of him climbing into the bed and shifting so close to her that she could feel his warmth.

"Can we talk, Una?" he had whispered.

She had adjusted the blanket higher over her shoulder and grumbled that they would talk in the morning.

It was nearly morning now, and Ewan lay on his back, one hand over his chest, the other tucked behind his head. He snored softly, his face relaxed in sleep in a way she hadn't ever seen it when he was awake.

She slipped silently from the bed and dressed. It was the last day of the handfast, and her heart was heavy. The night had passed in a slow fit as Una's mind turned over and over what to do. She still didn't have an answer.

She knew Ewan was only trying to protect her. She also knew that his fear of losing her was making him unable to see reason. But she couldn't live like that. She shouldn't have to. And yet, walking away wasn't nearly so easy a prospect as she would have thought a year ago. The truth was that, somewhere along the way, she had fallen in love with him. Horribly, irrationally, inconveniently in love with him.

They needed to talk. They needed to sit across from one another and each speak their piece and find a way to *make* peace between them. Because she *didn't* want to leave. Not really. She loved her life here. She loved the MacDonalds and the keep and Fiona and Fenella and Mathan and Calman and everyone else she had come to know.

She could go to the Stewarts. Perhaps she *should*. She had an obligation, and not just to herself and her bairn, but also to Blair. She had tried multiple times to broach the subject of sending for her friend, but every time, Ewan put it off with an excuse. It wasn't the right time. He couldn't spare the men. He needed to think about it.

Perhaps she had been naive in thinking it would be so easy to secret an enemy away. It's why she hadn't actually told Ewan *who* her friend was. Perhaps that was a mistake. Ewan might have welcomed him with gladness as a means to spite Malcolm Cameron. Or he might turn him away outright and leave Blair vulnerable to the greater world, which was not kind to loners.

Aye, they needed to talk. About the restrictions, about the rules, about listening to her expertise, about Ewan needing to talk to someone—anyone—about his worry so that the panic didn't live alone in his brain, consuming him alive. And she would talk about Blair by name and impress upon Ewan the importance of sending for him. She would demand that they make a plan *together*.

But before she could talk to Ewan about any of that, she needed to clear her head. She needed to gather more herbs and roots to replenish her supply before the ground became too hard and the baby was born. Digging and gathering were perfect activities for thinking, and she got some of her best ideas while doing so. She would go to the woods, she would do her work, and by the time she returned, she would have a plan of action for how to approach Ewan.

Una tucked her dagger into her boot and wrapped her plaid. The corridors were empty, and wasn't that a marvel. Perhaps the men were changing shifts, thinking it a safe time to do so since she usually wasn't up and about so early.

She ducked into the stable to check on Greer, who was sleeping in a pile with her puppies and Mathan. They hardly looked like puppies anymore, a tangle of long limbs and tails in the straw. Una smiled as she fondled Greer's ears. Greer made to follow her, but Una shook her head.

"I'll be back soon to visit with you, mo cridhe," Una said, scratching Greer's ears one more time before standing clumsily to leave, her belly making her feel ungainly and slow.

Hugging the wall and keeping to the shadows, Una crept to the gate, which had just been opened for the flow of people that came and went from the keep and its walls during the day. Stealth was not easy for a woman so close to delivering, but the stars aligned and she slipped through the gate and past the wall without being noticed. She hugged the curtain wall, lest the watch see her, until she could cut across the field to the forest.

A light frost had fallen in the night, making the ground sparkle in the dying moonlight. As she approached the forest, the sun broke over the horizon, sending spears of light piercing through the changing trees. She remembered riding through this wood more than a year ago, wrapped in Ewan's plaid. So much had changed.

Una sank to her knees and began breaking the earth with her digging stick, harvesting valerian roots and dusting them off. Her back ached, and she sat back on her heels to rub it. The morning was cold and clear, the forest quieter than usual. She needed to gather wild garlic now. She used the tree beside her for support as she stood, brushing the dead leaves from her gown.

She picked her way slowly through the forest, going deeper and deeper into the wood, farther from the keep. She'd come this far before and knew her way home. The babe was still, as she usually was when Una walked.

The keep would be awake by now, and Una knew Ewan had probably discovered her absence. If not yet, then soon, and then he'd be after her with every available man. Perhaps it had been selfish of her to slip away, but she needed the space to think, something she could not do with an entourage. What was more, there was no better proof of her fitness to be independent than returning safely after *being* independent. She wasn't going to fall or be kicked by a horse. She wasn't going to be anything but careful.

The garlic grew wild and abundant, and Una smiled at the bounty as she knelt and began digging, listening to the wind gently whistling through the barren trees. Further, water ruffled through a burn, not yet frozen, whispering against the rocks as it passed.

And then a twig snapped.

Had it been a man? A stag? Fear rose in her belly. But then she remembered that Ewan had men patrolling the lands surrounding the keep. No doubt it was one of his men. Who else would come this close?

She remembered her sgian dubh hidden in her boot and had bent to grab it when out of the dawn mist stepped a tall, looming shadow of a man. His face was obscured by a long, unkempt beard and shaggy hair that hung to his chest. But she would still know him anywhere.

"Blair?" she gaped, shocked beyond words.

His eyes darted around him, and he reached her in two long strides.

"Una, what the hell are you doing out here?" Blair said in a low growl. "Jesu, you've got to hide. Now."

"Hide? Why would I need to hide? And what the hell are *you* doing here?"

"There isnae time," he insisted, grabbing her by the upper arm and dragging her toward a fallen tree. "They must nae see you."

"Who, Blair? What in God's name is going on?"

"Keep your voice down," he said, his teeth clenched and his eyes wild. "If you have any sense at all, you'll get down now and nae make a sound."

In the near distance, hoofbeats. The shifting of a leather saddle in the cold air. Desperate, wild panic clawed at her as she realized that the sounds were not coming from the direction of the keep but from deeper in the woods.

The horses drew closer. That there was more than one was unnerving, but not as much as their silence. Were the MacDonald men looking for her, they would be calling her name and wanting her to find them. But judging by the slow plodding of the horses and the silence otherwise, she couldn't help but assume that these people did not want to be noticed.

"Una, dinnae drag your feet. Get your arse inside that hollow tree."

"I willnae fit!"

"You must try," he said, shaking her gently with the hand still gripping her bicep. "You must, Una."

But the hoofbeats drew closer. Una felt frozen on the spot, paralyzed by fear, unable to follow even Blair's simple commands.

"Goddamnit," he cursed under his breath just as a large bay horse stepped into the clearing.

"Ah, Blair! You are nae as useless as I thought!"

Una's blood went cold as she looked into the eyes of

Giffard, Laird Cameron's right hand and most trusted man. He was the captain of his guard, his closest advisor, and what most resembled a friend, if a man like Malcolm was capable of friendship.

"What do we have here?" he said, dismounting and walking toward her, his eyes glinting with malice. "Una? What a pleasant surprise! It has been too long!"

The words were friendly, but the tone made her shiver. Like a cow before the slaughter, Una looked out of the corner of her eye and saw shadows in the trees become clearer, men on horses. Dozens of them.

Giffard chuckled, gleefully rubbing his hands together. "Of all the boons my laird expected, this could nae have been farther from anything he dared to hope for. Una, how fortunate we found you! Now we can rescue you and bring you home."

"I willnae go anywhere with you, Giffard," Una spat.

Giffard clucked his tongue. "I cannae leave you here in enemy territory, so verra far from home. It wouldnae be right." He turned his gaze to Blair. "Bring her here."

Blair squeezed Una's arm before towing her closer to Giffard.

"Blair, I want you to ride ahead and send a man to fetch the laird."

"He has important business. Surely this can wait until he returns next week," Blair protested quietly, but Giffard cut him off.

"Ride ahead and send someone to fetch him now!" he barked before turning back to Una with a serpent's smile. "There is nae business more important than bringing one of his lost lambs home."

Blair clenched his jaw but stormed across the clearing, back in the direction from which he'd come. The men had dismounted and closed ranks around them. Before she could scream, Giffard had grabbed her wrist and spun her around so that her arm was twisted behind her back, her back to his front. He grabbed her other wrist and wrenched it back as well, bringing her to her knees.

Una felt as if she would be sick. Why had she left the walls without telling anyone that she was going? Joan would have kept a secret. She could have told her. As it was, nobody would know where she had gone or what had happened to her.

A single sob escaped her.

"Quiet," Giffard said.

Una looked up to see Blair glance over his shoulder at her before disappearing into the fog. She screamed, and with a blinding burst of pain at the back of her head, the world went dark around her.

CHAPTER 39

Ewan rolled over and reached for Una, startling when his hand brushed nothing but a cool sheet. Perhaps she had gone to the privy. He had demanded that she wake him whenever she needed to use it so that he could help her, but he also knew for a fact that she never did. He waited, focusing on his breath, until enough time had passed that she would have returned from the privy.

His hackles rose, but he forced himself to remain calm. Perhaps she had gone to the kitchen for an early breakfast. She had been hungry at odd hours lately. His entire day had already been spoken for, but he wouldn't be starting on any of those items until he talked to Una. He needed to apologize. He needed to tell her about the looming Cameron threat. Somewhere in the midst of their not speaking last night, he'd realized that she had a right to know.

He'd done the wrong thing for the right reasons. But that didn't make it the right thing.

He'd tell her everything and then he would apologize for being such a horse's ass. Perhaps she could help him. Perhaps she had a tincture for worry such as his.

With a sigh, he dressed and made his way downstairs. The Great Hall was filling as men made their way to the long tables to break their fast. His brothers and sister sat at the table on the dais, and Ewan wove his way through the crowd to reach them. As he sat, Catriona ladled oats into a bowl and handed it to him.

He ducked his head and ate.

Angus elbowed him in the side. "You look miserable, Ewan. What ails you?"

"I am fine," Ewan replied sullenly.

"It could be that our dear brother is so forlorn because his lady is upset," Kenneth said brashly, humor in his eyes.

"Drop it, Kenneth," Ewan growled.

"Wh-wh-what's the matter with Una?" Rabbie's deep concern was written plainly on his face in the furrow of his brow.

"She's fine, Rabbie," Ewan said, meeting his brother's eye. "She's just a wee bit… angry with me. Apparently, I've been unreasonable."

Cat choked on her oats, coughing loudly, and Kenneth's eyebrows shot high into his hairline.

Kenneth smiled. "What was it this time? Dinnae tell me she's angry about the wedding? Surely you are nae trying to interfere with her planning?"

"There has nae been any planning," Ewan gritted out.

"If you must know," Cat interjected saucily, "Una is angry with Ewan because he's been a menace of late and insists on treating her like a prisoner in her own home. Willnae let her leave. Willnae let her do her job. Willnae—"

"Her job is to be the lady of this keep. How can she be the lady of the keep if she's tromping about the land?"

"Her job, Ewan, is a healer. And she cannae do that confined to her chamber."

"She isnae confined to her chamber!" Ewan protested.

"Though she could do a fair number of things confined there," Kenneth said with a wink.

"Shut up, Kenneth!" Cat, Ewan, and Angus all said sharply in unison.

"Only because you ken she'd gut you like a fish if you tried to keep her there!" Cat hissed.

Ewan dropped his forehead to the table. Rabbie reached over and gripped his shoulder.

"You cannae protect her from everything, Ewan," Cat said, her voice softening.

"I've got to see her," Ewan said, sitting suddenly upright. He turned to see Joan hastening toward the table.

"Joan, are you well?" Cat asked, reaching for her hand.

"I am well. But m'laird, I cannae find Una anywhere. Is she still asleep?"

Ewan's body went cold and he shook his head.

"I went looking for her to ask for her advice on behalf of one of the servants. I've looked everywhere, all over the keep, and I cannae find her."

"Everywhere, Joan?" Ewan asked. "The stables?"

"Aside from the laird's chamber, I've turned this place upside down. Fiona and Fenella helped. If she isnae in bed, then she isnae here?"

Ewan tried to keep his face calm as he stood. Angus shot an uneasy look his way, and Kenneth's eyes were wide with shock.

"We should nae panic," Ewan said, mastering himself. "'Tis possible we've only missed her. Let's look in her usual haunts again. Kenneth, Angus, ask around the village. See if anyone has seen her. Rabbie and Connor, search the stable and outbuildings. Cat, stay here with Joan in case she returns."

"Where will you go, Ewan?" Cat asked as he stepped off the dais.

"To speak to the watch on the wall," he said over his shoulder, thinking that if they'd let her out without noticing or notifying him, he'd throttle them all.

"But it's freezing," Cat called after him, horrified. "Surely she wouldnae go out in this weather!"

"Someone might have needed her assistance. I am certain there is a perfectly logical explanation for where she has gone," he said with a confidence he didn't feel as he turned and left the Hall.

Behind him, he heard Cat clap her hands loudly. "Why are you lot still standing here? Be gone!"

A half hour later, Ewan descended the steps that led to the first watchtower. None of the guards on the wall had seen her leave. They hadn't seen *anyone* leave. That gave him hope that she was within the walls and they had just missed her. Perhaps she'd been in the stables with Greer or had gone to their chamber to fetch something after he'd gone.

But that hope began to crumble as he saw his brothers standing in the bailey, talking closely and quietly with David.

"Nothing?" Ewan asked as he approached.

"Nay," Angus said quietly. "Nae one in the village has seen her, and Rabbie says the only people in the stable are the master and grooms."

Ewan's heart pounded. He racked his brain trying to think of where else she might have gone. There was a small chance, the slightest of chances, really, that she could have slipped out without the guards noticing her, that she had gone to the woods to gather medicines, as she had done often before he'd confined her to the blasted keep.

"The woods," he said flatly.

"You think she snuck out? Hard for a lass in her condition

to sneak anywhere," Kenneth said, but without any of his usual jesting tone.

"If she kept to the shadows, aye. She's clever, and she'd have gone out of her way to avoid being seen." *Because of him.*

Guilt felt like poison in his veins. If anything happened to her, the blame rested squarely on his head.

He called for the stable master to ready his horse. Calman stamped impatiently as the groom saddled him. Ewan, his brothers, and David mounted their horses, and before Ewan even gave the command, Calman raced out of the bailey and through the gate as if his tail was ablaze, running over the dead grass toward the forest. Ewan leaned low over Calman's neck with Mathan close behind. They'd had to lock Greer and the puppies in the stable, and he'd heard her howling long after he'd passed through the gate.

"Fan out," he called over his shoulder as they approached the tree line. They searched a broad swath of the woods, following any path she might have taken and walking deeper into the forest than she was likely to have gone, just to be certain.

Una was not there.

Ewan's heart pounded. He racked his brain trying to think of where else she might have gone. She couldn't have gotten far, not in her condition. He pulled frantically on his hair and tried to think but panic made his thoughts hard to grasp. Anything could have happened to her. She had vanished without a trace.

David pulled his horse up close to Calman. "Ewan," he murmured. "You dinnae think—"

Ewan swallowed thickly. Because the possibility was entirely too terrible to consider. And yet what other possibility was there?

"Do you think she went back to her da?" Connor asked. "Is that it?"

"Nay!" Kenneth answered. "She once told me she'd die before she went back."

"What about to the Stewarts?" Angus asked.

Ewan shook his head. The Stewarts had been her backup plan. And it was very likely that she would want to go there now, especially after he had been such an unmitigated ass. But she wouldn't have gone without telling him.

"She would nae go there on her own." Ewan closed his eyes and fought back the bile rising in his throat. "I dinnae think she went anywhere on her own."

There was a long pause as they all considered that statement.

"You think she was taken," Angus asked.

Ewan looked at David, whose face was as drawn and tight as his felt.

"Ewan," Angus pressed, narrowing his eyes. "Do you have reason to suspect that Cameron took her?"

He didn't need to answer that from the way his brothers were glaring at him, no one more fiercely than Rabbie.

Ewan marshaled himself. He should have been more forthcoming with his brothers as well as Una, should have told them of his concerns. He'd kept it between himself and David and the men on watch. It wasn't that he didn't trust his brothers, but that he hadn't wanted to worry them.

He was a damned fool. He should have been up front when the first scouts had been seen. Una was a reasonable person. What was more, she would die before she returned to the Camerons. Hadn't she told him as much? She would have cooperated. Hell, she could have given him valuable insight. But it didn't matter now, and no amount of should-haves would change that.

"We'll split up. You three keep searching the woods just in case. Take Mathan and look for her, for a sign of something she left behind, a trail, anything."

"Sign of a struggle?" Kenneth offered.

"Anything," Ewan bit out. "David will ride with me."

"W-w-where will you go?" Rabbie asked.

"To catch her."

CHAPTER 40

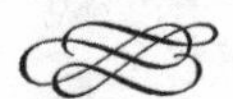

Una woke on horseback, unscathed except for her pounding head. The sun had crossed the midline of the sky, and Una thought it must be afternoon. The horse ran swiftly through the forest, piloted by a man who sat behind her. The air was damp and she felt a chill seeping through her clothes.

"Awake, now, are you?"

Giffard. Una's stomach rolled. He had been her second greatest tormentor during her handfast. Laird Cameron never allowed him to touch her, but he had allowed him to watch. And when Giffard would taunt her, Malcolm never stopped him. Once, when she was walking down a hallway, Giffard had pulled her into an alcove, his breath stinking of whisky, and would have done more than just talk if Blair had not happened to walk past and ask Una if she was available to stitch up one of the stable grooms who had cut his leg.

There had been other close calls, always interrupted by Blair, who once burned his hand on purpose as an excuse for her to leave with him. Blair had always been watching. Why hadn't she listened to him? Why hadn't she let him save her again?

Una felt the hard edge of her sgian dubh in her boot and was comforted to know that they hadn't found or taken it. It would do her no good right now, but who could say when she might need it?

"Take me back," Una said, mustering as much courage as she was able.

"Why would I do that, Una? Take you back to our enemies? In your delicate, precious condition? I couldnae possibly do such a thing."

Una shuddered as she felt his hot breath on her neck, the scratch of his whiskers against her skin. Giffard had her caged against his chest with his strong arms. He smelled her hair deeply and Una's entire body went stiff as a board.

"Laird MacDonald will come for you. There will be a war."

She wasn't entirely wrong. Ewan *would* come for her, and there *would* be war. But that would require Ewan to know where she was. How would Ewan know to look for her at the Cameron keep? The place she swore never to return to again? He wouldn't. When he had discovered her missing, he would have assumed that she'd run to the Stewarts. Hadn't she talked about it enough? Hadn't she told him that was her backup plan? That if, at the end of the handfast, she didn't want to marry him, that she would go there?

Ewan would never guess that she had been taken by the Camerons.

"I dinnae think he will, Una," Giffard chuckled. "You see, I've been watching that pup laird of yours for months now. Cameron wanted to see what he was up to. Turns out, a whole lot of nothing from what I've seen. Just a pathetic excuse for a laird up on crofter's roofs and soldiers running training drills in a field with wooden swords. Hardly worth monitoring at all, I told him. Imagine my surprise to see a certain raven-haired lass in the MacDonald forest then. How fortunate that you were able to escape their clutches."

He placed a big, gloved hand on her belly, the other still tightly holding the reins. "You've been busy, Una," he said and Una's whole body shuddered as she tried to shake off his hand.

He spoke into her ear, his breath sickeningly hot on her face. "I'm counting on a bit of a reward for bringing you in like this. Maybe I'll finally get my turn with you. Or perhaps I'll let the men ride on ahead, and you and I will have a little detour and finally become better acquainted."

She was going to be sick.

"Nay," he continued. "I willnae take you back. I'm taking you to Cameron, Una. I believe he'll be *verra* happy to see you."

"I mean nothing to him. Our arrangement is over."

"We shall see," he chuckled.

Hot tears stung Una's eyes as the heavy, strangling fear settled upon her. Her head hurt, her body hurt, the babe within her kicked hard into her ribs repeatedly until she was certain they would break. But she would not let Giffard see her cry. She would not feed him the food he liked best. Instead, she elbowed him in the gut.

He chuckled. "Glad to see you've still got spirit, Una. You wouldnae be much fun without it." But then his voice turned deadly serious. "Try that again, and I'll gag you and do as I please."

They stopped twice for Una to relieve herself next to the horse because Giffard would not let her out of his sight. She refused to feel humiliated, refused to give such a horrid man any such power over her. As night fell, they stopped the horses to rest, taking turns on watch. Giffard tied Una to him. At some point, he handed her an apple and his water skin and commanded her to eat and drink. The apple was mealy, but her growling stomach would not be ignored. She devoured it and drank greedily.

After a few hours rest, they mounted again and rode through the night. As dawn broke, she saw a familiar cottage appear from the mist. They would be riding past her childhood home on the road into the village. Perhaps she would see her father. He would see her with Giffard and know that something was terribly wrong. Perhaps he would get a message to Ewan. She could yet be rescued.

Una allowed herself to hope as she hadn't dared all day.

No doubt because of the commotion of so many horses, Fergus stepped out of the cottage. His eyes went wide, but she saw the mask descend just as quickly. Perhaps she had imagined his surprise. Una pleaded with her gaze.

Ewan. Go get Ewan, she mouthed silently.

Fergus narrowed his eyes, his brows knitting tightly together before he turned on his heel and stormed into the cottage, slamming the door behind him. As quickly as it had risen, her hope disappeared like a soap bubble against a stone.

"Someone didnae look too pleased to see you, Una," Giffard said, his glee evident.

Una said nothing. Her back and pelvis ached from riding, her ribs ached from the babe, her stomach rolled and turned, and her head hurt more than ever before. The skirt of the keep's wall loomed large to the right as they rode to the gate.

What fate awaited her? She could not say, but she did know one thing for certain. They would not break her a second time.

CHAPTER 41

They rode through the night, Ewan leaning hard into Calman with David close behind him. He didn't need to spur the horse on. As if sensing the danger, Calman rode as if his very life depended on it. When they reached the border of Cameron land, the sun was rising. A low fog blanketed the forest.

The animals needed rest, and Ewan needed to collect himself, to make a plan beyond charging into territory. But before he could make a plan, he needed to get a handle on himself. He would never find her if he was wild and reckless from his panic.

As Ewan relieved himself against a tree, he heard fast footsteps racing down the path. Someone was running clumsily toward them. Ewan dropped his plaid, unsheathed his sword from his belt, and slid behind a tree, gesturing to David, who dropped back behind a thicket.

A man ran into the clearing and immediately bent at the middle, his hands on his thighs, side heaving as he gasped for breath. Lank, gray hair hung down, obscuring his face, and the man coughed as he panted, spitting a wad of mucus into the leaves.

"Fuck," he cursed. "You cannae stop now. You'll never make it if you do."

Ewan recognized the hoarse croak even through the heavy breathing and stepped out from behind the tree.

"Oh, thank God!" Fergus said with a sob, spittle gathering at his mouth. "Did angels carry you here? I was comin' to find you."

"Where's Una?" Ewan said, his voice hard.

"They have her. They took her to the keep," he panted.

Ewan had suspected as much, but hearing it confirmed still made his blood run cold. Ewan cursed.

"You must go to her!" Fergus shouted. "You must ride to the keep and demand they give her back!"

Ewan felt a calm slide over him. He'd felt similarly when Connor had been wounded, where all of the loud, jangling panic that normally filled his brain went silent. His heart beat steadily. His breathing was even. And though he was absolutely *made* of feelings, he was able to think clearly for the first time in a very long time, the panic and worry morphing into something that felt a lot like composure.

As he thought, he heard David tell Fergus, "He cannae ride in one man alone. Or even two. They'll put an arrow through our hearts before we even get to the gates."

"So you're just going to abandon her?"

"Perhaps we can try diplomacy," David said. "You have the handfasting contract and a witness. The law would be on your side. We can bring Father Brian."

Ewan shook his head. "Today is the last day of the contract. Tomorrow, she is free. And we couldnae be back again before then with Father Brian."

David looked at his feet.

"We need more men," Ewan said. "We need as many men as we can spare."

It would take at least two days before he could return with any sort of fighting force. But what choice did they have?

"Let us hope she does nae begin her labors before we can return," David said and Ewan nodded.

"Begin her—" the words seemed to die in Fergus's mouth. "She is with child? What about the bairn? What if he tries to—"

Ewan forced his exhale out slowly through pursed lips as he took Calman's reins in his hands.

"At this late stage, he couldnae hurt the babe without risking Una," David said thoughtfully, shaking his head. "As long as she carries, they're both as safe as possible for anyone to be in that fox's den."

Ewan leveled a weary stare at David. "And we will pray that the bairn, unlike her mother, stays put."

"Oh, God help us, then," Fergus moaned.

A smile twitched at the corner of Ewan's mouth. Not because there was anything remotely funny about the situation, but because Una had never been governable a day in her life, and, for the first time, he allowed himself to imagine their child being just as wild, just as stubborn.

They mounted their horses and turned to go back the way they'd come when Fergus grabbed Calman's reins.

"Wait! I'm coming with you!"

"Nay," Ewan said, taking the old man's hand and holding it tight. "They dinnae have any idea that we ken where she is. If you disappear, someone might suspect you came to find me. We need surprise on our side. Stay put and keep an eye out, Fergus. Gather what information you can, but for God's sake, man, be discreet."

Fergus nodded wildly before turning and limping back

from whence he'd come. Before he left the clearing, he stopped and turned to look at Ewan. "M'laird..." he croaked, his voice cracking, "I ken that I havenae been the best father to her. But I only wanted her to be taken care of. Surely you ken that. And you... you love her, m'laird." It wasn't a question.

"Aye," Ewan said. "I do." He'd never spoken the words aloud, never told her. But they were true all the same.

"Well, at least we've got that on our side," Fergus said with a half-smile as he plodded away.

Ewan watched him go, his heart clenching in his chest. He jumped when David laid a hand on his shoulder. "Come, Ewan. We have quick work to do."

As they rode, they talked quietly about how many men-at-arms Ewan could call on such short notice, what supplies they would need, and how they could get within range of the Cameron keep without causing an alarm. Two days was a long time, and a great many things could happen before he could return to stage a rescue.

But he couldn't let himself think about those many things. He had to keep his mind focused on the plan. They would save her. He would leave the Cameron keep with her in his arms, or he would die trying. He closed his eyes and prayed for the first time since Connor's injury. He prayed to a God that he did not really know to keep Una safe, to watch over her, and to give her the strength to survive whatever lay in store.

And for God's sake, Una, dinnae do anything rash.

CHAPTER 42

The courtyard was empty as the Cameron contingent rode in. Giffard swung down off his black destrier and, more gently than Una had expected, lifted her off. He did, however, let his hands linger overlong on her ribs. When she slapped them away, he smiled. It was a slippery, leering smile.

Tossing his reins to a groom, Giffard walked toward the steps of the keep. When Una did not follow, another of Cameron's men—barely older than a boy—grabbed her arm and pulled her in Giffard's wake. As they entered the keep, Una saw the housekeeper, Maddie, standing in the shadows. Her heart leapt at seeing her old friend. Maddie flew to her side.

"Una! You must be frozen solid! We must get this damp cloak off of you and get you warm!" She clucked loudly, making a very physical display of removing Una's outer garments.

Maddie drew away from Una, her smile wide, and said brightly, "There! The laird isnae yet back, but I'll show you to your chamber." Her eyes were sharp and keen, locking on Una's when she spoke. Una nodded. "I believe we can take it from here, lads," Maddie continued, leading Una further into the keep, but the soldier did not leave. Rather, he followed them.

Maddie reached out and snatched her hand, chafing it between her own as they walked. Una savored the contact, bolstered by it. She was not completely without friends in this place. Una's feet felt heavier as they wound their way up the keep's tower to the chamber she had occupied for a year. Maddie opened the heavy door and ushered Una inside before turning to the soldier who made as if he would follow them in.

"I'm going to get her out of this wet gown. Surely you dinnae plan to be in the room for that?" Maddie asked with a high-quirked eyebrow. "I cannae imagine the laird appreciating that."

The young man scowled but nodded, and Maddie slammed the door in his face. He would stand just outside the door, of this Una had no doubt, but if they were quiet, perhaps she could speak with Maddie. The housekeeper bustled about the small chamber, pulling a shift out of a trunk under the window and stoking the fire.

"Blair sent a man to tell the laird that Giffard was escorting you. I had the boys lay a fire in here so that it would be warm for you." She held a finger to her lips before continuing to scurry from place to place in the room, chattering loudly but meaninglessly. "Verra well, lass, I see you dinnae feel like talking to me. Let's just get you dry and warm."

Una could barely hear Maddie's whisper in her ear. "Saints, lass. You shouldnae have come back."

Just as quietly, Una replied, "I didnae want to. Giffard took me."

"Where were ye that that devil could do such a thing?" Maddie hissed.

Una swallowed. "I was—am—handfasted to Laird MacDonald. I was walking in the woods beyond his keep. Giffard was watching, it seems."

"And he stole you away?"

"Aye."

Maddie was quiet for a moment as she began to peel the damp layers away from Una's body, her eyes returning time and again to Una's rounded belly.

"Cameron is at least a day's ride away. Perhaps your man will come? 'Tis nae so far to MacDonald land, is it?"

The tears fell in earnest now, fat, heavy drops that cascaded down Una's cheeks. "He doesnae ken where I am."

Maddie sighed and cocked her head to the side, biting her lips between her teeth. "Och, Una. I dinnae ken what Cameron has planned for you, but I fear for you, lass. I will do what I can to get a message out, but it will be difficult."

Una nodded, scrubbing her eyes with the heels of her palms.

"Until then, best you keep to this chamber. I dinnae trust Giffard with you in any time, but especially nae when his master is away. Bar your door and dinnae open it for anyone but me."

Una nodded and tried not to despair, but her heart felt heavy. Maddie helped to pass the clean shift over her head. The dry wool made her body feel better but did nothing to quiet her racing thoughts.

In the louder-than-normal voice she had employed earlier, Maddie said, "There now, lass. Rest. I'll return later with your supper."

Una mouthed *thank you* to the woman who had been such a good friend in this place. The heavy door closed behind her, and Una hurried to slam the bar down. On shaking legs, she shuffled to the bed and climbed onto it, bringing the covers up to her nose as she lay on her side.

She refused to allow the memories of this room to take over and instead thought of Ewan. She thought of him lying on his back by the loch, his hair an unruly, wavy halo around his head. His eyes were closed, and he was smiling. The sun was warm, the day was calm, and all was as it should be.

Exhausted and imagining the warmth of the sun on her face and Ewan's body at her back, Una fell into a deep, dreamless sleep.

CHAPTER 43

"Every able man is to meet me at the keep!" Ewan bellowed as Calman galloped down the road leading through the crofts. "Your lady has been kidnapped!"

He did not stop to answer questions. When they had reached MacDonald land, Ewan and David split up to reach more of his clansmen. His cries brought people out of their cottages, and an organized chaos ensued. In his years as laird, he had never issued a call to arms, and in his lifetime, he only remembered one of this magnitude. His father had worked hard to broker peace where he could and avoid warfare whenever possible. Always prepared, but always seeking another way. But there was no other way. Cameron would not accept diplomacy, and Ewan would tear down the Cameron stronghold stone by stone with his bare hands if that's what it took.

Blood pounded like a drum in his ears as he rode. Sweat coated Calman's flanks and neck, and Ewan felt his own perspiration sliding down his back as they sprinted through the cold air. He did not look behind him, but he knew that the men he had passed would be in short pursuit, following their laird to the keep.

Ewan heard shouts from the top of the wall as he neared the skirt, the gate opening at his approach. He leapt off Calman's back before the horse came to a full stop, and a stable lad took the reins, leading the horse off to a well-deserved dinner and cooldown. Angus and Kenneth ran to him from the steps of the gatehouse and Rabbie from the stables. It was early morning and the bailey was full of commotion and shouting as people flooded out of the keep and the other buildings within the wall and others poured in through the gate.

Ewan jumped onto a wagon so that he could be seen above the crowd. "Una has been kidnapped." The MacDonalds roared. Over the outrage, Ewan yelled, "By Malcolm Cameron." Impossibly, the noise escalated.

Ewan shouted above the din, and the crowd went silent as he spoke. "Every man who is able will meet me in the Great Hall at dusk, armed and ready. Their families will come to the keep and stay behind the safety of the walls. Go now and make your preparations. We will leave for the Camerons tonight." With that, he waded through the crowd and up the stairs of the keep, his brothers and David close on his heels. As he entered the Great Hall, Cat and Fiona ran up to him, tears in their eyes. Joan stood back.

"It cannae be true, Ewan!" Catriona cried.

"Aye. She has been kidnapped by the Camerons." Over Catriona's shoulder, Ewan met Joan's gaze. Her brows knit together, and she bit her lower lip.

"What can I do?" Cat asked.

Fiona chimed in, "Aye, what can we do? Give us a task, m'laird!"

"We need to make the Great Hall ready for a great number of people. And be sure there is food for all prepared."

"I shall go speak with Fenella. It will be done, m'laird," Fiona said before rushing away.

"And me, Ewan? What can I do?"

The ghost of a smile tugged at his mouth as he looked at his sister. "Cat, you can do what you do best. Make people feel safe and at home and welcome. There will be dozens, perhaps more, within the walls in the coming days. They will look to you for comfort and guidance."

He felt a stab of guilt, noting how grown up she looked. He'd asked the impossible of her a year ago in tasking her with piecing Connor back together and, in doing so, had yanked the last bit of her childhood away. And now he was asking her to do the job of someone twice her age.

But she did not look afraid. If anything, she stood taller, pulling her good shoulder back and lifting her chin. "Aye, Ewan. I can be the lady of the keep until our Una returns to us."

He swallowed against the rising lump in his throat and nodded. Out of the corner of his eye, Ewan noticed Joan slip through the door to the buttery. "I'll come find you before we leave in a few hours," he said and Cat hurried away.

"M'laird," David said, striding across the rapidly filling hall. "Any changes to the plan?"

Ewan shook his head grimly. It wasn't so much a plan as a choreography. They would leave when the moon was high in the sky. Ewan and David would lead, and the men would follow in groups of twenty, moving as quietly as possible. Ewan couldn't afford for Cameron to realize that the entire MacDonald clan was on its way, and he knew that the bastard would have watches placed throughout the woods surrounding his land.

Any Cameron man discovered was to be subdued or, if it was not possible to subdue them, dispatched. The MacDonalds would stay behind the tree line for as long as possible, and only when the forest ran out would they march en masse on the Cameron keep.

It was not a particularly finessed plan, but there wasn't time for one. The element of surprise was their best weapon. Cameron did not keep a standing army, and Ewan's men would outnumber his readied forces. They would cut down trees for the battering rams when they arrived.

David began grouping the men into twenty-man packs, trying to disperse them by skill, age, and weapon so there was balance among them. Ewan turned to his brothers.

"You three will stay here," he said, holding up a hand to silence their loud, immediate protest. "I willnae leave the keep unprotected. You will stay and keep our clan safe."

Angus scowled, but Rabbie nodded quickly. "We w-w-willnae let you down, Ewan."

Ewan put a hand on his shoulder and squeezed before turning to Kenneth. Always laughing, always joking—even when it was the wrong time—Kenneth looked as if he'd seen a ghost.

"If something happens, and I dinnae plan for it to," Ewan added quickly, "it all falls to you, Kenneth."

"Ewan, I—"

But Ewan cut him off with a shake of his head. "If ever the time comes for you to be laird, you will do a fine job of it."

Kenneth nodded, blinking rapidly. "Perhaps, Ewan. But see that it isnae right now."

Ewan's lips curved into a half smile. "Go now. Select your men who will stay with you and get to your posts. Dinnae close the gate until morning as there will be families making their way to the keep."

The afternoon flew by and the sky grew deep as pitch, made all the darker-looking by the brilliant full moon that shone like a silver dish against a black velvet cloth. Ewan and David rode in the front of the marching column, listening to the sounds of their horses against the background of muffled boots against the ground. Angus had been at the gate, counting and releasing each unit of men in time so that there was even space between them.

Once they reached the woods, they would fan out, covering a wide space as they closed in on the Cameron keep, performing whatever grisly reconnaissance was necessary along the way. Ewan and David would keep to the path. Let Cameron know he was coming. He would be expecting the foolhardy young son of his late enemy to rush in unprepared and alone. Ewan wanted Cameron to taste the sweetness of his own arrogance before both it and his life were snatched away from him.

Sweeter than that arrogance would be Ewan's revenge.

CHAPTER 44

Una woke to a knock on the door. She was groggy from having slept all through the previous day and night, her body needing the rest after the ordeal of being kidnapped and the long ride that had followed. Una went to the door, pressing her ear against the wood.

"Who is there?"

"'Tis Maddie, Una. I've brought you food to break your fast."

Relieved to hear Maddie's warm voice, Una lifted the bar and stepped back. Maddie entered the room carrying a tray in her arms and a basket at the crook of her elbow. She gestured to the chair, and Una sat as Maddie pulled up the table and laid out a spread of bread and cheese and a bowl of porridge. Una fell on the food, and Maddie glided around the room, making the bed and straightening.

"I finally found a gown that I believe will fit you. It laces on the sides. Helen in the kitchens wore it when she was carrying her last babe. She is shorter than you are, and 'tis quite humble, but it will serve better than your shift until your own gown is clean and dry."

Una nodded, her mouth full, as Maddie pulled the brown wool gown from the basket and laid it on the bed.

"I am sorry that it is so plain. Hardly befitting a laird's lady," she said, and Una shook her head. Maddie approached and bent to Una's ear.

"I wasnae able to get a message out, Una. I will keep trying, I swear it. But the only lad I trust hasnae been in the kitchen since you arrived."

Una's heart sank as this information confirmed what she, deep down, had already known—that if she was going to get out of here, she would have to save herself.

CHAPTER 45

They had traveled through the night and all through the next day as well. The light was nearly gone when Ewan entered the clearing. This was where they would wait and consolidate. Fergus's lanky body limped from behind one of the larger trees.

"I have news, Laird MacDonald," he said quietly, standing shoulder to shoulder with him as they watched men quietly filter into the clearing. Ewan grunted.

Fergus whistled, and a small, fair head popped up from behind the undergrowth. A boy, no older than eight or nine.

"Come, lad. And tell the laird your news."

The boy came, dutiful but hesitant, his eyes on his feet as he approached.

"He came and found me just after you left. I've kept him hidden in my cottage ever since," Fergus said, his voice like gravel. "Go on, lad. Laird MacDonald willnae hurt you."

"Laird Cameron is back," the boy said softly, shuffling his feet and staring at the ground. "He was away but rode back like the wind this afternoon. I am afraid for Una," the boy replied, meeting Ewan's gaze with watery eyes.

"You know her, then?"

"Aye. She tried to save my mother. When she— when she died, Una was living in the keep and got a job for me in the kitchen."

"And your father?"

"I dinnae ken him at all," he said, dropping his head in shame. Ewan exchanged a concerned look with Fergus, who nodded.

"What's your name, lad?" Ewan asked, coming to one knee in front of the boy.

"Ian, m'laird," he replied.

Ewan smiled. "That was my father's name. 'Tis a good name, lad. A strong name. You have proven yourself worthy of it. You were verra brave to try to help us find Una."

Young Ian's face lifted, his mouth open in surprise.

"She was kind to me, m'laird. She was kind to all of us. And I couldnae—" His voice broke.

Ewan placed a reassuring hand on the boy's shoulder, feeling every inch of his heart aching. Ian leaned into that touch, his small body nearly sagging with relief. Ewan squeezed the bony shoulder. "Well, young Ian. What do you think we should do next?"

Fergus gently pushed the boy on the shoulder. "You've yet to tell him the most important part, lad."

Taking a deep breath that puffed up his tiny chest, Ian said, "There is a secret passage. Lots of rooms have hidden doors that go to it, but it ends in a cave by the water." His words tumbled faster and faster in his excitement. "I can take you there. I've been all through it. I found it by mistake one night in the kitchen."

Ewan looked to David, who smiled widely, before turning back to the boy. "This passage wouldnae happen to lead to the laird's chamber, now would it?"

Ian nodded briskly, and Ewan clapped the lad on the shoulder.

"Have you any other family, Ian?"

"Nay, m'laird," Ian answered gravely.

"Would you like to come with us when this is all done, Ian? I'll see to it that you learn a trade, or I'll raise ye for the guard if that's more to your liking. You'll be welcome among the MacDonalds." He paused a moment before adding, "You'll be a hero."

Ian's eyes went wide, and he smiled, displaying several missing teeth.

"Now then, Ian. Can you take us to this cave?"

Ian turned quickly and made to charge across the clearing when Ewan caught his arm and pulled him back.

"Nae yet, lad," he chuckled. "We must wait for full dark."

Ewan began to hope as he scarcely had allowed himself all day. As his men filled the woods around the clearing and the sun set, Ewan and David walked about and issued orders. Only a small group would go to the cave. The rest would stay behind, ready for a fight, should one break out, with watches spaced between the clearing and the cave should reinforcements be needed.

Ewan was not one to murder a man in his bed, but he'd take Cameron however he could find him.

CHAPTER 46

Evening fell, and Una sat in a chair by the fire, knitting with the wool and needles Maddie had brought for her. Her finished supper tray sat beside her on the table. Her back ached fiercely, and she tried in vain to unclench her jaw as she speared the knitting needles through the yarn. The repetitive motion usually soothed her but not tonight. She could not shake the deep feeling of unease that hovered about her.

There had been a commotion in the bailey a few hours prior. Laird Cameron had returned, but, ever the cat, he had not yet summoned her. He always had been one to toy with his prey before dispatching it, and while Una was reasonably sure that that *particular* fate didn't await her—yet—she also couldn't begin to imagine why he wanted her here.

Someone pounded on the door, and the sudden boom of sound in the quiet space made Una jump and toss her knitting away. Whoever it was, it was not Maddie. Gripping the arms of her chair, she called, "Who is there?"

"Blair."

Una closed her eyes and took a deep breath. Her hands

rested on the large swell of her belly, and, as if feeling her touch, the baby kicked her right palm.

She rose and unbarred the door. Blair's huge frame filled the doorway, and he ducked his head as he entered the chamber. His thick hair was tied back with a leather strip, a few loose strands framing his face. Blair was a handsome man, albeit severe-looking, and the dark hair on his face, coupled with the dark hair on his head, made the Cameron blue eyes all the more striking and bright. But where Malcolm's eyes always glittered with what Una knew to be malice, Blair's eyes always looked sad, as if they had seen a thousand years go by and grown weary of the show.

He looked side to side before slipping into the room and standing with his back against the door. "What the hell were you doing at the MacDonalds'?" he snarled in a whisper. "You told me you were going to the Stewarts."

"I was! I was on my way there when Ewan intercepted me and begged me to come save his brother's life."

Blair nodded. "And then you stayed? Married?" He waved a hand at her midsection.

"Actually, another handfast."

Blair looked confused.

"To Laird MacDonald himself."

"Fucking hell," Blair muttered.

Una had always had the impression that Blair spoke just above a whisper because if he were to speak any louder, it would sound as if he were shouting on a battlefield. It was so low that sometimes it was hard to understand him if there were too many other sounds—his voice just became a rumble in the background. He was angry. He looked as if he *wanted* to shout.

But he'd been a good friend to her and she'd made a promise that she hadn't kept.

"I was going to send for you. But Ewan has been so fraught lately and there was never the right time and—"

Blair held up a hand and shook his head. "It probably wouldnae have worked anyway. It would have ended with me face down in the leaves with an arrow in my back."

Tears sprung to her eyes at that image. "If I get out, if I can..." What could she say? Because what were the odds? Not good. Not good at all, short of a miracle.

"Aye. If you get out," he said quietly. "Again."

Una nodded, and her voice cracked when she said, "'Tis good to see you again, Blair. You look well."

He held her gaze. "I wish you *didnae* look so well, Una. For your sake. I wish... well, it doesnae matter what I wish." He coughed into his hand. "I am to bring you to his solar. He was going to send Giffard to fetch you, but I told him that it was beneath his captain to run errands."

It's beneath the laird's brother, too, Una thought. But it didn't matter.

"I didnae want you alone with him. But I must deliver you now."

Una drew herself up to her full height, pulling her shoulders back and lifting her chin. "Well, no sense in delaying now, is there?" she said, sounding far braver than she felt.

But, perhaps, *feeling* brave was not so different than actually *being* brave. Blair followed her through the dim corridors. Just before they reached the door, Una stopped and looked back at him. She had no idea what awaited her on the other side. Blair's face looked pained as he stood in the dim hallway, his hands limp at his sides, as if he didn't know what to do with them.

"Una," he whispered, "I wish—"

"Me as well," she said, patting his shoulder. "You always were kind to me, and I dinnae think I ever thanked you properly. So.... thank you, Blair. You're a good man."

It felt so final. Like a goodbye. He nodded tightly, and she turned to the door. Blair reached out and grabbed her bicep, for the time it took to blink before dropping his hand.

"Una," he said, his voice almost inaudible. "Dinnae let him see you quake."

Una nodded and strode into Cameron's solar without knocking. Standing just inside the doorway, she leveled her eyes at the all-too-familiar person sitting at the table in the middle of the room. Malcolm Cameron looked the same as he had the day she'd left. Tall and sinewy, with dark, close-cut hair threaded through with gray. He had piercing blue eyes and thin lips that disappeared into the whiskers of a two- or three-week beard. Malcolm's leine was open across his pale chest. He stood as she entered, a cold smile spreading wide across his face.

"I didnae dare believe it when they told me. Una. My, my, my. You are quite a sight for sore eyes." He approached her and kissed her cheek.

"Why am I here, Malcolm?" she said, keeping her voice level, though the fear made it difficult.

Malcolm lifted an eyebrow and looked down at her, "Careful, lass. As I recall, you dinnae have leave to call me by my name."

"Verra well, *m'laird*," she said with a sneer. "Why am I here?"

He chuckled. "You've changed quite a bit since I've seen you last, Una. I hope that the MacDonalds have treated you well and taken good care of both you and my heir."

"Your heir?" Una spat, losing her composure, her mouth falling open. "I dinnae carry your heir!"

Malcolm tsked and went to the table, covered with documents. Una gasped as Giffard stepped from the shadows behind the door she'd just entered.

"Well, 'tis your word against mine, aye? I say you carry my

heir, and you say you dinnae. What will people believe? The word of the daughter of a penniless crofter who sold her to play whore? Or the laird he sold her to?"

His voice was honey, dark and rich and sweet. But poisoned. The bile rose in her throat. Malcolm Cameron had an incredible talent for saying vile words in such a genial way that you almost didn't notice how despicable he was. Almost. They had once made her cower

"It isnae possible, and enough people will remember that. I left here over a year ago. It cannae be your heir," she said, trying to get herself back under control. She needed to keep her wits about her.

"Well, now. That is interesting, lass. Because I have a document right here signed by witnesses that say that we were still handfast some eight months ago."

"I didnae sign that," she said through gritted teeth.

"Una," Malcolm said silkily, coming to stand before her. He rubbed a lock of her hair between his fingers before bringing it to his nose. "One X looks like any other."

He walked forward, forcing her to step backwards until her back was pressed against the wall next to the door. Giffard had moved and watched from the opposite corner of the room. Malcolm leaned in, smelling the skin below her ear as his hands came to her belly.

"Oh, Una. You have made me so verra happy," he whispered in her ear.

CHAPTER 47

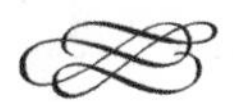

Una gasped as Malcolm palmed her rounded belly. He dropped his nose to the base of her neck and breathed deeply.

"So verra happy, lass," he repeated, punctuating each word with a kiss on her neck.

Una's skin crawled to the point where she wanted to claw it off her body.

"Giffard," Cameron said over his shoulder, "go and see to the gate. Be sure the guard is ready should Una's kidnapper come looking for her now that she's home safe and sound."

Leering as he passed, Giffard exited the room. It was hardly a relief—she still had Cameron pawing at her—but no situation was made better by Giffard's presence and now, with the numbers even, she felt as if she could at least think. Cameron grabbed her wrists and pinned them up against the wall as he continued to kiss her neck and shoulder.

"I can hardly believe my good fortune. 'Tis as if God himself willed it." Una felt his lips curl into a smile against her collarbone.

"A whole year. A whole year of doing my very best for

you, by you, with nothing. And yet you're away from home a few months, and look at what happened. 'Tis almost as if you didnae want to give me an heir."

She swallowed thickly as he kissed across her chest to the other side of her neck.

"For a time, I thought about letting Giffard have a go with you. He's gotten many a poor lass with child before. But I am a jealous man. I dinnae like sharing what is mine, even if it would benefit me."

A sob crept up Una's throat. She trembled against the wall.

"But, Una, what a gift you have given me. Now I have everything I've ever wanted."

He took both of her wrists in one hand, holding her jaw with his other. Dread settled heavily in her belly.

"I've never liked the MacDonalds, which makes this all the sweeter. I can piss off that whelp of a laird and, on top of that, get an heir *and* a bride."

"Nay," Una gasped, but Malcolm only gripped her cheeks more tightly, his fingers pressing painfully against her jaw, the flesh of her lips jutting outward from the force.

"Och, aye, lass. I've already summoned the priest. We shall marry tomorrow."

Her stomach rebelled, threatening to rid itself of its contents. She couldn't marry Malcolm Cameron. She *wouldn't* marry him. Nor would she subject her child to his caprice, his malice, his gleeful cruelty.

Since arriving at the Cameron stronghold, she'd been in shock, her mind a muddled, tangled mess. She felt herself drifting off to that safe space in her brain, where it was quiet, where she didn't notice his touch or attention. But then the baby kicked her hard in the ribs, and she sucked in a breath, launched back to the present.

Cameron pawed at her, and she wanted to scream for all

that it made her feel as if she couldn't breathe, but there was too much at stake. She needed to focus, to figure out a way out. She needed to save herself. If only she could buy more time.

"Then you'll be letting me go back to my chamber tonight?" she asked, feigning lightness.

"Why would I do that?"

Her mouth was dry. "'Tis bad luck for the groom to see the bride the night before the wedding.

He chuckled, and the sound froze Una's blood. "That is true of virgins, perhaps. But have you forgotten that I bought and took that prize long ago? I willnae wait till tomorrow to reclaim what's mine."

With that, he dropped her wrists and grabbed her face with both hands, pressing his lips to hers and forcing his tongue into her mouth. Una gagged and shoved him. He slapped her hard across the face. Her vision swam and her ears rang as she leaned against the wall for support.

"So it is to be like this again, is it, Una? You need to be broken in once more?" She dodged him, walking backwards across the room, sidestepping the chair he had vacated. "I didnae want to break your spirit twice, lass, but it seems that you require it."

She circled the table, cursing the clumsy state of her pregnant body as Malcolm advanced gracefully. "Apparently, Laird MacDonald doesnae ken how to keep a woman in her place."

What had been ice-cold fear slowly melted into a burning, white-hot fury that coursed through her and gave her strength. "He will come for me."

"Is that so?" he said through clenched teeth.

They circled the table again, each one trying to predict which way the other would go. Under normal circumstances, Una was fairly quick on her feet. But she hadn't calculated for the shift in her momentum from her belly. She stumbled, and Cameron grabbed her by the upper arms. He hauled her up and shook her.

"Aye," she spat, her voice full of venom. "He will come for me. Perhaps not today, but he will come."

"If that is true, then I'll be sure to put the pike with his head on it somewhere that you can easily see it. No doubt you'll have missed him."

She hated Malcolm Cameron. Down to the marrow of her bones, she hated him. And while she'd been afraid of him before, afraid of what he could do to her, what he *would* do to her, she realized in that moment that nothing short of his death would ever be enough to placate that burning rage.

Malcolm shook her again, cursing loudly in her face, spittle flying, before dragging her by her arms toward the bed. He threw her down upon it, tossing her skirts and shift up until she was bared from the waist down, her legs hanging off the bed. She kicked wildly as he placed himself between her thighs, fumbling with his clothing with one hand while the other gripped her wrists like a vice.

"You are mine, Una," he said through his clenched teeth. "You will say it."

"Nay," she shouted, still kicking, still struggling against her held wrists.

"*Say it*," he roared, still struggling with his belt. Frustrated, he tossed the front of his plaid to the side and leaned over her, crushing his mouth to hers and kissing her clumsily. Una felt the flaccid length of his cock against her thigh. His hip pressed against her boot, and she felt the outline of the sgian dubh dig into the outside of her ankle.

She had a chance—just one—to end this, to save herself and every other woman who would come after her from Malcolm Cameron. But she needed him relaxed. She needed him to believe that she was capitulating, that he had in fact "broken her," as he had said. And so she let her eyes appear vacant and drew her legs up higher, wrapping them around his waist. He groaned, the sound turning into a chuckle in the end.

"Now, there's a good lass. I'm glad you're finally starting to return to your senses," he said, panting, grinding against her sex.

Una mewled, reaching for her ankles, and Cameron buried his face in her neck, his body draped over her large belly. Before he could lift his head, Una squeezed her legs more tightly and moaned to cover the sound of her hand slipping her sgian dubh from her boot.

"It was always good with us, Una. Dinnae you remember? You fought me hard in the beginning," he said, pausing to thrust himself against her thigh, "but then you gave in and let me pleasure you. And I did pleasure you, aye?"

She moaned again in response, anything to keep him distracted. Una wrapped one arm around him, rubbing it up and down his back until she felt him relax even more against her, his lips grazing her neck.

"What a happy turn of events in an utterly dreary week, Una," he rasped against her throat.

She felt his ribs, palpating for the fleshy spaces between them. If she stabbed and hit bone, she was dead. He'd strangle her here. But if she stabbed lower, she would hit his kidneys. It would be fatal.

"Aye, Una. You remember how good it was. And so do I. I've thought of little else this year. Nae one else compared to you."

She clenched her teeth and took a deep breath. His cock grew hard between them, but Una did not wait for him to use it before she plunged the dagger under his ribs. Once, twice, three times, quickly striking at his kidneys with all her strength.

Malcolm roared and reared up to grab the dagger, but Una was quicker and plunged the small blade into the side of his throat. He took two steps back, and Una scrambled off the bed, placing as much distance between them as she could. He advanced on her, blood pouring from his wounds and flooding the floor. She dodged him, putting the table between them again. He lunged over it to grab her but at the last moment she jumped back and he crashed to the floor.

She held the sgian dubh in her hand, in case he rallied and came at her again. Her dress was drenched in blood, her hand and arm stained red. She could feel it under her fingernails. Una was well accustomed to blood—to the slippery feel of it between her fingers, the coppery smell, the way it bloomed bright red then deepened in color as the minutes passed. But never had she been covered with the blood of her own violence.

As she watched Malcolm try to turn onto his belly to crawl towards her, his life force pulsing out of him with every movement, she felt that violence keenly. It thrummed through her veins with a staggering heat. Her ears rang with it. He flopped onto his back, his breathing labored, making choking sounds as blood filled his throat. Una could not locate one grain of compassion for him.

Quite the contrary, she clenched her fist around the handle of her sgian dubh and resisted the urge to fall upon him with her blade and carve out his heart. The sudden image made her gasp and she stepped away, pressing her back against the far wall opposite the door, feeling the stones bite into her flesh.

Una clutched her free hand to her chest, her breathing heavy and hard as she watched him die. Her vision narrowed until all she could see was his body on the floor, the pool of blood around him widening, the edges seeping out to wrap around the legs of furniture. Her body began to shake violently, the heat of her anger replaced by intense cold as reality set in.

Suddenly, breathing seemed impossible as she gasped rapidly, feeling panic rise and grip her throat. There was no escape. The guards in the hall would not let her pass covered in blood, and Giffard and Blair would know that she was the last person to be in the laird's chamber. Blair was a good man but he was not in charge, and Giffard wouldn't hesitate to make her pay.

She would hang for this. Or worse, if Giffard had anything to say about it.

Una clutched her belly and tried to marshal her breathing, to figure out a plan. Just then, the tapestry next to Una was swept aside, and Maddie's head appeared from a dark recess. Both women clapped their hands over their mouths to stifle their shrieks.

"God in heaven, Una! Are you hurt? Is any of this blood yours?"

"Nay," Una panted, shaking with relief at Maddie's appearance. She'd heard rumor of the secret passages in the keep, but there had been none that led to her room and so she hadn't had a chance to explore. "'Tis all his blood."

Maddie's gaze slid from Una's face to where Cameron's body lay prone on the floor.

"Thank God," Maddie said, and as her friend flexed her shoulder, Una noticed the cudgel in her hand.

"Maddie?"

"I came prepared to do what I must to save you. But it seems you saved yourself."

Una felt the need to cry—she so desperately wished she could—but the tears wouldn't come, leaving her with a pit in her chest and an ache behind her eyes.

"We must hurry, Una," Maddie whispered. "It will nae be

long before they discover him, and you must be far from here by then."

Una nodded, and Maddie held the tapestry wider to allow her to pass into the shadows beyond. She bent to tuck the sgian dubh back into her boot before she followed Maddie into the passage. The tapestry flapped as it fell behind them, followed by the barely audible sound of Maddie closing the hidden door. A torch burned in a sconce on the wall, and Maddie grabbed it, holding her skirts and the cudgel in her other hand. She stepped past Una and began to descend a winding staircase into the dark.

Una picked her steps carefully. The torch helped, but it wasn't bright enough to clearly light the stairs, and it wouldn't do to fall. Maddie kept her brisk pace and led them down, down, down into the depths, passing landings along the way, which Una knew must lead to other chambers and passages. They were beneath the keep now. The air was cold and damp when the staircase ended and Una stepped off it into a shallow puddle.

"Mind your step, lass," Maddie whispered before turning sharply to the right and walking down what appeared to be a long, straight tunnel. They moved without speaking, the only sounds the soft, hasty shuffling of their shoes against the stone floor and the occasional drip of moisture from the ceiling. The passage stretched on and on, and Una picked her way across the uneven stones with as much speed as she could manage. She'd survived the belly of the beast. She couldn't afford to trip and fall now, especially not in her condition. The babe within her was blessedly still, lulled to sleep by her walking.

Creatures scurried around them, and Una tried not to think of rats and bats and other things that lurked in dark places as she hurried on. But in the distance, she could see stars. The tunnel was ending. Given how long they'd been walking, Una imagined it let out far beyond the walls. After all, these secret passages were built to help the residents of the keep escape in the event of a siege.

The moon was full and the sky was bright beyond the passageway. Just as they were about to exit, Maddie gasped and lunged backwards, pressing Una against the wall behind her and tossing the torch in a puddle of water.

"There are men outside the tunnel," she hissed in the sudden darkness.

"Cameron men?" Una asked, terror rising sharp and shocking.

"I couldnae see their plaids, lass. But nae doubt they saw the torchlight. You must hide here. I will go and speak to them. I'll tell them I got lost in the tunnels and found my way here."

"They'll never believe you, Maddie," Una insisted.

Maddie shook her head stubbornly, but Una knew what needed to be done. She would not let her friend, someone who had been so kind to her, be punished for her crime. She would likely hang for this crime. She grieved the fact that she would never see Ewan again or get to tell him that she had fallen in love with him. But if she could die knowing that Malcolm Cameron had been scoured from the earth, it would be enough. She could be at peace.

Una gripped her hand. "Maddie, you must listen to me. They dinnae ken you are here. I willnae allow you to hang beside me."

"I willnae abandon you," Maddie protested, taking Una's face in her hands. "They'll kill you for certain."

"Not yet. They'll wait till I deliver this babe, and that buys us more time. Perhaps you can get a message out with that lad you said you trust."

The men outside the tunnel grew louder, closer.

"I dinnae like it, Una. I cannae let you go out there alone."

She spoke the words around a sob, and Una grabbed her and held her close.

"We have no choice. Either I go out alone, or they come in and find us together. No sense in both of us hanging, Maddie. After all, you didnae kill him, I did."

"But I would have, Una," Maddie whispered through her tears. "I planned to. I—" she broke off, biting her lip.

A gravelly voice called out. "We know someone is in there. Come out, or we'll send a man after you." She heard the low rumble of other men speaking, the shifting of boots, and water cascading quickly over rocks. They must be near the river.

"Go, Maddie!" Una said, clutching her friend in one last hug.

With her heart in her throat, Una stepped out of the tunnel and into the brilliant moonlight. But even though the moon was full, she could not make out the colors of the men's plaids. She squinted at the group of men, searching for a face she recognized. Unease crept up her spine and over her scalp. Why were they staring at her? Why had no one grabbed her?

"God's bones, Una, is that you?"

A sob ripped from Una's throat as she turned toward the voice.

It couldn't be.

CHAPTER 48

In an instant, Ewan had Una in his arms, crushing her to his chest as he pressed his lips against the top of her head. Hot tears streamed from his eyes and fell into her hair. Una sobbed, gripping his leine in her fists. His shaky hands cupped her cheeks reverently before roaming over her body, checking for injury. Her clothes were sticky and wet, and when he drew his hands away, he saw that they were stained red.

"My God, Una. You're covered in blood."

She sobbed harder, pressing her face against his chest, but Ewan forced her to look at him. His voice was frantic. "Una, whose blood is this?"

"Cameron's," she whispered. "I stabbed him. Three times in the back before sticking him in his throat."

"Is he…"

"Dead, Ewan. I killed him."

With that, she began to tremble violently, clinging to his shirt. Ewan was awestruck. He'd come here, expecting to tear the keep down to save her when she'd been saving herself.

He'd never even considered that possibility, which shamed him. How had he ever doubted her?

Why hadn't he trusted her to handle the truth about Malcolm Cameron? Why hadn't he confided in her and asked for her thoughts on what would be the best course of action to protect her safety? She'd lived with the bastard for a year and survived. She knew him far better than Ewan. Another failure of intentions. He remembered what his mother had told him once. *"Ewan, mo cridhe. Well meant doesnae mean well done."*

The shame choked him almost as tightly as his relief. He didn't deserve to hold her so easily like this. He should have crawled to her on his knees over the rocks and begged her for the privilege.

Ewan brought one hand to the back of her head, holding her close. "You're so brave, mo ghraidh."

"I had to kill him, Ewan. I *had* to. He was going to claim the babe as his own and force me to marry him. He was—" She choked on a sob, and her eyes went wide. "We must leave. They'll hang me for this if they find me!"

She pulled away from him, grabbed his hand, and tried to drag him towards the forest. She was strong, but her belly threw her off balance, and when Ewan didn't move, she tipped backwards into him.

He wrapped his arms around her again. "Una, if you think I would let them take you now, you've lost your mind."

"Someone will pay, Ewan. Someone will have to pay," Una whispered, her eyes wide with fright.

"Aye. They will," boomed a deep voice from the darkness.

Una whipped around and, over her shoulder, Ewan saw Blair Cameron striding from the tunnel with a woman's arm in his grip. The relative quiet was broken by the sound of swords being unsheathed, the creaking of leather against staffs, bowstrings being drawn.

"Maddie!" Una cried. "Maddie, nay!"

"I tried to go back, but he was already in the tunnel, Una," the woman, Maddie, replied with tears in her eyes.

"Let her go, Blair!" Una shouted at him.

Ewan had seen Blair before. Cameron often sent his brother to deliver messages, a fact that had always confused Ewan. Tonight, there was a spark in Blair Cameron that had been missing every other time Ewan had seen him, as if he'd been animated and brought to life with the death of his brother. He still had that weary, long-suffering look about him, but his gaze was sharp, his shoulders back.

"You willnae take Una, Cameron. As long as I breathe, I willnae let you take her," Ewan said through clenched teeth. His blood ran cold as the big man sauntered toward them, seeming utterly unconcerned by the MacDonald arrows trained on him.

"Blair," Una whispered. "You ken what he would have done. You ken what he *did*."

Blair nodded. The gesture was so small that it would have been imperceptible from a distance. But Ewan saw, and he knew Una did too.

"Come with us," she said. "Run away. It was always the plan."

Ewan stared at her. The friend that she wanted him to shelter had been *Blair Cameron?* Why hadn't she said so? Probably because she hadn't trusted him enough to agree to help. More shame roiled through him.

"You could come with us, Blair," Ewan said, and Una smiled at him, her bottom lip trembling.

"I cannae do that," he said, sounding heavy. "I am the laird now."

He said as if it were a death sentence. Ewan understood. Sometimes it felt like his life had ended when he'd become laird and he'd become a mere occupation. Until Una, that is.

Una, who had breathed life and hope and peace back into his days.

He needed to get her away from here as quickly as possible. No matter that Blair was her friend. No matter that she seemed to trust him. Ewan didn't trust anyone with her safety right now when he barely trusted himself.

"We shall be on our way then," Ewan said.

Blair took a step forward and gripped the hilt of his sword. "I cannae let you do that."

"What is it that you want?" Ewan asked, drawing Una closer to his side.

Blair sighed. "That is the question now, aye? The clan will want retribution. They will want the laird avenged."

Ewan's hand tightened around the hilt of his claymore. "I have hundreds of men in the woods. What's to stop us from leaving right now?"

"I wouldnae need to stop all of them. Just the two of you." His rough voice was quiet. He almost sounded sad. Regretful. Ewan's jaw tightened, and he felt the hilt of his sword warming in his palm.

"Blair," Una whispered, her voice thick with tears. "Please. Dinnae do this. We are friends."

"Aye," Blair said. "We are friends. Which is why I willnae allow you to come to harm. But I must have something to show them, something in return to settle the debt."

Ewan knew that they could fight, he and Blair. They could settle the score now on this riverbed. But he also knew that there was a very strong possibility that neither of them would survive such a fight. And then what?

"What if..." Una said, stepping out of Ewan's hold. "I was meant to marry Laird Cameron. That's what he wanted. He wanted to claim my child as his heir. What if... what if I give you half? I will stay with you if you let the bairn go to her father when she's weaned."

Ewan dropped his sword in shock, something he had never done in his entire adult life. What had she said? *What the hell had she said?*

"Goddamnit! Why, Una? Why would ye offer such a thing?" Ewan shouted, feeling his helplessness and anger and fear coursing through his veins like a flood. He cupped her face in his hands.

She brought her own hands to his cheeks. "Because if I dinnae stay, you might die. Cannae you see that? I would rather live my life without you knowing that you're alive and well than live my life without you because you died for my crimes."

"Una, dinnae do this to me," Ewan whispered. He felt that old, familiar sensation, that caged animal in his chest that strained and threw itself against its confinement.

"'Tis a fair suggestion," Blair replied, and Ewan bit back a roar. "But I dinnae want you for a wife, Una. Nae offense. Neither do I particularly want to kill your man here."

"You could try," Ewan said, picking up his sword even as Una shoved against his chest.

Blair didn't flinch. He raised one large, dark eyebrow and crossed his arms.

Perhaps they could settle in trade. An alliance. Ewan would ask the utmost of his brothers. Perhaps there were two Cameron ladies in need of husbands. Such alliances were formed all the time. Angus would do it. Kenneth, too. And there was the MacDonald wool. They could arrange something in commerce.

Ewan's mind was racing, calculating what they could spare and trying to remember the Cameron family tree when a voice rang out from the crowd of men gathered. "I'll settle the debt. I'll be kept prisoner in Una's stead."

CHAPTER 49

Una would know that voice anywhere. What in God's name was Joan doing here? She scanned the shadowed crowd and saw a hooded figure threading through the men. She pushed back her hood with a brilliant smile, and Una choked on a startled laugh. Joan always had loved a dramatic entrance.

"Joan?" Blair and Ewan said in unison, their eyes wide, looking at one another as if surprised that the other knew her name.

"Dinnae look quite so shocked," Joan said with a smirk.

"You say that like finding my sister's lady-in-waiting among a fighting force is to be expected," Ewan said dryly, and Joan smiled beatifically at him.

"I've always had a knack for finding trouble."

"Trouble is an understatement, Joan," Blair growled. "You could have been killed."

"You could have been killed also, Blair, but you werenae killed and neither was I and so it doesnae matter," Joan said with a dismissive flick of her hand.

Una was confused. When had Joan met Blair? Una hadn't

met him until her handfast to his brother, and Joan had been her very best friend until they were both sixteen. How did *she* know him? How did she know him well enough to be so forward, to *tease* him?

Blair made a sound that was somewhere between a disgruntled huff and a growl. He stared at Joan, who stared back, a soft smile on her face. But Ewan wasn't paying attention to that sweet look on Joan's face.

"David," Ewan barked, "please escort Joan back to the wagons and see that she stays there."

Una watched as Joan turned to protest, but Blair lunged forward. "Dinnae touch her," he snapped at David and began to withdraw his sword from the sheath. It was a clear warning, and thankfully David stepped back.

"Joan has offered herself in Una's stead," Blair said.

"She doesnae get to make that choice," Ewan said through his clenched teeth.

Una shook her head. She loved him. She loved him for the laird he was and the laird he would become. He was so good, down to his core. He cared for his people and worried about them to his detriment. But he was also a hothead sometimes, and he often missed subtlety.

Like the way Blair was looking at Joan as if she was the relic he'd spent his whole life seeking. There was history. There was yearning. There was, perhaps, even *pining*. Una wrapped her hand around Ewan's arm to hold him back.

"I do get to make that choice," Joan said. Her tone was light, her eyes never left Blair's face. "I am a free woman. You are neither my father nor my husband or even my brother. You dinnae get to command me."

"I am your laird, Joan."

"And a verra good one, Laird MacDonald," she said. "But we are nae on MacDonald lands now, and you are nae my keeper. I offered myself in Una's stead, and I mean to see it through."

Ewan clenched his teeth so hard that Una heard his jaw pop. She wrapped her arm around his waist now and tucked herself close, trying to soothe him with her proximity. It didn't do much. Ewan was practically vibrating with fury.

"Joan, have you taken total leave of your senses?" he asked.

"Not at all, Laird MacDonald," Joan said. "It will be an adventure."

"Adventure?" Ewan nearly shouted. "You think a dungeon a good place for an adventure? Una, please, talk some sense into her," he protested, trying to encourage her into the fray.

Una lifted onto her toes and whispered into Ewan's ear, "Shhh. You are missing something. Watch them."

"She willnae be in the dungeon," Blair said, and Joan spun back to face Ewan.

"See, Laird MacDonald? I willnae be in the dungeon." She smiled, and Una rolled her eyes at how much fun Joan seemed to be having as the spoke around which all the chaos currently swirled. "Now, Laird Cameron, where will you have me? Shall I work in the kitchens?"

"You willnae be in the kitchens."

"Then perhaps you have a lady in need of a maid somewhere in that dusty keep of yours?"

"You willnae be anyone's maid either," he said darkly.

"The stables, then? Or perhaps I can serve in the guard? I've been told I have some skill with a staff."

Una rolled her eyes heavenward when Joan winked. Blair coughed into his hand.

"You willnae work here. I dinnae want you to work here," Blair said.

"I am confused, m'laird," Joan said, somewhat hesitantly.

"If I am nae to be a prisoner and I am nae allowed to work, what *am* I to do here?"

Blair took another step closer, and Una saw how very short Joan looked as she tipped her head back to look up at him. "I have something else in mind for you," he said, his voice husky and low.

Una heard Joan swallow. "And what might that be?"

"You'll be my wife," he said, stroking her cheek with a single, rough finger.

A twig snapped, sounding sharp and sudden in the quiet.

"Your wife?" Joan and Una said at the same time, though with far different inflections.

"My wife," Blair repeated, reaching out with his bear paw of a hand to trace the apple of Joan's cheek. "'Tis the only way. My brother intended to marry Una. Her proxy, a cousin we will say, will marry the new laird. Hopefully that will satisfy the clan enough to avoid war. But for a few people, there wasnae much love for my brother, so the politics should be easy enough to manage." He took a deep breath. "I hope."

He was right about most of the clan having no affection for his late brother. It was a common subject of conversation in the village. He would not be missed. Perhaps Blair was onto something. Una turned the possibility over in her mind.

"You only want to marry me for revenge," Joan said, her arms crossed over her chest as she looked up at Blair. "That isnae a good enough reason for me to marry."

"'Tis better than half the other reasons people marry," he snapped. But he leaned in close, whispering something in Joan's ear so quietly that Una couldn't make it out. In the moonlight, she saw Joan's mouth go slack, her eyes softening.

"And if I refuse to marry you?" Joan whispered.

Blair stepped away from her, the previously warm

expression on his face replaced with a detached coolness as he took a step towards Ewan, unsheathing his sword.

"Nay!" Una shrieked. Ewan growled, shoving Una behind him and raising his own sword.

"Oh, for the love of all that is good and holy in this world, stop!" Joan shouted, darting in front of Blair and pushing against his chest with both hands. He stopped, arrested. "You big brutes are so keen to kill each other. Maybe I should let you."

Una pressed her own palms hard into Ewan's chest, willing him to calm down, to be reasonable.

Behind her, Blair said, "I need your answer, Joan."

Joan sighed. "Saints alive. I will marry ye, Blair Cameron. If for nae other reason than to calm your goddamned bloodlust."

Something that might have been a smile briefly moved Blair's beard. "Maddie," he said without looking behind him, "please escort Joan to a chamber."

Maddie. In all the commotion, Una had forgotten about her entirely. She was exhausted, the energy and fear of the past hour having drained her as it wore off.

"You willnae cast Maddie out for helping me," Una pleaded.

"I dinnae ken what you're talking about. I found her alone in the tunnel with a torch. Perhaps she got lost on her way to find me."

Una had the energy to smile at him. Her eyes filled with tears.

"Thank ye, Bl—m'laird," Una said, knowing that she had more to say, that this might be her only chance. "And I am sorry. The plan. I… I meant to send for you. I tried, but it—"

Blair shook his head. "Everything happened the way it was meant, Una. I am happy for you."

"I am happy for you too, Blair," she said with a trembling voice.

He nodded and slid his sword back into his scabbard.

Joan looked up at Blair. "I'll be saying my goodbyes first."

IT ALL FELT SO FINAL. Saying goodbye to Blair. Saying goodbye to Joan. Who knew when she would see her again? It wasn't as if either of them knew how to write. And she didn't imagine that Ewan would oft be willing to take her to visit the bride of his enemy. Although perhaps they wouldn't be enemies any longer.

Joan rushed toward her and hugged her. Una squeezed her back as tightly as she could with her rounded belly between them.

In her ear, Una whispered, "If you dinnae truly want this, we will find a way to save you. I swear it."

Joan pulled back, looking up at her. "All will be well. You'll see, Una. I would have to marry sooner or later, and I could do far worse than marrying a laird, now couldn't I?"

Una smiled in spite of herself.

"Besides," Joan said, winking, "he's got all his teeth, and beneath all that hair, I'm sure he's still pleasing to look at."

Una grinned and hugged her friend once more. Joan curtsied to Ewan before walking toward Blair and Maddie.

"Have ye a torch, m'laird, or are we expected to grope our way back into the keep?" Joan asked.

Blair rolled his eyes and huffed something that might have been a chuckle. "There's a man with a torch just inside." With that, he turned to follow Joan and Maddie.

"Just one man?" Ewan called out.

Blair turned, his nose coming to a sharp point in profile. "Aye," he said over his shoulder. "I believed we could come to an understanding."

"What about Giffard?" Una asked.

"I plan to give Giffard his due. At long last," he replied, his eyebrows slamming down. Una didn't miss the tightening of his hand around his sword hilt. "In fact, it will be my second act as laird, after this bit of diplomacy. Be well."

CHAPTER 50

Una whipped around in Ewan's arms. "Ewan, my God. Am I dreaming?"

"Nay. But you've been living a nightmare these last days. Let's get you home."

Ewan pulled her close into his side. The trees were mostly bare and the moon shone brightly between the reaching branches. They walked in silence. Ewan heard the muffled steps of the men behind him and the light breeze that shook the bare trees. Just beyond the river, young Ian joined them. After showing them the tunnel, Ewan had instructed the boy to stay out of sight. He trotted alongside Una, glancing at her frequently.

Una kept up, but Ewan could see her losing strength as they neared the clearing where his men waited. He bent down and scooped her into his arms, ignoring her protests. She didn't protest long, resting her head on his chest, threading one hand around his back and gripping his leine as if that contact was the only thing holding her to him.

As they entered the clearing, David and Fergus approached. Having witnessed all, Ian retold the story of

Joan's disguise with great excitement, and for a moment, it seemed that everyone was talking at once. Ewan quieted the commotion with some difficulty, and after Una's father was satisfied that she was unscathed, Ewan lifted her onto Calman's back and climbed up behind her, settling her in his lap. He bundled her in blankets as the night was unseasonably cold. In a moment, she was asleep.

Ewan instructed David to ride in front and lead the column. He would ride in the middle of the group. As they picked a careful way along the path through the woods, Ewan kept looking at Una. She slept heavily, her body motionless in his arms as the shadows of trees swept across her face. Worry clenched his stomach like a fist. The sooner he got her home and warm, the better. The men were exhausted. He was exhausted. How Una had remained on her feet for so long was beyond him. But they couldn't afford to stop for the night.

And so they rode into the silent midnight. Ewan finally felt his body begin to relax. He had just reached down to pat Calman's flank when a sharp cry broke the silence.

CHAPTER 51

In an instant, Ewan's heart began beating at a fierce pace. It couldn't be happening now. Not when he had just gotten her back safely. He felt a gush of liquid against his thigh, and his heart threatened to stop beating altogether.

"Una, are you bleeding, mo cridhe?"

"My waters have broken," she panted.

How was he supposed to care for her like this in the middle of the woods in the dark of night? Shelter. They needed shelter. Up ahead, he knew, they would find the cave where he and Una had stayed the first night he'd met her. That night felt like a lifetime ago. The cave was small and hardly suitable for a woman in her condition, but he didn't know what else to do.

"Una," he rasped. "The cave. We will go to the cave."

"Nay," she groaned, adjusting herself on his lap. "We keep going."

"Una. Be reasonable, Una. We must—"

"We *must* listen to the only person here who has any knowledge about birthing bairns, and that is me," she snapped. "We keep going. It will be hours yet, and I dinnae want to have this babe in a cave, no matter how pleasant my last stay there was."

"But—"

"But nothing, Ewan," she said and then groaned loudly. "You havenae listened to a word I've said about this babe thus far, but you'll listen to me now. I willnae have this baby in that cave. If you insist on stopping, I'll walk home."

He was as annoyed as he was terrified. But the word "home" sent a tiny shiver of joy through him.

"Verra well, mo cridhe," he said softly, reaching for her hand. She took it, gripping it tightly. "We are at your command. What shall we do?"

Una closed her eyes and took a deep breath. "Send a man ahead to the keep. Tell Fenella we will need water boiling and clean linens, and make sure that Fiona has my kit ready. More clean linens"—she broke off on a groan—"on the bed."

Ewan squeezed her hand and shouted for a man to deliver the message. It was the only task she'd given him, all he could do. There was nothing else but to watch, his stomach in knots, as she labored in his lap on horseback. He offered words of encouragement and praised her, rubbing her back and letting her grip his hand so hard that his fingers felt in danger of breaking.

The night stretched on endlessly with Una's groans becoming louder and less controlled. His nerves became more and more frayed as their journey—and Una's labor—progressed. He tried to stamp the intrusive thoughts that loomed at the edges of his mind—memories of his mother, of her childbed, of— Nay. *Not every story has the same ending,* he told himself.

By the time they saw the walls of the keep rising from a late afternoon fog, Una was weeping. Ewan had tried multiple times to get her to eat, but she refused. He was bone-weary from his terror and lack of sleep, but he could not imagine how exhausted she must be. Halfway between the forest and the wall, Una wailed. "Ewan," she sobbed, "I need Father Brian. Send someone ahead and bring him to the keep."

Ewan clenched his jaw. He wanted to shout at her that she did not need a priest because she was not going to die. She *couldn't* die. Not when he'd just found her again. Not when they had only gotten started. But he could refuse her nothing.

The column of men had thinned significantly as people split off and made for their own homes. Ahead, he saw Ian riding behind Fergus, David beside them.

"David!" he shouted.

All three turned around sharply. Ian's eyes were as big as plates.

"Ride ahead and find Father Brian. Make sure he is at the keep when we arrive."

"Una," Fergus whispered, staring at her with haunted eyes.

"Please, David," Una cried, and Fergus nodded, urging his borrowed mount faster.

The bailey was full of commotion, and Ewan's entire family met them in the courtyard. Ewan felt as if he was underwater. The sounds around him were muted and muffled, difficult to make out, and it seemed as if he was fighting against heavy, soaked clothing as he dismounted and reached for Una. His ears rang and his heart pounded wildly in his chest as he gingerly coaxed her off of Calman's back. As soon as her feet touched the ground and she stood, her knees buckled. Ewan bent and scooped her into his arms, striding up the stairs of the keep.

He didn't stop to speak to anyone. He didn't notice who followed him. He didn't mark the steps as he usually did. It was all he could do to place one foot in front of the other and, before he knew it, he was carrying Una through the door and into the laird's chamber. Seeing the bed caused his heart to seize in his chest and his blood to run cold. His body shook as he laid Una on the mattress. She curled onto her side, her pale face damp with sweat.

"Father Brian?" she asked, gripping Ewan's hand. He went down to his knees beside the bed.

"I sent for him, mo ghraidh."

My love.

He'd never said it out loud before, never called her that. But he wanted her to hear it. He needed her to know. Just in case...

She nodded and closed her eyes, gritting her teeth against another labor pain, squeezing Ewan's hand until her knuckles went white. With that, the sob that he'd been holding onto all night broke free, and with it, his voice thick with unshed tears, "Dinnae leave me, Una."

At that moment, Father Brian burst through the door, Fiona, Fenella, and Cat on his heels. Ewan surged to his feet. It had been one thing for Una to ask for a priest, another thing entirely for Father Brian to appear, for Ewan to watch him deliver the sacrament that Una was requesting.

"Nay! Nay!" he shouted, feeling truly wild now. "You willnae give this woman last rites! She willnae die! I forbid it!"

"Ewan," Una's voice was shaky as she pulled on his hand. He turned. "I dinnae want last rites."

"You... What? What? What do you want with a priest, then?"

"I want to marry you."

"*Now*? You want to marry me *now*?"

She smiled weakly. "Before the babe comes. But if you dinnae want—"

His mouth dropped open, and he fell to his knees beside her, taking her hand in both of his now and bringing it to his lips. "Nay. Nay, mo ghraidh, I want to more than anything. I love you," he said, kissing her fingers. "I love you," he repeated against every knuckle. "I love you, Una."

Her smile turned into a grimace as another pain took hold, her back bowing off the bed.

"Help me, Ewan," she panted. "I need to move."

"Anything," he said. "Anything you need."

She told him she wanted to be on her hands and knees, wanted to be able to circle her hips and move, to take some of the pressure off of her back. He helped her to maneuver on the bed.

"Can... you... marry us... like... this?" she panted.

Father Brian, looking an alarming shade of red, stepped forth and said, "It isnae traditional, but if the laird insists, then—"

"I do," Ewan said.

Fiona hurried to Una's other side. "If you're going to do it, Father, best get on with it. I suspect we dinnae have much time before this babe joins our party."

Father Brian loped closer to the bedside on his long legs. "Well, there is a long version and a short version, but I imagine you will be wanting the short, aye?"

Una groaned loudly as another pain took her. "Short!"

"Verra well. Ewan, repeat after me...."

Ewan rubbed her back as he repeated after Father Brian.

I take you to be my wife.

I pledge to you the faithfulness of my body and the loyalty of my heart.

I will keep you in sickness and in health and in whatever condition you find yourself.

I shall nae forsake or exchange you for better or worse until the end.

Una spoke the same vows quickly, hurrying through the words while she was in between birthing pains, his hand on top of hers with their fingers laced. Once Father Brian pronounced them husband and wife, Ewan bent down and kissed Una, pressing his lips to hers and tasting the saltiness of both of their sweat and tears. But as soon as he stood, Father Brian began to gently pull him from the room.

"Nay," Ewan growled, wrestling his arm away from the old priest, "I will stay with her."

"It is nae done, m'laird," Fiona said gently. "I promise you that we shall take the verra best care of her."

Ewan struggled but felt more hands on him and turned to see Kenneth. His brother nodded and tilted his head toward the door.

"Una," Ewan called out, his voice ragged and hollow. "Hold fast, mo ghraidh."

"Dinnae fash, Ewan. You're stuck with me now," Una replied, in a moment of alarming calm, as Fenella began unlacing Una's bloody gown.

The door closed, shutting her away from him. He turned and saw his brothers in the hall. Rabbie sat with his back against the wall, his elbows resting on his bent knees, his head in his hands. Connor sat next to him, fidgeting with his plaid. Angus paced, scowling. Father Brian stepped around Ewan and Kenneth, bowed his head, and said, "If you need me, m'laird, I shall be in the Hall. I suspect that Lady Una's father will be relieved to know that I have nae given last rites."

Ewan nodded and began his own pacing. Angus moved further down the corridor to give him room. On the other side of the door, Ewan heard the women speaking muffled words of encouragement, weaving over and around Una's cries and groans.

Time crawled by, and just as Ewan was prepared to break

down the door, a sharp, little cry pierced the air. Rabbie and Connor scrambled to their feet, broad smiles on their faces. Even Angus, perpetually scowling, had an awed look on his face.

Ewan's fingers shook as he reached for the door handle. The last time he had entered this room following the cry of a newborn baby, the floor had been drenched with blood, the bedclothes a brilliant red, and his mother had lost all color as she lay dying on the sheets.

"It will be well, Ewan," Kenneth said softly, without any of the teasing behind which he normally hid. He placed a reassuring hand on Ewan's shoulder.

Ewan swallowed thickly against the lump in his throat. His eyes burned, his muscles shook. But he could wait no longer. With a deep breath, he eased open the heavy door, prepared to see the very worst.

The sight that greeted him, however, was not at all what he expected. Fiona bustled about the foot of the bed, gathering soiled linens. Fenella stoked the fire with brisk efficiency. And Cat fluffed pillows behind Una's back. They were so quiet. So calm. So *normal.*

Finally, his eyes traveled up the bed, and he saw Una.

My wife, he thought.

She lay propped up on pillows, a blanket drawn up to her chest. Peeking out from beneath the blanket, he saw a tiny head covered with hair as dark as Una's. He took a staggering step forward and saw the baby blinking and rubbing its small face against Una's skin, squirming and squeaking.

"Come," Una said with a weary smile, patting the mattress beside her. "Meet your daughter."

"My daughter," Ewan repeated as the air rushed from his body. He stumbled to the bed, speechless. He hesitated a moment before reaching out a shaking, scarred hand to touch the downy, soft head.

"She willnae bite, Ewan. Come closer," Una teased in a soft voice.

Ewan gently climbed onto the bed, curling his big body around Una and resting his head on her shoulder. Hesitantly, he ran one finger down the baby's spine, feeling the softness of her skin. Una shifted the baby to her breast and crooned to her as she latched. Ewan counted her toes and marveled at how, only minutes old, he could already recognize his feet on the babe.

"Are you both well, Una?" he whispered, mesmerized.

"Aye. Right as rain. Tired and hungry enough to eat something your size, but Fenella said she would fix me up straightaway."

Fenella chuckled from the doorway. "Aye, my sweet. I'll be back shortly with a tray of your favorites."

She left with Fiona on her heels. Cat stood by the fire, her eyes bright with tears and a smile stretching wide across her face. "Isnae she wonderful, Ewan? She's perfect."

"Aye," Ewan croaked. "They are."

"I believe I'll go tell our brothers about her. I am certain they are listening at the door."

Just before she exited the room, she said, "You were brilliant, Una. Absolutely brilliant."

Una smiled her thanks, and then they were alone. The fire crackled in the hearth, and the baby made small, contented sounds as she nursed. Una stroked gentle fingers down the baby's cheeks, as if she was the most remarkable thing Una had ever seen. Ewan understood because she was, without a doubt, the most remarkable thing *he* had ever seen.

"Have you thought of a name?" Ewan asked after a long moment of watching.

Una hesitated. "I have, but you're free to say nay."

"Ask me for anything in the world, Una," he said, feeling a

lightness in his heart for the first time in months. Una snorted.

"I thought we could name her Margaret, for your mother. And perhaps Joan as a middle name?"

"Margaret Joan MacDonald," Ewan murmured. "Aye. It suits her."

Una smiled and sighed, resting her cheek against the top of Ewan's head. Margaret fell asleep and unlatched, her tiny mouth hanging open. It reminded Ewan of how his brothers looked when they slept, and he smiled. Una gently transferred Margaret into Ewan's arms. He gazed down at his sleeping daughter, who looked so much like her mother already that it stole his breath.

"I hope Joan is happy," Ewan said absently as she shifted downward, snuggling close.

"I believe she will be." She looked up at him. "And you, mo ghraidh? Are you happy?"

Ewan took a deep breath. How could he possibly communicate an answer to that question? He felt as if he was *made* of happiness.

"Ewan?" Una asked sleepily, her head heavy against him.

He turned and kissed her crown, lingering with his lips in her hair and smelling deeply.

"Aye, Una. I am the happiest man in the world."

EPILOGUE

The brisk, spring wind whipped Una's black hair behind her like a banner as she strode across the field between the forest and the keep. The sun was high in the sky, shining brilliantly with no clouds to block its warmth. Una turned her face up and closed her eyes. It was the perfect day.

After months cooped up in the keep with a newborn who liked nothing more than to nurse, Una had finally snuck away, leaving Margaret with Fiona and Fenella. The hours in the quiet forest had been as good as medicine for her, but her aching breasts told her it was time to return home.

Greer had accompanied her, along with her brood. The nine puppies—now nearly full-grown dogs—were gangly and enthusiastic, bowling into each other and, on occasion, their mother, earning them a sharp nip on the heels. The pups were an assortment of white and gray, some solid, some with patches of color. But all had shaggy coats like their father, albeit shorter. The sight of the pack of them never failed to make Una smile.

Una had just bent to remove her skirts from one of the

pup's mouths when she heard rapid hoofbeats. Though there had been no threat on the MacDonald lands since Ewan had formed an alliance with Blair and the Camerons, history taught her to be wary of riders approaching. She bent and removed her sgian dubh from her boot, but just as she stood, she saw Ewan's blond head rise above the crest of the hill, Calman's gray head bobbing happily as he ran.

He pulled up, and Calman stopped a few paces from Una, whinnying as the pups ran to him, running around and under him.

"What are you doing out here, mo ghraidh?" Ewan asked with narrowed eyes.

Una dropped her basket and put her hands on her hips, her anger flashing hot and immediate. "I told you nae fewer than ten times that I was coming today, I told Angus, I told Kenneth, I told David, I told the watch at the gate, I told Fenella and Fiona, I—"

She broke off when she saw the smile teasing at the corner of Ewan's mouth.

"You're an arse, Ewan MacDonald."

"Aye," he said, smiling in earnest now, his eyes crinkling. "But you love me."

She couldn't deny it. She did love him. She loved their family and the life they were building together. She loved the kind of father he was, as patient and caring as he was as laird. Imperfect, to be certain, but always striving to be better, always trying.

"I was just heading home," she said, shielding her eyes against the bright sun.

"Care to take a detour?" he asked suggestively, an eyebrow tilted high.

She felt her lower belly heat at the thought. But she felt the dull ache in her heavy breasts sharpening.

"I cannae go," she said. "I must feed Margaret."

He nodded his head, though his disappointment was obvious. She felt it too.

"But perhaps," she began and his eyes sharpened, "perhaps Fiona and Fenella would be willing to take her back once I'm done."

"Och, Una, I dinnae think you will have to work hard to convince them. Come, we can ride home together."

"I am perfectly capable of walking, *m'laird,*" she said, still loving to vex him.

His hands tightened their grip on the reins. It was subtle, but she did not miss it. "For now," he replied, his voice low and dark, dripping with promise.

And it turned out that Ewan had been correct. Once Margaret had finished nursing, Fiona and Fenella whisked Margaret down to the kitchens with nary a backward glance. Calman remained saddled, tied to a post near the keep, and Ewan and Una raced down the steps to him. They took off at a gallop through the gate and headed toward the loch, Una riding behind Ewan with her arms wrapped tightly around him.

She loved to ride like this, feeling the muscles of his abdomen flex and shift with Calman's gait, feeling his strong back moving under her cheek. New spring grass grew around the loch, and Calman bent his head to eat as soon as they stopped. Ewan jumped off the horse and reached up for Una. She braced her hands on his shoulders as he lifted her down.

He slid her against his body, trapped between man and beast, as he lowered her to her feet. Una felt the heat from his body as he caged her against the saddle. Ewan's hardening cock pressed against her stomach, and in an instant, his mouth was on hers. She melted into him, gripping his leine in her fists and levering herself closer, rubbing against him.

His fingers wrapped behind her neck, thumbs pressing into her jaw. He moaned into her mouth.

"Saints, Una," he said against her lips. "The things you do to me."

Una took his bottom lip between her teeth. Ewan grabbed her arse and pulled her tightly against him. With shocking grace, Ewan had her on her back on the ground. He thrust his hips against her, and Una sucked in a breath as she felt him through the layers of fabric that separated them. Her hands traced the muscular curves of his back, pulling him closer, loving the way his body flexed under her hands.

"Inside me, Ewan," she whispered against his neck.

"Nay, Una," he growled. "It's been too long since I had you without rushing. I want to savor this."

"And it's been too long since I've had you at all," she replied, biting his earlobe sharply and then soothing the flesh with her tongue.

He groaned, but his hands made quick work of pulling her skirts up around her waist. Una reached for his cock and fit it against her entrance. She held her breath as he slid into her channel with short, deepening thrusts. Her hands gripped his arse under his plaid and pulled him hard against her until he was fully sheathed.

She mewled as he shifted his hips and ground against her pearl. She tried to hold him at that angle, but he wasn't having it. Every time she felt the wave of her release beginning to rise, he would change his pacing or stop thrusting as deep. Una grew frustrated and whined loudly, thrashing her head from side to side.

"Why will you nae let me finish?" she cried.

"Why should I reward your impatience?" he replied wickedly, running the tip of his tongue from her ear down to the base of her throat and continuing his maddening rhythm of hard, slow thrusts that shook her to the core but did not give her the speed or friction to chase her own release.

She reached down between them with her hands but Ewan snatched them away.

"Nay. I will give it to you," he said in a rasp.

He lowered his head to nip at her wool-covered nipple. The sensation of his teeth against the fabric against the sensitive, pebbled flesh made her cry out.

"Please, Ewan. Please. Dinnae make me beg," she whined.

Una bucked against him. His hand skated down her belly, and his thumb found her pearl and began to make tight, firm circles around it. Ewan's mouth returned to hers, and he kissed her with renewed fervor.

The climax rushed over her. She felt it down to her toes, her feet nearly cramping in her boots. Ewan thrust harder and faster, and Una felt boneless beneath him. With a guttural sound, Ewan withdrew quickly and spent his seed in the grass beside her. He collapsed, rolling onto his side to face her. The air was cold enough to fog their breath as they panted. He reached for her and kissed her slowly.

"That was nae what I had planned, Una," he said, breathing heavily.

"You were hoping for something a little more tender?" she said with a smile.

"Hardly," he replied. "But I was planning to draw it out a bit more than that. I never get to take my time anymore. It seems that anytime I get close, a certain someone wakes up."

"Well, bairns do that."

He laughed. "Aye, that they do. It seems, then, my only course is to make up for missed opportunities."

And he did, until not even his body over hers was enough to keep the chill from her skin and the sun began to set low in the sky. They rode back to the keep together, one of his arms wrapped tightly around her as he held the reins in the other. Una leaned back against him, and he nuzzled her neck. They would go home and play with Margaret, whose world expanded every day. They would dine with their family. And they would sleep, with Una wrapped around him like a vine, her head on his chest and her hand clasped in his over his heart.

Una smiled. It was more than enough.

The End

WANT TO READ MORE?

Want more from the Highlands?
Visit **www.elizamacarthur.com/newsletter** for bonus content, new release info, and more!

ACKNOWLEDGMENTS

Somehow writing acknowledgements is always harder than writing the book itself. It feels especially hard right now during an ADHD medication shortage. I'm going to keep these short this time. If you slipped through the cracks in my chaotic memory, I love you, I love you, I LOVE YOU, and I appreciate you more than I can express. (And I'm sorry about the whole chaos memory bit, too.)

First off, as always, I want to thank my mom for being absolutely terrible at hiding her romance paperbacks so that I could find and read them. She was the first person to read this book seven drafts ago because nobody knows historicals like she does. It's changed a lot since then, Ma, but I promise I listened.

Special thanks to my husband, a real life romance hero. Thanks for all of your love and support (and mass quantities of crab rangoon) while I locked myself in the writing cave to bring this one across the finish line. You're so money and you don't even know it.

To my other biggest cheerleader, my sister, thanks for always making me feel like what I'm doing is important. I think the old man would be proud of us.

To my friends (in alphabetical order because that is visually satisfying), Caitlin, Danielle, Elizabeth, Em, Emily, Emma,

Erin, Erin, Gloria, Jennifer, Jessica, Lara, Megan, Melissa, Nellie, [REDACTED], Rux, Sam, Sarah, Sarah, Victoria and the rest of both the MacCoven and Crane Coven, I love you to the moon. Thank you for your friendship and care.

Special thanks to Sarah Estep, who read this book three versions ago and not only told me that it was worth fixing, but bullied me into doing so.

To Kels, thank you for designing a cover so gorgeous I screamed so loudly upon opening it that my husband came running to rescue me. (And thanks for being a top notch friend, too.)

The biggest of thanks to my editor, the incomparable Sarah at Lopt & Cropt for taking so much care with every version of this book and giving me all the gentle pushes I needed.

As always, thanks to my grad school mentors, who taught me how to show AND tell.

To my Patreon subscribers, your generosity made this book possible and I couldn't have written this book without you.

And last but not least, to the bookish community. Anyone who has ever flown into my DMs with words of encouragement or humor or support, anyone who has wrecked my TBR, and all of the people who are changing the genre we so deeply love and how we talk about it for the better. I appreciate you.

ABOUT THE AUTHOR

Eliza MacArthur is a writer of romance and humor. She lives in the mid-south with her husband, two feral werewolf children, and dogs. She is fueled by decaf coffee and a good grumpy/sunshine trope.

She cut her teeth stealing romances from the cabinet under her mom's bathroom sink (where all good Midwestern moms kept their Julie Garwood paperbacks in the 90's.

ALSO BY ELIZA MACARTHUR

Elements of Pining

Soft Flannel Hank

'Til All the Seas Run Dry

The Laird's Holdings

Hold Fast

Visit www.ElizaMacArthur.com for more information.

Printed in the USA
CPSIA information can be obtained
at www.ICGtesting.com
CBHW060544011024
15135CB00003B/57